The Great New England Sea Serpent

THE GREAT NEW ENGLAND
Sea Serpent

An Account of Unknown Creatures

Sighted by Many Respectable Persons

Between 1638 and the Present Day

J. P. O'Neill

DOWN EAST BOOKS

Copyright © 1999 by Junella Pusbach O'Neill

Illustration on p. 120 from *Cape Cod*, by Henry David Thoreau,
Dudley C. Lunt. © 1951 by W. W. Norton & Company, Inc.

Illustration on p. 221 © by Douglas Henderson. Originally
published in *Living with Dinosaurs*, by Patricia Lauber (Bradbury Press).

ISBN 0-89272-461-7

Book Design by Phil Schirmer, Ribeck Design
Printed and bound at Versa Press, East Peoria, Ill.

2   4   6   8   9   7   5   3   1

DOWN EAST BOOKS / CAMDEN, MAINE
Book orders: (800) 766-1670

LIBRARY OF CONGRESS CATALOGING-IN-PUBLICATION DATA

O'Neill, J. P. (Junella Pusbach), 1958-
    The great New England sea serpent : an account of unknown
creatures sighted by many respectable persons between 1638 and
the present day / J. P. O'Neill
        p.   cm.
    Includes bibliographical references and appendixes
    ISBN 0-89272-461-7 (pbk.)
    1. Sea monsters—New England. 2. Tales—New England. I. Title.
GR106.054 1999

For WillieO and Maeve

Contents

*Among the fishermen with long experience, some claim to have seen in the sea
animals like beams of wood, black, round and the same thickness throughout.*
—Aristotle, Historia animalium

*In view of all this testimony, and particularly that of so many intelligent and
respectable citizens of Gloucester, what shall we say—that this monster was indeed a
visitor from that "gloomy and pathless obscure," the home of "Salamander,
snake, dragon—vast reptiles that dwell in the deep?"*
—John J. Babson, History of the Town of Gloucester, Cape Ann, 1860

*The most striking fact about sea-serpents is their tendency to
appear when news is dull and the reporters and correspondents of the
newspapers are decidedly in need of something startling.*
—New York Times, September 1, 1879

*Scores, perhaps hundreds, of trustworthy mariners of all ranks, in both the navy
and mercantile services, have seen what they believe to be such a creature,
but they refuse to publish any account of their observations, knowing
that they will be insulted and publicly gibbeted as fools and liars if they do....*
—W. Matthew Williams, circa 1884

*I have no hesitation in saying that nobody ever saw a sea serpent. Why? For the
excellent reason that there is none to see.... The sea serpent is a myth. It does not
receive the attention of scientific men because they have real things to attend to.*
—Dr. David Starr Jordan, president, Stanford University, 1893

*The case of the sea serpent represents not so much a study in marine zoology as of
human psychology. Give a subject a high sounding name, cover it with ridicule, procure
from some eminent person a statement condemning it (it matters not how little that
eminent person knows of his subject) and it then becomes necessary to produce the
most unimpeachable evidence to obtain even a hearing for arguments in favor of it.*
—Dr. Maurice Burton, British Museum of Natural History, 1953

*When sometime a true sea serpent, complete and undecayed, is found or caught,
a shout of triumph will go through the world. "There you see," men will say,
"I knew they were there all the time. I just had the feeling they were there."*
—John Steinbeck, The Log from the Sea of Cortez

Introduction

One of the great unsolved mysteries of sea serpent lore....
The Gloucester monster simply cannot be encompassed
by any rational explanation.
—Richard Ellis, *Monsters of the Sea*, 1994

In August 1817, members of the New England Linnaean Society found themselves in the unique position of conducting the first ever scientific investigation of an unknown marine creature, supposed to be a sea serpent, that had appeared in the harbor at Gloucester, Massachusetts.

This was not the first sighting of a strange creature in the Gulf of Maine; nor was it the last. However, that August remains singular in that it was the first time that men of scholarship and means had an opportunity to conduct a scientific study of a creature thought to exist only in myth.

Eager to "collect evidence with regard to the existence and appearance of any such animal," the members of the investigative committee of the Linnaean Society set about gathering sworn statements from a variety of credible witnesses. Residents of the town of Gloucester, who were less inclined to scholarship, pursued the evidence with every available weapon. The creature remained elusive.

As recorded in the published report of the Linnaean Committee in 1817, the witnesses' accounts agreed that the creature "was said to resemble a serpent in its general form and motions, to be of immense size, and to move with wonderful rapidity; to appear on the surface only in calm bright weather; and to seem jointed or like a number of buoys or casks following each other in a line."

Similar descriptions of a creature bearing little resemblance to any known animal had been reported as early as 1638 and would be repeated over and over again for the next 150 years.

My first encounter with the great sea serpent came when I was ten or eleven years old. What had taken me to the Swampscott Public Library, and what drew me to Waldo Thompson's little clothbound book entitled *Swampscott: Historical Sketches of the Town* (1885), I cannot now say. I do know that the sixth chapter, "The Sea Serpent, Seen in 1638 at Cape Ann; in 1793 at Mount Desert; in 1819, 1820 and 1849 at Swampscott" (which curiously makes no mention of the Linnaean Society's investigation), had a deep and lasting impact. I simply never looked at the ocean in the same way again.

In the years that followed my introduction to the creature in Thompson's book, the Loch Ness monster was undergoing intense scrutiny. New books appeared almost annually, each confidently predicting that the next expedition to the loch would produce evidence of an unknown animal hidden in its peat-stained depths. I read the accounts with enthusiasm, but it was the ocean that I scanned with eager eyes—hoping, always wondering. So, when the opportunity to prepare a manuscript on the New England sea serpent presented itself, I was primed with almost thirty years of avid interest in the subject.

Beneath the murky waters of sea serpent lore are shoals of misinformation. Apart from the principal researchers on the subject—Dr. Antoon Oudemans, Rupert T. Gould, and Bernard Heuvelmans (who coined the term *cryptozoology* in an effort to apply scientific principles to the study of "hidden" animals)—few writers, it seems, have looked at charts or maps, local history, or original accounts. Many have been content to quote (and sometimes misquote) earlier authorities, extracting the juicier bits without attribution. No one has been more shamelessly plundered in this way than Heuvelmans, whose 1965 work, *In the Wake of the Sea-Serpents*, is an encyclopedia of worldwide sightings, thoughtfully and scientifically analyzed.

As disgraceful as this piracy is, it seems to me a far greater crime to copy the material and still get it wrong. Misspelled place and proper names, misquotes, and misleading partial quotes, used either to bolster the thesis that sea serpents exist or make ridiculous even the myth, do neither side any favors.

Though the guilty shall remain nameless, one particularly egregious error involves testimony originally collected by a folklorist who dedicated his small book to another well-known folklore writer. The better-known writer in turn quoted the testimony but got one essential word wrong. Instead of the witness seeing "three bends" in the creature, the second writer (in a much more widely available book) wrote that the witness saw "three heads." This mistake not only makes the witness seem like a fool, it lends false support to the theory that most sightings are "the figment of a vulgar mind."

I encountered one "historian" who trod right on the line of plagiarizing Rudyard Kipling's *Captains Courageous*, then credited the book to Robert Louis Stevenson.

Another writer reported the early-nineteenth-century sightings off the Fox Islands in Maine as having taken place at the "Fix Islands." Not only are there no Fix Islands in Maine, there are none anywhere in the world. In reporting other sightings, the same writer roamed the globe in the most confusing manner possible, hopping back and forth across the Atlantic (where many seaports have the same names) without mentioning that he was changing continents.

This book, then, is an attempt to present in a coherent context an account of the creature(s) seen in the Gulf of Maine and adjacent waters. To avoid any unconscious bias on my part, I have left most of the testimony and newspaper reports intact. Wherever possible, with the aid of willing colleagues, I have used original sources. Errors (there are bound to be a few) are my own. Tracking the ownership of the sea serpent images used in this book, even those reproduced in relatively recent publications, has often proved as difficult as finding the elusive creatures themselves. Every effort has been made to obtain the images from their original sources or from an authorized library or institution.

Of the other sea serpents observed throughout the world (they are numerous; I refer the reader to Gould's *The Case for the Sea-Serpent* and to Heuvelmans's book, which though out of print can be found in many libraries), only two, the *Daedalus* and *Valhalla* creatures, make their way into these pages in detail. Although these sightings took place far from the Gulf of Maine, they enter this story because of the players: the *Valhalla* encounter because it involved two trained naturalists, and the *Daedalus* sighting because it pitted a British naval captain against one of the most celebrated comparative anatomists of the day.

In the interest of space, sightings in Connecticut, New York, and the Chesapeake Bay area are mentioned only briefly. A compelling amount of material exists for those locations, which are the particular province of my esteemed colleague Gary S. Mangiacopra. Gary, more than anyone, has done exhaustive research on these sightings, yet even he, with all his years of applied study, assures me that we have barely scratched the surface.

It is clear from the information we do have that throughout the nineteenth century and the first thirty years of the twentieth, fishermen, coasters, local residents, and newspaper editors—even those who didn't "believe" in sea serpents—were well aware that something unexplained was making apparently seasonal visits to the New England coast.

How many more sightings occurred, and when and where they did, may never be known. Still we have tantalizing references in the extant material to "first one this year" or "also first seen last year," indicating that there may be dozens (maybe hundreds) of other reports in the morgues of local daily and weekly newspapers and on microfiche in libraries from Cape Breton to Cape Hatteras. Many of the newspaper accounts cited in this book, which had been previously overlooked, were collected in a single scrapbook at the Cape Ann Historical Association. Several others were found by Wayne Wilcox in yet another scrapbook at the Calais Free Library in Calais, Maine. This leads me to hope that other similar archives may yet be revealed.

For the sea serpent doubter, this means little. Even if one were to uncover every scrap of yellowing newsprint with a fading report of an unknown creature, there will always be some who will not be convinced. Not that there haven't been mistakes and misidentifications; there have been. I have included some. However, as will be shown, most of the sightings included in this book come from seemingly trustworthy witnesses who at first thought they were seeing something they could explain—an overturned dory, a school of porpoises, an unmarked shoal, a whale—and only upon closer examination discovered that whatever they were seeing was not explainable as one of those.

Science wants—demands—a specimen: a perfectly reasonable and responsible position. No definite identification can be made without something to examine. But the absence of a carcass or skeleton is not proof positive that what the witnesses have described can be explained as mirages, seaweed, drifting spars, or sharks, dolphins, or whales (take your pick) swimming in a line, especially when those witnesses are experienced fishermen with considerable knowledge of local marine life.

Nothing but a specimen living or dead will convince the skeptics. But this book was not written to persuade. The people who live by and of the sea in New England have been seeing something strange in the water for three hundred years, and whatever it is, or was, they called it a sea serpent. This book, then, is for all the people who look at the sea and wonder.

I

1751 — 1815

On the Surface of the Dark Water

All this evidence, I think, cannot fail to establish that a large Sea Serpent has been seen in and near the Bay of Penobscot.

—Rev. Alden Bradford, Wiscasset, Maine, 1804

What combination of vision, courage, hubris, and avarice must the early European explorers have possessed to sail west across the wide Atlantic toward what they believed was the Orient, leaving behind them the known world. Before them, they hoped, lay the enticements of Asia: ancient cities, silks, and spices. In between, if what maps they had or had seen were to be believed, lay huge wastes of open ocean inhabited by the most dire beasts imaginable.

The Basques could have told the explorers that the North Atlantic offered no passage to Asia. They'd been fishing the cold waters of the Grand Banks for several centuries, growing rich on Catholic Europe's observance of restrictions against eating flesh on Fridays.

A series of shoals rising from the continental shelf, the Grand Banks were, until the latter half of the twentieth century, one of the richest fishing grounds in the world. Here, between Grand Bank, off the southeast coast of Newfoundland, and Georges Bank, off Cape Cod, the cold Labrador Current meets the warm Gulf Stream in shallow water, producing a plankton-rich environment that draws the great baleen whales, basking sharks, herring, halibut, haddock, mackerel, and "the sacred cod."

Detail of a map of Iceland by Ortelius circa 1570 depicting the creatures believed to inhabit the sea.

But the Basque fishermen who came ashore only to dry or salt their catch left no records of their voyages. At the end of each season they abandoned their shelters and stages, filled their holds with cod, and kept the news of the bountiful Banks and the incidental continent to themselves.

So the merchant explorers who came in search of gold or silk or sassafras found not the riches of Cathay but a vast land of thick forests, islands covered with birds, and waters filled with infinite numbers of fish. Each claimed the land for the king or queen who had sanctioned his voyage, mapped and named prominent features of the coast, then sailed home with news of a great continent awaiting conquest.

If there was an oral tradition of a monster in the sea among the native people of Maine, it may no longer be known. Of the twenty or so related Algonquian tribes that once inhabited Maine, only the Penobscot and Passamaquoddy survive in numbers. A virulent epidemic in 1616-17 (probably a combination of illnesses brought by the Europeans) virtually wiped out the coastal tribes from the Penobscot River in Maine as far south as Cape Cod, Massachusetts. However, a petroglyph on a large rock jutting into the Kennebec River at Embden, Maine, certainly suggests that someone long ago either saw or dreamed of a creature remarkably similar to the one that hundreds of people would later describe. In addition to the "dragon" on this large rock that juts into the Kennebec at what was probably a portage point, there are hundreds of figures, including humans, animals, canoes, and abstract motifs.

Many centuries after an unknown shaman pecked the enigmatic dragon into the rock on the riverbank, a Penobscot Indian by the name of Joseph Nicolar recounted a tale in which the Wabanaki folk hero Klose-kur-beh[1]—"the man from nothing"—slays a sea serpent with the help of May-May, the Wabanaki name for the red-headed woodpecker.

Roslyn Strong, of the New England Antiquities Research Association, who has investigated the petroglyphs and the Klose-kur-beh legend, points out that the serpent depicted at Embden has an unusual feature for a North American "dragon": an arrow shape at the tip of its tail. (Roslyn Strong)

This sea serpent tale does not appear in other written versions of the Klose-kur-beh adventures; nevertheless, Nicolar stresses in his preface to *The Life and Traditions of the Red Man* (1893) that he has recorded "all the pure traditions which have been handed down from the beginning of the red man's world to the present time."

As Nicolar tells it, Klose-kur-beh is the man to whom the Great Spirit gave the knowledge of tools necessary for survival: the canoe and the bow and arrow. After passing along these skills to "the man" and "the woman," Klose-kur-beh began a journey to subdue the animals of the earth. After many adventures, Klose-kur-beh built himself a canoe and:

> . . . upon returning to his people . . . by way of the sea he found the waters
> very dark in color. . . . As he moved along he saw a serpent at a long dis-
> tance, as it lay on the surface of the dark water. Upon nearing the monster
> it raised its head and began to run out its fire-like tongue rapidly at him;
> by this action he was well aware that this was another deadly enemy; so
> he steered his canoe directly for the monster and the serpent reared up in
> a fearful manner and seemed ready to crush the canoe and the man, but
> at that moment "May-May [the] Red headed wood pecker," flew between
> the man and the serpent. . . . "Be quick and take your bow and shoot the
> arrow at the smallest part. . . ."

Six times Klose-kur-beh shot at the serpent and six times the arrow
bounced off. On the seventh try,

> . . . the bird flew in advance of the arrow and with its beak pointed to
> Klose-kur-beh where to aim. Klose-kur-beh obeyed and sent the arrow
> swiftly to the spot very near the end of the tail; this broke the serpent's
> back bone which caused him to recoil in death.

Klose-kur-beh then dipped the arrow in the blood of the serpent and
marked the head of the woodpecker as a sign of true friendship, whereupon
May-May told Klose-kur-beh:

> I have been watching your enemies and I have seen that the serpent was
> very mad . . . and his wrath was so great that he came here where he
> thought no power could reach him because when the rush of clouds and
> wind comes he can sink himself to the bottom out of harm's way, and
> here he has been waiting many times seven moons for your coming . . .
> but now the monster is gone and his dead body you will see no more.

Nicolar's portrayal of the sea serpent is markedly similar to eyewitness
descriptions of an unknown marine creature in the Gulf of Maine written
both before and after Nicolar's book was published. Was the "dragon"
among the Embden petroglyphs meant to depict Klose-kur-beh's serpent
with his arrow in its tail, was it simply a creature of imagination, or was it
a representation of a living creature known to the Penobscots?[2]

One might be forgiven, after reading the following accounts, for supposing that the only individuals with any real interest in sea serpents in

eighteenth-century Maine were men of the cloth. In fact, it is quite likely that these encounters would be totally unknown today but for the interest of the clergy. Although recording strange phenomena may seem to be an unusual use of a minister's time, it was not uncommon. During this era, the clergy were among the few with sufficient education, interest, and leisure to dabble in natural history and write about the world around them.[3]

The majority of Down-Easters would, in contrast, have been fully absorbed in the hardscrabble pursuit of making a living. Although many could read, far fewer wrote more than was necessary in the keeping of daybooks in which they recorded their finances and family events. Many had come to Maine (then still part of Massachusetts) after the Revolution, having obtained their land as compensation for service in the Continental army. Others who settled in the region did so as a means of evading the restrictions of living in the more puritanical society of the Commonwealth.

Establishing themselves near the banks of rivers, these hardy, headstrong souls perched their small, family-centered communities on the edge of what was still largely wilderness. They fished, farmed, and felled trees, using the rivers to transport timber to local mills, then to the shipyards at Bath (Maine), Boston, and Essex (Massachusetts). They trapped or traded for furs, wove their own cloth, grew their own food, and were, except for procured luxuries such as rum and sugar, almost wholly self-sufficient.

Still, many of these communities were so small that they could not provide a living for a "whole minister." It is likely that Machiasport, situated on the far northeastern Maine coast, was one of these. It was there in 1801 that the Reverend Abraham Cummings discovered that a proselytizing ghost by the name of Nelly Hooper Butler had turned up among his flock.

The ghost, at first known only from the odd and irritating noises emanating throughout the home of one Captain Abner Blaisdel, had finally identified herself on January 2, 1801, through a disembodied voice in the cellar.

Curious people began turning up at the Blaisdel home, where Nelly held forth in a voice described as "shrill, but mild and pleasant." However, it was not until May that she took form, appearing as "a shining white garment" to an assembly of twenty.

Nelly's gatherings grew to include as many as two hundred listeners. She

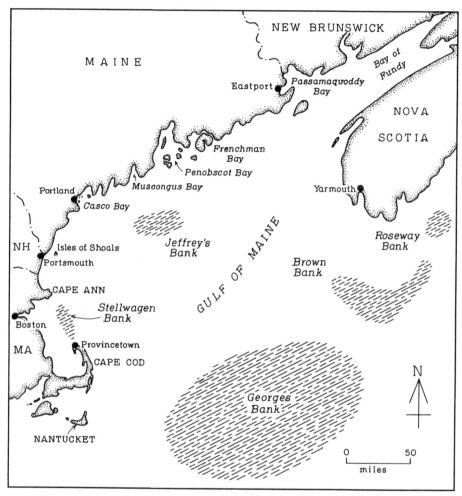

The Gulf of Maine, including major fishing banks.   Map by Marie Litterer

preached and made predictions (including the death of Mrs. Blaisdel and the remarriage of Nelly's widowed husband to Blaisdel's daughter Lydia), apparently knowing a bit more about the moral behavior of the congregates than was comfortable.

At last, the Reverend Mr. Cummings, who did not believe in ghosts, decided that something ought to be done. Nelly was, after all, trespassing on his territory. Cummings began interviewing eyewitnesses and found, among the hundred or so who gave sworn testimony, that their stories were remarkably similar. Many included Nelly's oft-quoted claim: "Although my body is consumed and turned to dust, my soul is as much alive as before I left my body."

In spite of this earnest message, Cummings was convinced that the whole thing was a hoax perpetrated by Captain Blaisdel. On his way to confront Blaisdel, Cummings had an encounter of his own. A group of white rocks rose from the ground, took the outline of a globe, then "resolved into the shape and dress of a woman." Though very small at first, the apparition grew "and now appeared glorious, with rays of light shining from her head all about, and reaching to the ground."

Nelly Butler never appeared or spoke again, and the Reverend Mr. Cummings, formerly a skeptic, now a convert, spent the remainder of his life as a missionary.[4] It was while engaged in some duty relating to his mission a year later that the reverend, accompanied by his wife, daughter, and a young woman of their acquaintance, had an encounter with an "extraordinary sea monster."

It will surprise no one that the story of Cummings's visitation at Machiasport does not ordinarily precede the story of his observation of an unknown marine creature in Penobscot Bay. The former can do nothing to enhance the credibility of a witness with regard to the latter, an already suspect phenomena. We are fortunate, then, that the ghostly encounter does not seem to have negatively affected his trustworthiness with the Reverends Alexander McLean and Alden Bradford. If circumstances had been otherwise, this narration of the incident, and the others that Cummings subsequently recounted, might never have come to light.

My Dear Sir,

With peculiar pleasure I comply with your request though the urgency of my affairs must excuse my brevity. It was sometime in July 1802 that we saw this extraordinary sea monster, on our passage to Belfast, between Cape Rosoi and Long Island [now Cape Rosier and Islesboro]. His first appearance was near Long Island. I then supposed it to be a large shoal of fish with a seal at one end of it, but wondered that the seal should rise out of the water so much higher than usual; but, as he drew nearer to our boat, we soon discovered that this whole appearance was but one animal in the form of a serpent. I immediately perceived that his mode of swimming was exactly such as had been described to me by some of the people on Fox Islands [North Haven and Vinalhaven Islands], who had seen an animal of this kind before, which must confirm the veracity of their report. For this creature had not the horizontal, but an ascending and descending serpentine motion. This renders it highly probable that he never moves on land to any considerable distance and that the water is his proper element. His head was rather larger than that of a horse, but formed like that of a serpent. His body we judged was more than sixty feet in length. His head and as much of his body as we could discover was all of a blue colour except a black circle around his eye. His motion was at first but moderate, but when he left us and proceeded toward the ocean, he moved with the greatest rapidity. This monster is the sixth of the kind, if our information be correct, which has been seen in this bay within the term of eighteen years. Mrs. Cummings, my daughter and Miss Martha Springs were with me in the boat at that time, and can attest to the above description.

I continue yours in Christian affection,

Abraham Cummings

Rev. Abraham Cummings's report is remarkably lucid and, apart from the details he furnishes about the creature, reveals something about the author himself. He is an able boatman, familiar with the region and local wildlife. Although he has heard reports of a sea monster, he has not really believed them and so does not leap to conclusions upon seeing something unusual. He at first supposes that he's seeing a shoal of fish and a seal, both of which are commonplace. It is only after his observations convince him that he is seeing a single creature that he permits himself to make a study of its form, color, and movement and to indulge in some speculation about its nature. The skin of the creature being "all of a blue colour" is unusual, but the rest of the description will soon become familiar. It is interesting to note that although his parishioners have seen the creature, it is his encounter "which must confirm the veracity of their report."

When the story of this sighting came to the attention of the Reverend Alexander McLean, he wrote to Cummings asking for additional details, which were duly supplied in the above letter. McLean then forwarded the letter to the Reverend Alden Bradford, of Wiscasset, along with a note, which read in part:

One of the same kind was seen above thirty years ago, by the deceased Capt. Paul Reed, of Boothbay, another was seen in Muscongus Bay in time of the American war, two miles from the place where I lived then, and another soon afterwards off Meduncook [now Friendship]. These were all I ever heard of seen on this coast. . . .

Although Rev. Bradford was not inclined to believe the reports, he collected all the information he could with regard to sea serpent appearances.[5] He in turn wrote to Abraham Cummings asking if perhaps there might not be some other explanation for what he'd seen—say, perhaps, a school of porpoises swimming Indian file. Cummings replied:

I can recollect nothing material which would render my description of the animal more convincing. . . . Who ever saw fifty or sixty porpoises moving after each other in a right line and in such a manner that those who formed the rear were no larger than haddock and mackerel, and none but the foremost shewed his head? Who ever saw a serpent's head upon a porpoise or a whale? We saw him swim as far as from Long Island to the Cape before he disappeared. His head and neck all the time out of the water. Now whoever saw a porpoise swim so great a distance without ever immerging at all?

Having rebutted the porpoise theory, Cummings went on to note all he knew of previous sightings:

Two young men on Fox Island, intelligent and credible, saw an animal of this kind about five years since, as they then informed me. They told me that the serpent which they saw was about sixty feet long, and appeared to have an ascending and descending motion. A few years before, perhaps ten years since, two of those animals were seen by two other persons on that island, as their neighbors informed me. About twenty years since, two of those serpents, they say, were seen by one Mr. Crocket, who then lived upon Ash Point. This is the best information you can obtain from

Your Friend and Servant,

Abraham Cummings

Apparently convinced, Bradford in 1804 sent his findings to the Honorable John Quincy Adams, corresponding secretary of the American Academy of Arts and Science, with a letter that read in part:

> As one object of the Academy is to notice and preserve discoveries in Natural History, I am induced to communicate to the Society the following account of a Sea Serpent which I have lately collected. . . . There have been vague reports of an animal of this description having been seen in or near Penobscot Bay. But little credit however, was attached to the story, and no particular authentic account has yet been given to the public on the subject. . . . A few months ago I happened to hear related the story of one, which was seen in the Bay of Penobscot in 1802. And for my own satisfaction, I have been inquisitive relative to the truth of the account, and to the general evidence of the existence of the animal. . . . All this evidence, I think cannot fail to establish the fact that a large Sea Serpent has been seen in and near the Bay of Penobscot. The existence of such a Monster can no longer be reasonably disputed.

Bradford went on to admit that it was not known if the creature was a permanent resident or "whether he coasts further south or north during a part of the year. . . . Nor is it known on what species of fish he subsists." In closing he wrote with considerable, if misplaced, confidence:

> By this communication I have it in view only to furnish evidence of the actual existence of the animal. It will probably operate in favour of further information, and lead to a particular history of this hitherto undescribed Serpent.

Accompanying the letter was all the evidence the good reverend could assemble, including Cummings's letters as well as a letter from Captain George Little, of the frigate *Boston*, and the testimony of Captain Eleazar Crabtree.

> Marshfield, 13th March 1804

> Sir,

> In answer to yours of the 30th of January last, I observe that in May 1780, I was lying in Round Pond in Broad Bay, in a public armed ship. At sunrise, I discovered a large Serpent, or monster, coming down the Bay, on the surface of the water. The Cutter was manned and armed. I went myself in the boat, and proceeded after the Serpent. When within a hundred feet, the

marines were ordered to fire on him, but before they could make ready, the Serpent dove. He was not less than from 45 to 50 feet in length; the largest diameter of his body, I should judge, 15 inches; his head nearly the size of that of a man, which he carried four or five feet above the water. He wore every appearance of a common black snake. When he dove he came up near Muscongus Island—we pursued him, but never came up within a quarter of a mile of him again.

A monster of the above description was seen in the same place by Joseph Kent, of Marshfield, 1751. Kent said he was longer and larger than the main boom of his sloop, which was 85 tons. He had a fair opportunity of viewing him, as he was within ten or twelve yards of his sloop.

> I have the honor to be, sir,
>
> Your friend and humble servant.
>
> George Little

Captain Crabtree signed his testimony, which Rev. Bradford recorded as follows:

Capt. Crabtree, now of Portland (late of Fox Islands, in the bay of Penobscot)[6] declares, that in the year 1777 or 1778, upon information of a neighbor, that a large Serpent was in the water, near the shore, just below his house, and having often been told by individuals that they had before seen a similar sea-monster in that quarter, and doubting the correctness of their reports, was induced to go down to the water to satisfy his own mind—that he saw a large animal, in the form of a Snake, lying almost motionless on the sea, about thirty rods [a rod is equal to 16.5 feet] from the bank where he stood—that his head was about four feet above the water—that from the appearance of the animal he was about 100 feet in length—that he did not go off to the animal through fear of the consequences, and that he judged him to be about three feet [in] diameter. He also says that before that time, many people, living on those islands, on whose reports he could depend, had declared to him that they had seen such an animal—and that more than one had been seen by several persons together.

Perhaps the Honorable John Quincy Adams, to whom this material was sent in good faith, had heard about Cummings and the ghost, or perhaps, like so many men of science who would follow, he just didn't believe in sea serpents.[7] Whatever the reason, the evidence was "mislaid" and did not become public until sixteen years later, when Jacob Bigelow revived it in the *American Journal of Science and Arts*.

The following story of Edward Preble's Revolutionary War-era encounter with the creature (near where it was seen by Cummings) comes to us through the pen of James Fenimore Cooper in his *Lives of Distinguished American Naval Officers* (1846).

A native of Portland, Maine, Preble ran away to sea at age sixteen, two years before he chanced upon the creature while serving aboard the twenty-six-gun ship *Protector* (Commander John Foster Williams). In July 1779, *Protector* was one of seventeen ships and twenty-four transports under the command of Commodore Dudley Saltonstall that participated in the ill-fated Penobscot Expedition against the British base at the partially complete Fort George at Majabagaduce, Maine, in present-day Castine.

A staggering blow to the Revolutionary navy, the "Bagaduce Blunder" ended when a reinforcing British squadron sailed into the bay and the colonial commanders blew up their own ships, sending 140 badly needed cannon to the bottom of the bay. Never since has the American navy lost so large a percentage of its fleet at one time.

The way Cooper tells it, Preble's encounter with the serpent apparently took place at the start of the expedition.

> Preble related the affair substantially as follows: The *Protector* was lying in one of the bays on the eastern coast . . . awaiting the slow movements of the squadron. The day was clear and calm, when a large sea serpent was discovered outside the ship. The animal was lying on the water quite motionless. After inspecting it with the glasses for some time, Captain Williams ordered Preble to man and arm a large boat, and endeavor to destroy the creature; or at least go as near to it as he could. . . . The boat thus employed pulled twelve oars, and carried a swivel in its bows, besides having its crew armed as boarders. Preble shoved off, and pulled directly towards the monster. As the boat neared it, the serpent raised its head about ten feet above the surface of the water, looking about it. It then began to move slowly away from the boat. Preble pushed on, his men pulling with

all their force, and the animal being at no great distance, the swivel was discharged loaded with bullets. The discharge produced no other effect than to quicken the speed of the monster which soon ran the boat out of sight.

There is no question that in after-life, Preble occasionally mentioned this circumstance to a few of his intimates. He was not loquacious, and probably saw that he was relating a fact that most persons would be disposed to doubt, and self respect prevented his making frequent allusions to it. . . . Preble stated it as his opinion that the serpent he saw was from one hundred to one hundred and fifty feet long, and larger than a barrel.

This length, though it staggers the imagination, will be reported again and again, as will the creature's speed in eluding capture and its habit of lying still on the surface of the water.

Cooper's retelling of Preble's encounter was not published until 1846, by which time sea serpent appearances had received significant scientific and popular attention. As Cooper noted: "When it is remembered that Preble died long before the accounts of the appearance of a similar serpent, that have been promulgated in this country, were brought to light, it affords a singular confirmation of the latter."[8]

Further confirmation appeared amid numerous sightings of a similar serpent at Gloucester, Massachusetts, in 1817. In the atmosphere of scientific inquiry accompanying the sightings at Gloucester, a number of eighteenth-century accounts were dredged from memory and offered as corroborating evidence. This one was written by William Lee, "former consul at Bordeaux, now in the treasury department," to Dr. Samuel L. Mitchill, who had served in the House and Senate and was a principal founder of the Lyceum of Natural History in New York.

September 2, 1817

Dr. Mitchill,

On a passage I made from Quebec, in 1787, in a schooner of about eighteen tons burthen, while standing in for the Gut of Canso, the island of Cape Breton being about four leagues distant, one of the crew cried out "a shoal a-head!" The helm was instantly put down to tack ship, when to our great astonishment, the shoal, as we thought it to be, moved off, and as it passed athwart the bow of our vessel, we discovered it to be an enormous Sea Serpent, four times at least as long as the schooner. Its back was of a dark green color, forming above the water a number of little hillocks, resembling a chain of hogsheads. I was then but a lad, and being much terrified ran below until the monster was at some distance from us. I did not see his head distinctly; but those who did, after I had hid myself in the cabin, said it was as large as the small boat of the schooner. I recollect the tremendous ripple and noise he made in the water, as he went off from us, which I compared at the time to that occasioned by the launching of a ship.

My venerable friend, Mr. _____ [sic], of your city [New York], was a passenger with me at the time. He will corroborate this statement and probably furnish you with a better description of this monster; for I well recollect his taking his stand at the bow of the vessel, with great courage, to examine it while the other passengers were intent only on their own safety.

At Halifax, and on my return to Boston, when frequently describing this monster, [I] was laughed at so immoderately that I found it necessary to remain silent on the subject, to escape the imputation of using a traveller's privilege of dealing in the marvelous.

William Lee

Mr. Lee would certainly have found a sympathetic listener in James Fenimore Cooper, who made this observation in connection with Preble's sighting:

There appears to be an indisposition in the human mind to acknowledge that others have seen that which chance has concealed from our own sight. Travelers are discredited and derided merely because they relate facts that lie beyond the circle of common acquisition; and the term "travelers' stories" has its origin more in a narrow jealousy than in any prudent wariness of exaggeration.

A letter to the *Salem Gazette* dated August 3, 1793, and signed by Captain Crabtree (whose relationship to Eleazar Crabtree, if any, is not known) reports a sighting on the coast of Maine:

On the 20th of June last, being on my passage from the West Indies, in the morning, having just made Mount Desert Island, distant nearly ten leagues, I suddenly got sight of a serpent of an enormous size, swimming on the surface of the ocean, its head elevated about six or eight feet out of the water, rather prone forward. That part of the body which was out of the water I judged to be about the size of a barrel in circumference, but the head larger, having some resemblance of a horse's. According to the most accurate computation, which I made in my mind of his length, I think it could not be less than from fifty-five to sixty feet, and perhaps longer. That part of the body which was not elevated, but of which I had a distinct view several times, was longer than the part out of the water; the body of a dark brown.

The same paper reported that "a party, well prepared, was to have sailed from Marblehead, on Saturday morning, for the purpose of attacking this animal which by last accounts was near Kettle Island, a short distance this side of Gloucester Harbour."

Reverend William Jenks collected two other sightings from this period, the first of which took place sometime prior to 1809 as reported by Charles Smith, a Boston attorney formerly of Bath, who had been told by a Captain Lillis that he had once seen a "very singular fish" off the coast. "It appeared more like a snake than a fish and was about forty feet long. It held its head erect, had no mane and looked like an ordinary serpent."

The second account "respecting a sea serpent of the Penobscot" was reported by. . . a Mr. Staples of Prospect, of whom I inquired as I passed, was told by a Mr. Miller of one of the islands that he had seen it; and "it was as big as a sloop's boom and about sixty or seventy feet long."[9] He told me also that about 1780, as a schooner was lying at the mouth of the river or in the bay, one of these enormous creatures leaped over it between the masts—that the men ran into the hold for fright and that the weight of the serpent sunk the vessel "one streak" or plank. The schooner was of about eighteen tons. . . .

The latter of these reports in which the creature leaps between the masts may be a fabrication, or it may be a true story that was somehow distorted in the retelling, because the common reports of the sea serpent do not include anything like this behavior.

Although the following sighting did not occur in the Gulf of Maine, the account presents (apart from the gills) a near perfect composite picture of the New England sea serpent regarding its appearance, color, speed, and apparent curiosity about the ship that had it under observation. Mid-Atlantic encounters, as it turns out, were fairly common and were reported with some regularity throughout the nineteenth century.

This account appears in an extremely rare volume entitled *A Particular Account of a Monstrous Sea-Serpent, the Largest Ever Seen in America*, published by Brattleboro Book Store in 1817.[10]

> Being bound to St. Petersburg in the *Washington* of Newbury-port, in the year 1811, about the last of July, being then in lat. 60° 40' N. and long. 7° 40' W (in the vicinity of the Faeroe Islands), I discovered something about three or four miles distant, about two points on the weather bow, which appeared like a mast, as it rose and sunk in a perpendicular manner, once in about eight or ten minutes. I kept the vessel directly for it, and after looking at it with my glass, I observed to my mate that it was a wreck, as I could see the timbers &c. sticking up, but as we approached nearer, I found what appeared like timbers to be a number of porpoises and black fish [pilot whales] playing and jumping around a large Sea Serpent, which we had supposed to be the mast.
>
> He appeared to keep the same motion of rising and sinking from the time of his first coming in sight, till we lost sight of him astern, and his motions and progress were very moderate, and appeared to be making his way to the N.N.E. and the above fish playing round him, as long as we could see him with a glass. It is supposed he was in sight of us about an hour and a half. I had a number of fair views of him, and went abreast of him; he came up about 30 feet from the vessel, and rose about 15 feet above the surface, with his head bent a little forward but did not appear to be startled, but turned his head, as if to view the vessel.
>
> His head was formed somewhat like that of an eel, only more blunt, his back was nearly black, and his belly a muddy white or grey; he had a sharp looking eye, about as large as that of a horse; his mouth was about 15 inches in length, and he was big round as a barrel, or rather less, and generally rose about 15 feet above the surface; he had eight creases on the under part of his neck, which came half way round, which I supposed

to be his gills; his head appeared to be from 18 to 24 inches in length, he had no appearance of any fins or scales, but was smooth like the skin of a porpoise.

John Brown, 3d.

Four years after Captain Brown's sighting, Captain Elkanah Finney encountered a similar creature in the water near his home in Plymouth, Massachusetts. The following is his statement given on oath.

About the twentieth of June 1815, being at work near my house, which is situated near the sea shore in Plymouth, at a place called Warren's cove, where the beach joins the mainland, my son, a boy, came from the shore and informed me of an unusual appearance on the surface of the sea in the cove. I paid little attention to his story at first; but as he persisted in saying that he had seen something very remarkable, I looked towards the cove, where I saw something which appeared to the naked eye to be drift sea weed. I then viewed it through a perspective glass, and was in a moment satisfied that it was some aquatic animal, with the form, motion and appearance of which I had hitherto been unacquainted. It was about a quarter of a mile from shore, and was moving with great rapidity to the northward. It then appeared to be about thirty feet in length; the animal went about half a mile to the northward; then turned about, and while turning, displayed a greater length than I had before seen; I supposed at least a hundred feet. It then came towards me, in a southerly direction, very rapidly, until he was in a line with me, when he stopped and lay entirely still on the surface of the water. I then had a good view of him through my glass, at the distance of a quarter of a mile. His appearance in this situation was like a string of buoys. I saw perhaps thirty or forty of these protuberances or bunches, which were about the size of a barrel. The head appeared to be about six or eight feet long, and where it was connected with the body was a little larger than the body. His head tapered off to the size of a horse's head. I could not discern any mouth. But what I supposed to be his under jaw had a white stripe extending the whole length of the head, just above the water. While he lay in this situation, he appeared to be about a hundred or a hundred and twenty feet long. The body appeared to be of a uniform size. I saw no part of the animal which

I supposed to be a tail. I therefore thought he did not display to me his whole length. His colour was deep brown or black. I could not discover any eyes, mane, gills or breathing holes. I did not see any fins or legs. The animal did not utter any sound, and it did not appear to notice anything. It remained still and motionless for five minutes or more. The wind was light with a clear sky, and the water quite smooth. He then moved to the southward, but not with so rapid a motion as I had observed before. He was soon out of my sight.

On the following day, Captain Finney rose early in the hope of seeing the creature again. He was rewarded for his effort. For about two hours he was able to watch it diving again and again, before it swam off toward the Gurnet Lighthouse.

There was a fresh breeze from the south, which subsided about eight o'-clock. It then became quite calm, when I again saw the animal about a mile to the northward of my house, down the beach. He did not display so great a length as the night before, perhaps not more than twenty or thirty feet. He often disappeared and was gone five or ten minutes under water. I thought he was diving or fishing for his food. He remained in nearly the same situation and thus employed for two hours. I then saw him moving off, in a northeast direction, towards the lighthouse. I could not determine whether his motion was up and down, or to the right and left. His quickest motion was very rapid, I should suppose at a rate of fifteen or twenty miles an hour. Mackerel, menhaden, herring, and other baitfish abound in the cove where that animal was seen.

Captain Finney's encounter was not recorded until two years later, in the fall of 1817, when his testimony was solicited by the Committee of the Linnaean Society as part of its historic investigation of the creature at Cape Ann.

CHAPTER 1 NOTES

1. This is Nicolar's spelling; the name is also sometimes spelled Gluskabe or Glooscap.

2. Ten years before Nicolar's book was published, Charles G. Leland published *Algonquin Legends*, in which he reports that he discovered five versions of a "ghastly and repulsive legend" that he had collected from Gov. Topmah Josephs of Peter Dana Point, Maine, in Rink's *Tales and Traditions of the Eskimo*. Leland's story, entitled "Of the Woman who loved a Serpent that lived in a Lake," is a cautionary tale in which a woman embraces a sea serpent "of immense size" and dies from the poisons that enter her body.

3. During roughly the same period in England, Dean William Buckland, of Oxford University, and the Reverend William D. Conybeare, vicar of Axminster, made significant contributions to the as yet unnamed science of paleontology. In 1824, Buckland described *Megalosaurus*, the first of what would come to be known as dinosaurs; in 1823, Conybeare, with Henry De La Beche, described the first plesiosaur.

4. Cummings later published a book, *Immortality Proved by the Testimony of Science* (1859), about his own experience and the testimony of the witnesses.

5. Curiously, in 1809, another clergyman, the Reverend William Jenks, had been collecting testimony concerning sea serpent appearances for his *Manuscript Notes on the District of Maine*. He turned over the account to the Linnaean Society in September 1817.

6. The westernmost point of North Haven Island (one of the Fox Islands) is called Crabtree Point.

7. John Quincy Adams was not a believer in the supernatural, as he noted in his journal circa 1799 when, while serving as representative to the court of the King of Prussia, he was astonished to discovered that the royal family believed in ghostly apparitions and all that "farago" and wondered that this family could be related to Frederick the Great.

8. Preble ultimately achieved the rank of commodore, the highest rank in the U.S. Navy prior to the Civil War; he has been called by some the father of the American navy, because so many competent commanders received their training from him.

9. Today the term *sloop* applies to a single-masted sailboat. However, in the seventeenth and eighteenth centuries a sloop was a small two- or three-masted ship carrying up to sixteen guns.

10. The only known original is owned by the Vermont Historical Society. I am deeply indebted to Gary S. Mangiacopra for his expert sleuthing and for providing me with my photocopy.

2

1817 – 1818

The Creature at Cape Ann

*If we now wish to examine strictly the very existence
of the great marine serpent, we must admit that it would be
difficult to deny that there has appeared in the sea
off Cape Ann a sort of animal of very large size, much
elongated and swimming rapidly.*

—Henri-Marie Ducrotay de Blainville,
Professor of Zoology and Comparative Anatomy, Paris, 1818

Projecting nine miles into the Atlantic roughly forty miles north of Boston is a rocky peninsula that was known to the native people as Wingaer-sheek. Explored variously by Cabot, Verrazano, and Gosnold, this cape was already well known to Basque, Breton, and Portuguese fisherman as Cabo Santa Maria when in 1605 Samuel de Champlain renamed it Cap Aux Isles and described a magnificent harbor there, which he called Le Beauport (now Gloucester).

Nine years after Champlain's exploration of the region, Captain John Smith would call it Tragabigzanda, after a Turkish courtesan, a name that for obvious reasons did not catch on, though it survives as a street name in Gloucester. Upon Smith's return to England, Prince Charles (later Charles I) renamed the peninsula, for the last time, in honor of his mother, Ann. Smith, incidentally, had better luck with the name he gave to the territory formerly known as North Virginia; he called it New England.

When Cape Ann was first seen by the early European explorers, it was a granite promontory covered with trees. Some of the earliest explorers mention Indians, but by the time Smith was conducting his exploration of the region, many of the coastal tribes had disappeared or been seriously diminished by disease.

Although the deepwater port attracted potential settlers, the rocky terrain did not lend itself easily to farming. Early attempts to establish a settlement failed, at least in part because farmers rarely make good fishermen and fishermen are loath to farm, and the season for one often overlaps the other. Most moved on to the better established village of Salem. It was not until 1633, according to Gloucester historian John Babson, that the beginnings of a settlement took root. Then in 1642, Rev. Richard Blynman arrived with several families from the Plymouth Colony, established a plantation, and gave it the name Gloucester.

From the beginning, the men and women of Gloucester looked to the sea to provide food and commerce. Indeed, the harbor at Gloucester, shielded as it is almost entirely from the wrath of the Atlantic, placed the settlers in a most enviable position for foreign and coastwise trade. In due course it would become America's premier fishing port. The sea would indeed provide, but it would exact a terrible price.

John Josselyn recorded the first account of a sea serpent sighting in American waters, circa 1638, in *An Account of Two Voyages to New England*:

> They told me of a sea serpent, or snake, that lay quoiled up like a cable upon a rock at Cape Ann; a boat passing by with English(men) on board, and two Indians, they would have shot the serpent, but the Indians dissuaded them, saying that if he were not killed outright, they would all be in danger of their lives.

Obadiah Turner recorded a similar incident on September 5, 1641, in which he described a serpent seen off Lynn, Massachusetts:

> Some being on ye great beache gathering of clams and seaweed wch had been cast thereon by ye mightie storm did spy a most wonderful serpent a shorte way off from ye shore. He was as big round in ye thickest part as a wine pipe; and they do affirm that he was fifteen fathoms or more in length. A most wonderful tale. But ye witnesses be credible, and it would

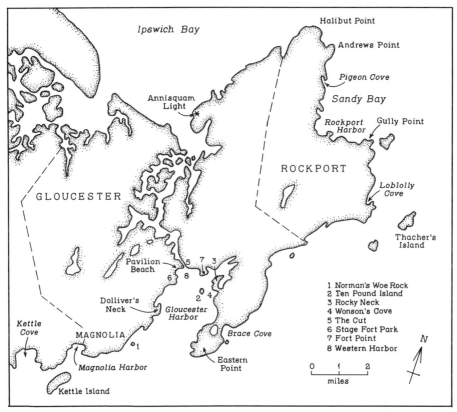

Cape Ann coastline.   Map by Marie Litterer

be of no account to them to tell an untrue tale. Wee have likewise heard
yt Cape Ann ye people have seene a monster like unto this, whch did there
come out of ye sea and coile himself upon ye land mch to ye terror of
them yt did see him.

Another early reference to a creature at Cape Ann is in the 1793 report accompanying Captain Crabtree's letter to the *Salem Gazette* that citizens of
Marblehead were preparing to attack the creature, last seen "a short distance
this side of Gloucester."

Then came the extraordinary events of August 1817.

On August 6, two women claimed they'd seen a sea serpent entering Gloucester Harbor. No one took them seriously, although several fishermen had
also reported seeing something similar. Then the captain of a coasting ves-

sel was laughed out of Lipple's auction room when he reported a sixty-foot-long sea serpent at the entrance to the bay. He was soon to be vindicated.

Several days later, Mrs. Amos Story, "a woman held in high esteem for her veracity," saw what appeared to be a tree trunk washed up on the rocks of Ten Pound Island. She quickly obtained a telescope in order to observe it more closely, and as she watched, it moved. She was then momentarily distracted by some domestic chore, and when she looked again it was gone.

On August 10, Lydia Wonson saw the creature from her home near Rocky Neck. Watching it with a good spyglass for nearly half an hour, she saw it draw itself into a coil, then extend itself again with sixty to seventy feet showing on the surface of the water. It looked, she later told Captain C. L. Sargent, like the buoys of a seine (a fishing net weighted on the bottom and buoyed with cork spaced at regular intervals along the top).

The same day, near the cove that makes up the isthmus of Rocky Neck, William Row watched, from "a stone's throw away," as the creature came into the cove in the company of two sharks. He saw "100 feet of the creature borne on the water" and thought it seemed to be fishing "as he moved rapidly and frequently put his head out of water as if to swallow his game." By way of description, he said that "its head was as broad as a horse or more so, but not quite as long."

Local mariner Amos Story "saw a strange marine animal . . . at the southward and eastward of Ten Pound Island," also on August 10. According to his sworn statement,

> It was between the hours of twelve and one o'clock when I first saw him, and he continued in sight for an hour and a half. I was setting on the shore, and was about twenty rods from him when he was the nearest to me. His head appeared shaped much like that of the sea turtle, and he carried his head from ten to twelve inches above the surface of the water. His head at that distance appeared larger than the head of any dog I ever saw. From the back of his head to the next part of him that was visible, I should judge to be three or four feet. He moved very rapidly through the water, I should say a mile in two or, at most, in three minutes. I saw no bunches on his back. On this day, I did not see more than ten or twelve feet of his body.

Susan Stover and her father saw the creature the same day. It was so near the shore, Susan reported, that her father "took off his hat that he should not frighten him."

Shipmaster Solomon Allen III saw the creature for three days' running, beginning on August 12. Unlike the others who gave their testimony, he claimed to have seen "fifty distinct portions" of the eighty- to ninety-foot-long "rough, scaly" creature and thought it moved from "right to left."

> His head formed something like the head of a rattle snake, but nearly as large as the head of a horse. When he moved on the surface of the water, his motion was slow, at times playing about in circles, and sometimes moving nearly straight forward. When he disappeared, he sunk apparently directly down, and would next appear at two hundred yards from where he disappeared, in two minutes.

Asked how often and for how long a time he saw the creature, Allen replied,

> I was in a boat on the 12th and was around him several times, within one hundred and fifty yards of him. On the 13th I saw him nearly all the day, from the shore. I was on the beach, nearly on a level with him and most of the time he was from one hundred and fifty to three hundred yards from me. On the 14th, I saw him but once, and had not so good a view.

By August 14, the creature was big news, and people began turning up at the harbor with their spyglasses to have a look. From her house early that morning, Mary Row saw the animal in rapid motion between Rocky Neck and Ten Pound Island. She felt sure she saw plainly a hundred feet of him on the surface of the water; its head, out of the water, resembled that of a horse.

The same day, Samuel Wonson saw it swim with great rapidity from Norman's Woe and "'brot too' abreast of me perfectly still at about 100 fathoms distance." (There are six feet to a fathom, making this six hundred feet.) Wonson said that the serpent passed between his house and Ten Pound Island, so near that his children were alarmed and ran into the house.

The creature then moved farther into the harbor, where it was seen in the area of Western Harbor known as Pavilion Beach (where the famous fisherman's statue now stands), with Stage Point (Stage Fort Park) at one end and Fort Point at the other.

At roughly the midpoint of Pavilion Beach is an area known as The Cut, which joins Gloucester Harbor to the Annisquam River. Mrs. Moore saw the creature there, close to Piper's Rocks; because she was "without previous knowledge of there being a serpent in the water, she trembled like a leaf and stood some time in agitation to view."

John Somes, who owned a ropewalk (a long covered walkway or building where rope and cordage are made) on The Cut just at the highwater mark, saw the creature pass repeatedly across the harbor. He was certain he could not be mistaken in describing what he saw, which was sixty to seventy feet of the creature, its head and neck having every appearance of a snake. Joseph Moores, who saw the creature while he was standing by Mr. Somes's ropewalk, claimed that it "put his head near his tail and [I] could plainly see one part of him move one way and the other in a contrary direction."

Ship's carpenter Matthew Gaffney shot at the creature on August 14:

> I was in a boat, and was within thirty feet of him. . . . I had a good gun, and took good aim. I aimed at his head, and think I must have hit him. He turned toward us immediately after I had fired, and I thought he was coming at us; but he sunk down and went directly under our boat, and made his appearance at about one hundred yards from where he sunk. He did not turn like a fish, but appeared to settle directly down, like a rock. My gun carries a ball of eighteen to the pound; and I suppose there is no person in town, more accustomed to shooting, than I am. I have seen the animal at several other times, but never had so good a view at him as on this day. His motion was vertical, like a caterpillar.

Gaffney responded to additional questions put to him by Lonson Nash:

> Q: Did he appear more shy after you fired at him?
>
> A: He did not, but continued playing as before.
>
> Q: Who was in the boat with you when you fired at the serpent?
>
> A: My brother Daniel, and Augustin M. Webber.

In spite of being shot at by Mr. Gaffney, the creature did not appear any the worse for wear when Epes Ellery saw it from "an eminence, near low water mark, and about thirty feet above the level of the sea," along with "fifteen or twenty persons" a little after sunset on the same day. Ellery said, "He appeared to be amusing himself, though there were several boats not far from him."

The next day, near what is now Magnolia Harbor, aboard the schooner *Hazard* at anchor off Kettle Island, Joseph Lee of Manchester encountered the monster. Lee's account is one of the very few that survives in original and unedited form, giving us a glimpse of the creative spelling of the day:

> On the 15th day of August, 1817, I had the pleasure of seeing the Sea Serpent. I was on bord of scooner Hazard laing to anchor off little [Kettle] island between the town of Manchester and Cape Ann. I judge that I was abought one hundred and fifty yards from him. But to have a better view of him I went into the boat and went as near him as I though it safe. I was within twenty yards of him. I thought it not safe to go any further. I then turned back on bord of the scooner again. I saw him in the above fashen. He was about one hundred feet in length as nie as I could judge. His bigness around I could not essertain. I saw him twenty minnets.

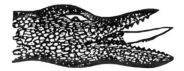

Joseph Lee's sketch of the head of the creature he saw from the *Hazard*, published in the *Gloucester Daily Telegraph*, September 29, 1875.

William Saville saw the creature from the windmill on August 17. He said that the creature became alarmed by the noise on shore, sank in the water, and was seen no more.

John Johnston, Jr., was the last to see the creature on the evening of the seventeenth.

> . . . between the hours of eight and nine o'clock, while passing from the shore in a boat, to a vessel lying in the harbour . . . I saw . . . a serpent, lying extended on the surface of the water. His length appeared to be fifty feet at least, and he appeared straight, exhibiting no protuberances. . . . He remained in the same position, till we lost sight of him. We approached so near him that I believe I could have reached him with my oar.

On August 18, two serpents were reportedly seen "at play" in the harbor, a circumstance that was to have interesting consequences. Reports of more than one sea serpent seen together are extraordinarily rare. Bernard Heuvelmans, writing in 1964, remarked that altogether he had found accounts of no more than a dozen such sightings.

Later on August 18, between five and six o'clock, William Pearson was in a sailboat in the harbor with James P. Collins when he saw a solitary creature coming out of Webber's Cove.

> The serpent passed out under the stern of our boat, towards Ten Pound Island; then he stood in towards us again, and crossed our bow. We immediately exclaimed, "here is the snake!" From what I saw of him I should say that he was nothing short of seventy feet in length. I distinctly saw bunches on his back, and once he raised his head out of the water. . . . His velocity at this time was not great; though at times I have seen him move with great velocity, I should say at the rate of a mile in three minutes, and perhaps faster. . . . He turned very short, and appeared as limber and active as the eel, when compared to his size . . .

Curiously, Pearson, who saw ten to twelve distinct "portions," also reported, "From where I judged his navel might be, to the end of his tail, there were no bunches visible."

That same day, the serpent put on a show for Colonel Thomas Handasyd Perkins and a friend, as recorded in this letter, dated October 13, 1820, to John P. Cushing.[1]

> Wishing to satisfy myself on a subject of great import of which there existed a great difference of opinion, I myself visited Gloucester. . . .
>
> All the town was, as you may suppose, on the alert: and almost every individual in town, both great and small, had been gratified at a great or less distance with a sight of him.
>
> The weather was fine and the sea perfectly smooth, and Mr. Lee and myself were seated on a point of land [Eastern Point] which projects into the harbor, and about twenty feet above the level of the water, from which we were distant about 50 or 60 feet. . . .
>
> Whilst thus seated, I observed an agitation in the water at the entrance of the harbour, like that which follows a small vessel going five or six miles an hour through the water. As we knew there was no shoal where the water was thus broken, I immediately said to Mr. Lee that I had no doubt that what I had seen was the sea-serpent in pursuit of fish. . . .

In a few minutes after my exclamation, I saw on the opposite side of the harbor, at about two miles' distance from where I had first seen, or thought I saw, the snake, the same object, moving with a rapid motion up the harbor on the western shore. As he approached us, it was easy to see that his motion was not that of the common snake, either on land or in the water, but evidently the vertical movement of the caterpillar. As nearly as I could judge, there was visible at a time about 40 feet of his body. It was not, to be sure, a continuity of body, as the form from head to tail (except the apparent bunches appeared as he moved through the water) was seen only at three or four feet asunder. It was very evident, however, that his length must be much greater than what appeared, as, in his movements, he left a considerable wash in his rear.

I had a fine glass, and was within from one-third to half a mile. The head was flat in the water, and the animal was, as far as I could distinguish, of a chocolate color. I was struck with an appearance at the front part of the head like a single horn, about nine inches to a foot in length, and of the form of a marline-spike.

There were a great many people collected by this time, many of whom had before seen the same object and the same appearance. From the time I first saw the animal until he passed by the place where I stood, and soon after disappeared, was not more than fifteen or twenty minutes.

I left the place fully satisfied that the reports in circulation, although differing in details, were essentially correct.

Perkins, who would later admit when asked if he had ever known anyone who had seen the sea serpent, "unfortunately I have," was a wealthy Bostonian who amassed a fortune in the China trade. The "Merchant Prince of Boston" earned his rank in the Massachusetts Militia and later served in both the state Senate and House of Representatives. Among many who would benefit from his wealth was the New England Asylum for the Blind, now Perkins School for the Blind.[2]

Perkins's letter is the first in which we learn that the creature was seen by hundreds of spectators; it will not be the last of such accounts. One can imagine the excitement of the citizenry if Perkins is correct that "almost every individual in town had been gratified with a sight of him." There were at the time more than six thousand residents of Cape Ann, though exactly how many lived in the town of Gloucester is not definite, because the census did not then differentiate between Gloucester and Rockport.

The oddest part of Colonel Perkins's account is the description of the foot-long marlinespike horn. (A marlinespike is a pointed metal tool used for splicing rope or twine.) The only other person to mention the "horn" was William Foster, a merchant, who saw the creature on August 14 and 17. Foster testified that on the seventeenth he watched the creature with a glass from a distance of about forty rods: "As he drew near, and when opposite to me, there rose from his head or the most forward part of him a prong or spear about twelve inches in height, and six inches in circumference at the bottom and running to a small point."

Questioned as to whether the prong might have been the creature's tongue, Foster replied that he "thought not, as I saw the prong before I saw the head."

James Mansfield in turn swore he'd seen "a strange creature, of enormous length, resembling a serpent" a little before six o'clock in the evening on August 15. He noticed no ears, horns, or other appendages but agreed with many others that its "sinuosities" were vertical.

On August 18, the Linnaean Society of New England called a special meeting to establish a committee to "collect evidence with regard to the existence and appearance" of the sea serpent. The committee appointed by the society included botanist and physician Jacob Bigelow; the Honorable John Davis, judge of the U.S. District Court for Massachusetts; and naturalist Francis Gray, Esq.

All three men were graduates of Harvard, where Bigelow taught medicine and applied science. He invented the term *technology*, publishing his "applications of science to the useful arts" lectures in 1829 under the title *Elements of Technology.* Davis had been, at twenty-seven, the youngest delegate (he was from Plymouth) at the Massachusetts Convention, which ratified the U.S. Constitution. He was highly respected for his wise and judicious handling of legal matters during the Embargo and War of 1812 and is said to have been the first person to use the term *pilgrim* to describe the settlers at Plimoth

Plantation. Davis was also a close friend of John Quincy Adams, whom Gray had served as unofficial secretary when Adams was minister to Russia.

Newly established at the close of the War of 1812, the Linnaean Society was named for eighteenth-century Swedish naturalist Carl von Linne, or Carolus Linnaeus, who created the framework for the modern system of taxonomic classification. The membership consisted of a small group of scientific-minded men whose exclusive Saturday evening meetings provided those in attendance (usually about twenty persons) with an opportunity to discourse on "curious facts and ingenious observations" concerning natural history.

Membership was by invitation only, though the society had many "corresponding members" who sent reports and specimens of new minerals, flora, and fauna for their collection. It was common practice in the eighteenth and nineteenth centuries, when travel was hazardous and expensive, to rely on reports of local correspondents when conducting scientific inquiry. This helps explain why, although any one (or all) of the committee members could have made the trip to Gloucester by water or stagecoach, none did.

They wrote instead to the Essex County justice of the peace, the Honorable Lonson Nash, asking that he "examine upon oath some of the inhabitants of that town with regard to the appearance of this animal, to make the examination as early as possible, to request the persons examined not to communicate to each other the substance of their respective statements, until they were all committed to writing, to have these statements signed and certified in due form, and sent to us." The committee members also provided Nash with a list of twenty-five questions "to be proposed, if not rendered unnecessary by the statement given." (See Appendix B.)

Nash had himself seen the creature on August 14 from a distance of 250 yards, at which point he perceived "eight distinct portions, or bunches" on the creature's back and estimated its overall length at from 70 to 100 feet. He accepted "most cheerfully" the task of collecting affidavits, which he did from "men of fair and unblemished character." They included Solomon Allen III, Epes Ellery, William H. Foster, Matthew Gaffney, John Johnston, Jr., James Mansfield, William B. Pearson, and Amos Story.

Europe too was on the alert. On August 20, Colonel Perkins's brother, S. G. Perkins, wrote to his friend Edward Everett in Paris, telling him of the first sightings of the creature on August 6 and mentioning that the captain and crew of a vessel from Newfoundland Bank had sighted the creature off Cape Ann Harbor on the eighteenth. Everett, who had been in Europe for several years studying at Gottingen, where he received the first Ph.D. ever awarded to an American, eagerly collected news of the sensational sea serpent for his colleagues in the European scientific community.

In response to the growing public interest in Boston, on August 22, 1817, a broadsheet (quoted in full below) was printed and sold by Henry Bowen of Devonshire Street. The large single side of newsprint was a composite of articles from several newspapers.

A Monstrous Sea Serpent,

The largest ever seen in America,

Has just made its appearance in Gloucester Harbour.
Cape Ann, and has been seen by hundreds of
Respectable Citizens.

The Editor of the Salem Gazette, says: We have in our possession an extract of a letter from John Low, E.q. to his son in this town, dated Gloucester, Thursday afternoon, August 14, 1817.

"There was seen on Monday and on Tuesday morning playing about our harbor between Eastern Point and Ten Pound Island, a SNAKE with his head and body about eight feet out of the water, his head is in perfect shape as large as the head of a horse, his body is judged to be about FORTY-FIVE or FIFTY FEET IN LENGTH. It is thought that he will girt about 3 feet round the body, and his sting is about 4 feet in length.

"While writing the above a person has called in to say that there are two to be seen, playing from the Stage-head into the harbor inside of Ten Pound Island.

"The spectators are Mr. Charles Smith, Mr. John Proctor and several others. A number of our sharp shooters are in pursuit of him but cannot make a ball penetrate his head. Another party is just going in pursuit with guns, harpoons &c. Our small craft is fearful of venturing out a fishing.

"The above can be attested to by twenty different people of undoubted veracity."

In addition to this account the Salem Register states that the Serpent is extremely rapid in its motions which are in all directions, that it shews a length of 50 feet, that a man who discharged his musket within 30 feet of the Serpent says its head is partly white and that he hit it, that a large sum had been offered for it, that "it appears in joints like wooden buoys on a net rope almost as large as a barrel, that musket balls appear to have no effect on it, that it appears like a string of gallon kegs 100 feet long."

The editor of the Register quotes an account of a Sea Serpent seen on the coast in 1746, something like it. It had a head like that of a horse, and as he moved he looked like a row of casks following in a right line.

The Boston Daily Advertiser, in speaking of this *Monstrous Serpent*, says—We have seen several letters from Gloucester, which describe a prodigious Snake that has made its appearance in Cape Ann Harbour. It was first seen by some fishermen, 10 or 12 days ago, but it was then generally believed to be the creature of the imagination. But he has since come within the harbor of Gloucester, and has been seen by hundreds of people. He is declared by some persons, who approached within 10 or 15 yards of him, to be 60 or 70 feet in length, round and the diameter of a barrel. Others state his length variously from 50 to 100 feet. His motions are serpentine, extremely varied, and exceedingly rapid. He turns himself around almost instantaneously. He sometimes darts forward, with his head out of the water, at the rate of a mile in 3 minutes, leaving a wake behind of a half a mile in length. His head, as large as the head of a horse, is shaped somewhat like that of a large dog, is raised about 8 feet out of the water and is partly white, the other part black. He appears to be full of joints and resembles a string of buoys on a net rope, as is set in the water to catch herring. Others describe him as like a string of water casks. His back is black. Various attempts have been made, without success, to take him. Four boats went out on Thursday, filled with adventurous sailors and experienced gunners, armed with muskets, harpoons, &c. Three muskets were discharged at him from a distance of 30 feet; two balls were thought to hit his head, but without effect. He immediately after plunged into the water, and disappeared for a short time, after which he moved off to the outer harbor, and was seen no more that night. A number of persons are employed in making a net of cod-line, of sufficient size to take him. It is conjectured that he has resorted to this harbor for the purpose of preying upon a very numerous shoal of herring, which has lately appeared there. If he is instrumental, as is supposed, in driving these herring into the harbor, he has rendered an essential service to the town.

The Salem Gazette of the 19th inst. [meaning "instant," or "of the current month"] says, "We are informed, that on Sunday this creature was seen playing sometimes within 15 or 20 feet of the shore, affording a better opportunity to observe him than before occurred. Gentlemen from Gloucester state that he appeared to them even of greater magnitude than had before been represented, and should judge from their own observation that he was as much as 150 feet in length, and as big round as a barrel. They saw him open an enormous mouth, and are of the opinion that he is cased in shell."

The following day, the *Boston Centinel* reported that "Capt. Beach, who appears to have examined [the creature] very often, and sometimes in favorable situations, says his head is the size of a common bucket. He has seen him with his mouth open, his under jaw and teeth like a shark's, his head round, with apparently very thick scales and its whole appearance very terrific."

No one pursued an affidavit from Captain Beach, and no one among the

Perhaps it was Captain Beach's statement that influenced the artist who prepared this depiction. It is certainly unique and bears no resemblance to any of the other descriptions or sketches. (Fortean Picture Library)

dozens of other witnesses, even those with marine spyglasses, mentioned a round head, sharklike teeth, or thick scales.

According to Colonel Perkins, a Mr. and Mrs. Mansfield reported seeing the creature partly on land on August 22:

> The animal was stretched out partly over the white sandy beach, which had four or five feet of water upon it, and lay partly over the channel. . . . He said he had made up his mind as to the length of the snake, but wished the opinion of his wife on the same subject. . . . She thought him the length of the wharf behind their house. . . . Mr. Mansfield said he was of the same opinion. The wharf is 100 feet long. It is to be observed that the person above spoken of had been such an unbeliever in the existence of this monster that he had not given himself the trouble to go from his house to the harbor when the report was first made of such an animal being there. . . .

On August 23, Amos Story saw the creature again, as he later recounted to Nash:

This was in the morning, about seven o'clock. He then lay perfectly still, extended on the water, and I should judge that I saw fifteen feet of him at least. . . . I continued looking at him about half an hour, and he remained still in the same position, until I was called away. Neither his head nor tail were visible. His colour appeared to be a dark brown and when the sun shone upon him, the reflection was very bright.

On August 25, the creature was reportedly seen feasting on alewives at Kettle Cove, and three days later it was spotted off Eastern Point. The animal might still have been hovering along the coast feeding on herring, but Nash felt that his work on a subject "calculated to excite much interest at home and abroad" was done. By August 28, he had completed his interviews and was addressing a letter with his findings to the Linnaean Society. In his report, Nash said that the "deponents were interrogated separately, no one knowing what the others had testified, and though they differ in some few particulars, still, for the most part they agree." Nash noted having confirmed Matthew Gaffney's account with Gaffney's brother Daniel, who was also in the boat, though he differed with Solomon Allen concerning the bunches or protuberances and "as to the motion of the animal. His motion is vertical."

I think Mr. Allen is likewise mistaken as to the distinct portions of the animal that were visible at one time. I saw, at no time, more than eight distinct portions, though more have been visible; still I cannot believe that *fifty* distinct portions were seen at one time. I believe the animal to be straight, and that the apparent bunches were caused by his vertical motion.

Unbeknownst to Nash, as he was preparing his report, the schooner *Laura,* bound from Newburyport to Boston, was becalmed two miles east of Eastern Point, where its crew members were among the last to see the creature at Cape Ann that August.

On August 30, two of the *Laura's* crew appeared before Justice of the Peace Joseph May at Boston to give their sworn statements, which from their similarities suggest that they got their stories together before testifying. Of the three men on board, Robert Bragg, having been the first to spot the creature, and not being engaged at the helm or in other business, had it in sight the longest.

[A]bout ten o'clock A.M. . . . being on deck . . . looking to windward, I saw something break the water, and coming very fast towards us. . . . The animal came about 28 or 30 feet from us, between the vessel and the shore, and passed very swiftly by us; he left a very long wake behind him. About six inches in height of his body and head were out of the water, and I should judge about 14 or 15 feet in length. He had a head like a serpent, rather larger than his body and rather blunt; did not see his eyes; when astern of the vessel about 30 feet, he threw out his tongue about two feet in length; the end of it appeared to me to resemble a fisherman's harpoon. He raised his tongue several times perpendicularly, or nearly so, and let it fall again. He was in sight about ten minutes. I think he moved at the rate of 12 or 14 miles an hour; he was of a dark chocolate colour, and from what appeared out of water I should suppose he was about two and a half feet in circumference; he made no noise; his back and body appeared smooth; a small bunch on each side of his head, just above his eyes; he did not appear to be at all disturbed by the vessel; his course was in the direction for the Salt Islands; his motion was much swifter than any whale that I have ever seen, and I have seen many—did not observe any teeth; his motion was very steady, a little up and down. To this account I am willing to make oath.

William Somerby corroborated this account in all its particulars, adding only that he thought the tongue

. . . extended two feet from his jaws—the end of it resembled a harpoon. He threw his tongue backwards several times over his head, and let it fall again. I saw one of his eyes as he passed; it appeared very bright, and about the size of the eye of an ox. . . . The motion of the body was rising and falling as he advanced, the head moderately vibrating from side to side. The colour of his tongue was light brown.

The following day, Sewell Toppan, master of the schooner, also appeared before Joseph May to testify.

I heard one of my men call to the man at the helm, "what is this coming towards us;" being engaged forward, I took no further notice till they called out again. I then got on top of the deck load, at which time I saw a singular kind of animal or fish, which I had never before seen, passing by our quarter, at a distance of about forty feet. . . . The motion of his head was sideways and quite moderate; the motion of the body, up and down. I have seen whales very often; his motion was much more rapid than whales, or any other fish I have ever seen; he left a very long wake behind him; he did not appear to alter his course in consequence of being so near the vessel. . . . I have been to sea many years and never saw any fish that had the least resemblance to this animal.

In contrast to the passivity of the Linnaean Committee members, General David Humphreys, upon hearing news of the creature, journeyed to Gloucester from his home in Humphreysville, Connecticut, arriving on August 29 too late to catch a glimpse of the creature. The sixty-seven-year-old general, known by the sobriquet "Belov'd of Washington," was a distinguished statesman, a writer of somewhat flowery patriotic poetry, and an avid amateur naturalist. In spite of having served with distinction in the Revolutionary War as Washington's aide-de-camp and having had the honor of receiving Cornwallis's colors at Yorktown, Humphreys had also sought a fellowship in the Royal Philosophical Society.

It was to Sir Joseph Banks, president of the Royal Society, that the general addressed his findings, which he simultaneously prepared for publication as *Letters from the Hon. David Humphreys, F. R. S. . . . to the Rt. Hon. Sir Joseph Banks . . . Containing some Account of the Serpent of the Ocean, frequently seen in Gloucester Bay* (New York, 1817). One letter contains the following report:

> [According to] the stories told with great simplicity and apparent truth by the women and children who had the best advantage for viewing [the serpent], he seemed to them an awful-looking, shocking, great, black, creature—with a head almost as large as a horse's—with frightful, glaring eyes, nearly as big as the rim of a midling-sized tea-cup—his tongue and tail being like a snake's, his motion in diving and playing quick as lightning— that they shuddered with fear in beholding, yet could not help looking at him as long as he continued in sight; and that he had something rough and sometimes shining all over his body.

Humphreys further ventured that, "The fishermen and whalemen, with which Cape Ann and Marblehead abound, may doubtless be reckoned in the class of the most bold, enterprising, and dexterous mariners in the world." He added that "more than 5000 dollars had been offered for the spoils of this Leviathan."

It was apparently to these bold mariners that Humphreys was looking when, as Chandos Michael Brown points out, he portrayed the pursuit of the creature as an epic drama, asking, "Who will dare to put a hook in his nostrils, transfix his sides with a spear, or engage in single combat with Vulcanean arms the monarch of the deep, in his own element?"

On September 1, the Linnaean Society Committee sent a letter to Samuel Davis, of Plymouth, asking him to procure "any evidence which may exist respecting a remarkable animal, denominated a *Sea Serpent*" as "an appearance of this sort is mentioned as having been noticed by some persons at Plymouth two or three years since."

Captain Finney's testimony regarding his 1815 encounter, "duly authenticated," was forwarded to the society together with a letter in which Davis remarked of Finney, "He has been from his youth accustomed to a seafaring life—in the fishing employ, and in foreign voyages—has frequently seen whales, and almost every species of fish." Further, Davis added, "Certain house carpenters, who were at work on a building near the spot, also saw it, as well as many others—these persons dwell with emphasis on the long and distinct wake made in the water by the passage of the fish. As to the point of time, it must have been from known data between the 18th and 25th of June. And I would remark that this is exactly the season when the first setting in of mackerel occurs in our bay."

The next day the committee wrote to Nash thanking him for his "very acceptable labors . . . in giving some precise and accurate conceptions on a subject peculiarly exposed to exaggeration and mistake."

On September 10, the creature was reportedly seen sleeping off a meal of baitfish in the vicinity of the Half Way Rocks (a landmark off Marblehead halfway between Boston and Cape Ann), where it was "coiled up on the surface of the water reposing after a hearty breakfast of herring." There were no further reports at Gloucester that autumn.

Then, nearly a month after the creature had last been seen in the vicinity of Cape Ann, a similar creature was reported in Long Island Sound. At ten o'clock on the morning of October 5, Thomas Herttell viewed with a spy-glass from his house at Rye-Neck, New York:

> . . . a long rough dark looking body, progressing rapidly up sound [toward
> New York City] against a brisk breeze and a strong ebb tide. . . . His back,
> forty to fifty feet of which was seen above the surface of the water, ap-
> peared to be irregular, uneven, and deeply indented . . . creating a swell be-
> fore him not unlike that made by a boat towed rapidly at the stern of a
> vessel.

On October 3, James Guion was standing on a point of land on the east side of Mamaroneck Harbor when he saw something similar "a little dis-tance from the rocks, usually called the Scotch Caps . . . going with great ra-pidity up sound." The report of the two sightings, published in the *Columbian Centinel*, was written by Herttell, who had been somewhat disconcerted by others having taken the liberty of using his name in association with the creature. The Linnaean Committee included it in their report, also mention-ing that on October 5 the creature was "seen by some persons at or in the vicinity of the lighthouse on Sand's Point."

The great sea serpent had not been reported at Cape Ann for almost two weeks, and it is possible that the entire episode would have dwindled into an obscure, if sensational, memory had it not been for the coincident ap-pearance of a strange, misshapen snake near Loblolly Cove.

On September 27, Goreham Norwood and a Mr. Colbey, responding to the shrieks of Colbey's young son, speared and stoned a three-and-a-half-foot-long "serpent" with humps on its back about ten or twelve rods from the sea near Loblolly Cove (a mile and a half from Sandy Bay village in what is now Rockport).

Because the creature was different from any animal they'd ever seen, Col-bey and Norwood brought the carcass to the village to be examined. It being training day (a mustering of local men with their weapons and a great social occasion), many people had an opportunity to view it. The odd appearance of the creature, together with its discovery in such close proximity to the sea, prompted considerable speculation. Hadn't there been two sightings of the creature on September 22 in shallow water near the shore? Hadn't there been reports of more than one serpent playing in Gloucester Harbor? Perhaps the creature had not come to Cape Ann for the fishing after all; perhaps it had come to spawn.

The dead serpent was sold to John Gott of Sandy Bay, then was acquired by Captain Beach, Jr., who exhibited it for a few days at his house before presenting it to the Linnaean Society for examination, with a promise to donate it to "their cabinet."

This use of the term *cabinet,* now obsolete, refers to the early origins of museums; as Francis Bacon wrote in his *Gesta Grayorum* (1594), a "learned gentleman" might obtain a "goodly, huge cabinet [in which] whatsoever Nature hath wrought . . . and may be kept . . . shall be sorted and included."

The society's collection of miscellaneous (and unsorted) specimens was open to the public, free of charge, on Saturdays at the "new south market house" in Boston. It need hardly be said that the spawn of the sea serpent would have added greatly to the society's prestige.

The Linnaean Committee now wrote to Nash asking him for additional information about the capture. He duly supplied this in a letter indicating that he "supposed the young serpent to be the progeny of the remarkable Sea Serpent." He recommended that the "young serpent ought to undergo the severest scrutiny, and I doubt not the investigation by your society will be thorough and satisfactory to the public."

Lonson Nash's confidence was deeply misplaced.

The fact that the "serpent" from Loblolly Cove resembled a common black snake a good deal more than it did the monstrous creature in the harbor, and that people were now scouring the local beaches for other "young" and had found none, might have given pause. Undaunted, the committee, after dissecting the carcass and having detailed anatomical plates made for their publication, concluded that, although "this animal approaches most nearly to the *Coluber constrictor*" (the aforementioned black snake), it must instead be a close relation.

Overriding their own sensible objections to any connection between the two creatures, they named their specimen *Scoliophis atlanticus* (Atlantic humped snake), adding, "It is worthy of remark that nearly all the circumstances with regard to the appearance of the Great Serpent, stated by the deponents as facts, agree with the structure of *Scoliophis*. . . . Supposing that the species of the two serpents is the same, it is not improbable that one is the progeny of the other."

This supposition was to make the committee a laughingstock. *Report of a Committee of the Linnaean Society of New England Relative to a Large Marine Animal Supposed to Be a Serpent Seen Near Cape Ann Massachusetts* resulted in considerable excitement on both sides of the Atlantic. Alas, the "Atlantic humped snake" was shortly to be identified by William D. Peck, professor of natural history at Harvard, and ichthyologists Samuel L. Mitchill and Alexandre Lesueur as nothing more than a deformed black snake. It was a bitter blow from which the Linnaean Society would never recover. Five years later, the society donated their specimens to Harvard and disbanded; only Bigelow continued to pursue the serpent.

The improbable progeny as it appeared in the committee report of the Linnaean Society of New England in 1817. *Scoliophis atlanticus* was in reality a diseased black snake.

Lesueur, who when still in his twenties had taken part in an expedition that yielded 2,500 new species, may even have regretted the role of debunker when he also declared, "As to the famous and gigantic sea serpent, of which this is supposed to be the young, if it comes back next summer I have firmly decided to go and see it for myself."

Whether or not Lesueur proved true his word to go and see it for himself is not known, but the next summer the creature (or something like it) did return. On June 21, 1818, Shubael West, master of the packet *Delia* (also reported as the *Delta*), claimed he'd seen a sea serpent about two leagues from Cape Ann battling a large humpback whale. Although he swore his testimony before Kennebec County (Maine) justice of the peace Ariel Mann on June 27, this report is considered by some to be suspect, in part because the creature is said to have raised its head and tail simultaneously twenty-five and twenty feet, respectively, in the air.

Because the packet was three-fifths of a mile from the combat, it is possible that what the fifteen to eighteen persons on board saw was *two* creatures in a struggle with the whale. Perhaps the creature(s), which were certainly neither prey nor predator of the humpback, were attempting to drive it off from a school of herring or mackerel, upon which both feed.

There was a sighting of a similar creature off Long Island, New York, in mid June and others in late June and early July in Casco Bay, off Portland, Maine. By the end of July, Cape Ann residents were reporting that the creature had returned, and there it remained until the middle of August.

In the summer of 1818, it was not a scientific society but Gloucester resident Captain C. L. Sargent of the merchant marine who collected testimony, most of it from the previous year. Sargent's handwritten notebook, *The Sea Serpent, Evidence About It,* is in the archives of the Cape Ann Historical Association; his reports (evidently taken from acquaintances, including women, whom he considered trustworthy) are short summaries and provide few details or dates. Still, it is from him that we learn that Joseph Moores, who had observed the creature the previous summer, saw what to all appearances was the same creature in July near Muscle Point at about a hundred yards' distance. Using a compass, Moores took bearings and calculated the animal to be 120 feet long. Lydia Wonson also saw it, though not as distinctly as during the previous summer.

William Sargent saw it on July 25; some fishermen went after it with muskets on the twenty-ninth; and on the thirtieth a Captain Webber and other whalers came within yards of it but could not make a harpoon penetrate. On this occasion the creature came so close to the boat that when it submerged, the whalers said, it almost sank them.

On August 12, fisherman Timothy Hodgkins and three companions saw the creature from a boat while returning to Gloucester from Newburyport. Hodgkins at first thought the creature was a school of pilot whales. He changed his mind when he saw the animal up close: It approached his boat, dove under it, and reappeared a mere ten yards away. Hodgkins counted twenty bunches five feet apart and calculated that "his whole length could not be less than one hundred and twenty feet," adding, "I believe he is perfectly harmless, and might be easily caught. . . ."

Testimony of Susan Stover

About the 10th Aug. 1817 in Company with her father near the shore by the house saw the serpent very near his head in very plain of the shape of a dogs he was so near the shore her father took off his hat that he should not frighten him cannot say how long he was saw him ~~turn in the water~~ the parts pass in opposite directions. —— has not seen him this year

Testimony of Lydia Wonson

Augt. 10th 1817 standing in the house first saw him between the house & ten pound Island appeard about 60. or 70 feet on the surface of the water lookd like the buoys of a seine saw him draw himself up into a coil and extend himself again, and this with a good spy glass, nearly ½ an hour he was plainly & fairly in view his head out of water about as large a horses head. saw the same creature

A page of testimony collected by C. L. Sargent, unusual because it contains accounts from two women, Susan Stover and Lydia Wonson. (Cape Ann Historical Association)

Harmless or not, the thing was not easily caught (even with a price on its head), as subsequent events were to show. General Humphreys, who had died that February, would certainly have applauded the dexterous mariners who yielded to "the hope of having the glory of killing him . . . with the certainty of being well remunerated for their expense and hazard."

Hooks and traps were baited and set in response to news of a reward, and the public and eager mariners waited. Then on August 16, a large number of people saw the creature in the vicinity of Squam (Annisquam) Lighthouse. It was only a matter of time before the reputations of the mariners would be put to the test.

Reports of the beast having been spotted off Squam Bar on August 19 touched off a major monster hunt, as reported by Colonel Perkins:

> Believing that the possession of the sea-serpent would be a fortune to those who should have him in their power, many boats were fitted out from Cape Ann and other places in the neighborhood of his haunts. . . . Among others a Captain Rich…of Boston took command of a party, which was fitted out at some expense, and went into the bay, where they cruised along shore two or three days without seeing the serpent.

Then at last the creature was spotted. The chase lasted seven hours, with the beast maintaining a safe lead until it dived under the whaleboat of Captain Richard Rich. The captain reported the incident as follows:

> Squam River, Aug. 20th, 12 o'clock. After several unsuccessful attempts, we have at last fastened on this strange thing called the Sea Serpent. We struck him fairly but the harpoon soon drew out. He has not been seen since, and I fear the wound he received will make him more cautious how he approaches these shores. Since my last [letter], yesterday, we have been constantly in pursuit of him; by day he always keeps a proper distance from us. . . . But a few hours since I thought we were sure of him, for I hove the harpoon into him as fairly as ever a whale was struck, he took from us about 20 fathoms (180 feet) of warp before we could wind the boat, with as much swiftness as a whale. We had but a short ride when we were loose from him to our sore disappointment.

Captain Rich and his crew, though disappointed, did not give up.

On September 10, the *Boston Weekly Messenger,* edited by Nathan Hale, nephew of the patriot of the same name, ran a piece under the headline "The Sea Serpent."

> We lament, in common with the public, the disappointment of the hopes that had been raised by the report of the capture of this remarkable animal. Capt. Richard Rich and his party on Thursday last [September 6] ter-

minated a cruise of nearly three weeks in pursuit of the Serpent by the taking of a fish . . . which, from its singular appearance in the water, they had been led to believe was the Sea Serpent so often described. The intelligence of the capture of this fish, and the assurance of some of the crew, who either believed or wished to believe that this was in fact the animal which has been the object of so much curiosity and speculation, occasioned a general belief that the leviathan of the deep had yielded to the skill and enterprise of our seaman. The rumor produced a very great excitement in this town, and in proportion as curiosity was raised, disappointment has been severely felt. . . .

According to Colonel Perkins, "Thousands were flocking to see this wonder, when it was found to be no other than a large horse macquerel, which (though a great natural curiosity) . . . very much disappointed those who had been induced to visit it."[3]

The *Boston Weekly Messenger* continued:

The inquiry naturally arises, can this fish, or any number of them, be the monster so often described as a Sea Serpent? We answer decidedly no. . . . The existence of some remarkable animal in our waters last summer, particularly near Cape Ann, was proved by the most satisfactory testimony. . . . The descriptions which we have had this season of the Serpent have been less consistent and satisfactory, and undoubtedly often exaggerated. But neither these exaggerated descriptions nor the error of persons who by mistake have been pursuing what had nothing of the remarkable and characteristic appearance of the Sea Serpent ought to lead us to suspect all former testimony. On this subject we are happy to publish the following remarks of a correspondent:

Mr. Hale—

Since the great excitement occasioned last summer by the appearance on our coast of an animal supposed to be a marine serpent, public expectation has been on the watch for the return of so extraordinary a visitor. Whether the same animal has since been seen in our waters, or whether the name sea serpent has been this year applied to objects unlike the original one, is a point on which opinions differ. It is not surprising that to persons prepared to see this aquatic monster, almost every unusual marine phenomena should be identified with the expected serpent. . . .

As we may not this season be gratified with a nearer interview with his serpentine majesty than through the person of his representative the Thunny, it may be well to examine how far the pretensions of the latter give him the right to be considered a legitimate connexion of the former.

The Thunny (Scomber thynnus) is found in almost all seas. . . . It is extremely voracious, feeding on herring and other small fish. It frequents the shores in the spawning season, swimming in vast shoals with great swiftness, accompanied by a hissing noise. They are said to form in swimming a regular parallelogram. The size of the Thunny is usually from 2 to 10 feet in length, and the back and belly considerably convex. . . .

It does not seem probable that a single fish of this kind could produce, by any means, appearances like those ascribed to the sea serpent. . . .

The correspondence of the two appears specious. But those of us who have never seen the one nor the other are obliged to make up our own opinions from the representations of those who have been more fortunate as spectators. . . .

Everyone allows that the phenomenon at Cape Ann harbor last summer had a head. This was carried several feet above the water; it was seen by many, accurately described by a number, and actually fired at, from the distance of about a rod. Now a feature of this kind could not well belong to a train of separate animals, unless one travelled in the air and the rest in the water. Again, the Gloucester Serpent was often seen at rest, as well as in motion, with great length of back uncovered by the water. This was repeatedly described as being 40 or 50 feet in length, not only by the spectators at Cape Ann, but by Judge Herttell and others of New York, who reported his appearance in Long Island Sound.

The appearance of shoals of the Thunny is said to be a thing by no means unfrequent. It is hardly probable that in a maritime town like Gloucester, a great portion of whose inhabitants are sailors, familiar with every sea, that any common marine phenomena should have passed as new.

(Signed) M.

A contemporaneous image of the sea serpent at Cape Ann. (Nahant Historical Society)

A week later (September 17), Hale decided to give the captain a chance to explain himself:

> We conceive it to be a duty we owe to Capt. Rich as well as our readers, to publish the following communication. Capt. Rich with a very laudable spirit undertook the arduous and apparently hazardous enterprise of drawing the monster from his hiding place, and of solving, if possible, an important problem in natural history. If the public have been disappointed by the result of his enterprise, it is not his fault. On the contrary he ought to have the credit of the best intentions, as well as of skillful and bold exertions.

Hale goes on to quote from the testimony provided by Amos Story, Solomon Allen, Lonson Nash, and Matthew Gaffney the previous year, then inserts a disclaimer before quoting Rich's account:

> We leave it to our readers to conclude whether the above testimony, made deliberately on oath by men of respectability, is utterly false and ground-

less. If so we should be glad to know on what grounds human testimony is to be credited. We have no doubt that Capt. Rich has taken an animal which he and others believed to be the Sea Serpent; but whether he has taken the animal described by the above deponents, we entreat our readers to judge for themselves.

Capt. Rich's Statement

Sufficient time having elapsed for the public mind to cease fermenting, I now offer my statement of facts, without comment leaving it for others to judge of the good or ill that it may produce.

Having been fully satisfied in the belief of the existence of a Sea Serpent (although I must acknowledge, I at first doubted), and feeling confident that the means were within the power of man, if rightly used, to overthrow this monster—I determined on a trial—so proceeded to Gloucester and completed my expedition. Presuming I had a formidable foe to contend with, I was well prepared for attack. While selecting my crew I took none but men of respectability and integrity, and among the whole of eleven, eight had seen the supposed Serpent. Some of these had made oath to the account already published of his existence, appearance and character. I selected such men, in order that I might not be deceived, should he make his appearance, having never seen him myself.

When all was in readiness, information was brought us that the Serpent was off Squam Bar. We immediately proceeded thither, where on our arrival we were assured he had been seen, and that we might expect his appearance whenever it should be perfectly calm. The next day brought with it dead calm, with the much wished for appearance of the Serpent. My crew all agreed to a man that what we saw was the "supposed Serpent," which had been seen both at that place and at Gloucester Harbour.

I was perfectly satisfied, so precisely did it answer the description that had been given of him, and had I never approached nearer, I could have given testimony upon oath that I had seen a Serpent not less than 100 feet in length. We did not keep at a distance "and wonder at what we saw." Our object was to take it so we accordingly gave chase. . . .

After many attempts we at length fastened to him. We soon found that he possessed great strength, but he reappeared and we succeeded in taking him. We felt convinced that we had caught the creature which had caused so much wonder. I brought it to Boston, not doubting that those interested would be satisfied with what I had done. . . .

If I am asked—how is it possible for a Fish like this to produce such a wonderful appearance, I can only answer: His peculiar movement and his velocity produced a greater deception than I ever saw before, and that describing his body as being like kegs fastened together, struck me so forcibly, that had I not followed it up and discovered the deception, I should have given my testimony to the long list already given, of the existence of a Sea Serpent on our coast.

I now take my leave of the public, hoping they will do me the justice to say that I used no deception.

Richard Rich

Captain Rich's claim that he had not intended to dupe the public notwithstanding, many went away feeling they'd been hoaxed. More damning still, the creature did not reappear that summer, or if it did, the sighting went unreported.

In his own way, Captain Rich did more to discredit the reports of the sea serpent than had the black snake blunder of the previous summer. The serpent had become a fish and quite a common one at that.

CHAPTER 2 NOTES

1. Perkins's letter to Cushing was not published until November 25, 1848, when it appeared in the *Boston Daily Advertiser* in response to the debate being waged in London over the *Daedalus* affair.

2. One of the most famous teachers in history, Ann Mansfield Sullivan was a student at Perkins School for the Blind. In 1887, having undergone surgery to restore some of her vision, she left the school to undertake the education of Helen Keller.

3. A horse mackerel, as the bluefin tuna (*Thunnus thynnus*) was then known, is a fast, elegantly streamlined fish weighing up to 1,200 pounds. When hooked it will battle for hours at the end of 130-pound test line, making it a favorite of sport fishermen, who value the species for its size and fight. Today, bluefin tuna carry a high dollar value per pound, making them widely hunted for the Japanese sushi market. Many conservationists consider them endangered, although efforts to protect the bluefin have, as of this writing, been sidelined by powerful commercial and governmental lobbies.

3

1819 – 1825

Sightings at Nahant and Swampscott

*Probably the stuffed skin of this monster is never destined
to adorn the walls of any museum, or his remains to repose
in any pickle other than his native brine.*

—Waldo Thompson, *Swampscott: Historical Sketches of the Town*, 1885

By 1819, the scientific community of Europe had had an opportunity to observe with polite condescension the rise and fall of the Linnaean Committee's *Scoliophis* and the reports of Captain Rich's horse mackerel. Their courteous disdain for the methods of their upstart counterparts was, however, nothing compared to the contempt of the committee's own countrymen, particularly in the South.

On May 12, 1819, a play called *The Sea Serpent, or Gloucester Hoax: A Dramatic jeu d'esprit in Three Acts* premiered at the Charleston Theatre in Charleston, South Carolina. The playwright, Charleston native William Crafts, had graduated Harvard College in 1805 and by coincidence had been in Cambridge to give the Phi Beta Kappa address at commencement there in the summer of 1817.

Crafts, who died quite young only seven years later, was considered by his Harvard contemporaries to be one of its most brilliant belles lettres scholars. Having had an opportunity to witness the folly of the Yankee naturalists firsthand, Crafts took on the sea serpent phenomenon of the previous two years with caustic humor. The sea serpent of the play is a hoax invented to bring notice to the town of Gloucester. No one escaped Crafts's satiric wit, as seen in the lines of the character Justice Portly (Lonson Nash).

> For sceptic appetites I'll make a feast
> One thousand affidavits at the least . . .
> Let a new sign upon my door appear:
> Snake! Snake! Snake affidavits taken here!
>
> Let Salem boast her museum, and her witches
> Her statues Newb'ry, Marblehead her riches—
> We from them all the shining now will take,
> The snake and Glo'ster, Glo'ster and the snake!

Cynicism and scorn notwithstanding, by mid June 1819 the sea serpent was back in New England waters and had been seen by two experienced mariners who offered their own "snake affidavits" to Justice of the Peace Theodore Eames, of Boston, on June 9.

Commander Hawkins Wheeler and Gersham Bennett, of the sloop *Concord* of Fairfield (Connecticut), while on passage from New York to Salem on June 6, saw "something that resembled a snake" at about five o'clock in the morning, fifteen miles northwest of Race Point and within sight of Cape Ann. Wheeler described the sighting:

> The weather was good and clear—it was almost calm, with a light air of wind from the S. The vessel was going about two knots—I had a fair and distinct view of the creature, and from his appearance am satisfied that it was of the serpent kind. . . .

Gersham Bennett's testimony provides additional details.

> I was on the deck of the sloop, sitting on the hatches—the man at the helm made an outcry. . . . I immediately arose and went to the side of the vessel, and took a position on the rough-tree, holding on by the shrouds; there I saw a serpent of enormous size and uncommon appearance upon the water. His head was about the length of the anchor stock above the surface of the water, viz. about seven feet. I looked at the anchor stock at the time, and formed my opinion by comparing the two objects. . . . I had

I think as good a view of the animal as if I had been within two rods of him. The color of the animal throughout, as far as could be seen, was black, and the surface appeared to be smooth, without scales—his head was about as long as a horse's and was a proper snake's head—there was a degree of flatness, with a slight hollow on the top of his head—his eyes were prominent, and stood out considerably from the surface, resembling in that respect the eyes of a toad, and were nearer to the mouth of the animal than to the back of the head. I had a full view of him for seven or eight minutes. He was moving in the same direction with the sloop, and about as fast. The back was composed of bunches about the size of a flour barrel, which were apparently three feet apart—they appeared to be fixed but might be occasioned by the motion of the animal, and looked like a string of casks or barrels tied together—the tail was not visible, but the part which could be seen was, I should judge, fifty feet in length—the motion of the bunches was undulatory, but the wake of his tail, which he evidently moved under water, showed a horizontal or sweeping motion, producing a wake as large as the vessel made. He turned his head two or three times slowly round, toward and from the vessel, as if taking a view of some object on board. I went up on the rigging, for the purpose of taking a view of him from above; but before I had reached my station, he sunk below the surface of the water, and did not appear again.

On June 11 and 12, five days after its encounter with the *Concord*, the creature was reported on the south shore off Cohasset, and at Scituate on June 30. In August some soldiers on guard at Fort Independence in Boston saw something similar, but the creature's best show was reserved for the seaside town of Nahant.

In early colonial times, Nahant—a peninsula of about fifteen square miles jutting south into the Atlantic above Boston—was used as a grazing area for animals belonging to the residents of adjacent Saugus, now Lynn. By the time "His Snakeship," as the newspapers now referred to the creature, began to make his appearances there, Nahant was gradually being transformed from a quiet fishing village to a place frequented by the well-to-do of Boston wishing to escape the summer heat. According to Lewis's *History of Lynn* (1829): "Nahant is much visited by persons for the improvement of health and by parties of pleasure. . . . Two steamboats are constantly running from Boston during the pleasant season."

So it was that during the pleasant season of August 1819, the sea serpent was seen by hundreds of residents and resort visitors, among them Samuel Cabot, who recorded his experience in this letter to Colonel Thomas H. Perkins, apparently at Perkins's behest.

Brookline, August 19, 1819

Dear Sir,

I very willingly comply with your request to state what I saw of the Sea Serpent at Nahant, on Saturday last, particularly as I happened to see it under favourable circumstances to form a judgement, and to considerable advantage in point of position and distance.

I got into my chaise about 7 o'clock in the morning, to come to Boston, and on reaching the long Beach observed a number of people collected there, and several boats pushing off and in the offing. I was speculating on what should have occasioned so great an assemblage there without any apparent object, and finally had concluded that they were some Lynn people embarking in those boats on a party of pleasure to Egg Rock or some other point.

I had not heard of the Sea Serpent being in that neighborhood, and I had not lately paid much attention to the evidences which had been given of its existence; the idea of this animal did not enter my mind at the moment.

As my curiosity was directed towards the boats to ascertain the course they were taking, my attention was suddenly arrested by an object emerging from the water, at the distance of about one hundred or one hundred and fifty yards, which gave to my mind at the first glance the idea of a horse's head. As my eye ranged along I perceived, at a short distance, eight or ten regular bunches or protuberances, and at a short interval three or four more. I was now satisfied that the Sea Serpent was before me, and after the first moment of excitement produced by the unexpected sight of so strange a monster, taxed myself to investigate his appearance as accurately as I could.

My first object was the Head, which I satisfied myself was serpent shaped, it was elevated about two feet from the water and he depressed it gradually, to within six or eight inches as he moved along. I could always see under his chin, which appeared to be hollow underneath, or to curve downward. His motion was at that time very slow along the Beach, inclining towards the shore; he at first moved his head from side to side as if to look about him. I did not see his eyes, though I have no doubt I could have seen them if I had thought to attend to this. His bunches appeared to me not altogether uniform in size, and as he moved along some appeared to be depressed, and others brought above the surface, though I could not perceive any motion in them. My next object was to ascertain his length. For this purpose I directed my eye to several whale boats at about the same distance, one of which was beyond him, and by comparing the relative length, I calculated that the distance from the animal's head to the last protuberance I had noticed, would be equal to about five of those boats. I felt persuaded by this examination that he could not be less than eighty feet long; as he approached the shore and came between me and a point of land which projects from the eastern point of the beach, I had another means of satisfying myself on this point.

After I had viewed him thus attentively for about four or five minutes, he sunk gradually into the water and disappeared; he afterward made his appearance for a moment at a short distance.

My first reflection after the animal was gone was that the idea I had received from the description you gave of the animal you saw at Gloucester, in 1817, was perfectly realized in this instance; and that I had discovered nothing which you had not before described. The most authentic testimony given of his first appearance there seemed to me remarkably correct; and I felt as if the appearance of this monster had been already familiar to me.

After remaining some two or three hours on the beach, without seeing him, I returned towards Nahant; and in crossing the small beach had another good view of him for a longer time, but at a greater distance. At this time he moved more rapidly, causing a white foam under the chin, and a long wake, and his protuberances had a more uniform appearance. At this time he must have been seen by two or three hundred persons on the beach and on the heights on each side, some of whom were very favorably situated to observe him.

> I am, very respectfully,
>
> Your obedient servant
>
> Samuel Cabot

Cabot's account, with its flattering reference to the "descriptions you gave of the animal" being "perfectly realized in this instance," is a product of a more polite age and an acknowledgment of the ridicule to which Perkins (and other witnesses) had no doubt been subjected. Cabot was not a trained naturalist, but he nevertheless attempted to provide the most accurate description possible so that his observation of the creature would bolster the earlier claims.

Cabot's efforts to defend the dignity of the other witnesses is clearly echoed in the letter of James Prince, Esq., marshal of the district, who presented his "unvarnished" version of the events in a letter to Judge Davis, who had been a member of the Linnaean Society Committee two years earlier. Whether or not Judge Davis was pleased by being reminded of a painful subject is another question altogether.

> My Dear Sir,
>
> I presume I may have seen what is generally thought to be the SEA SERPENT—I have also seen my name inserted in the evening newspaper at Boston on Saturday, in a communication on this subject. For your gratification, and from a desire that my name may not sanction any thing beyond what was actually presented and passed in review before me, I will now state that, which in the presence of more than two hundred witnesses, took place near the long beach of Nahant on Saturday morning last:
>
> Intending to pass two or three days with my family in Nahant, we left Boston early on Saturday morning. On passing the half way house on the Salem turnpike, Mr. Smith informed us the Sea Serpent had been seen the evening before at Nahant beach, and that a vast number of people from Lynn had gone to the beach that morning in hopes of being gratified with a sight of him. . . .
>
> I was glad to find that I had brought my famous mast-head spy glass

with me as it would enable me, from its form and size, to view him to advantage if I might be so fortunate to see him. On our arrival on the beach, we associated with a considerable collection of persons on foot and in chaises; and very soon an animal of the fish kind made his appearance nearly in this attitude and manner.

His head appeared about three feet out of the water; I counted thirteen bunches on his back—my family thought there were fifteen. He passed three times at a moderate rate across the bay, but so fleet as to occasion a foam in the water—and my family and self, who were in a carriage, judged he was from fifty feet, and not more than sixty feet in length. Whether, however, the wake might not add to his appearance of length, or whether the undulation of the water, or his peculiar manner of propelling himself, might not cause the appearance of protuberances, I leave for your better judgement.

The first view of the animal occasioned some agitation, and the novelty perhaps prevented that precise discrimination which afterward took place. As he swam up the bay, we and the other spectators moved on, and kept nearly abreast of him; he occasionally withdrew himself under the water, and the idea occurred to me that his occasionally raising his head above the level of the water was to take breath, as the times he kept under water was on the average of eight minutes. And after being accustomed to view him, we became more composed; and his general appearance was as above delineated. . . .

I had several distinct views of him from the long beach so called, and at some of them the animal was not more than a hundred yards distance. After being on the long beach with other spectators about an hour, the animal disappeared and I proceeded on towards Nahant; but on passing the second beach, I met Mr. James Magee of Boston with several ladies in a carriage . . . and we were again gratified beyond even what we saw in the other bay; which I concluded he had left in consequence of the number of boats in the offing pursuing him—the noise of whose oars must have disturbed him, as he appeared to us to be a harmless timid animal. We had here more than a dozen different views of him, and each similar to the other; one, however, was so near that the coachman exclaimed, "Oh, see his glistening eye!"

I feel satisfied of the correctness of my decision that he is sixty feet long, unless the ripple of his wake deceived me—nor, my dear Sir, do I undertake to say he was of the Snake or Eel kind; though this was the general impression of my family, the spectators and myself. Certain it is, he is a very strange animal. I have been accustomed to see Whales, Sharks, Grampuses, Porpoises and other large fishes, but he partook of none of the appearances of either of these: The Whale and the Grampus would have spouted, the Shark never raises his head out of the water, and the Porpoise skips and plays; neither have such appearances on their backs, or such a head as this animal. The Shark it is true has a fin on his back, and often the fluke of his tail is out of the water; but these appendages would not display the form and certainly not the number of protuberances which this animal exhibited, nor is it the habit of the Shark to avoid a boat.

The water was extremely smooth, and the weather clear; we had been so habituated to see him that we were cool and composed. The time occupied was from a quarter past eight to half past eleven; a cloud of witnesses exceeding two hundred, brought together for a single purpose, were all alike satisfied and united as to appearances and of the length and size of the animal. . . . I must conclude there is a strange animal on our coast— and I have thought [that] an unvarnished statement might be gratifying to a mind attached to the pursuit of natural science, and aid in the inquiries on a controverted question, which I hope will have interested you. I have ventured on the description, being also induced to hope that if anything of the marvelous is stated as coming from me, you will correct it.

> Accept the respects and attention of,
> Dear Sir, yours sincerely,
> James Prince
> Nahant, Aug. 16th, 1819

What is most interesting about Prince's account is that he is not surprised by a strange creature appearing in the water. He has, on the contrary, set out to see it and is glad to have with him his "famous mast-head spy glass." He and his family arrive at the "long beach," presumably in an open carriage, and encounter "a considerable number of persons on foot and in chaises" who have similarly come to see the creature. When the creature moves off up the bay, one can imagine the carriages jockeying for position as they follow it, keeping "nearly abreast." One can assume there was a festive atmosphere on this warm, clear August Saturday. All in all, it was a pleasant family outing.

"The Prince and Cabot accounts were published in the papers," Joseph E. Garland points out in his book *The North Shore,* "and revived the sensation a hundredfold. Probably it was only coincidence that Prince was the first treasurer of the Massachusetts General Hospital and a close friend of the chairman of the board—the doyen of sea serpent sighters, Colonel Perkins—who happened also to be Sam Cabot's father-in-law."[1]

Happily, testimony regarding the serpent did not rest solely with the relatives and business associates of Colonel Perkins. Perkins could not possibly have influenced Obadiah Turner, who 178 years earlier had written:

> Ye Indians doe say yt they have manie times seen a wonderful big serpent
> lying on ye water, and reaching from Nahauntus to ye greate rock wch we
> call Birdes Egg Rocke; wch is much above belief for yt would be nigh upon
> a mile. Ye Indians, as said, be given to declaring wonderful things, and it
> pleaseth them to make ye white people stare. But making all discounte, I
> doe believe yt a wonderful monster in forme of a serpent doth visit these
> waters.

Nor is it likely that Perkins was responsible for the journal entry dated January 14, 1858, in which Henry David Thoreau provides another witness at Swampscott by the name of Buffum, who claimed to have seen the serpent twenty times. Thoreau says that at one time Buffum was "within fifty or sixty feet of [the serpent], so that he could have touched him with a very long pole, if he had dared to." Thoreau indicates that Buffum was unclear as to the year of his sighting (1817 or 1819), but because he saw the serpent at Swampscott along with several hundred other witnesses, and he mentions Prince, we can conclude that the sighting was in August 1819.

Another witness, Nathan Chase, provided this account of his sighting to

J. B. Holder in 1881. Holder later published it in an article entitled "The Great Unknown," written for *Century Magazine* in 1892.

I saw [the serpent] on a pleasant, calm summer morning of August, 1819, from Long Beach, Lynn, now called Nahant. The water was smooth and the creature seemed about a quarter mile away; consequently, we could see him distinctly and the motion of his body. Later in the day I saw him again off Red Rock. He then passed along about one hundred feet from where I stood with his head two feet out of the water. His speed was about that of an ordinary steamer.

What I saw of his length was about sixty feet. It was difficult to count the humps, or undulations on his back, as they did not all appear at once. This accounts in part for the varied descriptions given by other parties. His appearance on the surface was occasional and but for a short time. The color of his skin was dark, differing but little from that of the water, or the back of any common fish. This is the best description I can give of him from my own observation. I saw the creature just as truly, though not as clearly, as I ever saw anything. I have no doubt that the uncommon, strange rover, which has been seen by hundreds of men and boys, is a form of snake, Plesiosaurus, or some such form of marine animal.

The sea serpent illustration that accompanied the Chase account as published in *Lynn and Surroundings* by Clarence Hobbs. (Nahant Historical Society)

Chase has the advantage, writing some sixty-two years later, of having had the opportunity to observe the rise of a new field of scientific study—paleontology—when attempting to identify the creature.

The first complete skeleton of a plesiosaur was excavated from the chalk cliffs of Lyme Regis, Dorset, England, in 1823 by Mary Anning, who has been described as "the greatest fossilist the world ever knew." Anning was born into a family that supplemented its meager income by fossil hunting, and upon the death of her father she continued to do so as a principal means of support.

The Reverend William D. Conybeare, who had done a preliminary reconstruction of the plesiosaur in 1822 based on a disembodied skull, was pleased to discover that when the full skeleton was unearthed, it "confirmed the justice of my former conclusions in every essential point. . . ."

Although fossil and geological evidence point to the extinction of these marine reptiles some 65 million years ago, the theory that sea serpents and lake monsters are descendents of the giant swan-necked creatures continues to provoke discussion to the present day.

Giant snake or relic marine reptile—whatever the creature was—it appears to have remained for some time at Nahant before moving on to Cape Ann, where the schooner *Science* was surveying the harbor. Reverend Cheever Felch, who taught navigation to the midshipmen, was at the time chaplain of the seventy-four-gun man-of-war *Independence*. The somewhat defensive tone of his letter to the editor of the *Boston Centinel* suggests that he too was well aware of how the information might be received. [2]

Gloucester, Aug. 26, 1819

Dear Sir,

Others having taken in hand to give some account of the Sea Serpent, I know not why I should not have the same liberty. Being on this station, in the United States schooner *Science*, for the purpose of surveying this harbor, we were proceeding this morning down the harbor in the schooner's boat, when abreast of Dallivan's Neck, William T. Malbone, Esq. Commander of the schooner, seeing some appearance on the water, said, "there is your Sea-Serpent," meaning it as a laugh on me, for believing in its existence; but it proved to be no joke.

The animal was then between thirty and forty yards distance from us. Mr. Malbone, Midshipman Blake, myself, and our four boatmen had a distinct view of him. He soon sunk, but not so deep but we could trace his course. He rose again within twenty yards distance of us, and lay some time on the water. He then turned, and steered for Ten Pound Island; we pulled after him, but finding that he was not pleased with the noise of our oars, they were laid in and the boat sculled. We again approached very near him. He continued some length of time, plying between Ten Pound Island and Stage Point.

As he often came near the Point, we thought we could get a better view of him there than from the boat, of which he seemed suspicious. Mr. Malbone and myself landed; and the boat was sent to order the schooner down, for the purpose of trying what effect a twelve pound carronade would have upon him. [A carronade was a small, short-range ship's cannon originating at the Carron Iron Works in Scotland circa 1779.]

He did not remain long after we landed, so that I was unable to effect my intention of ascertaining, accurately, his length, with my instruments. From my knowledge of aquatic animals, and habits of intimacy with marine appearances, I could not be deceived. We had a good view of him, except the very short period while he was under water, for half an hour.

His colour is dark brown with white under the throat. His size we could not accurately ascertain, but his head is about three feet in circumference, flat and much smaller than his body. We did not see his tail; but from the end of the head to the fartherest protuberance was not far from one hundred feet. I speak with a degree of certainty, from being much accustomed to measure and estimate distances and length. I counted fourteen bunches on his back, the first one say ten or twelve feet from his head, and the others about seven feet apart. They decreased in size towards the tail. These bunches were sometimes counted with and sometimes without a glass. Mr. Malbone counted thirteen, Mr. Blake thirteen and fourteen, and the boatman about the same number.

His motion was sometimes very rapid, and at other times he lay nearly still. He turned slowly, and took up considerable room in doing it. He sometimes darted under water, with the greatest velocity as if seizing prey. The protuberances were not from his motion, as they were the same whether in slow or rapid movement. His motion was partly vertical and partly horizontal, like that of fresh water snakes. I have been much ac- quainted with snakes in our interior waters. His motion was the same.

I have given you in round numbers, one hundred feet, for his length, that is, what we saw; but I should say he must be one hundred and thirty feet in length, allowing for his tail. There were a considerable number of birds about the Sea Serpent as I have seen them about a Snake on shore. That there is an aquatic animal in the form of a snake is not to be doubted. Mr. Malbone, till this day, was incredulous. No man would now convince him that there was not such a being. The sketch or picture [by] Mr. Prince is perfectly correct. I could not, with my own pencil, give a more correct likeness.

> With respect,
> Your obedient servant,
> Cheever Felch

According to J. L. Homer:

About this time the infidels of the South began to laugh at the Yankees, and to insinuate that they were too credulous on the subject. The [Columbian] Centinel resented the insult, and threw back in their teeth the burning words, *southern scoffers* [emphasis added] in the following para- graph from a September issue: "It is perhaps owing to [the sea serpent's] harmlessness that he has not long since been taken. Had he exhibited the ferocity at first attributed to him, or occasioned the death of a single sea- man or fisherman, the whole coast would have been alive with his adver- saries, and our southern scoffers, if they pleased, [would] have long since seen his skeleton decorating the hall of our Linnaean Society."

Whether it was the sea breeze or the unusual wildlife that drew Colonel Perkins to the north shore of Nahant we do not know, but that fall he pur- chased a plot of land overlooking Eagle Rock and began construction of a stone cottage. The following summer, he and his large family took up resi-

Colonel Perkins's stone cottage overlooking the bay. (Nahant Historical Society)

dence and enjoyed, as Garland points out, the only sighting of that summer at Nahant, "obligingly from his terrace."

The sighting by the Perkins family may have been the only one at Nahant, but a short distance up the coast, in Swampscott, the creature appeared on August 5, 1820, as reported from Salem. [3]

> On Saturday last about 1 o'clock in the afternoon, the Sea Serpent was distinctly seen again from Phillips Point [now Little's Point], by Mr. Richard Phillips, his wife and family and the younger men at work in the shoemaker's shop near Mr. P's house; also by Mr. Heath and family from the Beach, about a quarter of a mile from the Point, and by Mr. Ingalls, a respectable man, whose shop is near the beach and can command a full view of the sea. . . . Three intrepid young men, at work in the shop, whose names are Jonathan B. Lewis, Andrew Reynolds and Benjamin King, embarked in a boat, and came within about thirty yards of him. . . . He was also seen Sunday afternoon by several persons residing at the Beach and Point.

One of the young men at work at the shop, Andrew Reynolds, appeared before Justice of the Peace John Prince, Jr., and gave this statement:

On Saturday, the fifth day of August inst., about 1 o'clock P.M., I discovered in the water near Phillips Beach, at Swampscut, an animal different from any that I had ever seen before; he was lying on the surface of the water, which was at that time very smooth, and appeared to be about 50 or 60 feet long. . . . We took a boat and rowed towards him . . . and had a very distinct view of him. He had a head about two feet long, and shaped somewhat like an egg, which he carried out of the water when he was moving. There were several protuberances on his back, the highest point of which appeared to be seven or eight inches above the level of the water. He was perfectly black. When we first drew towards him, he was moving westerly from Phillips Point, and as we drew near to him, he turned and moved to the eastward, and when we got within about thirty yards of him he sank under the water and disappeared.

News of the Phillip's Beach sighting traveled all the way to New York City and was reported in the *New York Daily Advertiser*. [4]

We congratulate the public on the safe arrival of the "Old Serpent" of the ocean at his usual station in Massachusetts Bay. This may now be fairly considered the monster's summer residence, and will probably be re-peated from year to year, unless some hardy whalemen should succeed in fastening a harpoon to his scaly side. His presence will at least serve to break up the monotony of the papers, for some time past devoted almost exclusively to the queen of England and her affairs. We have no hesitation in acknowledging our obligations to the "Snake" for this visit; and hope at the same time that no evil-minded person will endeavor, by fair means or foul, to change this formidable animal into an insignificant horse-mackerel—at least without first satisfactorily accounting for the twenty-three bunches on his back of the size of a ten gallon keg: it being physi-cally impossible to place so many of them, and of such size, upon the back of a fish not more than ten feet in length.

The *Advertiser*'s sponsorship of "this formidable animal" was echoed the same year by former Linnaean Committee member Jacob Bigelow, who wrote the following in his "Documents and Remarks Concerning the Sea Serpent" in the *American Journal of Science and Arts*. [5]

As the friends of science can have no object in view more important than the attainment of truth it is proper to submit . . . some additional evidence . . . which has come to light since the publication of Capt. Rich's letter. . . . It is to be hoped that the unsuccessful termination of Capt. Rich's cruise will not deter others from improving any future opportunities which may occur for solving what may now perhaps be considered the most interesting problem in the science of Natural History.

Such opportunities were few in 1821. There was apparently only one sighting at Nahant, although Francis Joy spotted an unknown creature in the vicinity of Nantucket Island sometime that summer, and on August 2 a customs inspector named Samuel Duncan saw another from a whaler near Portsmouth Harbor in New Hampshire.

Later that month, the *Eastport Sentinel* carried this report datelined Boston, August 13, 1821:

The Sea Serpent—Was seen yesterday about ½ past 12 o'clock by the officers, crew and passengers of the schooner *Cash* (Capt. Beal) from Bowdoinham. He was first seen by Mr. Asa B. Hagins, a passenger, about 1½ miles northeast of the Graves [an appropriately named series of rock ledges in Massachusetts Bay] moving towards Nahant; his motion was slow and apparently playful, with his head raised from the water about three feet. The circumference of the animal was about the size of a common barrel; his head shaped like that of a horse and the protuberances on his back were about six feet apart. The sail on the schooner was taken in, and the Serpent kept in distinct view more than 30 minutes; his length appeared about 60 feet, but having no glass on board it could not be ascertained with certainty.

To these facts Capt. Beal, Mr. Sampson, the mate and Mr. Hagins are ready to testify, and authorize this statement.

Predictably, the Perkins family saw the creature from the stone cottage in 1822. Realizing Nahant's potential as a fashionable watering place, Colonel Perkins was inspired to form a syndicate there for the purposes of buying land and building a hotel. One wonders if it was he who, envisioning the lure to future guests, tipped off the Boston press that the creature had returned.

The Nahant Hotel, which had cost an impressive sixty thousand dollars, opened on June 26, 1823. Visitors in June and July of that year who'd come hoping to spot the serpent from one of the broad porches were to be disappointed. There were, however, compensations. Guests could choose between hot and cold fresh- and saltwater baths, and there were billiards rooms, a bowling alley, and a choice of sailing, fishing, riding, and swimming. Those wanting refreshment were served by the dining room, which could accommodate 124 persons.

Three gentlemen from Duxbury by the name of Weston saw the creature in Plymouth Bay sometime that July, but it showed up only once at Nahant. On July 12, it was seen by a local fisherman, Francis Johnson, Jr., in Lynn Harbor.

> I heard a noise in the water, and saw, about four rods distant, something resembling the head of a fish or serpent, elevated about two feet above the surface, followed by seven or eight bunches, the first about six feet from the head, all were about six feet apart, and raised about six inches above the water. It then [moved] eastwardly, at the rate of five miles an hour, with an undulating motion, like that of a caterpillar; its color was dark like that of a porpoise. I firmly believe what I saw to be the animal hitherto described as the "sea serpent."

The creature turned up again in early August, but not in Nahant. The *Salem Gazette* reported that the sea serpent had been seen off Squam Bar on August 6 and in Sandy Bay Harbor on the seventh. As many as fifty witnesses gave the usual description and reported firing upon it, but the balls did not seem to penetrate.

Four days later, members of the Ruggles family, of Bristol County, Massachusetts, were enjoying a swim on Plum Island beach in Newburyport when they were startled by the appearance of a huge animal. The creature came up a few yards from shore, where just a few moments previously they'd been bathing. They then watched it for more than half an hour as it moved up the shore in the direction of Shad Cove, where they lost sight of it.

The only reference to a sighting in 1824, which appears in Bernard Heuvelmans's *In the Wake of the Sea-Serpents*, indicates that a sea serpent was seen by two gentlemen from Plymouth in the vicinity of Little Boar's Head.

The creature apparently made no Massachusetts appearances at all in 1825, not even to the Perkins family, which would seem to mitigate against them fabricating the phenomenon. However, writer James L. Homer, who often stayed at Nahant, hinted that "it has been insinuated—with what truth I am unable to say—that the people of Nahant themselves, the hotel keepers, or some wag of an editor for them, often raise the cry of sea-serpent! when, in fact, his majesty was more than a thousand miles off."

Homer had written truer words than he knew, for although no one at Nahant claimed to have seen the serpent, it was, in fact, not a thousand but some four hundred miles north in Nova Scotia. There, according to Heuvelmans, a sixty-foot creature matching the descriptions given at Gloucester and Nahant was seen on July 15 in Halifax harbor from the shore by a farmer named Goreham and his family and also from a boat by a William Barry and several companions.

CHAPTER 3 NOTES

1. On August 28, a sighting was reported in the *Eastport* (Maine) *Sentinel*; Prince had a brother living in that city. The newspaper also carried a snippet datelined Liverpool (England), June 21, that reported with considerable enthusiasm the arrival in that port of the steamship *Savannah*, "the first ship on this construction that has undertaken a voyage across the Atlantic."

2. "Dallivan's Neck" referred to in the first paragraph of the letter is Dolliver's Neck, and the commander's name ("William T. Malbone" in the letter) is sometimes spelled Melborne, from which one could assume that the good reverend hadn't the best penmanship.

3. The Mr. Ingalls referred to in the sighting is probably the descendant of Francis Ingalls, one of a pair of enterprising brothers who left Salem in 1629 "with leave to go where they would." Ingalls settled in an area known as M'squompskut, now Swampscott, where he established the first tannery in New England in 1632.

4. The reference to the queen of England reflects the fact that the exploits of Britain's royal family were headline news then, as now. In this case, it was Queen Caroline, whose estranged husband, George IV, had recently succeeded his father, George III (Mad King George), after a regency of nine years. George IV refused to allow poor Caroline to attend

his coronation, and unsuccessfully attempted to divorce her on the grounds of infidelity. When George died ten years later without a legitimate heir, he was succeeded by his brother William IV, who reigned for seven years and also died without legitimate issue. The crown then passed to their niece, a girl of eighteen who would become England's longest-reigning monarch, and whose name would define an era: Victoria.

5. The additional evidence referred to in the article includes the material gathered by Rev. Alden Bradford in 1804; the Prince, Cabot, and Felch letters; and the testimony of Wheeler and Bennett.

4

1826 — 1848

His Snakeship

We hail thee welcome, thou King of Snakes....
Again thrice welcome thy noble Snakeship. A New York
Captain having seen thee, thou shalt no longer be called a
nonentity, a horse mackerel, or a base counterfeit,
but the true Leviathan of the great deep.

—*New York Spectator*, June 1826

On June 17, 1826, the captain and some passengers of the *Silas Richards*, while on passage from Liverpool to New York, encountered an unknown creature at latitude 41°30′ north, longitude 67°32′ west, in the vicinity of Georges Bank.

Upon arriving in New York, the captain, Henry Holdredge, submitted a letter to the *New York Mercantile Advertiser*.

Dear Sirs—If you should deem the following statement worthy of insertion in your valuable journal, the veracity of it can be attested by the undersigned. . . .

While standing by the starboard bow, looking at the unruffled surface of the ocean, about 7 o'clock P.M., I perceived a sudden perturbation in the water, and immediately on that an object presented itself, with its head above the water about four feet . . . which position it retained for nearly a minute, when it returned to the surface and kept approaching abreast of the vessel, at a distance of about fifty yards. I immediately called to the passengers on deck, several of whom observed it for the space of eight minutes, as it glided along slowly and undauntedly past the ship at the rate of about three miles an hour. Its colour was a dark dingy black with protuberances similar to the above sketch [unfortunately not printed in the *Advertiser*]; its visible length appeared about sixty feet, and its circumference ten feet. From former accounts which have been given of such a monster, and which have never been credited, this exactly corresponds, and I have no doubt but it is one of those species called Sea Serpent. It made a considerable wake in the water in its progress.

I remain your obedient servant,

Henry Holdredge, Captain

One of the passengers, William Warburton, an employee of Barclay & Bros., of London, was asked by his employers to provide his personal account of the sighting. The following excerpts are taken from his letter to Robert Barclay, Esq.

The captain and myself were standing on the starboard side of the vessel, looking over the bulwark, and remarking how perfectly smooth was the surface of the sea. It was about half past 6 o'clock P.M. and a cloudless sky. On a sudden [sic] we heard a rushing in the water ahead of the ship. At first we imagined it to be a whale spouting; and turning to the quarter from whence the sound proceeded, we observed the serpent. . . .

I must premise that I never had heard of the existence of such an animal. I instantly exclaimed, "Why, there is a sea snake." "That is the sea serpent," exclaimed the captain, "and I would give my ship and cargo to catch the monster."

I immediately called to the passengers, who were all below, but only five or six came up. . . . The remainder refused . . . saying there had been too many hoaxes of that kind already. I was too eager to stand parleying with them, and I returned to the captain.

In the same slow style the serpent passed the vessel at about the distance of fifty yards from us, neither turning his head to the right nor left. As soon as his head had reached the stern of the vessel, he gradually laid it down in a horizontal position with his body, and floated along like the mast of a vessel. That there was upwards of sixty feet visible is clearly shown by the circumstance, that the length of the ship was upwards of one hundred and twenty feet, and at the time his head was off the stern, the other end (as much as was above the surface) had not passed the main-mast. . . . After he had declined his head, we saw him for about twenty minutes ahead, floating along like an enormous log of timber.

Warburton also noted that two days later the creature (or one like it) was seen by another vessel off Cape Cod about two hundred miles from the *Silas Richards*'s position.

It was actually three days later that Captain Peter Daggett reported in the *Boston Palladium* having seen a sea serpent three leagues south of Cape Cod Light. (A league is the equivalent of three nautical miles, or 6,080 feet.) Captain Charles Godspeed, master of the sloop *Iris*, wrote up his account of a similar creature, forty to fifty feet in length, in the same vicinity and submitted it to the *Hartford Times*:

As he neared us we perceived his head about 4 feet above the level of the water, making his course athwart our bow. . . . We stood for him with about a three knot breeze, but found we could not overtake him. The above can be testified by myself and seven others on board.

There was also an unusual report in the *New York Post* from an individual identifying himself as "the Supercargo of a vessel recently returned from the East Indies." The name of the ship that was "surrounded for several hours by a number of Sea Monsters" while at latitude 40° south, longitude about 20° east, is not given, nor is the description much help in clarifying the identity of the creatures. The writer does indicate that the serpents "carried their heads three or four feet out of the water; their bodies appeared of an irregular shape, resembling a sunken rock, and were covered with barnacles." However, the "eight or nine" thirty- to forty-foot creatures also had "tails forked like a fish's," which is hard to interpret. Still, the writer also made a point of saying that "some of them at a short distance off exactly resemble the representation, and their appearance generally was similar to the description I have seen of the Sea Serpent, which appeared on our coast some time since."

The Reverend J. G. Wood also reports that the *Lynn Mirror* carried a brief mention of the creature having been in Nahant sometime during the summer of 1826. Then, on Christmas Day of that year, the captain and crew of the *Gold Hunter,* on passage from Wales to New York, had an unknown creature in sight for about forty minutes a bit farther out in the Atlantic. As reported in the *New York Gazette,* Captain Knowles said that, when first sighted, "its head was elevated about six feet out of the water, and directed towards the bow of the vessel. Night coming on, it was lost sight of. Its color was black." He described the creature as "80 or 90 feet long, its head about the size of a bullock's without the horns; the circumference of the body was about equal to that of a barrel, tapering to the tail to about the thickness of a topmast, and smooth; it was suddenly rounded at the end and was destitute of fins."

The following July (1827), the captain and passengers of the sloop *Levant* reported a similar creature in Vineyard Sound off Gay Head, Martha's Vineyard. They claimed that they had had "a very near and distinct view of the monster, and could not have mistaken it for any known species of fish."

Some citizens and scientists might sneer at the idea of a sea serpent, but Yale University professor Benjamin Silliman, a distinguished American geologist and chemist, did not. Silliman became a champion of sorts, writing of the creature in the *American Journal of Science:* "To us it seems a matter of surprise that any person who has examined the testimony can doubt the existence of the Sea-serpent."

On the other side of the Atlantic, Scottish botanist William J. Hooker expressed a similar point of view in the *Edinburgh Journal of Science.* "It [the sea serpent] can now no longer be considered in association with hydras and mermaids for there has been nothing said with regard to it inconsistent with reason. It may at least be assumed as a sober fact in Natural History. . . . We cannot suppose that the most ultra-skeptical can now continue to doubt with regard to facts attested by such highly respectable witnesses."

Yet, the ultraskeptical did continue to doubt, and even deny, the existence of the sea serpent. Nor was the creature cooperating; there appear to be no records of even a single sighting in New England during the next three years. It was not until July 1830 that a vague report mentions a "strange animal," from sixty to a hundred feet in length, somewhere off the New England coast.

The best appearance that summer took place a few miles from the mouth of the Kennebunk River, where on July 21 a sixty-foot-long creature startled three fishermen when it came within six feet of their boat. Only one of the three, a man named Gooch, was bold enough to remain on deck, where he "returned the glances of his serpentship, for a considerable length of time." Gooch, who the paper claimed was "a man whose statement can be relied on," said the serpent "raised his head about four feet out of the water, and looked directly into the boat." By way of description, Gooch said that "his skin was dark gray and covered with scales; he had no bunches on his back. When he disappeared he made no effort to swim, but sank down apparently without exertion."

The following June (1831), another of the creatures turned up in Boothbay Harbor, Maine. This one was estimated to be 150 to 200 feet long. The *Wiscasset Yankee* published a compelling account of the sightings and noted that it was "the same monster, probably, that visited the same harbor last year about this time." The creature seen in 1831 was first noted on Sunday by Mr. Chandler, keeper of the harbor light. However, on Tuesday, "the nearest and most accurate view of this monster was had . . . from a northerly part in the western harbor so called, very near the dwelling of Marshall Smith, Esq." Smith and his brother had an excellent opportunity to inspect the creature, because it passed them at a distance of only 60 feet. The creature also cruised back and forth 150 feet from another ten to twelve men watching from Mr. Smith's wharf.

The description given of the creature in the *Wiscasset Yankee* agrees in many respects with those from Gloucester fourteen years earlier, including its color—brown on the back, yellow-brown on the belly—and its ability to make hairpin turns.

> Most of them [the witnesses] would be willing to testify under oath that his length could not be less than 200 feet . . . his general form . . . resembled that of an eel, more than any other animal known. . . . All agreed that there were no bumps on his back, but his undulating motions in swimming were like a leech or bloodsucker which gave his back precisely the

appearance of bumps hitherto described by those who have seen him. The shape of his head which was most distinctly seen was compared to a snake's—flat on the top, and tapering before and behind. Although of such immense length, he made several very short quick turns, from which it may be inferred his body cannot be very large in circumference. His head and tail in one of these turns appeared within less than 20 feet of each other. Neither dorsal nor lateral fins could be discovered by anyone.

The animal was also seen in Boothbay Harbor that summer by a Captain Walden and the crew of the revenue cutter *Detector*.

The following year, an article in the *Lynn Weekly Messenger* (August 1832) carried an account of the sea serpent seen on July 27. Many of the weeklies in this era used reports culled from other newspapers to fill out their editions. This report is credited to the *Boston Advocate*; the bracketed statement is probably an editorial note corroborating the account with a local sighting on August 2 or 9.

On the 27th ult.[1] a sea serpent was seen by a boat's crew of four persons for 15 minutes in a southeasterly direction from Nahant about 2½ miles. He passed from the northeast between them and the land circularly, to the southward and the eastward. Many bunches on his back were seen, supposed about forty in number. He moved spirally like the land serpents, and raised his head (barrel size) apparently 4½ feet above water at an angle of seventy degrees. It was nearly calm, and in going through the water the object made a wake equal in length to a vessel of 300 tons in rapid progress. It has been said that porpoises will make such an appearance, but our informant (one of the four who was in the boat) says it is impossible to be deceived in this respect, because the serpent (as he supposed him to be) disappeared two or three times and always re-appeared in the same position from the head, and he was positive that his movements were spirally. The skipper of the boat was Mr. Washington Johnson.

We give the above statement as related to a gentleman of this city, by a man who is well known to be respectable and cautious in his assertions.

—*Boston Advocate*

[His Snakeship is stated to have been seen off Nahant on Thursday by 150 persons.]

The following spring, on May 15, 1833, five officers of the British Army, and their man-of-war's man, encountered a sea serpent while salmon fishing near Mahone Bay, Halifax, Nova Scotia. The following is an account of their adventure, written by Henry Ince, which ultimately made its way into the *Zoologist* in London.[2]

[We were] focused on a shoal of grampuses [grampus is a generic name for any number of small toothed whales related to dolphins; in this case, it might mean either pilot or killer whales] that seemed to be quite agitated. Indeed the excited fish approached our craft so closely that several of the men playfully fired at them with their small caliber rifles.

Our attention was presently diverted from the whales and such "small deer" by an exclamation from Dowling, our man-of-war's man, of "Oh Sirs, look here!" We were startled into ready compliance, and saw an object that banished all other thoughts, save wonder and surprise.

At the distance of from a hundred and fifty to two hundred yards on our starboard bow, we saw the head and neck of some denizen of the deep, precisely like those of a common snake, in the act of swimming, the head so far elevated and thrown forward by the curve of the neck as to enable to see water under and beyond it.

The creature rapidly passed, leaving a regular wake, from the commencement of which, to the fore part which was out of the water, we judged the length to be eighty feet.

We were all taken aback at the sight, and with staring eyes in speechless wonder, stood gazing at it for a full half a minute.

There could be no mistake, no delusion, and we were all perfectly satisfied that we had been favoured with a view of the true and veritable sea serpent, which had been generally considered to have existed only in the brain of some Yankee skipper, and treated as a tale not much entitled to belief.

Dowling's exclamation is worthy of record: "Well, I've sailed in all parts of the world, and have seen rum sights in my time, but this is the queerest thing I ever did see." And surely, Jack Dowling was right!

It is most difficult to give correctly the dimensions of any object in the water. The head of the creature we set down at about six feet in length, and that portion of the neck which we saw at the same, the extreme length at between eighty and one hundred feet. The neck in thickness equaled the bole [trunk] of a moderate size tree.

The head and neck were a dark brown or nearly black colour, streaked with white in irregular streaks. I do not recall seeing any part of the body.

Such is the rough account of the sea serpent, and all in the party who saw it are still in the land of the living: Lyster in England, Malcolm in New South Wales with his regiment, and the remainder still vegetating in Halifax.

Signed: W. Sullivan, Captain, Rifle Brigade

A. Maclachlan, Lieutenant R.B.

G. P. Malcolm, Ensign, R.B.

B. O'Neal Lyster, Lieutenant, Artillery

H. Ince, Ordnance Storekeeper, Halifax

One can't help but like Henry Ince, his slight against Yankee skippers notwithstanding. His first reaction is "wonder and surprise," and, unlike some earlier witnesses who are so confident in their judgments as to seem conceited, Ince admits that it is difficult to give correctly the dimensions of any object in the water.

Three days later, the creature (or a close relation) turned up about twenty miles from Cape Cod Light. In his account, later published in the *Essex Register*, Thomas Bridges, of Salem, wrote that on May 18 while fishing from the schooner *Mechanic*, on passage from Salem to Philadelphia in a calm sea, they discovered something in the water that they at first took to be an empty hull.

> We, however, found the object to be alive, and soon saw very plainly that it was the Sea Serpent. He came directly towards the vessel, and passed within 12 or 15 yards of us, going quite slowly so that we had an excellent view of him. He appeared to be about 80 feet long, judging from the length of our vessel. . . . His color was a rusty black—appeared at a distance to have a great many humps but as he came near, I rather thought it was only his undulating motion which gave that appearance. . . . As he passed us, he turned his head a little on one side to look at us; he swam with his head out of the water. We saw him fairly, for more than half an hour—he

was seen by all on board as well as myself—and the mate made an entry of it in the log book at the time.

It was then, as it is today, a crime to enter any untruth in a logbook.

One hundred years later, the *Boston Evening Transcript* of August 21, 1933, revived a story of the next sighting of that summer, which originally appeared in the Boston *Post* of July 7, 1833:

REAL SEA SERPENTS RELIABLY DESCRIBED OFF NAHANT BY CAPTAIN PORTER OF CONNECTICUT

Captain Porter of the steamboat *Connecticut* states that on his passage up from Portland on Sunday morning [July 5], about 10 o'clock, four miles N.E. of Nahant, he saw three Sea Serpents, one of which was about 100 feet long and the other two between sixty and seventy. On his passage down, on Friday evening, he and his passengers saw the Serpent spoken of in yesterday's [Providence] *Journal* [taken] from the [Boston] *Transcript*. Capt. Porter, until within a few days, has been an unbeliever in the existence of Sea Serpents; his description of the monsters he saw agrees in the main with those which have heretofore been given in public.

The Sea Serpent in verity—Extract of
a letter to a gentleman in Boston.

"Portland, July 6

Dear Sir—I arrived in safety this morning, at 8, having passed an hour or more of yesterday afternoon among a shoal of Sea Serpents, three of which measured from 80 or 90 to 120 or 130 feet. I distinctly saw them with the naked eye, and afterwards carefully examined [them] through a glass. They were lying full length on the water occasionally lifting their heads four or five feet above the surface and showing twenty or thirty bunches or snake-like undulations at a time. Their heads bore a resemblance to the pickerel's, and the crease of their mouths, marking the division of the jaws, was like that of a common snake. The engine of the boat was stopped, and for three quarters of an hour we had a cool and deliberate view of the monsters. Such ____ looking objects I never beheld."

Since the above was received we have conversed with several people who came up in the *Connecticut* yesterday and they all state that they saw,

about ten o'clock yesterday morning, a little below Nahant, three or four
of the Serpents, one of which was certainly 100 feet in length.

Captain Porter's story was supported by those of Jacob Cook and James M.
Needham, of the schooner *Charles of Provincetown*, who reported that they too
had seen a sea serpent one and half miles east of Nahant and had hailed the
Connecticut to tell them to be on the lookout.

The creature returned to Nahant in 1834, where it was seen in early August by a Captain Goodrich and the thirty passengers of a Portsmouth, New
Hampshire, packet. They were within eight miles of Nahant when the
hundred-foot creature raised its head three to four feet above the surface
about twenty rods away. It seemed frightened by the noise of the boat and
moved off at a speed of fifteen to twenty knots. Other sightings that year
put one in Penobscot Bay near Castine, where it was seen by a schooner's
crew, and another off Gloucester.

In the spring of 1835, Captain Shibbles and the crew of the brig *Mangehan*
saw the creature ten miles from Race Point Light, at the eastern tip of Cape
Cod. Watching it through a glass, they saw a head and neck with "something
that looked like a mane upon the top of it" raised seven to eight feet above
the water. One of the sailors claimed he'd seen a similar creature the year
before at Gloucester.

On June 17 of that year, the creature appeared again, also off Cape Cod,
eight miles from Chatham Light, as reported by the master and crew of the
brig *Mary Hart*. The master, John Nichols, said that at eight o'clock that
morning, "we saw within a cable's length [120 fathoms, or 720 feet] of us
something lying in the water, resembling the shape of a snake." It was black,
about forty feet long, and carried its head above the water "while its body
bent with the waves of the sea."

Later that year, in October, seven men rafting lumber from a wreck off
Great Point, Nantucket, saw a creature that fit the "description of the sea serpent not long since seen off Nahant."

On November 17, the fishing schooner *Dove*, while on passage from Boston
to Kennebunk, "fell in with his marine majesty, the sea serpent, cruising
near the half-way rock." Captain Peabody reported that he had a fair view of

EXCLUSIVE OFFER

$9 off

Oil Change

COME BACK. SAVE BIG.

We're in your neighborhood

$9 off

Valvoline™ Full-Service Conventional Oil Change*

106022614

10602261A

Hurry in now and save big on an oil change

Exclusive savings for you!

3987 Vineyard Dr, Dunkirk

✔ **Save on your next visit**

$9 off
EXP: 9/17/2014

Valvoline™ Full-Service Conventional Oil Change*

NA567

$11 off
EXP: 9/17/2014

Valvoline™ Full-Service Full Synthetic or Synthetic Blend Oil Change**

NA568

Sun	Mon	Tue	Wed	Thu	Fri	Sat
closed	8:00am–6:00pm	8:00am–6:00pm	8:00am–6:00pm	8:00am–6:00pm	8:00am–6:00pm	8:00am–5:00pm

15684290 - 08/11/

Valvoline Instant Oil Change

90 Earhart Dr Ste 4
Amherst, NY 14221

*************AUTO**5-DIGIT 14048
The Spell Household
or Current Resident
756 Deer St
Dunkirk, NY 14048-2606

30055

him at a distance of about four rods and that "several protuberances appeared along his head, which was elevated three or four feet above the water; but as the schooner neared him he settled under the water, his wake indicating him to be sixty or seventy feet in length."

The following summer (1836), an unbelieving Captain Black of the schooner *Fox* of Sedgwick, Maine, saw a creature in the inlet between the mainland and Mount Desert Rock, as reported in the *Bangor Commercial Advertiser*. Captain Black and two other crewmen were within fifty yards of the sixty-foot creature for an hour. Black's description of a head like a land snake held two or three feet above the water is most typical, including the fact that when the schooner attempted to approach the creature, it became alarmed, sank down, then reappeared some distance away.

July 1839 found the creature back in the familiar territory off Nahant. The *Boston Centinel* reported that on the afternoon of July 10, Captain Sturgis of the revenue cutter *Hamilton* saw the creature in a smooth sea while cruising between Cape Ann and Boston.

Nearly two weeks later, on July 22, fishermen from a dozen or more boats in Wells Bay, Maine, reported sighting a hundred-foot creature that resembled "a long row of hogsheads or barrels with perhaps a foot or eighteen inches space between each of them." The editor of the *Kennebec Gazette* noted that the observers were "credible men, not over credulous."

In early August, the creature was apparently following the fish inshore. At least that's what the crew of the schooner that spotted the serpent three miles off Portsmouth Harbor thought. Evidently the fishing was good, because the creature was next seen by a Mr. Chapman a short distance up the coast at Braw Boat Harbor (now Brave Boat Harbor), between Kittery and York, Maine. It was raising its head six to seven feet above the water as it "passed leisurely along, across the entrance of the mouth of the harbor."

It could have been the same or another creature that was reported during the second week of August off Kennebunk Harbor, where the fishermen complained that the fish had deserted all their old feeding grounds and were only to be found inshore. On August 13, a gentleman from Cape Neddick, when about a mile and a half outside the harbor, saw what he supposed was a school of sharks at a distance of about thirty feet. He quickly revised his opinion, "convinced that it must be the huge marine monster that was visiting this coast. . . . [The creature's length] was not less than one hundred feet; he had bunches or humps on his back about the size of a common barrel, with flippers at each end of them; was covered with scales the size of a common plate; had a small head, resembling somewhat that of a snake; passed through the water with great velocity and his motions resembled those of a snake. . . . [The gentleman] had often seen shoals of various kinds of fish, such as whales, sharks, etc., but this resembled no marine animal, or cluster of marine animals, which he had ever before met. . . ." There were other boats in the vicinity, and the creature spent some minutes dodging them before making off in an easterly direction while the boats' crews pulled for shore.

Daniel Remich, in whose *History of Kennebunk from its Earliest Settlement to 1890* this last account appears, states that, "This marine wonder has not visited Wells Bay, so far as is known, since 1839. He has not, however, forsaken the coast of New England. . . . He still 'roams at large in the wide waters,' eluding all efforts for his capture, and discordant descriptions of him are still given by 'eyewitnesses.'"

On August 15, the creature had moved a short distance south, to the mouth of the Piscataqua River, which forms the boundary between New Hampshire and Maine. Here, a confirmed nonbeliever, Boarding Officer[3] George Bell, Esq. (a man with some seventy years on the water), saw a forty-five-foot serpent from his boarding boat "about half a mile from the Western Sister, not far from Whale's Back Light." Two witnesses in another boat were nearer to the creature and estimated its length at closer to sixty feet. The *Portsmouth Journal* noted that Bell, who was "perfectly acquainted with all the common sea animals on our coast," had "up to this week been a studied unbeliever. . . . He is convinced now, and like a worthy old gentleman has come forward and given his testimony."

On August 30, the Boston *Mercantile Journal* ran the following story of a "remarkable fish" seen the previous Friday by Navy Lieutenant John Bubier, off Deer Island at the entrance to Boston Harbor. The story was printed horizontally to accommodate the foot-long sketch of the sea serpent, which Lieutenant Bubier estimated to be between 120 and 135 feet in length.

Mr. Bubier is an experienced officer, having entered the service in 1813, and is familiar with the appearance of inhabitants of the sea, in every quarter of the globe; yet in all his "goings down" to the mighty deep, he has never seen any thing bearing any resemblance to this animal before. He is positive that it could not have been any species of Fish with which he is acquainted. There were in the boat with him several men belonging to the Navy Yard, one of whom, with a readiness which bears testimony to his courage and simplicity, grasped the boat-hook and stood ready to grapple with the monster! It may not be improper here to state that Lieutenant Bubier has been heretofore incredulous in relation to the existence of a Sea serpent on our coast.

SEA SERPENT, as seen off Deer Island, near Boston Harbor, by Lieut. Bubier, of the U. S. Navy.

The "remarkable fish" seen off Deer Island by Lieutenant Bubier. "A sketch of his Majesty's appearance was taken at the time, of which the above is an exact copy." (*Mercantile Journal,* August 30, 1839)

Cheek by jowl with this account was another five and a half column inches devoted to the question "is there a sea serpent?" The writer thought not, invoking the usual explanations of seaweed and porpoises and capping it all off with Captain Rich's capture of the horse mackerel in 1818.[4]

Still, the same issue of the *Mercantile Journal* also carried a snippet from the *New York Commercial* indicating that residents of Gotham would give all their "old shoes" if His Snakeship would select the waters off Sandy Hook for its summer visits. "We hear that it is in contemplation to change the name of the Boston watering-place from Nahant to *Snake-haunt*—the vicinity being so extensively patronized by the sea-serpent. The notion tickles the Bostonians."

That same August, British consul Thomas Colley Grattan saw the serpent two days in a row from the terrace of a Boston hotel, declaring in his book *Civilized America* that "above a hundred persons saw it at the same time. . . . One of the spectators, Dr. Amos Binney, a gentleman of scientific attainments [he was a zoologist], drew up a minute account of it which is deposited in the archives of one of the Philosophical Societies of Boston."

By September, the creature had again moved north; it was seen on September 3 by Concord Patten from aboard the schooner *Columbia*, bound for the Kennebec River from Newburyport.

Four days later, Captain David Smith of the Sag Harbor schooner *Planet* encountered the creature about thirty miles off Seguin, coming into the Kennebec. The captain and all hands had a "distinct view" of the creature, which came within forty feet of the vessel:

> They could see his whole length. His color and shape were very nearly like a black snake, without anything that looked like fluke or fins. Most of the time he had his head out of the water four or five feet. He was as long as the schooner, about 70 feet, and his body appeared as large as a barrel, but the captain thought it was larger in the middle. . . . His body appeared smooth—nothing like bunches on his back, as some have described him. They were probably deceived by his undulatory or wriggling motion in swimming, his back appearing above the water at regular distances.

Despite being an experienced whaler and having a harpoon on board, Captain Smith did not pursue the creature because he lacked the necessary lines and lances for capture.

The last sighting of 1839 took place on November 2, when the creature was spotted off Boon Island, Newburyport, by Captain Sawyer in the schooner *Alfred*, of Newburyport. Sawyer at first thought he'd seen a boat, but as the schooner approached, an unknown creature raised its head ten feet above the water, then quickly sank out of sight.

A series of storms that December devastated the maritime communities of New England. The first storm hit hardest at Gloucester on December 15, when would-be rescuers watched in impotent horror as vessels that had sought refuge in the harbor were battered by the savage gale. Ripped from their anchors, more than half of the ships were pounded to pieces in the surf while desperate crewmen clawed their way into the rigging, only to be swept away when strength and will gave out.

Scarcely had the people of Gloucester, Provincetown, and Boston absorbed the full extent of the destruction when a week later (on December

22) another storm hit, to be followed on the twenty-seventh by yet another. The "Triple Hurricanes of '39" sank more than 120 vessels, some with all or most of their crew, and another 218 ships were dismasted and left derelict.

Perhaps it was a part of one of those doomed vessels that Captain Samuel L. Fears, of the Gloucester schooner *Phoenix*, assumed that he was seeing when he encountered what he took to be a floating spar on a trip to Boston in March 1840. Intending to haul it aboard, he was startled when the "spar" raised its head and thrust out a long tongue.

Later that year, in July, a sixty-foot creature appeared near Cohasset, on the south shore of Massachusetts, where it was watched for half an hour by five or six people, among them a sea captain. The witnesses said the creature approached within thirty rods (about five hundred feet) of the shore, and its motion appeared to be caused by lateral fins or the motions of its tail under the water.

Three years later, on May 12, 1843, Captain Cotton of the schooner *Brilliant* watched a seventy- to eighty-foot sea serpent for an hour about fifteen miles off Cape Ann. The creature was said to have held its head eight feet out of the water.

It was only many years later that Gloucester resident Joseph O. Proctor, Sr., reported his encounter with "this much talked of creature" to George Woodbury. It was on a Sunday afternoon in August 1844 that he, along with Robert O. Fears, William Gaffney, and one or two other boys, went to Manchester (now Manchester-by-the-Sea, between Gloucester and Beverly) in a small boat. Knowing that any such excursion on a Sunday was strictly forbidden, the boys told no one of their experience.

The sea was smooth and the weather hot, Proctor said, when suddenly about three hundred feet away they saw a mouse-gray serpentlike head raised above the surface of the water. The creature did not appear frightened and calmly looked around. The boys were terrified and made all haste to get away, fearing they might be attacked. They saw the animal plainly, and it seemed to be a long serpent. Finally it disappeared. Mr. Proctor gave no estimate of the length of the creature.

That same summer, a similar creature was fired on by a gentleman at Boothbay, Maine, whereupon it dove and was not seen again.

Geologist J. W. Dawson collected the following sighting from Merigomish, Nova Scotia, for Sir Charles Lyell, who then included it in his book, *A Second Visit to the United States of North America* (1850). The sighting took place in August 1845.

It was about 100 feet long, seen by two intelligent observers nearly aground in calm water, within 200 feet of the beach, where it remained in sight for about half an hour, then got off with difficulty.

One of the witnesses went up a bank in order to look down upon it. They said it sometimes raised its head (which resembled that of a seal) partially out of the water. Along its back were a number of humps or protuberances, which, in the opinion of the observer on the beach, were true humps, while the others thought they were produced by vertical flexures of the body. Between the head and the first protuberance there was a straight part of the back of considerable length and this part was generally above water. The colour appeared black, and the skin had a rough appearance.

The animal was seen to bend its body almost in a circle and again to unbend it with rapidity. It was slender in proportion to its length. After it had disappeared in deep water, its wake was visible for some time. There were no indications of paddles seen. Some people who saw it compared it to a long string of fishing-net buoys moving rapidly about.

In the course of the summer, the fishermen on the eastern shore of Prince Edward's Island, in the Gulf of St. Lawrence, had been terrified by this sea monster. . . .

Dawson was also told that in October 1844 a similar creature swam past the pier at Arisaig, a short distance up the western coast of Nova Scotia from Merigomish, where it was "attentively observed by Mr. Barry, a millwright of Pictou. Barry told Mr. Dawson he was within 120 feet of it, and estimated its length at sixty feet, and the thickness of its body at three feet. It had humps on the back, which seemed too small and close together to be bends of the body."

Sir Charles Lyell had more than a passing interest in sea serpents, though he was certain that they were nothing more than misidentified basking sharks. It was he who reported that after the year 1817, "every marvelous tale was called a snake story, and when Colonel Perkins went to Washington twenty years ago and was asked if he had ever seen the sea serpent, he answered that he was one of the unfortunate individuals who saw it himself."

Lyell was also an early proponent of a theory originated by James Hutton, a Scottish physician, who claimed that the earth was gradually and continually changing. This theory, like those later proposed by Charles Darwin, was considered to be virtually heretical. The Bible was then the accepted source of all facts concerning the creation of the earth and its creatures.

Although the discovery of fossil creatures such as Iguanadon and Megalosaurus in the 1820s were posing perplexing questions not entirely answered in Genesis, many people, scientists included, believed that species thought to be extinct could still exist in some unexplored regions of the world. Indeed, Meriwether Lewis, when he set out on his journey of discovery in 1803, had fully expected that he might encounter a mastodon.

Forty years after Hutton proposed his theory, Lyell convincingly demonstrated that structural changes in the earth were the result of gradually occurring phenomena such as erosion. Lyell's theory in turn influenced Darwin, who reasoned that if the earth could change form by natural processes over a long period of time, so too could living species.

In the summer of 1846, James Wilson and James Boehner saw a steel gray creature between seventy and a hundred feet long from a schooner in St. Margaret's Bay, Nova Scotia. Naturalist Rev. John Ambrose reported the sighting in 1864:

> They saw what they at first thought were the floats of a long net, which began to move, leaving a wake as large as that of a schooner.
>
> They now perceived the object to be a large Serpent, with a head about the size of a barrel, and a body in proportion, and with something like a mane flowing down its neck. It carried its head erect, with a slight inclination forward.
>
> A fisherman belonging to Mill Cove now came rowing with all his fast decreasing strength to the schooner, and having barely leaped in over the side, fainted with terror on the deck.

A similar creature was seen by George Dauphiney, of Boutilier's Point, at Hackett's Cove, also in St. Margaret's Bay.

A mid-Atlantic sighting sometime prior to 1846 was reported by Captain Christmas of the Danish navy. Christmas observed what he believed to be a sea serpent in the company of porpoises between Iceland and the Faeroe Islands, where Captain Brown had seen the creature thirty-five years earlier, also in the company of porpoises.

Having been seen at least once almost every year since 1815, the sea serpent, though doubted by some, was for others an accepted fact. One can imagine, then, the sensation that ensued when in 1845 a German immigrant fossil collector by the name of Albert C. Koch claimed that he had found the skeleton of a 114-foot sea serpent *in situ* in Alabama. For the modest price of twenty-five cents, this "gigantic fossil reptile" was available for viewing at the Apollo Saloon on Broadway in New York City. There, mounted in a posture calculated to suggest the sea serpent, was the fabulous skeleton that Koch had the effrontery to call *Hydroargos sillimani*, "Silliman's Master-of-the-Seas," named for Yale professor Benjamin Silliman, who, it will be recalled, had gone on record in favor of the sea serpent in 1827.[5]

The credulous New York press was duly dazzled by what the *New York Dissector* termed "the serpent of the Deucalion deluge,"[6] but the skeleton was soon revealed to be a hoax. Examination of the teeth and vertebrae proved that it was not a giant reptile at all but a mammal, or rather several mammals. Koch, it was shown, had assembled the bones of no less than five extinct whales (most of them from *Basilosaurus*, also known as *Zeuglodon*) in order to produce his marvelous creation. Not in the least amused, Silliman demanded that his name be removed.

Unabashed, "Dr." Koch renamed his counterfeit creature *Hydroarchos harlani* (for Dr. Richard Harlan, who had first described Basilosaurus) and packed it off to Europe, where it was again proved to be a fake. King Wilhelm IV of Prussia was suitably impressed with *Hydroarchos*, however, and purchased the skeleton for his museum, providing Koch with a stipend for life.

Charlatan or showman, Koch was not entirely without talent; he was the first to suggest that humans and mastodons had lived contemporaneously when he discovered stone blades amid the remains of the gigantic elephan-

The illustration that accompanied "Doctor" Koch's description of *Hydroarchos*. Koch's "Ruler of the Sea," although impressive, was actually cobbled together from fossil whale bones. (Koch, 1845)

tine creature *Missourium*. Koch added extra bones to the skeleton, which he also took on a tour of Europe before selling it to the British Museum. The museum removed the extraneous bones and assembled for display a near perfect mastodon.

Naturally, the Koch hoax had a resoundingly negative impact on the sea serpent's reputation. It took great courage, then, on the part of Edward Newman, editor of the *Zoologist* of London, to open the columns of his journal to reports of the sea serpent, one of which would become a defining moment in the history of the subject: the sighting from Her Majesty's Ship *Daedalus*.

CHAPTER 4 NOTES

1. Meaning "ultimo," or in the month that preceded the present.

2. An editorial note states that it was forwarded by W. H. Ince, who had received it from his brother, Commander J. M. R. Ince, of the Royal Navy. It had been written by their uncle Henry Ince, ordnance storekeeper at Halifax, Nova Scotia.

3. A naval or revenue officer designated to board and inspect a ship arriving from a foreign port.

4. Almost lost amid all this discussion of the sea serpent is a single column inch reporting that the U.S. surveying brig *Washington*, "manned chiefly by boys apprenticed to the Navy," had captured and carried into New London, Connecticut, a suspicious "Low, Black Schooner"—the *Amistad*. In 1841, former president John Quincy Adams defended the Africans who had revolted against their captors and attempted to sail the *Amistad* back to Africa. Adams argued that a human's right to liberty superseded maritime law and the dubious property rights of the slavers. The Supreme Court concurred with only one dissent.

5. Koch also had a little problem with his Greek. *Hydroargos* translates to something like "bright shining water." He later corrected this to *Hydroarchos*.

6. According to Greek mythology, Deucalion (a son of Prometheus) and his wife, Pyrrha, were the only survivors of a flood created by Zeus to punish mankind for its wickedness. Their son Hellen was said to be the founder of the Hellenic race.

5

A Brief Digression
on the Debate Concerning a Sighting from
Her Majesty's Ship *Daedalus*

Perhaps no incident in all sea serpent literature proved as controversial as the sighting of an unknown marine creature in the south Atlantic by the captain and crew of HMS *Daedalus* in August 1848. Although the sighting occurred far from New England waters, it is included here because it became a defining moment in the history of the subject. Its notoriety was due, in no small part, to the fact that it provoked a public debate, carried on in the newspapers, between an officer of Her Majesty's Navy and one of the most exalted zoologists of the day.

On October 10, 1848, the (London) *Times* (among others) ran an article under the headline "Naval Intelligence," datelined Plymouth, October 7, reporting that between the Cape of Good Hope and St. Helena, while on passage to England from the East Indies, the captain and crew of the frigate *Daedalus* had seen a sea serpent.

The story might have ended there had not the Admiralty quite naturally called upon the captain to elucidate the incident, which had not been recorded in the ship's log. Captain M'Quhae complied with a letter to Admiral Sir W. H. Gage, which subsequently appeared the *Times* on October 14:

Her Majesty's Ship Daedalus

Hamoaze, Oct. 11

Sir—

In reply to your letter of this day's date, requiring information as to the

The sea serpent seen from HMS *Daedalus* on August 6, 1848. The engraving was made from a drawing executed under the direction of Captain M'Quhae and affirmed by the other witnesses. (Fortean Picture Library)

truth of a statement published in The Times newspaper, of a sea-serpent of extraordinary dimensions having been seen from Her Majesty's Ship *Daedalus*, under my command, on her passage from the East Indies, I have the honour to acquaint you, for the information of my Lords Commissioners of the Admiralty, that at 5 o'clock p.m. on the 6th of August last, in latitude 24°44'S., and longitude 9°22'E., the weather dark and cloudy, wind fresh from the N.W., with a long ocean swell from the S.W., the ship on the port tack, heading N.E. by N., something very unusual was seen by Mr. Sartoris, midshipman, rapidly approaching the ship from before the beam. The circumstance was immediately reported by him to the officer of the watch, Lieutenant Edgar Drummond, with whom and Mr. William Barrett, the Master [navigator] I was at the time walking the quarter deck. The ship's company were at supper.

On our attention being called to the object, it was discovered to be an

enormous serpent, with head and shoulders kept about four feet constantly above the surface of the sea; and as nearly as we could approxi-
mate by comparing it with the length of what our main top-sail yard
would show in the water, there was at least sixty feet of the animal a fleur
d'eau ['twixt wind and water], no portion of which was, to our perception,
used in propelling it through the water, either by vertical or horizontal
undulation. It passed rapidly, but so close to our lee quarter that had it
been a man of my acquaintance I should have easily recognized his features with the naked eye; and it did not, either in approaching the ship or
after it had passed our wake, deviate in the slightest degree from its
course to the S.W., which it held on at the pace of from 12 to 15 miles per
hour, apparently on some predetermined purpose.

The diameter of the serpent was about 15 or 16 inches behind the head,
which was, without any doubt, that of a snake, and it was never during
the 20 minutes that it continued in sight of our glasses, once below the
surface of the water; its colour, a dark brown with a yellowish white about
the throat. It had no fins, but something like the mane of a horse, or rather
a bunch of sea weed, washed about its back. It was seen by the quartermaster, the boatswain's mate, and the man at the wheel, in addition to
myself and the officers above mentioned.

I am having a drawing made of the serpent from a sketch taken immediately after it was seen, which I hope to have ready for transmission to
my Lords Commissioners of the Admiralty by to-morrow's post.

> I have the honour to be, sir
>
> Your obedient servant,
>
> Peter M'Quhae, Captain

Unable to obtain a copy of the sketch, which the *Illustrated London News*
had copyrighted, Edward Newman's *Zoologist* then published the private
notes of Lieutenant Edgar Drummond:

In the 4 to 6 watch, at about 5 o'clock, we observed a most remarkable fish
on our lee quarter, crossing the stern in a S.W. direction; the appearance of
its head, which, with the back fin, was the only portion of the animal visible, was long, pointed, and flattened at the top, perhaps ten feet in length,
the upper jaw projecting considerably: the fin was perhaps twenty feet in

the rear of the head, and visible occasionally; the captain also asserted that he saw the tail, or another fin, about the same distance behind it; the upper part of the head and shoulders appeared of a dark brown colour, and beneath the under jaw a brownish white.

It pursued a steady undeviating course, keeping its head horizontal with the surface of the water and in rather a raised position, disappearing occasionally beneath a wave for a very brief interval, and not apparently for purposes of respiration. It was going at a rate of perhaps from twelve to fourteen miles an hour, and when nearest was perhaps one hundred yards distant: in fact it gave one quite the idea of a large snake or eel.

No one in the ship has ever seen anything similar, so it is at least extraordinary. It was visible to the naked eye for five minutes, and with a glass for perhaps fifteen more. The weather was dark and squally at the time, with some sea running.

Then the debate began.

Evidently someone asked the eminent anatomist Sir Richard Owen if the creature seen from the *Daedalus* could have been a marine dinosaur. He responded, then sent a copy of his letter to the *Times*, which published it on November 14. The sketch he refers to, which he provided but was not published by the *Times*, showed the head of the creature from M'Quhae's sketch attached to the submerged body of a large seal.

The sketch will suggest the reply to your query "whether the monster seen from the Daedalus be anything but a saurian?" If it be the true answer it destroys the romance of the incident, and will be anything but acceptable to those who prefer the excitement of the imagination to the satisfaction of the judgement.

I am far from insensible to the pleasures of the discovery of a new and rare animal, but before I can enjoy them certain conditions, e.g. reasonable proof or evidence of its existence, must be fulfilled. I am also far from undervaluing the information which Captain M'Quhae has given us of what he saw. When fairly analysed, it lies in a small compass; but my knowledge of the animal kingdom compels me to draw other conclusions from the phenomena than those which the gallant captain seems to have jumped at.

He evidently saw a large animal moving through the water, very different from anything he had before witnessed—neither a whale, a grampus, a great shark, an alligator, nor any other of the larger surface swimming creatures which are fallen in with in ordinary voyages. . . . No fins were seen (the captain says there were none; but from his own account he did not see enough of the animal to prove the negative). . . . "So much of the body as was seen was not used in propelling the animal through the water, either by vertical or horizontal undulation." A calculation of its length was made under a strong preconception of the nature of the beast. The head, e.g., is stated to be "without any doubt that of a snake"; and yet a snake would be the last species to which a naturalist conversant with the forms and characters of the heads of animals would refer such a head as that which Captain M'Quhae has transmitted a drawing to the Admiralty, and which he certifies to have been accurately copied in the *Illustrated London News* for October 28, 1848, p. 265.

The foregone conclusion, therefore, of the beast's being a sea-serpent, notwithstanding its capacious vaulted cranium, and stiff, inflexible trunk, must be kept in mind in estimating the value of the approximation made to the total length of the animal, as "at the very least 60 feet." This is the only part of the description, however, which seems to me to be so uncertain as to be inadmissible, in an attempt to arrive at a right conclusion as to the nature of the animal.

The more certain characters of the animal are these: Head, with a convex, moderately capacious cranium, short obtuse muzzle, gape of the mouth not extending farther than to beneath the eye, which is rather small, round, filling closely the palpebral aperture; colour, dark brown above, yellowish white beneath; surface smooth, without scales, scutes, or other conspicuous modifications of hard and naked cuticle. . . . Nostrils not mentioned, but indicated in the drawing by a crescentic mark at the end of the nose or muzzle.

All these are characters of the head of a warm-blooded mammal; none of them are those of a cold-blooded reptile or fish. Body long, dark brown, not undulating, without dorsal or other apparent fins; "but something like the mane of a horse, or rather a bunch of sea-weed washed about its back."

. . . If an opinion can be deduced as to the integuments from the above indication, it is that the species had hair, which if it was too short and too close to be distinguished on the head, was visible where it usually is the longest, on the middle line of the shoulders or advanced parts of the back. . . . Guided by the above interpretation, of "the mane of a horse, or a bunch of sea-weed," the animal was not a cetaceous mammal, but rather a great seal.

But what seal of large size, or indeed of any size, would be encountered in latitude 24˚44' south, and longitude 9˚22' east—viz., about three hundred miles from the western shore of the southern end of Africa? The most likely species to be there met with are the largest of the seal tribe, e.g. Anson's sea lion, or that known to the southern whalers by the name of "Sea Elephant," the *Phoca proboscidea*, which attains the length of from 20 to 30 feet. These great seals abound in certain of the islands of the southern and Antarctic seas, from which an individual is occasionally floated off upon an iceberg. The sea lion exhibited in London last spring, which was a young individual of the *Phoca proboscidea*, was actually captured in that predicament, having been carried off by the currents that set northward towards the Cape, where its temporary resting-place was rapidly melting away.

When a . . . *Phoca proboscidea* or a *Phoca leonina* is thus borne off to a distance from its native shore, it is compelled to return for rest to its floating abode after it has made its daily excursions in quest of the fishes or squids that constitute its food. It is thus brought by the iceberg into the latitudes of the Cape, and perhaps further north, before the berg has melted away. The poor seal is compelled to swim as long as strength endures; and in such a predicament I imagine the creature was that Mr. Sartoris saw rapidly approaching the *Daedalus* from before the beam, scanning, probably, its capabilities as a resting-place, as it paddled its long stiff body past the ship. In so doing, it would raise a head of the form and colour described and delineated by Captain M'Quhae, supported on a neck also of the diameter given; the thick neck passing into an inflexible trunk, the longer and coarser hair on the upper part of which would give rise to the idea, especially if the species were the *Phoca leonina*, explained by the similes above cited. The organs of locomotion would be out of sight. The pectoral fins being set on very low down as in my sketch, the chief impelling force would be the actions of the deeper immersed terminal fins and tail, which would create a long eddy, readily mistakable by one look-ing at the strange phenomenon with a sea-serpent in his mind's eye for an indefinite prolongation of the body.

It is very probable that no one on board the *Daedalus* ever before beheld a gigantic seal freely swimming in the open ocean . . . but the creative powers of the human mind appear to be really very limited, and, on all the occasions where the true source of the "great unknown" has been detected—whether it has proved to be a file of sportive porpoises, or a pair of gigantic sharks—old Pontoppidan's sea serpent with the mane has uni-formly suggested itself as the representative of the portent, until the mys-tery has been unraveled.[1]

I have no unmeet confidence in the exactitude of my interpretation of the phenomena witnessed by the captain and others of the *Daedalus*. I am too sensible of the inadequacy of the characters which the opportunity of a rapidly passing animal, "in a long ocean swell," enabled them to note, for the determination of its species or genus. Giving due credence to the most probably accurate elements of their description, they do little more than guide the zoologist to the class, which, in the present instance, is not that of the serpent or the saurian.

A larger body of evidence from eye-witnesses might be got together in proof of ghosts than of the sea serpent.

Sir Richard Owen, gifted anatomist, royal hobnobber, coiner of the term *Dinosauria*, and all-around curmudgeon, was at that time curator of the Hunterian Museum. In his book, *In the Wake of the Sea-Serpents*, Bernard Heuvelmans writes of him: "Owen was then forty-five years old and had a great, and largely deserved, reputation, which he misused shamelessly in settling zoological questions in the most peremptory fashion. He had come to regard himself as the pope of his subject, and his excommunication of Darwin and his Theory of Evolution will give some idea of his strictly con-servative mind. Darwin called him 'one of my chief enemies (the sole one who has annoyed me).'"

Captain M'Quhae would certainly have agreed.

Never mind that one does not, as a rule, run in with alligators in the course of an "ordinary voyage." Never mind that Owen's geography is a bit off. He seems to have called upon his own "creative powers" in painting us a very affecting picture of a seal, lost and alone in the wide ocean looking for a place of refuge, his iceberg having melted away.

The sea elephant, *Phoca proboscidea*, has an extremely distinctive face. If M'Quhae is to be believed at all that, had the creature been a man of his acquaintance, he should have "easily recognized his features with the naked eye," he must then have noticed the characteristic nose that gives the sea elephant its name.

Then there is that nasty bit about the ghosts. If only the Reverend Mr. Cummings had been available for comment. He is the only person, so far as is known, ever to have seen a sea serpent *and* a ghost.

One would expect a captain in the Royal Navy to be able to give as good as he got, and so it was that an unrepentant M'Quhae made this reply in *The Times* of November 28, 1848.

> Professor Owen correctly states that I "evidently saw a large creature moving rapidly through the water very different from anything I had before witnessed, neither a whale, a grampus, a great shark, an alligator, nor any of the larger surface-swimming creatures fallen in with in ordinary voyages." I now assert—neither was it a common seal nor a sea elephant, its great length and its totally differing physiognomy precluding the possibility of its being a "Phoca" of any species. The head was flat, and not a "capacious vaulted cranium"; nor had it a "stiff inflexible trunk"—a conclusion to which Professor Owen has jumped, most certainly not justified by the simple statement that "no portion of the 60 feet seen by us was used in propelling it through the water, either by vertical or horizontal undulation."
>
> It is also assumed that the "calculation of its length was made under a strong preconception of the nature of the beast"; another conclusion quite contrary to the fact. It was not until after the great length was developed by its nearest approach to the ship, and until after that most important point had been duly considered and debated, as well as such could in the

brief space of time allowed for so doing, that it was pronounced to be a serpent by all who saw it, and who are too well accustomed to judge of lengths and breadths of objects in the sea to mistake a real substance and an actual living body, coolly and dispassionately contemplated, at so short a distance too, for the "eddy caused by the actions of the deeper immersed fins and tail of a rapidly moving gigantic seal raising its head above the water," as Professor Owen imagines, in quest of its lost iceberg.

The creative powers of the human mind may be very limited. On this occasion they were not called into requisition, my purpose and desire being, throughout, to furnish eminent naturalists, such as the learned Professor, with accurate facts, and not with exaggerated representations, nor with what could by any possibility proceed from optical delusion; and I beg to assure him that old Pontoppidan having clothed his sea-serpent with a mane could not have suggested the idea of ornamenting the creature seen from the *Daedalus* with a similar appendage, for the simple reason that I had never seen his account, or even heard of his sea-serpent, until my arrival in London. Some other solution must therefore be found for the very remarkable coincidence between us in that particular, in order to unravel the mystery.

Finally, I deny the existence of excitement, or the possibility of optical illusion. I adhere to the statement, as to form, colour, and dimensions, contained in my official report to the Admiralty; and I leave them as data whereupon the learned and scientific may exercise the "pleasures of imagination" until some more fortunate opportunity shall occur of making a closer acquaintance with the "great unknown"—in this case surely no ghost.

Ten years later, the *Daedalus* monster was still a topic of discussion. In a letter to the *Times* dated February 12, 1858, Captain Smith, of the ship *Pekin*, described how he had once been deceived by a piece of seaweed twenty feet long and four inches in diameter. Captain Smith had no doubt, so he wrote, that the *Daedalus* sea serpent "was a piece of that same weed." The following day, the *Times* published this reply.

Sir,

Observing in your paper of yesterday's date a letter from a correspondent on the marine animal commonly called the "sea serpent," in the concluding paragraph of which he mentions that he has no doubt the object seen from Her Majesty's Ship *Daedalus* in the month of August 1848, when on the passage from the Cape of Good Hope to St. Helena, was a piece of the same sea weed observed by himself, I beg to state that the object seen from Her Majesty's ship on that occasion was beyond all question a living animal, moving rapidly through the water against a cross sea, and within five points of a fresh breeze, with such velocity that the water was surging under its chest as it passed along at a rate, probably, of not less than 10 miles per hour.

Captain M'Quhae's first impulse was to tack in pursuit, ourselves being on a wind on the larboard tack, when he reflected that we neither could lay up for it nor overhaul it in speed. There was nothing to be done, therefore, but to observe it as accurately as we could with our glasses as it came up under our lee quarter and passed away to windward, at its nearest position being not more than 200 yards from us; the eye, the mouth, the nostril, the colour and form all being most distinctly visible to us.

We all felt greatly astonished at what we saw, though there were sailors among us of 30 or 40 years standing, who had traveled most seas and seen many marvels in their day. The captain was the first to exclaim: "This must be that animal called the sea-serpent," a conclusion we all at last settled down to. My impression was it was rather of a lizard than a serpentine character, as its movement was steady and uniform, as if propelled by fins, not by an undulatory power. It was in sight from our first observing it about 10 minutes, as we were fast leaving one another on opposite tacks with a freshening breeze and the sea getting up. I feel, Sir, I have already occupied more of your time and space than is justified, and have the honor to remain your obedient servant.

An officer of Her Majesty's Ship "Daedalus"

CHAPTER 5 NOTE

1. Erik Ludvigsen Pontoppidan, bishop of Bergen, devoted a chapter in his 1752 *The Natural History of Norway* to reports of unusual creatures in northern seas including mermaids, sea serpents, and the legendary kraken.

6

1849 – 1885

"I have seen the Sea Serpent"

It does require some courage to face the alternative of being either ridiculed as an ignorant fool, or denounced as a contemptible imposter, but such is the ordeal through which all have to pass who venture to assert that they have seen the sea-serpent.

—Rev. J. G. Wood, 1884

There were still a few men of science willing to go on record in favor of the sea serpent, among them the Swiss American naturalist Louis Agassiz, who, perhaps as a result of the ongoing debate over the *Daedalus* affair, addressed the question of the sea serpent at a speaking engagement in Philadelphia in March 1849.

> I have asked myself in connection with this subject whether there is not such an animal as the Sea-serpent. There are many who will doubt the existence of such a creature until it can be brought under the dissecting knife; but it has been seen by so many on whom we may rely, that it is wrong to doubt it any longer.

Among those upon whom one could rely was Colonel Thomas Handasyd Perkins, to whom Agassiz would soon be related. Agassiz married Elizabeth Cabot Cary, Perkins's granddaughter, the following year.[1]

When the colonel died four years later, Elizabeth's parents moved a small foursquare house known as the Butter Box onto the family property. During the summer months the Agassiz family shared the house with Elizabeth's sister Mary and her husband, Greek scholar Cornelius Felton, who was a professor at, and later president of, Harvard. Agassiz attached a laboratory to the Butter Box where he conducted research on local marine life, none of which, unfortunately, was the sea serpent.

In the summer of 1849, the creature was spotted in St. Margaret's Bay, Nova Scotia, as reported by Rev. John Ambrose. According to Ambrose, when Joseph Holland, Jacob Kedy, and other fishermen were on South West Island at the entrance to the bay, they saw what looked like a sixty-foot-long snake about as large around as a "puncheon," or cask.

> It was proportioned like an eel, i.e. tapering towards the extremities, with no caudal fin perceptible, but one very high fin, or row of spines, each of about an inch in diameter at the base, erected along its back, serving indeed for a dorsal fin, like the folding fin of the *Thynnus vulgaris* [now *Thunnus thynnus*], or albicore. This spinal erection seemed to occupy about one third of its length, each end of it being about equidistant from the Serpent's extremities; and at a distance, somewhat resembling, in size and appearance, the sail of a skiff. The animal's back was covered with scales, about six inches long and three inches wide, extending in rows *across* the body, i.e., the longer diameter of the scale being in the direction of the circumference of the body. The color of the back was black. The men had no opportunity of seeing the belly, but what the Americans would call "a smart chance" of becoming acquainted with the inside of it; for the creature, perceiving the boat, raised its head about ten feet above the water, turned towards it, and opened its jaws, showing the inside of its mouth red in color and well-armed with teeth about three inches long, shaped like those of a catfish. The men, now thinking it high time to terminate the interview, pulled vigorously for shore, followed for some distance by the snake, which at length gave up the chase and disappeared.

Bernard Heuvelmans considered this report suspect, in part because of the description of a distinct dorsal projection along the back that does not correspond with that on any known marine animal living or extinct. However, references to a similar feature will turn up again in later descriptions, particularly those of the *Valhalla* (1905) and *Philomena* (1912) creatures. It might also be worth considering the reference to this "spinal erection" being like a tuna's "folding fin." The bluefin tuna does in fact possess the ability to retract its first dorsal fin, as well as its pectoral and pelvic fins, to reduce drag when putting on a burst of speed. Because this is a second- (possibly third-) hand account, and because no information as to weather conditions or the witnesses' proximity to the creature were provided, we can only speculate. But *if* the dorsal projection seen on the creature at St. Margaret's Bay *could* be folded back against the body, it might appear as a row of humps when not erect.

Swampscott resident John Marston saw the creature about two hundred yards offshore from Nahant Beach on August 3, 1849 and gave this statement sworn before Waldo Thompson, justice of the peace in Swampscott:

> While walking over Nahant beach in common with many others who had been aroused by the excitement, I saw in the water . . . a singular-looking fish in the form of a serpent. His head was out of the water, and he remained in view about twenty minutes, when he swam off towards King's Beach. . . . I saw the whole body of the serpent, not the wake but the fish itself. It would rise in the water in un undulatory motion aand then all his body would sink except for his head. then his body would rise again. I have been constantly engaged in fishing since my youth. . . . I have seenn all sorts of fishes and hundreds of horse mackerel, but I never saw anything like this.

Three years were to pass before one of the creatures was sighted on the north shore of Massachusetts at Rockport, in August 1852. Another report that month put the creature on the south shore in Hull. Four years later, on March 30, 1856, a mid-Atlantic encounter was recorded in the log of the *Imogen*, in which it was reported that "an immense snake" was seen at latitude 29°11′ north, longitude 34°26′ west, possibly heading for the Azores.

In a journal entry dated June 14, 1857, Henry David Thoreau records two sightings, reported to him by his friend Benjamin Marston Watson, which were later abstracted from his *Journals* for the book *Cape Cod*.

> B. M. Watson tells me that he learned from pretty good authority that Webster once saw the sea serpent. It seems that it was first seen in the Bay between Manomet and Plymouth Beach, by a perfectly reliable witness

The sea serpent as depicted by Henry Bugbee Kane in W.W. Norton's 1951 edition of Thoreau's *Cape Cod.*

(many years ago) who was accustomed to look out on the sea with his glass every morning. . . . One morning he saw this monster, with a head something like a horse's raised some six feet above the water, and his body the size of a cask trailing behind. He was careering all over the bay, chasing the mackerel, which ran ashore in their fright and washed up and died in great numbers. . . .

Webster had appointed to meet some Plymouth gentlemen at Manomet and spend the day fishing. . . . After the fishing was over he set out . . . in his sailboat with Peterson . . . and on the way they saw the sea serpent, which answered to the common account of this creature. It passed directly across the bow only six or seven rods off, and then disappeared. . . . Webster, having had time to reflect on what had occurred, at length said to Peterson, "For God's sake never say a word about this to any one, for if it should be known that I have seen the sea serpent, I should never hear the last of it, but, wherever I went, should have to tell the story to everyone I met." So it had not leaked out till now.

It might come as a surprise that the Webster referred to in this passage is none other than celebrated orator Daniel Webster,[2] although when the incident took place is not certain. (Webster died in 1852.) That we should find these two famous men in the company of the sea serpent is extraordinary indeed. Webster's sentiments, sadly, are not. Increasingly, we will find the world less and less credulous on the subject, which perhaps explains why reports of the sea serpent suddenly grew scarce.

Had the Koch hoax and the *Daedalus* debate closed people's minds to sea monsters? Or had the New England creature temporarily decamped, enjoying perhaps a sojourn in some other waters? Were the changes in the North Atlantic fisheries to blame? Whatever the reason, the sea serpent would not be reported in the Gulf of Maine for twenty years.

According to Gloucester historian John Babson, "The first 'great year' of the mackerel fishery was 1825, in which year a single jigger, carrying eight men, took over thirteen hundred barrels." The autumn of 1830 and 1831 brought mackerel in almost unbelievable abundance, and an amazing 51,000 barrels of the fish were packed in Gloucester. Still, Babson noted, "The mackerel is a capricious fish and its habits are not understood even by the most experienced fishermen. . . . They began to be scarce in Massachusetts Bay, and finally to avoid the coast, so that since 1850 hook-fishing for mackerel in our own waters has proved a total failure. The enterprise of the fishermen, however, has pursued them into their distant retreats in the Bay Chaleur." (Bay Chaleur is in the Gulf of St. Lawrence, separating New Brunswick from Quebec.)

The innovation of the purse seine in the late 1840s dramatically altered the fortunes of the mackerelers. Because *Scomber scombrus* is a schooling fish, the new method, compared with hook fishing, quickly caught on.

A school of mackerel having been spotted, the seine boat of thirty to forty feet would be lowered from the schooner and the net (weighted on the bottom and buoyed on top) would be laid out in a circle. Once the net surrounded the mackerel, it was drawn in, forming a pouch. The schooner then sailed alongside the seine boat and dipped a barrel or two of fish from the seine at a time. Like most fishing it was an exercise in patience, precision,

Purse seining for mackerel. (*The Fisheries and Fishery Industries of the United States*, 1887, G. Browne Goode, et al.)

and finesse. Naturally, not every set of the seine produced a deck load of fish. If the mackerel spooked, they could break through the net, and the entire effort would be wasted. There were, however, compensations: It was a summer fishery, and a companionable one by some accounts.

The halibut fishery was also making its debut. Between 1830 and 1850, halibut were populous inshore; however, increased fishing caused a coincident decline, and soon it was necessary to travel to the Grand Banks for the giant flatfish. Cod, haddock, and halibut were all fished in a more or less similar manner on the Banks. These were dory fisheries, a dangerous and often deadly business.[3]

Rowing out from the ship as much as two miles before beginning their set, a pair of dory mates would lay out a trawl line of from 375 fathoms (2,250 feet) for halibut to about 1,700 feet for cod. Buoyed and anchored at one end, the trawl line, with between three hundred and six hundred baited hooks dangling from it on "gangings," was let out over the stern from a trawl

Hauling in the halibut. (*The Fisheries and Fishery Industries of the United States*, 1887,
G. Browne Goode, et al.)

tub (a round wood bucket about the size of an ordinary laundry basket) until
it might stretch for a mile and more before the second anchor and buoy
were set. Two, maybe twelve, maybe twenty-four hours later, the mates
would be back "housekeeping," first searching out their buoy, then pulling
in the anchor. Halibuters used a hurdy-gurdy in the bow to haul in their
lines loaded with the fish, which reached up to seven feet in length and
weighed as much as three hundred pounds. (The largest halibut ever
recorded was a whopping seven hundred pounds.)

Codfish quickly resign themselves to their fate, rarely making a fuss once
hooked; halibut are less philosophical and need to be persuaded to come to
dinner. Halibuters therefore carried a killing stick in their dories to convince
the reluctant giants with a smack or two on the head.

Once the dory (made, incidentally, more seaworthy by a full load) was
rowed back to the ship and its contents were emptied over the rail, the
process was repeated, many times a day if the weather was fair and the fishing good. When the catch was in it was time not for rest but for dressing
down—gutting, cleaning, and icing the fish.

In a perfect world, the crew of the schooner would soon find its hold

packed with fish and would set sail for home. But the world is seldom perfect. Men were caught on the lines and dragged overboard, and dories cap-
sized or went astray in the dense, deceptive, impenetrable fogs that quickly
turned the world into illusion. The fog muffled the sounds of the ship's bell
or horn and obscured the lanterns lit to guide the dory men home. If the sea
got sloppy and rough . . . well, it might only be a matter of time. When the
schooner sailed into port, she'd be carrying her flag at half-mast to let those
on shore know that some of the crew wouldn't be coming home.

During the Civil War, nothing so frivolous as reports of sea monsters
made its way into New England newspapers, which now focused on reports
of the conflict, the wounded, and the dead. Gloucester sent 1,500 men to the
war, 127 of whom did not return. In that city, however, it was not Johnny
Reb but Georges Bank that was the most dreaded widowmaker.

Gloucester historian John J. Babson completed the writing of his *History
of the Town of Gloucester, Cape Ann* in 1860, so it carries no report of the war, but
in a paragraph of rare emotion Babson recounted the terrors of Georges
Bank with profound feeling.

> Many of the vessels engaged in the George's [sic] Fishery make great voy-
> ages; but at what a fearful expense of human life is the business carried
> on! and how little is it to be wondered at that none but the stoutest hearts
> will brave the perils and hardships of the employment! Twenty-five men
> in three schooners, in the last spring alone, found in it a watery grave, and
> also an unknown end; for no tidings ever come from the missing George's
> fishermen. After they have been out three or four weeks, friends begin to
> inquire anxiously of returning mariners for husband, son, brother or fa-
> ther, and watch from the hills in agonizing suspense; but nothing comes
> save the moan of the sea, which sounds their requiem.

In the second year of the war, Georges claimed 19 schooners and 162 men.
A terrible gale on February 24 took 120 lives in a single night. By war's end
there would be still more Gloucester men with only the "moan of the sea"
for their requiem. And despite their bravery and the adversity they endured,
many would be remembered only by the widows and orphans they left
behind.

In contrast, Swampscott historian Waldo Thompson reported that on December 22, 1865, "The surrender of the stained and tattered banners, borne by the soldiers of Massachusetts, to the keeping of the State, was one of the most imposing, and at the time, affecting occasions incident to the war. . . . There were two hundred and sixty-nine flags in all . . ."

> And many saw the waving flags
> The fluttering flags, the tattered flags,
> Red, white and blue, shot through and through,
> Baptized with battle's deadly dew.

The only sea serpent reported along the New England coast during the late 1860s turned out not to be a sea serpent at all. When an unusual thirty-five-foot creature was killed in Carrying Place Cove, Eastport, Maine, in August 1868, local fishermen thought it was some kind of shark. That didn't stop newspapers from printing highly apocryphal accounts of a sea serpent. The story even appeared in *Harper's Weekly* accompanied by a curious illustration showing well-dressed residents strolling alongside a large shark-shaped creature with leglike flippers.

Local resident Warren Brown promoted himself to captain and took the preserved hide on the road, first as the "Great Shark Dog Fish" and later as the "Great Utopia Lake Sea Serpent," though it bore no resemblance to the creature sighted there.[4]

Phineas T. Barnum, always on the lookout for a possible exhibit, paid twenty-five cents to see the creature at the Boston Zoological Institute and estimated that alive it would have been worth a million dollars. But in the January 23, 1869, issue of *Harper's Weekly*, there appeared a letter from Professor Gill of the Smithsonian, who put the creature in its proper zoological framework. It was a basking shark after all.

The actual sea serpent had, for whatever reason, not been reported in New England waters for fifteen years. There had been other sightings, however. In May 1863, the *Athenian* reported a sighting between the Cape Verde Islands and the Canary Islands. In November 1869, the captain and crew of the bark *Scottish Bride* claimed to have seen a pair of sea serpents at latitude 38°16' north, longitude 74°09' west, sixty miles from Delaware Bay.

The following May, a ninety-foot creature was shot at (apparently without effect) when it raised its head above the surface of the water in the Hudson River near Grant's Island, eighty miles upriver from New York City. This last location is perplexing. What was a large oceangoing creature doing eighty miles from the sea in fresh water? Still, the witnesses' description of a sea serpent covered with scales raising its head ten to twelve feet above the water certainly sounded familiar, even if the location was not.

Five years after the sighting in the Hudson River, the creature was back in its traditional waters, where it showed itself frequently in the summer of 1875. On the evening of July 17, Captain Garton, pilot of the steamer *Norman*, spotted a strange animal off Plymouth apparently pursuing a swordfish.

> The head of the monster was raised at least ten feet above the ocean but remained stationary only a moment, as it was almost constantly in motion; now diving for a moment, and as suddenly reappearing to the same height.
>
> The submarine leviathan was striped black and white, the stripes running lengthways, from the head to the tail. The throat was pure white, and the head, which was extremely large, was full black, from which . . . protruded an inch or more a pair of deep black eyes, as large as ordinary saucers.
>
> The body was round, like a fish barrel, and the length was more than one hundred feet. The motion was like that of a caterpillar, with this exception: that the head of the snake plunged under the water, whereas the head of the worm merely crooks to the ground.

As it happened, a passenger on another steamer bound from Boston to Philadelphia gave a similar account except for certain details, including a fin on its back and small fins on the side. (The Reverend J. G. Wood, who uncovered these accounts, suggested that the side fins may have been flippers.) This time the creature was being attacked by the swordfish.

> When the swordfish first attacked him he reared his head at least ten feet above the water, and then dove down once more. These actions he kept repeating so that we had a fine opportunity to scrutinize him. His head was rather flat and closely resembled that of a turtle. The fin we first observed on the back, several feet from the head, while small fins protruded on each side. The body was at least eighty inches in diameter, and presented

a shiny surface, covered with large coarse scales. When he moved his head the water seemed to boil as he rapidly clove his way through the wave, so that by far the largest portion of his body must have been under the water. We estimated his length to be at least sixty feet. . . .

On August 3, 1875, the *Boston Advertiser* printed an anonymous letter describing an encounter with a sea serpent in Nahant Bay. The letter writer claimed to have chased the creature around the bay for two hours, during which time he shot at it, without apparent effect, at least twenty times. He would not presume to estimate its length but assumed "there must have been an immense power somewhere to enable it to raise such a head and neck, slowly, such a distance (8 feet) above the surface." He further stated that a school of blackfish (a species of small whale) remained in its company the whole time. In closing, he wrote: "No one in this neighborhood ever saw anything like it before, and if it was not the original sea serpent, I should like to know what it was."

It transpired that the letter writer was Francis W. Lawrence, who kept his yacht *Princess* at Swampscott, which had also entered the resort business. The man's brother, Rev. Arthur Lawrence, rector of St. Paul's Church in Stockbridge, Massachusetts, had been with him at the time and supplied the following account to Rev. John George Wood.

A party of us were aboard the yacht *Princess*, and while sailing between Swampscott and Egg Rock, we saw a very strange creature. As nearly as we could judge from a distance of about one hundred and fifty yards, its head resembled that of a turtle or a snake, black above and white beneath. It raised its head from time to time some six or eight feet out of the water, keeping it out from five to ten seconds at a time. At the back of the neck there was a fin, resembling that of a black-fish, and underneath, some distance below its throat, was a projection which looked as if it might have been the beginning of a pair of fins or flippers, like those of a seal. But as to that, we could not be sure, as the creature never raised itself far enough out of the water to enable us to decide. Its head seemed to be about two and a half feet in diameter. Of its length we could not judge, as only its head and neck were visible. We followed it for perhaps two hours. It was fired at repeatedly with a Ballard rifle, but without apparent effect, though one ball seemed to strike it. It was seen and watched by the whole party upon the yacht.[5]

Answering a list of thirty-four questions prepared by the Boston Society of Natural History, the Reverend Mr. Lawrence added a few details. They

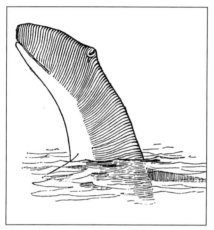

The unknown creature seen from the yacht *Princess* at Swampscott in 1875. (*Atlantic Monthly*, June 1884)

thought it had moved at six knots and faster. They saw no scales but mentioned well-defined nostrils such as those of a turtle. Its eyes were on the top of its head, and,

[j]ust above the water its neck seemed to broaden out as if into fins or flippers which were under the water. I should suppose it to be one of the saurian family. It seems to me neither a fish, snake, or turtle. If such a thing as an ichthyosaurus is extant, I should think this creature to be one of the same family.

Lawrence's report was added to material gathered by Rev. J. G. Wood for an 1884 article in *Atlantic Monthly*, in which he provided confirmation of the reverend's account with those of J. Kelsoe and J. P. Thomas of Swampscott.

Mr. J. Kelsoe, of Swampscott, who was fishing, passed within a few hundred yards of the animal while the chase was going on, and repeats all Mr. Lawrence's statements. He was near enough to observe on the dark surface of the creature two elongated white marks, about six feet in length, six inches wide, and having the ends rounded. Mr. J. P. Thomas, of Swampscott, saw the same creature and said that it came slowly out of the water, like a large mast.

In early August, there was a report of the creature in the vicinity of Gloucester. Another account from Wells Beach, Maine, describes a "veritable sea serpent," with a head like a shark, which grasped a cable rope and dragged a boatload of fishermen through the water at tremendous speed. Such uncharacteristically aggressive behavior makes this report extremely suspect, at least as concerns the New England creature.

Another encounter in the summer of 1875 comes from Captain Frederick York, of the schooner *Emily Holden*. The *Boston Herald* reported that on August 22 the vessel, while attempting to get a closer look at something that appeared to be a cross between an eel and a whale off Matinicus, on the Maine coast, struck the creature, whereupon it lashed at them with its tail and disappeared.

On August 30, the creature displayed itself to a small crowd for twenty minutes off Salisbury Beach, just north of Newburyport, Massachusetts. Captain Coffin, of the steamer *Everett*, also reported seeing it that afternoon. Then, on September 15, an unidentified creature got itself stuck in the mud at Brown's Wharf in Portland Harbor but freed itself before low tide.

On September 29, the *Gloucester Telegraph* carried an article that referred to the incident at Portland and mentioned that earlier in the month the creature had been seen off Race Point, Cape Cod, chasing porpoises. It also reported another sighting off the Maine coast.

> About the first of last month one of our skippers saw a sea-serpent about twenty miles off Mt. Desert Rock. The captain came on deck and looking to windward saw the sea-serpent with his head elevated about ten feet above the water. The crew were called on deck, and all but one, who remained below, saw the sight and corroborate the master's story. The serpent was about one hundred and fifty feet long, and turned his head from side to side as if taking observations.

The same article indicated that "Joseph Wonson of East Gloucester has witnessed the marvel several times, seeing the serpent under different conditions, sometimes appearing smooth and again exhibiting the customary bumps." No dates were given for Wonson's sightings.

All these reports of the creature in the summer of 1875 led the *New York Times* to run an editorial in which the writer, remarking that although the country had been "singularly free of epidemics" during recent months, the New England coast had been "visited with unprecedented severity by that strange disease, the culmination of which is the seeing of a sea serpent." Noting that isolated towns from Maine to Connecticut had reported sightings, the writer went on to state: "There is, indeed, no reason to suppose that seeing the sea serpent is a contagious malady, and we are as much in the dark as to the way in which the disease spreads as we are as to its origins."

The "disease" was apparently temporarily arrested, for the next report of the creature was not until two years later, when George S. Wasson saw it from his yacht *Gulnare* while in the company of his friend B. L. Fernald. The Reverend J. G. Wood reported that Wasson recounted the July 15, 1877, incident this way:

> The day was hazy, with a light breeze from the southeast. When we were, as I should judge, about two miles off the mouth of Gloucester harbor, the monster came to the surface about an eighth of a mile to leeward of us. I was looking that way and saw him appear, but Mr. Fernald did not, the first time. He immediately noticed the surging noise made, and, turning, exclaimed, "What ledge was that which broke?" This is exactly what the sound most resembled—a heavy groundswell breaking over a submerged ledge. And the creature itself looked, both in shape and color, more like a ledge covered with kelp than anything else we could think of, though from the extreme roughness of the surface I remember that we both spoke of its being somewhat like a gigantic alligator. The skin was not only very rough, but the surface was very uneven, and covered with enormous humps of varying sizes, some being as large as a two-bushel basket. Near one end was a marked depression, which we took to be the neck. In front of this the head (?) rose out of the water perhaps half as high as the body, but we saw no eyes, mouth fins, or the slightest indications of a tail. It impressed us above all as being a shapeless creature of enormous bulk. I suppose its extreme height out of the water might have been ten feet, certainly not less: and as it disappeared the water closed over it with a tremendous roar and surge and spray, many feet in the air. The water for a large space where it had been remained white and seething with foam for some little time. From the way the water closed over it, and the great commotion caused by its disappearing, we judged of its immense bulk, and we also concluded that it went down perpendicularly. It apparently rose in the same way. The largest whale I ever saw did not make a quarter part of the noise and disturbance in the water that this creature did. In concluding I will add that Mr. Fernald has followed the sea for fifteen

years as a fisherman, and is perfectly familiar with all the cetaceans that appear on our coast.

Rev. Wood asked Wasson to complete the Boston Society of Natural History's questionnaire, which he did, noting that the creature was brown, its speed was five to six knots, and between forty and sixty feet had been visible. Wasson was a marine painter, and one can't help wishing that the watercolor depiction he made for Wood survives. If it does, its whereabouts are unknown.

The very same day, J. T. Gardham, of Nantasket, also saw a sea serpent, which was reported in the *New York Herald*.

> It was between two and three o'clock that my attention was called to an unusual appearance on the water, in the direction of Gun Rock, about a half a mile distant. I immediately procured a powerful opera glass, with which I proceeded to investigate the phenomenon, and I, with others, unmistakably saw a sea serpent or some monster of the deep not generally known to natural history. The head was distinctly visible and raised about 8 inches above the water line. The formation of the head, owing to the distance, I could not define, but at intervals, it seemed to be enveloping in white sea foam as if in the act of spouting. The length of his snakeship seemed to be about forty feet and I counted twenty fins, or something like them, projecting out of the water about three inches, one foot apart, from the head to where the tail was supposed to be. He was first seen approaching the shore between Minot's Light and Gun Rock at a very rapid rate, and in a straight line, until he suddenly whirled around and faced the sea. This he repeated twice and finally disappeared, apparently heading for Nahant. He was seen for one-half hour.

A correspondent from Port Chester, New York, wrote to the *New York Times* on September 1 summarizing the sightings of that summer. According to the writer, in addition to the sighting in Nahant the creature had been spotted off Norwalk and Greenwich, Connecticut; Watch Hill, on Fire Island; and Port Chester, New York—all on Long Island Sound.

In 1878, the creature, or something very much like it, was again frequenting the coast of Connecticut, because there are reports of sightings off Rocky

Point, Greenwich; somewhere between Huntington, Long Island, and Stratford; and off Bridgeport, about a mile southeast of Black Rock Lighthouse.

Many of the accounts that follow would likely have been forgotten if not for George W. Woodbury, whose bound scrapbook somehow found its way into the Cape Ann Historical Association archives, where it is listed as Scrapbook #15.

Nothing is known about Mr. Woodbury or the year his scrapbook was acquired by the historical association. His collection seems to have been the result of an avid and long-standing interest in all manner of marine mysteries. In addition to the articles and firsthand testimony on sea serpent sightings, the scrapbook also contains accounts of the *Mary Celeste* and other ghost ships, as well as the occasional article on paleontological discoveries.

If there were some in his household and among his friends who shook their heads and wondered what could be done about poor George and his everlasting sea serpents, others indulged his unusual hobby by sending him their own statements and clippings. In the following letter, dated September 15, 1931, George N. Whipple supplied Woodbury with the details of his encounter. An accompanying note written on Whipple's stationery reads: "Dear George, Here is something to make you happy. Merry Christmas!"

> I have seen the Sea Serpent. Although I have related the circumstances many times, I have refrained from putting it on paper on account of not being sure of the date. It must have been in the summer of one of the late seventies, probably seventy-eight, the year I graduated from College.
>
> A party of us had gone down the Park River from Byfield for a picnic on Plum Island Bluff. There were, as I remember it, two dory loads of us, both boys and girls. The tide was low at noon. While sitting on the ledge of the Bluff after luncheon, we all saw what appeared to be a huge snake, swimming to and fro not far from the shore, apparently bewildered by the shallow water, and seeking a chance to find its way out to sea. We watched him for sometime, not only with the naked eye, but through a pair of opera glasses.
>
> We saw his head distinctly, which was shaped like that of a snake, and many folds appeared above the water in his sinuous motions. He finally

came in so close to the shore that two of us rushed down to our dory, and rowed out in the hope of heading him off and driving him ashore, but before we reached him, he had disappeared and we saw no more of him.

Among Mr. Woodbury's collection (which is sometimes vague as to dates and sources) are some accounts (such as Whipple's) that have never before been published in any survey of sea serpent sightings. Even more tantalizing is the fact that the collection hints at so much more. It is hoped that Mr. Woodbury's scrapbook is not unique. Perhaps there are others, stowed away in attic trunks, still awaiting discovery.

An interesting encounter that took place in Massachusetts Bay in 1878 was not revealed until eight years later. Evidently emboldened by two well-documented sightings at Cape Ann in 1886, B. A. Colonna, of the U.S. Coast Survey, submitted an extract of a report of a sea serpent to the journal *Science*. The report was written by Captain Robert Platt, of the U.S. Coast and Geodetic Survey schooner *Drift*, to his superintendent.

> [On] August 29, while becalmed off Race Point, Cape Cod, almost four hundred yards from the vessel, we saw a sea monster, or what I suppose has been called a sea-serpent. Its first appearance was that of a very large round spar two or three feet in diameter, from twelve to fifteen feet high, standing upright in the sea, but in a few minutes it made a curve and went down. It was visible about three minutes; the second appearance, about half an hour after the first, the monster came out of the water about twenty-five feet, then extended to about thirty-five or forty feet and about three feet in diameter; when out about forty feet, it curved and went down, and as it did so a sharp dorsal fin of about fifteen feet in length came up. This fin was connected to the monster, for the whole animal moved off with the same velocity. I looked at it with a good pair of glasses. I could not tell whether it has a mouth or eyes; it was brownish color. I enclose to you a sketch made by me and submitted to all on board who saw the animal, and they all agree that it is a fair representation of the animal as it appeared.

In an accompanying statement, Colonna notes: "Captain Platt is a trained observer, whose daily occupation at that time was to record just what he saw, and nothing more or less. I know Captain Platt so well that I have never doubted the existence of such a monster from the time his report was made known to me; and if others have been skeptical, I hope that recent events have proved the matter beyond question."

The following year, 1879, began with an out-of-season sighting on January 2 near Greenwich, Connecticut. That June, what may or may not have been another creature was seen two miles off Cape Ann Light. A more recognizable specimen (about a hundred feet long and moving at about seven knots) was seen in the Gulf of St. Lawrence, between Nova Scotia and Prince Edward Island, by the schooner *Louisa Montgomery* in July. The *Privateer* spotted a creature in the mid-Atlantic on August 5. The remaining reports of that summer of sightings from the Grand Banks to New Jersey contain details that either indicate mistaken identity or a size so huge as to be absurd.

The first sighting of 1880 took place in June when the creature was seen in Massachusetts between Cohasset and Scituate by Henry W. Goodwin and his family, watching from Green Hill:

> It came quite near the land, passing between the Black Rocks, and from
> then in a straight course toward Minot's. It remained above water until
> half way to Minot's when it disappeared and was not seen again. The head
> of the animal appeared to be several feet above the water, and its body was
> at least 25 feet in length. As it passed through the water it left a long wake
> behind it. Its motion was very rapid. Faster than any steam boat.

Late that August, a report from Merigomish, Nova Scotia, stated that a crew of mackerel fishermen saw something unknown to them. They said it was seventy to a hundred feet long and made waves like a steamer. In October, a questionable encounter occurred off New London, Prince Edward Island, although the animal seems to have been too small, twenty feet, and uncharacteristically aggressive to have been the New England creature.

The schooner *Edward Waite* of Portland, Maine, had a more familiar encounter four years later, on February 18, 1884, near Cape Henry, North Carolina, north of Cape Hatteras. That creature, which was seen for half an hour in clear weather by the officers and crew, was said to be ninety feet in length, swimming with its horse-shaped head out of the water and leaving a long, wide wake. The mate, William Page, whose report of the incident was printed in the *Philadelphia Record*, said that the most remarkable feature of the animal was its bright, saffron-colored eyes "half as big as a man's hand." Page was certain it was a sea serpent.

Ten days later, in Lower New York Bay, three Staten Islanders reported seeing a floating spar coming from the direction of the Quarantine Islands. When they rowed out to investigate, they found the spar to be not lumber at all but a living creature. Apparently disturbed by the sound of an oar carelessly shipped, it raised its head—the size of a powder keg—a yard from the boat, then bit into the oar that the men used to drive it off.

The only encounter in the summer of 1884 was recorded in the log of the *Silkworth*, whose captain and crew one moonlit night spotted a creature with a head like that of a conger eel in the Gulf of St. Lawrence while on their way to Quebec.

Rev. J. G. Wood's article entitled *The Trail of the Sea-Serpent* appeared in the *Atlantic Monthly* in June of that year. The *New York Times* responded with a scathingly critical editorial suggesting that the sea serpent had "prostituted his great length and imposing name to the service of watering place hotels."

For two years the sea serpent abandoned its local haunts, so it was not until 1886 that the Reverend Mr. Wood was somewhat vindicated by renewed interest in that most elusive denizen of the deep.

CHAPTER 6 NOTES

1. Elizabeth Cary Agassiz helped found Radcliffe College and served as its president from 1894 to 1902.

2. Webster began his political career as a representative from his home state of New Hampshire. He later moved to Massachusetts, which he represented in the House and Senate, and twice served as Secretary of State. The Peterson referred to here was Seth Peterson, Webster's right-hand man on fishing and gunning trips and one of the pallbearers at his funeral.

3. Handlining—fishing over the rail of a vessel—was another method.

4. Lake Utopia, in St. George, New Brunswick, is only one of dozens of lakes worldwide where unusual creatures have been sighted. There are two highly regarded books on the subject: *In Search of Lake Monsters*, by Peter Costello (1974, now out of print), and *In the Domain of the Lake Monsters*, by John Kirk (Key Porter Books, 1998). The latter reports the suggestion that the Lake Utopia creature—"Old Ned," which is said to resemble a giant snake—may enter the lake via the Magaguadavic River, which flows into the Bay of Fundy.

5. That party included, besides Rev. Arthur Lawrence, Mrs. Lawrence, Francis W. Lawrence, Mrs. Mary Fosdick, and two sailors—Albion W. Reed and Robert O. Reed.

7

1886 – 1929

"Sighted Her, by Crikey!"

If any of you or your friends wish to preserve your peace of mind,
I would suggest that if you ever see an animal of this character, unless
you can produce the animal as evidence, never mention the fact.
—Judge Sumner D. York, Rockport, Massachusetts, 1886

The sea serpent sightings of 1886 began, as one might expect, at Cape Ann and coincided exactly with the late appearance of mackerel in the region. A little before seven in the evening of July 24, as Albert W. Tarr and his wife were seated on the piazza of their cottage near Gully Point in Rockport, Mrs. Tarr noticed the creature and called it to the attention of her husband. According to one newspaper report, Mr. Tarr, who was a teller at the Rockport National Bank, was "sweeping the horizon with his glass when he saw a strange object approaching in the water from the direction of Gap Head. The water was as smooth as glass, and the fish, or whatever it was, looked so peculiar that he immediately called to the occupants of the adjoining cottage."

Within a few moments, the Tarrs were racing with their daughter to the shore, accompanied by the three young lawyers who were staying in the cottage next door (Sumner York, Charles Russell, and Edward Battis).

Notice of the event was sent to the *Boston Journal* by a local physician, Dr. John E. Sanborn, who after "a somewhat judicial examination of the evidence" undertook to prepare a statement of the events, which was published in the issue of July 27, 1886.

> All six rushed to the shore and were astonished to witness along the surface of the perfectly still water a long series of huge folds or curves, as of an enormous body moving slowly along, or as the little girl at once expressed it, "a great big eel, Papa!"
>
> The sea was calm as a pond, not the slightest wave, and it being broad daylight and the animal about, as they estimate, five or six hundred feet from the shore, their opportunity for observation was excellent.
>
> The folds or curves of the animal were about ten or twelve in number, and they estimate his length at certainly a hundred feet. The course he made was at first obliquely toward the spectators, but as he approached the head of a small cove, he lifted his head often out of the water and gradually swayed off, and slowly moved out toward the open sea. He thus described a sort of horse shoe curve of a mile and a half or so, giving the spectators, now increased to nine (Mr. and Mrs. John G. Moseley of Salem and a visitor), a good chance for leisurely inspection as he was in sight from ten to fifteen minutes. . . . He did not raise his head vertically or even obliquely out of the water, as in the usual typical legend, and serenely "survey the landscape o'er," but in his progressive, curving motion lifted his head out with the first curve of his body, his head dipping in and out of the water as he passed on. Once or twice he disappeared entirely from the surface, but soon came up again a few rods in advance. . . . Other persons at a farther distance also saw the monster. Some of the spectators have been all their lives familiar with every known style of fish and could not be deceived.

Skeptics might scoff and scientists sneer, but Phineas T. Barnum knew his audience. He quickly fired off a letter to the *Journal* in which he offered twenty thousand dollars for the capture, dead or alive, of such a specimen. He added: "If it should be only half or two-thirds the estimated length of the Rockport sea serpent I will pay pro rate, the reptile to be delivered preserved in a fit state for stuffing and mounting. If captured it will, of course, be added to my Greatest Show on Earth and eventually be permanently placed in the Barnum Museum of Natural History at Tufts College."

Of course.

Two and a half weeks later, the creature turned up again at Rockport, this time off Pigeon Cove. Almost fifty years later, William Pool, who was a boy at the time, related what had occurred in a letter to Marshall Saville.

> My father and I were surveying land just west of Mr. Putnam's cottage on the extreme end of Andrew's Point. I was the first to discover the serpent, [and] I called father's attention to it. He took a good look and said, *"That is the Sea Serpent!"* He then called Mr. Putnam and some others that were nearby.

Granville Putnam, master of the Franklin School in Boston, quickly heeded the call.

> I was engaged in the study of Professor Farlow's work upon algae, when I heard the voice of Calvin W. Pool, town clerk of Rockport, at the door of my cottage at Pigeon Cove, saying, "There is something strange in the water; I think it is the sea-serpent." I quickly took up my station upon the rail of my piazza, so that my marine glass was about fifty feet above the water and but thirty-six feet from the shore.

Virginia Henderson, who was a girl at the time, was visiting with her sister and brother-in-law, Rev. and Mrs. David H. Brewer, at the Way Cottage.

> We were all at midday meal, when we heard people shouting and saw all our neighbors rushing to the rocks. We promptly did the same and beheld, to our amazement, the cause of the excitement: a sea-serpent in the flesh, rounding Andrews Point and swimming with great speed towards Halibut Point.[1]

From his piazza, Putnam noted the following:

> He was about one-fourth of a mile from where he was seen last month. . . . It was a dead calm, a smooth sea, with a bright shining sun so that there was the best possible opportunity to observe his motions. . . . The creature was advancing in a northerly direction and but little more than an eighth of a mile from me. I watched most attentively for about ten minutes.

The younger Pool remembered it differently:

> The wind I should say was fresh north which made a heave to the sea and the serpent was travelling straight into the eye of the wind. At times we

could see lengths of ten or twelve feet of portions of the body between the
waves. At no time was the whole of the body under the water.

Virginia Henderson's recollection was more like Putnam's:

The sea was like glass, so we could plainly see his long black body moving
with vertical undulations through the water; his head, reared, cutting the
sea into one wake. The noise he made churning through the water, a quarter mile from shore, was like the swish of a modern speed boat.

Putnam further noted:

The head was frequently raised out of the water, and the movement was
a vertical one, showing some ten to fifteen ridges at once. I should say
that he was at least eighty feet in length.

Henderson agreed, pointing out that they did not depend on mere guess-
work to determine the size of the serpent:

Mr. Pool, a surveyor, had set up his theodolite on the rocks and he aided
us in this estimate of the size of the huge snake. Also the schooner *Annie
M.*, Captain Fears, master, which we knew to be forty foot long, was cruising nearby.

The younger Pool went on to describe its color:

[T]he body was a light French gray or looked as a salmon looks when it is
taken from the water. We watched until it reached a place about a mile off
shore from Mr. Putnam's house where it encountered heavier seas and
gradually disappeared in deep water.

Its color was darker, according to Putnam:

The color was a dark brown, and it appeared to be somewhat mottled with
a lighter shade—none of the forty or more persons who saw it detected
anything that looked like a fin or flipper. Its movement was not that of a
land serpent, but of a vertical one—from my elevated position, I could
plainly see the movements of the body. . . . Its course was direct, its speed
uniform, at not more than five miles an hour.

William Pool also emphasized the creature's method of travel:

There is no question in my mind, but that it was the real sea serpent. There
wasn't anything invented at that time to travel in a straight line as the sea
serpent did. It was not a log, spar or mast as it was traveling too fast to be
anything of this sort.

This never-before published sketch of the sea serpent was drawn by Virginia Henderson at the bottom of her handwritten account in the Woodbury scrapbook from the Cape Ann Historical Association archives.

The elder Pool agreed:

> I am well acquainted with the movements of porpoises, puffers, sharks, and other sea animals common on this coast and feel full sure that it was not one of them. After it disappeared a school of porpoises passed, rolling in their peculiar way and showing their fins.

Putnam too mentioned the porpoises:

> After [the serpent] had disappeared, and while we were still looking, a school of porpoises passed, so that we had a chance to compare their appearance with that of the serpent. I speak of this, as it has often been said that the former was mistaken for the latter. I shall never doubt that the sea serpent is fact.

Virginia Henderson wrapped it up:

> Quite a crowd was assembled on the rocks. We were tense and spellbound as he swam toward Halibut Point and disappeared from view around that point. Mr. Granville B. Putnam, principal of a Boston grammar school, was our star witness.

Star witness and loyal champion, for which he was rewarded by another

David Brewer's sketch from the Woodbury scrapbook. (Cape Ann Historical Association)

sighting on August 19, also in the company of the Reverend and Mrs. David Brewer. Doubted, mocked, flayed in the *New York Tribune*, a quixotic Putnam later asserted that he had "never regretted that I offered my report to the public."[2]

When the news of a second sighting at Rockport reached P. T. Barnum, he sent another letter to the *Boston Journal*:

> The Pigeon County [he means Pigeon Cove; it is Essex County] testimony proves what has before been previously established, the existence of a monster sea serpent, and I hope ere long to pay $20,000 for one as named in my offer through your columns last week.

Good old P. T. never did get his serpent, despite the proffered reward and an editorial in the *Washington Post* declaring that "One must now be captured. The feat cannot be impossible." The editorial also exhorted "zoological students of the country to attend to this duty and perform it. To add a unique marine monster to our knowledge of the world's life is far more important than to discover an imaginary Pole in the palaeocrystic desert of the North."

Although Robert Peary finally reached the North Pole in 1909, zoological students of the country never did undertake the capture of the unique marine monster.

Remaining reports for 1886 and for several subsequent years come primarily from Long Island Sound and the Connecticut River, except for a five-day period (August 29 to September 2) during which the creature was again seen in New York's Hudson River, where "the head stood right up straight for a second or two, as if the animal wanted to breathe, then it sunk out of sight."

Another report from early September of that year places the creature back in a more customary haunt off Cape Cod. Interestingly, the witnesses suggested that the animal had resorted to Herring Cove because the sun had raised the water temperature in the cove above that of the open water.

In October it was back in Long Island Sound. In early December, the Danish steamer *Thingvalla*, while in the company of pilot boat number 11, spotted something thirty miles off Nantucket that the captain thought was a "queer whale." The skipper of the pilot boat, James Hanman, who had come right alongside it, insisted it was no whale.

Another creature matching the classic description was reported by lobsterman G. Courland Paine off the Connecticut coast near Fisher's Island Sound in February 1887.

Then on July 22, 1887, two Philadephians vacationing at Fort Popham, on the Maine coast, encountered a long, black creature while enjoying a moonlight swim. The animal caused such phosphorescence in the water that a crowd gathered and subsequently witnessed the creature in combat with "some sort of fish" for a quarter of an hour before both disappeared. The following morning, the steamer *Percy L.* reported a dying whale stranded on a sandbar. People who went to examine the dead whale (no species given) reported that its flesh was torn and gashed.

Although it seems highly unlikely that the sea serpent caused the death of the whale, it should be remembered that Shubael West reported a similar incident in June 1818 off Cape Ann. Descriptions of the New England creature do not seem to suggest that any species of whale is a natural enemy; however, there could be rare instances in which the two might come into conflict, perhaps in dispute over prey or in defense of their young.

An appearance in Long Island Sound in mid July was followed by one on July 29, when the creature was seen off Nahant by residents and fishermen;

it was outrunning the pursuing boats, which would have followed it further but for squally weather.

The creature was spotted in the mouth of the Connecticut River by Captain Sherman, of the schooner *Coral*, in March 1888. On June 3, two fishermen reported the animal off Jones Beach on Long Island as it was going through the water "like a steam yacht." Two weeks later, the mate George Thomas of the *Alice Hodges* told a *Baltimore Sun* reporter that he had seen a hundred-foot sea serpent in the vicinity of Nags Head, North Carolina. "I am convinced it was a sea monster. I have sailed for the past 16 years and I have seen some queer things, but the object was the most curious I ever saw."

On June 20, the creature was seen "northward of Georges Shoals and about 190 miles from Boston" by the steamer *Venetian*. The commanding officer, Mr. Muir, reported: "It was unlike any animal I ever saw. It couldn't have been a shark. It certainly was not the back of a whale, although we had seen plenty of whales for two days."

The creature next appeared in July and August, twice in two weeks, between Watch Hill, on Fire Island, New York, and Point Judith, Rhode Island, apparently the first ever recorded sightings in that state. The crew of the tug *Sanford* reported seeing "an immense monster . . . swimming rapidly . . . his head elevated some six feet and showing a long back-fin, which projected for many feet along the surface."

In 1889 there was a sighting at latitude 44° north, longitude 42°40' west, by the American liner *British Princess*. The first officer, Captain Smith, reported that he and the fourth mate had seen the creature on May 4 at dawn from the bridge. According to Smith it was a "large black obstacle, sticking out of the water in a perpendicular position—like a long spar or a river buoy." Later that May the creature was again reported in the Hudson River.

At the Island Beach life station in January 1890, crewman Howard Potter spotted what he thought was lumber from a wrecked schooner, only to have a sixty-foot snakelike creature swim off to the north. In early July, the creature turned up at Nantasket, on the south shore of Massachusetts. In September it was seen nearby, at Marshfield, where witnesses watched from the beach as it was fired upon by George and P. H. Edson and Joseph E.

Whidden, who chased it from two boats. They claimed to have lassoed it with a painter, but when it became clear that they could not kill it with their guns, they cut the line. The creature swam off, leaving a large wake.

On August 9, 1891, Mate Opt and Seaman Jacobsen, of the British schooner *Gold Hunter*, had a strange creature with a prominent dorsal fin in sight for ten minutes in clear weather about thirty miles east-southeast of Cape Ann. Simon Borden, an assistant court clerk from Fall River, Massachusetts, saw another unknown creature later that summer in Vineyard Sound, between Martha's Vineyard and the Elizabeth Islands.

In 1892, Dr. Antoon Oudemans published *The Great Sea Serpent: A Historical and Critical Treatise* to mixed reaction. Intending to reach the widest possible audience, the Dutch biologist had written the book in English, but his imperfect command of the language was compounded by printing errors, and the critics were less than forgiving. There were, however, some zoologists who praised the book, in which Oudemans had analyzed 162 of what he considered legitimate sea serpent sightings, among them the creature that had come to be known as the "Gloucester Sea Serpent." It is frequently referred to by this name even today, though, as we have seen, it did not confine itself to the waters off Cape Ann.

First Officer Peters of the steamer *American* arrived in New York with the story of a strange encounter off Newfoundland at 43°55' north, 56° west, southwest of Grand Bank. Peters's account was reported in the *New York Herald* on December 7, 1893:

> I have been at sea man and boy these twenty-one years and I know that what I saw was a big fish or snake. He moved with a wavy motion. He bent his back into arches until he looked like a lot of crank shafts. You could see the humps plainly. They rose and fell with a steady beat.

Peters estimated that its chocolate-colored body was a hundred feet long and as big around as a sugar barrel. He watched it move in arches through the water for five minutes before going to get the captain. By the time they returned, it was gone.

In June 1896, there were two sightings in St. Andrews Bay, New Brunswick. In late July, a creature with bulging eyes, traveling at great speed with its head six feet above the water, was seen by fishermen nearby, in the Bay of Fundy.

Also in late July, an unusual creature was reported off Cape Ann as being the sea serpent. Granville Putnam made a different identification in a letter to the *Cape Ann Breeze*. "I have the pleasure of reporting the appearance . . . of a fine specimen of the white whale off Andrews Point," wrote Putnam, who had seen the sea serpent in almost the same location ten years before. "He was quite in shore and came frequently to the surface, blowing as he came. He was on his way out of Ipswich Bay and was headed toward the Salvages."

Although it is rare for Beluga whales *(Delphinapterous leucas)* to stray so far south of their customary home in Arctic waters, it is reassuring that Putnam, whose credibility had been questioned in connection with the sea serpent, was able to identify it and did not hesitate to do so.

Professor R. H. Mohr and his son, who were vacationing at Swampscott, reported a sea serpent in Nahant Bay on August 10.

> I was awake at daybreak. The morning was an exceptionally fine one, and my son and myself decided to take a sail for an hour or so in our yacht, and see the sunrise. The ocean looked like glass in its smoothness, and just enough air was stirring to move us along at a fair rate of speed. We sailed along toward East Point, Nahant, then came about and passed Egg Rock about a quarter of a mile when suddenly we heard a sound like that of escaping steam from the exhaust on a boiler, and another like the side wheels on a paddle steamer. We looked for a boat near us and saw none. I observed at the same time a splash in the water just a few feet back of us, and called my son's attention to it, saying he would have a chance to see a porpoise play.
>
> Then up came a head resembling that of a seal, except that it was somewhat larger and had a horn about a foot in length projecting out of its forehead. The eyes were large and bright, and it seemed to gaze at us as if in curiosity. Then the head disappeared.
>
> We had not gone far when the head appeared again, and this time it was followed by an immense loop, and another and another, and a fourth

which did not come wholly out of the water, as did the others, and we then discovered that the steam-like sound which first attracted our attention came from this creature.

Each loop was crowned with a thick fleshy fin, and the thing moved not by jumps and starts, but with a measured wheel-like motion, which produced the sound like the side wheels of a steamer boat, while from the mouth came the other sound.

The creature was so powerful and so rapid in its movements that we concluded we had better get out of its way as quickly as possible. My son took the oars and I hauled the sails close and took the tiller and headed for the Swampscott weirs, the nearest point. The creature circled our boat and disappeared.

Quite relieved, we continued our course, and had gone about a mile and a half when we again heard the steaming sound, and to our surprise saw the thing in advance of us ploughing along through the water. I headed the boat to port to avoid running into it just in time to avoid it, and so near were we to it that we could almost touch it with an oar.

It circled us again, and then spread itself about thirty feet on the surface of the water across our bow. This time there was no mistaking what it was.

There it lay, long glossy and black, its skin looking like that of a porpoise, with fins along its back about three or four feet apart. It remained in that position two or three minutes, and then it plunged under water and appeared again far away from us, making its way out to sea.

The following summer, John Kirk, of Marblehead, saw the creature while fishing near the Half Way Rocks on July 10, and there was another report from Long Island Sound on August 7.

In 1898, Albert G. Wass, of Addison, Maine, was in a boat with his brother Robert when they saw a serpent, as reported in a letter to George Woodbury dated February 12, 1933.

Robert and I were on board the A-1 copper-bottomed sloop *Nancy Hanks* bound from S.E. Rock Fishing Ground to N.E. Harbor about four or five miles southwest from Schoodic Point in the mouth of Frenchman's Bay, when a black object having the appearance of a ledge just awash, or a whale's back loomed up at less than a quarter of a mile ahead. We could see and hear what seemed to be a spar buoy with its base held stationary, spanking its length on the surface of the water with a circular motion, at varying intervals of from two to five seconds.

At first we thought it must be a whale being attacked by a thrasher or swordfish, but, on nearer approach, we were convinced that it was something different from what we had ever encountered. When we had reached a proximity of about 100 yards (and, believe me, that was close enough!), the monster straightened itself out to a form resembling a seventy-five-feet string of hogsheads. Whether the body was creased in sections or the color markings camouflaged it as such, I am not sure. It carried its head, which was like that of a horse, six feet higher than its body, the motion of its swimming was like an eel, and its speed, at least, twenty knots. The absence of fins and the eel-like shape of the tail settled all doubt that this could be any known type of whale.

At first glance it seems that the Wass brothers saw a very different species of creature than the one seen by Professor Mohr and his son two years earlier off Swampscott, but that might not be the case. Professor Mohr reported that they were near enough to the creature that they could almost touch it with an oar, whereas the Wass brothers never got closer than a hundred yards. It is possible that the "fins along its back about three or four feet apart" reported by Mohr resembled (from a far greater distance) the "seventy-five-feet string of hogsheads" reported by Albert Wass. It is also possible that the horn that Mohr reported (like the one mentioned by Colonel Perkins back in 1817) belonged to either a male or a female of the species, and the Wass brothers saw its opposite. Albert Wass's comment about "the absence of fins" may mean that he did not see a distinct dorsal, pectoral, or caudal fin, which would identify the creature as a known whale, because he qualifies his description of the back "resembling a . . . string of hogsheads" by saying, "Whether the body was creased in sections or the color markings camouflaged it as such, I am not sure."

In November 1898, a cyclonic storm slammed into the New England coast with winds measured at ninety miles per hour before they shattered the instruments at Provincetown, Massachusetts. Dozens of schooners were wrecked at Vineyard Haven, Provincetown, and Block Island (Rhode Island) in the gale, named for the paddle wheel steamer *Portland*, which was lost with 160 souls somewhere off Cape Cod. The Portland Gale hit hardest on the south shore of Massachusetts. When it was over, it would be remembered as the most devastating storm ever to hit the East Coast, taking 400 ships and at least as many lives.

The loss of more than 70 percent of the commercial fishing fleet of New England is one possible explanation for a reduction in sightings over the next few years. Another is the changes in the ships and the fishing practices. By the early 1900s, diesel engines were beginning to replace coal-fired steam engines. The top-heavy "clipper-schooners," which had taken an enormous toll on the fishermen (1,614 of whom lost their lives at sea between 1880 and 1897), were soon to become a memory.

In the fisheries, the otter trawl, with its flexible weighted base, would soon supplant its older sibling the beam trawl, which required a flat bottom for efficient fishing. It was probably not known then that the otter trawl, although exceptionally good at harvesting deepwater fish such as cod, was also wreaking havoc on the ecosystems of the ocean floor. Even if it had been known, it is unlikely that anyone would have stopped using it, because the annual haul of fish continued to rise. In the face of such abundance, probably no one even imagined that this was the beginning of the end.

In July 1899, the passengers and crew of the ocean liner *New England* spotted a creature off the coast of Newfoundland, as reported in the *Gloucester Times and Cape Ann Advertiser* of July 25 under the headline "Passengers on Steamer *New England* Sighted Great Lizard." According to the newspaper report, while the steamer was on passage from Liverpool to London, a strange forty-five-foot-long monster with a "carinated back" projecting six feet out of the water was sighted at 7:45 A.M. when the ship was in latitude 45°37' north, longitude 58°09' west.

The Captain said that his attention was called to an object off the starboard bow, which he first made out to be a ship's boat or part of a derelict. He bore two points out of his course to ascertain just what the object was, believing it might be a wreck with some poor sailors in need of assistance. The steamer approached to within about 40 feet of the object, which still had the appearance of a submerged wreck. Suddenly a thin stream of water was thrown in the air and the animal—for it proved to be one— moved off at right angles to the ship, going through the water at an eight knot clip. . . .

Its head was visible for only a few seconds when it raised it from the water to gaze unconcernedly at the big ship as she approached. The neck was elongated and the head hooded.

The captain did not say it was a sea serpent, but acknowledged it was the strangest animal he had ever seen in his 40 years' experience at sea.

. . . One of the saloon passengers said that he believed it was a giant sea lizard.

If not for the elongated neck, the animal seen by the passengers and crew of the *New England* could be assumed to have been a whale that was spouting. The description of the head as "hooded" is unusual and, in the absence of additional details, hard to interpret. Does it mean that the creature looked like a cobra? Or did the observers perhaps see a walrus or some kind of large seal with rolls of fat that might resemble a cowl?

Twentieth-century reports frequently contain peculiar and confusing descriptive details such as these, and some of them can seem downright bizarre. There are several possible reasons for this. One is that the sober, earnest statements and carefully prepared correspondence of the nineteenth century are not characteristic of the twentieth century. Most of the reports that follow are second- or even third-hand accounts written for newspapers and therefore subject to editing for space and content. Competition between the numerous dailies of the early twentieth century may have led some writers to embroider their accounts to suit the tastes of their readership. Taken as a whole, however, the reports are distinctly lacking in the type of sensational details one might expect from this topic.

Terminology will present its own set of complications, as we have already seen in the discrepancies between the Mohr and Wass accounts, which might agree more than is at first evident. What one person might call a fin would to another person be a flipper; one person's "hump" might be another's "carinated back." One interesting element of the twentieth-century vocabulary associated with the creatures is that their motion in swimming is almost never described as "undulating vertically." The creatures are no longer described as moving through the water "like a caterpillar"; instead they "glide" away or swim rapidly out of sight.

One possible explanation for some differences in descriptive details is the perspective of the witnesses when viewing the creature. More often than not, the creature when seen from land or a fishing boat will be described as snakelike. In contrast, when seen from the greater height of an oceangoing ship, the creature will give the appearance of an upturned boat. Although this is not uniformly true, the viewer's perspective does seem to have been a factor and should perhaps be taken into account when significant discrepancies are evident.

Sightings were reported in Long Island Sound and again in the Hudson River in 1901, but the following summer the creature was back in Maine.

In early July 1902, Captain Chapman and Mate Drinkwater, of the schooner *Kitty Lawry*, while in the vicinity of Mark Island, Maine, saw "what appeared to be a huge snake, going along at steamboat speed and turning its head from side to side as if taking a survey of the bay."

Unfortunately, no descriptive details accompany the report of another sighting a week later by George Sherman, of Gilly's Harbor, Islesboro, in Penobscot Bay, near where the Reverend Mr. Cummings had seen the creature one hundred years earlier.

On July 10, there was a report from Halifax, Nova Scotia, that while entering Sydney Harbor, the yacht *Wacouta* had found a two-hundred-foot sea serpent in its path. That seems an extravagant length but perhaps appropriate in the moment; the yacht was owned by tycoon J. J. Hill, president of the Great Northern Railway.

On July 15, the *Daily Evening Item* (Lynn, Massachusetts) reported the sea serpent off Nahant:

Mrs. Laura Wagniere Catches a Glimpse of the Monster of the Deep. Two Friends of Eugene Brann While Out Sailing See Him Close To. Ancient Ocean Summer Visitor Seen in All of His Official Glory.

The sea serpent has again reared its horrid head off Nahant, and its inhabitants are on the lookout for another glimpse of the monster of the deep. . . . It was seen in repose, moving its enormous and slimy bulk through the water with the dignity of age and reputation. It was seen in action, snorting and bellowing, gnashing its sharp and gleaming teeth and with a greenish yellow lustre in its fiendish eyes.

It was not a mere glimpse that the observers obtained, as some of the people who saw the fearful creature watched it for fully 20 minutes. They were on shore, and could in safety keep their fascinated eyes fixed upon the monster that since the times of hoary antiquity has roamed the seas and, though often seen, always eluded capture. The party who were embarked on the element where he, she or it was sporting had a better chance for observation, but fled in terror from the terrible monster and have not yet recovered fully from the shock to their nervous system.

THE MARINE MONSTER SEEN OFF NAHANT,
According to Descriptions of a Nahant Woman, Swampscott Fishermen and Marblehead Yachtsmen.

The Daily Evening Item added this educational drawing to their account of the Wagniere sighting.

It transpired that the creature had twice been seen in Nahant Bay, once from shore on Friday evening and again on Monday morning by yachtsmen from Marblehead. Laura Wagniere, who saw it on the evening of July 11 from "a piazza overlooking the sea" in the company of her husband and several friends, reported her experience in a letter to the *Boston Transcript*. Wagniere's mostly matter-of-fact account provides a rare opportunity to compare an eyewitness statement with the somewhat more lurid newspaper report.

> [W]e were suddenly attracted by something unusually long and dark in the water. . . . Little by little we became aware that it was no raft, neither was it a shoal of fish, but in reality an extraordinarily long, living and terrible creature of the deep . . . which was gliding slowly but surely through the water. After moving along for some time steadily, it changed its course making an enormous circuit. . . . Its head appeared from time to time above the surface, and seemed to be flat and long. . . . I should say [the creature] measured anywhere between eighty and a hundred feet, possibly more. Its color was indicated by certain dark spots which rose to the surface at regular distances, and suggested the undulatory motion of a serpent. . . . For my part I am glad to have seen with my own eyes a rare specimen of the deep, which until yesterday seemed only to be a legend in the annals of the history of Nahant. One would like to know about its hiding place and where it drags out its lonely existence. This may forever remain one of those great mysteries which no human being will be able to solve.

Later that summer, the creature was again seen in Long Island Sound. The following year, on August 24, 1903, the *Gloucester Daily Times* reported:

Sea Serpent Seen: Monster 50 Feet Long Reported Off Louisburg

The Captain of a schooner which arrived at Louisburg, C.B. [Cape Breton] on Wednesday claims he saw a sea serpent off that port the day before. The monster was fifty feet long and was throwing up a heavy sea in his wake. The presence of a monster of this kind may account for the exceptionally large schools of mackerel which have made their appearance around the Cape Breton coast near that place the last few days.

More likely it was the other way around, and the "monster" was following the fish. Either way, this behavior seems to be characteristic and was first reported in 1817 at Gloucester. Other reports of the creatures turning up during a run of herring or mackerel come from Plymouth, Massachusetts, in 1815; Kennebunk, Maine, in 1839; Rockport, Massachusetts, in 1886; and Nahant Bay in 1947.

A report from the summer of 1903 puts the creature a bit farther south, where it was seen by three ladies at Wood Island, Maine.

Still another 1903 report puts the creature at the mouth of the St. Croix River on the United States–Canada border. Walter Greenlaw (described as a "total abstainer" and an elder in the Presbyterian Church) and his brother were startled a little after noon by a peculiar noise and saw a huge animal swimming toward them. They quickly pulled for shore, and the animal shot past them, leaving a "torpedo-boat trail." A short time later it reappeared, headed back for Passamaquoddy Bay with its head out of the water. The two were unable to describe the creature except to say that its eyes "were of remarkable size and as green as starboard lights." A party of schoolchildren from Robbinston, Maine, who had been swimming in the river rushed ashore screaming as the creature approached, and would not reenter the water. A veteran boat pilot of the St. Croix River, Captain Stanson, declared that he'd seen a similar creature in practically the same spot fifteen years before.

The report falls apart in the last two paragraphs, however, when it states that a small boat belonging to the steamer *Queen* had been bitten in two forty years earlier, and that sea serpents, although acknowledged by scientists to be rare, live to be three to four hundred years old and, traveling at speeds up to "150 knots an hour," can "shoot across the Atlantic in less than 24 hrs. time."

Most stories of sea serpent sightings appear in newspapers during the summer months, or what has been called "the silly season." The term implies that real news gets the summer off and, as Bernard Heuvelmans points out, "acts of God, and follies of mankind were also on holiday." This is not true, of course—hard news never takes a vacation—but sea serpents do get reported more often (although not exclusively) between May and September. In the Gulf of Maine this is probably due to the migration of fish, though it may also be because the North Atlantic is not especially hospitable to humans (and possibly not to sea serpents) during the winter months. Nevertheless, Second Officer H. A. Dawes, of the steamship *Columbian*, reported a curious encounter on December 1, 1904, about forty miles off Sable Island.

The *Boston Transcript* ran the story under the headline " **He Really Saw a Sea Serpent: H. A. Dawes, Second Officer of the *Columbian*, Tells of His Experience in a Signed Statement**"

> ... The sky was overcast, but the air was clear, and he had a perfect view of the creature. He says that it was about 80 feet long, 5 feet across the back, while about twenty feet from the head was a fin about three feet across and twelve feet high, pointed at the top. The head was high and pointed, and tapered down to a flat nose, with a wide mouth and thick lips. The eyes were about the size of a saucer, and were bright and glaring. ... When the creature was abreast of the ship, it raised itself from the water, shook itself and then sank its body under the water, leaving the fin still sticking out. Mr. Dawes is a perfectly matter-of-fact, unimaginative steamship officer, and there seems not the slightest reason to doubt his statement.

Maybe not, but the next one is a doozy.

In June 1905, the Newton Journal Publishing Company of Newton, Massachusetts, offered for sale, at the modest price of ten cents, a fourteen-page booklet whose cover announced: "The Old Orchard Sea Serpent—8th Wonder of the World—Discovered at Old Orchard, Maine; A Graphic and Illustrated Description of the Huge Monster that came ashore at Old Orchard, Maine in June 1905. The Most Marvelous Mammal in Creation."

According to the pamphlet, a "huge monster" had washed ashore on June 7 and been discovered by F. E. Sidelinger. Those statements appear to be the last that might loosely be considered reliable. The creature described in the pamphlet is certainly fantastic: "A sea serpent with no teeth, 150 feet long with eyes as large as watermelons, a heart the size of a beer keg, and a tongue fifteen feet long." The booklet claims that "[i]ts presence startled the scientific world," which it most certainly would have done had it been, as was claimed, "half fish, half lizard, three million years old and preserved in polar ice ever since."

A contemporaneous newspaper report indicates that the "creature floated

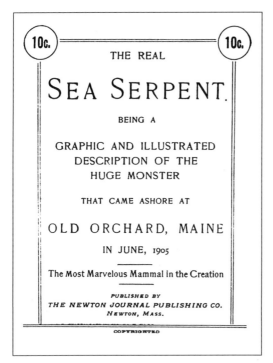

The title page of F. E. Sidelinger's pamphlet.

in on the crest of Wednesday night's high tide," and that "2000 people flocked to the shore unable to believe from others' reports that the sea serpent, long a mystical, half-legendary leviathan, had proved a reality."

The creature apparently stank, which did not deter the resourceful Mr. Sidelinger from hauling the head, jawbone, and one vertebra into the village and putting them on display in a tent "nearly as big as Ringling Bros. Circus."

To a meandering and incoherent text, which included a thumbnail history of sea serpents, Mr. Sidelinger added some titillating details. He claimed it was a "lady" creature, offering as evidence "mammae (each weighing 85 pounds, with nipples as long as a telephone receiver) and the extraordinary length of its tongue." Two extremely grainy photographs and a sketch used to illustrate the booklet were claimed to be "not only genuine but the only ones extant." (They are also of little use in identification.) The booklet concludes with the speculation that it was "barely possible that [the creature] is allied to the genus Balanoptera of Zenglodundt variety, considered by naturalists the longest animal in creation."

It is not only barely possible but quite likely that it *was* the remains of a Balaenoptera, probably a blue whale, *Balaenoptera musculus,* which are rare but not unknown in the Gulf of Maine.

What it most assuredly was not was one of the "Zenglodundt variety." Creative spelling aside, Sidelinger is referring to a carnivorous ancient whale, *Basilosaurus cetoides,* from the Middle and Upper Eocene, 35 to 40 million years ago. When Sir Richard Owen examined the teeth of a specimen that Dr. Richard Harlan had named *Basilosaurus* (King of Reptiles), he pointed out that its teeth were those of a mammal and, with characteristic arrogance, promptly renamed it *Zeuglodon* (yoked teeth), which has been causing confusion ever since.

Basilosaurus certainly looked like a traditional sea serpent, with its forty-five- to fifty-foot elongated body. Albert Koch used its bones when fabricating his "Master of the Seas," and Rev. John G. Wood was among many who suggested these primitive whales as the likeliest candidate for the sea serpent. The whale had, however, no neck to speak of, and its five-foot-long wedge-shaped head does not correspond to Sidelinger's description. Finally, it never was considered to be "the longest animal in creation." That distinction belongs on land to *Seismosaurus* and in the sea, because no carcass of the New England creature has ever been preserved and examined, to the blue whale.

(Once reaching lengths of more than a hundred feet, the mighty blues eluded early harpooners by their size and speed, but the factory ships of the twentieth century have all but done them in. Now classified as endangered, with pollutants threatening their food source, blue whales have a bleak future. Scientists fear that the remaining population may simply be too small to recover.)

One might have thought that the exhibition of one of these rare and remarkable creatures would have been enough for Mr. Sidelinger. However, the back cover of the booklet is most telling. It is an advertisement for F. A. Sidelinger & Co. Real Estate Agents, offering "Ocean front lots in first class locations" and "Business opportunities of every description."

Sidelinger certainly knew about business opportunities and had capitalized on a rare stranding with true entrepreneurial spirit.

The headline of a report in a Gloucester newspaper of July 12, 1904, stated:

Off Nantasket: Sea Serpent Has Arrived for Summer Sojourn.
Fisherman Will Take Oath That He Saw 70-Foot Monster.

Henry Edwin Hatch, an unassuming fisherman of Gun Rock, Nantasket, who bears an unquestioned reputation for integrity, says he is ready to make affidavit before any justice of the peace that while in a boat with his wife about one mile off Simons Farm Beach on the morning of Monday, July 10, he saw a sea monster about 70 feet long with about 40 humps or curves about the size of a man's body along its back and head, which it occasionally raised above the surface of the water, as large as a nail keg.

The monster, which resembled a serpent in the sinuous movements, with great rapidity passed within 100 feet of the boat, furiously lashing the sea and leaving a wide wake in its course.

When Hatch and his wife first noticed the thing, only four or five humps were visible as it sped in the direction of Black Rock, which lies off the coast where Hull and Cohasset join.

Then it turned back, passing the boat at a greater distance seaward, where it finally disappeared.

But no matter how others may take Mr. Hatch's story, there is one man, Ambrose B. Mitchell, a lobsterman of Hull village, who will doubtless place absolute credence in it, for several years ago he had almost an identical experience, and his description of the monster that now seems to have inhabited these waters for a long time is practically the same.

Corroboration of this story came in 1969 when John J. Gaulding, of North Weymouth, Massachusetts, reported to historian and folklorist Edward Rowe Snow that on July 12, 1905, Cohasset fisherman George Cole was knocked from his dory by a seventy-foot sea serpent that was apparently attempting to disentangle itself from the lines of a lobster trap. Having overturned the boat, the sea serpent made no further attempt to harm Cole, who was able to swim the dory back to Cohasset Beach. Gaulding also mentioned the Hatch and Mitchell accounts; even the day and month are the same, though he was off by one year, which is understandable after more than half a century.

On August 5, 1905, the creature was seen by Major General H. C. Merriam near Wood Island Light, Maine. Merriam described the sighting in a letter to Dr. Frederick A. Lucas, of the United States National Museum in Washington, D.C.

We were startled by a loud splashing in the water some distance off our stern, and were looking in that direction [when] we saw what appeared to be a monster serpent. Its head was several feet above the surface of the

On April 15, 1905, *The Daily Evening Item* (Lynn, Massachusetts) carried this cartoon. Evidently the keeper of the Egg Rock Light, Captain George L. Lyon, had complained that something or someone was stealing his chickens, and the newspaper responded with this entertaining but unlikely solution to the mystery.

water, its long body was plainly visible, slowly moving towards our boat by a sinuous or snake-like motion. . . . The animal continued its course, passing entirely around our boat . . . keeping a distance of about three hundred yards. . . . It swam at a steady and rapid rate—not less than twelve miles an hour, keeping its head uniformly about four feet out of the water and apparently intent upon examining our craft on all sides. It had no dorsal fin unless it was continuous.

The color of its back appeared to be brown and mottled, shading down to a dull yellow on its belly. The head was like that of a snake, and that part shown above the surface—that is the neck—appeared to be about fifteen or eighteen inches in diameter. . . . I estimated its length at sixty feet or more. During all the time occupied in swimming around us, which must have been at least ten minutes, the head remained uniformly above the surface of the water and then it quietly dove and disappeared.

December 1905 produced one of the most extraordinary sightings of a sea serpent ever, if for no other reason than that the observers, Michael J. Nicoll and E. G. B. Meade-Waldo, were trained naturalists, although their primary field of study was ornithology. The sighting took place off Parahiba, Brazil, but the description of a creature with a long neck, about the thickness of a man's body, raising its head seven to eight feet out of the water will by now be familiar.

Both Fellows of the Zoological Society of London, Nicoll and Meade-Waldo were guests of the Earl of Crawford on board his yacht *Valhalla* when Nicoll spotted something unusual in the water and called it to Meade-Waldo's attention, saying, "Is that the fin of a great fish?"

Meade-Waldo reported:

> I looked and immediately saw a large fin or frill sticking out of the water, dark seaweed brown in colour, somewhat crinkled at the edge. It was apparently about six feet in length and projected from 18 inches to 2 feet from the water.
>
> I got my field-glasses on to it and almost as soon as I had them on the frill, a great head and neck rose out of the water in front of the frill; the neck did not touch the frill in the water, but came out of the water in front of it, at a distance of certainly not less than 18 inches, probably more. The neck appeared about the thickness of a slight man's body, and from 7 to 8 feet was out of the water; head and neck were all about the same thickness.
>
> The head had a very turtle-like appearance, as had also the eye. I could see the line of the mouth, but we were sailing pretty fast, and quickly drew away from the object, which was going very slowly. It moved its head and neck from side to side in a peculiar manner: the colour of the head and neck was dark brown above, and whitish below—almost white, I think. When first seen it was about level with the poop of the yacht and on the starboard side. . . .

In a letter written in 1929 to Rupert Gould, Meade-Waldo added: "It made a wave as it went along, and under water behind the neck I could see a good-sized body. As we drew ahead we could see it swing its neck from side to side and it lashed the sea into foam."

The creature seen from the *Valhalla*, based on the sketch of M. J. Nicoll. (*London Illustrated News*, 1906; Fortean Picture Library)

Nicoll later reported that on the following day the first and third mates, Mr. Simmonds and Mr. Harley, witnessed something making a commotion in the water:

> . . . as if a submarine was going along just below the surface. They both say most emphatically that it was not a whale, and that it was not blowing, nor have they ever seen anything like it before. After they had watched it for several minutes, it "sounded" off the port bow, and they saw no more of it.
>
> This creature was an example, I consider, of what has been so often reported, for want of a better name, as the "great sea serpent". . . .

The following report from St. Croix Island at the head of Passamaquoddy Bay was discovered in Miscellaneous Scrapbook #8 at the Calais (Maine) Free Library by Wayne Wilcox. The scrapbook was compiled by W. W. Brown from two local newspapers, the *Calais Advertiser* and the *St. Croix Courier*. It is not known in which paper the story appeared on September 5, 1907.

THE SEA SERPENT
Three Men in a Boat Made His
Close Acquaintance on Sunday Last

Two Calais men and one from Boston became intimately acquainted with the Champlain sea serpent last Sunday. Edward Carver was at his cottage at DeMonts and with him were Henry Gillespie and a Boston man. The sea serpent was seen playing around a buoy near the Canadian shore and the trio put out in a boat to investigate , carrying a loaded rifle stowed in the bow of the boat.

When they had nearly reached the buoy, they rested a while to investigate. But the monster of the deep "saw them first" and came within a couple of feet of the boat to investigate. Just then all three men lost interest in everything but "Home sweet home" and put on the biggest spurt of speed that they could summon for the American shore.

The pace did not bother the serpent a bit and it kept them very close company until shallow water was reached.

The men talked it all over for a while and came to the conclusion that the big fish is a man-eating shark.

In a little while he was seen again at his old play about the buoy and the temptation came to them to try another encounter, in the hope of getting a shot at long range.

They had reached well out into the stream again, when all at once the monster was seen to be headed their way and coming just as if he had no other object in living than to reach their boat.

In less time than it takes to tell it he was beside them again and the Boston man was thinking longingly of his absent friends.

The others concluded that as the big fish seemed willing to keep at a distance of two feet from their boat they would just try one shot at him and await further developments.

With Mr. Gillespie at the oars, Mr. Carver secured the rifle and resting it on the gunwale of the boat he took careful aim and fired.

They are confident that the shot went home for the big fellow made a mighty splash for a second or two and then disappeared for the remainder of the day at least.

The absence of descriptive details makes this an extremely perplexing account. On one hand, the creature's curiosity and apparent speed argue for it being the New England monster. On the other, the men's assessment that it was a man-eating shark argues for it actually being some sort of selachian, perhaps a basking shark. The willingness of the three men to go back into the water after the creature also seems a bit implausible. It is impossible to reach a definite conclusion.

The mention of the Champlain sea serpent is also puzzling. There have been more than three hundred sightings of "Champ," as the Lake Champlain creature is known, and most descriptions given of it are similar to those of the New England creature. But how the writer thought that a creature from a landlocked lake got to the sea is another question entirely.

The most intriguing item is in the final paragraph: "Some people down the way tell a story of having enticed the serpent clear across the river one day by feeding it herring from the boat. They are commencing to think that he is harmless and are a little inclined to regard him as a pet."

If this seems unlikely, consider this item reported in the *Essex Register* at the height of the sea serpent frenzy in 1817: "We are told he actually received herrings when offered to him."

One weird detail appears in this unsourced report dated October 1909 from the Woodbury scrapbook:

SAW SEA SERPENT
So Captain and Crew of Schooner *Warren M. Goodspeed* Aver.

If Capt. George Perry and the crew of sch. *Warren M. Goodspeed* did not see the sea serpent yesterday, they certainly gazed upon something that looked mightily like the real thing and which, all hands solemnly declare, they never saw the like of before.

At T. wharf, Boston, this morning Capt. Perry and his men told of what they had seen. They were about ten miles off Highland light and were coming along headed for market when someone spied the queer thing in the water and close at hand.

In a jiffy, every pair of eyes on board was gazing at the sight. It was big and long, whatever it was, and had a hump sticking out of the water. The head was not visible, but following behind the hump for a distance of fully 12 feet was what appeared like a tail, long and slender, the tip of the tail being round, perfectly round in shape and white in color, contrasting strongly with the dark shade of the rest of the body in view.

A round white ball on the tip of the tail would seem to be a most inefficient adaptation on a creature presumably built for speed. Yet this feature has been mentioned before, in 1826, by the crew of the *Gold Hunter* and will be mentioned again by the skipper of the *Calvin Austin* in 1921. It's a puzzler.

On August 25, 1910, this report appeared in the *Gloucester Times*:

SIGHTED SEA SERPENT

The captain of the fishing steamer *Bonita*, which arrived at Portland on Monday with 100 barrels of sardine herring, reports that when off the Brown Cow, just this side of Small Point, on Saturday last, he passed within 50 yards of an immense sea serpent, apparently 80 to 90 feet in length, the color of the fish being black with large white spots. The serpent was plainly visible for several minutes, and evidently has a penchant for the *Bonita*, as her captain was the first to see it in the summer of 1909.

The mention of spots on the creature is somewhat uncommon, but they are mentioned occasionally, as are light-colored streaks or stripes on the side of the head and neck. They should not be taken to mean that the creature was covered with polka dots, rather that some witnesses note whitish patches on some of the creatures. Humpback whales have light patches such as these on their flukes. Because no two patches are exactly alike on the whales, the markings greatly assist marine biologists in identifying individuals.

Although many writers refer to the sea serpent in the singular and as a male, it stands to reason that reports dating back to 1639 could not all refer to a single individual. Discrepancies in descriptive details such as coloration, length, and anatomical features can be explained by what was probably a very small population of the creatures comprising juveniles and adults of various dimensions and appearance. Or it could mean that there were more than one kind.

One cryptozoologist[3] who subscribed to this theory was Ivan T. Sanderson, a Scottish zoologist trained at Cambridge. In 1947, Sanderson wrote an article for the *Saturday Evening Post* entitled "Don't Scoff at Sea Monsters."

That article elicited reports of many previously unknown sightings, such as the one that follows. According to Mrs. F. W. Saunderson, while aboard a steamer on passage between New York and Portland, Maine, in the summer of 1912 or 1913, the following incident occurred, which she communicated in a letter to Ivan Sanderson dated March 15, 1947:

> Off the starboard there emerged an enormous head supported by a huge eel-like body on a long neck about the size of a barrel. It rose about twenty feet above the water, giving the effect of a gigantic eel standing on its tail and about half submerged. It remained erect for half a minute or so and the head seemed to turn slowly as if the monster were taking a good look at its surroundings. Then it slipped slowly backward into the water leaving scarcely a ripple.

On August 24, 1912, the *Gloucester Daily Times* reported the creature's demise:

THE GREAT SEA SERPENT IS NO MORE!

Gloucester Skipper and Crew Credited With Its Killing

Captain John A. McKinnon and his crew have killed the sea serpent according to the Portland *Argus*. It was 60 feet long and has a big fin like a leg of mutton sail, put up a desperate fight, exhausting the crew and—oh, well, here's what the *Argus* says:

> The sea serpent which has been a frequent visitor to our coast for the past 20 summers, and an object of dread to all fishermen, will be seen no more, having been killed on Sunday last off Cape Porpoise by the crew of the Boston fishing steamer *Philomena*, once the George F. West steam yacht of the same name, after a desperate combat, lasting two hours.
>
> Capt. John A. McKinnon, the master of the *Philomena*, one of the best known mackerel killers on the coast, was a busy man yesterday afternoon taking out a fare of mackerel at Commercial wharf which he had just secured off the lightship, but delayed his departure from the dock long enough to give a brief account of the affair, which occurred on Sunday forenoon.
>
> A small school of mackerel in the seine boat were pulling in the seine when a commotion was noticed among the fish, and the sea serpent, which had evidently been under the seine, made its appearance alongside

the boat to the alarm and disgust of the crew, who had never seen anything like it before. . . . [I]t became entangled in the seine, tearing it to pieces, and then started off at a 2.40 gait with the boat, seine and everything in tow, all the mackerel estimated at about 40 barrels, getting away.

Seeing that something was wrong, the fishing steamers *Victor* and *Ethel*, which were fishing in the same location, came to the assistance of the *Philomena*'s men and a pretty stiff fight ensued, the combined crews of the three steamers joining in the attack on the serpent, knives, boat hooks, clubs and anything that came handy being used.

At last one of the *Philomena*'s men armed with a knife a foot long reached a vital spot, and after a great splashing the serpent succumbed. Capt. McKinnon describes the sea monster as being from 50 to 60 feet in length, its body which resembled in size and shape an immense tree trunk being black with rough skin covered with barnacles. It had what the fishermen call a hammer head and an immense fin on the back resembling a leg of mutton sail and nearly as large.

The skipper was afterwards sorry that he did not tow the serpent into port, but with a badly exhausted crew and a wrecked seine he concluded it best to cut him adrift. Called "Big Ben" by the fishermen, and dreaded by them so much that they invariably pulled up stakes when he put in an appearance, he has been seen every summer along the coast for many years, although its existence has been doubted by many. On one occasion it ventured into this harbor, and was seen by many at the islands. The defunct serpent has been the theme of countless jokes in times gone by, and has been celebrated in poetry and prose.

It might be tempting to dismiss this tale because the idea that a sixty-foot animal could be finally done in by a foot-long knife seems unlikely. However, this comparatively peaceable creature attacked by the crews of three fishing boats was probably done in by the combined effects of many wounds, with the knife delivering the coup de grâce.

Although the description of a "hammer head" leaves one wondering if the fishermen meant it had a head like the head of a hammer or if it resembled a hammerhead shark, other elements of the story seem perfectly logical. The mackerel are "pulling in the seine," evidently spooked by the creature as it

This account is accurate as I remember it.

John a. MacKinnon

Gloucester, August 24—1933,

60 feet long and had a big fin like a leg of mutton sail, put up a desperate fight, exhausting the crew and— oh, well, here's what the Argus says:

"The sea serpent which has been a frequent visitor to our coast for the past 20 summers, and an object of

CAPT. JOHN McKINNON,
Whose Crew Is Credited with Killing

On this newspaper clipping in the Woodbury scrapbook is a notation made by Captain MacKinnon himself in 1933: "This account is accurate as I remember it." (Cape Ann Historical Association)

rises toward them from the depths. Perhaps the creature is unable to see the net and becomes entangled as it swims up on a closely packed meal. If the leg-of-mutton sail appears as an odd detail, we have only to look at Michael Nicoll's drawing of the *Valhalla* creature for a similar depiction.

On the other hand, it is difficult to fully explain why MacKinnon would not put himself to the effort of towing in this much sought after prize. Could he possibly have failed to appreciate the financial rewards that could have accrued from the capture of this creature? Or was it, as the newspaper seems to suggest, pure Yankee pragmatism that made him cut his losses and head for home? Of all the reports thus far encountered, this is easily the most frustrating. Did Captain MacKinnon and the crew of the *Philomena* do battle with and kill a true sea serpent? Or do we place them in the company of Captain Rich and the whale men with a misidentified common creature? We shall never know.

What is known is that twenty-one years later, George Woodbury confirmed the report with Captain MacKinnon. There is a notation in the margin of the scrapbook that reads: "This account is accurate as I remember it. [signed] John A. MacKinnon, Gloucester, August 24, 1933."

On August 30, 1913, the Allan Line steamer *Corinthian* had an encounter with a sea serpent while on passage from London to Montreal. The second officer, G. Batchelor, who was officer of the watch at the time, sent an account of his experience to Dr. Antoon Oudemans, extracts of which follow.

At 4.30 a.m. in the cold gray dawn of August 30th 1913, on The Grand Banks of Newfoundland . . . while casting my eyes around the horizon I picked up an object about a mile off right ahead. The best conjecture I could make as to its nature was that it was a fishing boat laying end on to us. In the dense and extensive fogs which sweep over the fishing banks sailors frequently become separated from their schooners and many starve for days before they are picked up. I had such an accident in mind as I watched the object ahead. When it suddenly disappeared beneath the surface, being still unenlightened I thought of tragedy. Suddenly, however, after I had meditated a moment upon serious things something surprising showed itself about two hundred feet away from the ship.

First appeared a great head, long fin-like ears and great blue eyes. The eyes were mild and liquid, with no indication of ferocity.

Following sad eyes came a neck, it was a regular neck alright, all of twenty feet in length which greatly resembled a giraffe.

The monster took its time in emerging, but it kept emerging so long that I wondered what the end would be.

The neck . . . seemed to be set on a ball-bearing so supple was it and so easily and rhythmically did it sway while the large liquid eyes took in the ship with a surprised, injured and fearful stare. . . . Three horned fins surmounted its bony head, probably for defense and attack or for ripping things up. The body was about the same length as the neck very much like that of a monster seal or sea-lion with short water-smoothed fur. . . . The tail was split into two large fins. . . . Its colour scheme was good, although some might think it giddy; light brownish-yellow tastefully spattered with spots of a darker hue.

For a minute the creature inspected the *Corinthian* with its roving gaze, and then it disappeared, showing its after-works as it dived. Its whole attitude while in sight was that of one "moving about in worlds unrealized." It seemed to be trying to comprehend a curiosity which it had good reason to believe might be a new danger. I almost felt a tenderness for it, and never have I experienced such a

The curious creature seen from the *Corinthian* as sketched by G. Batchelor. (Reproduced from *In the Wake of the Sea-Serpents*, by Bernard Heuvelmans)

minute in my life. Down in my room I had a camera and a rifle. Yet I was the only one on the bridge besides the quartermaster at the wheel. I don't mind confessing that I wavered between my duty and my desire for some kind of a shot. Finally I stayed, but I don't know whether I should take full credit for that or not because I hated to lose sight of the thing. As it watched me it churned the water into foam and spray with its huge front fins. As it went out of sight it emitted a piercing wail like that of a baby. Its voice was altogether out of proportion with its size.

The strange creature is either a native of the Arctic regions which has come down with the streams which bring the ice-bergs, or else of the mile-down bottom of the sea. . . . From its general appearance I surmise that it grubs on jelly-fish and the plant growth at the bottom of the sea. What does it really live on? But as to that we can't tell, because it is something new to us, and its food would probably be just as strange.

Zoologically speaking, as I got a good view of the creature when diving, I could only describe it as identical with Sauropterygia [an order of extinct marine tetrapods including plesiosaurs] . . .

The location of its appearance was Lat. 47°51′N. Long. 48°30′W. and I am of the opinion that the wreck of the *Titanic* a few degrees south from the position I saw the monster may have had something to do with its presence.

What the poetic officer of the *Corinthian* thought the wreck of the *Titanic* had to do with the creature's appearance is anyone's guess. One certainly can't blame this sentimental account (or the sketch he drew to accompany it) on an overeager reporter.

The following newspaper reports, both of which were discovered in the Woodbury scrapbook, are the only known accounts of the sea serpent in New England waters during the First World War.[4] The first appeared in the *Gloucester Times* of June 12, 1914, under the headline "**Saw Sea Serpent Near Thatchers.**"

The crew of the British sch. *Flora M.* told an amazing story when their vessel reached Boston late Wednesday from Port Wade, N.S. [Nova Scotia]. Off Cape Ann Tuesday afternoon, while the two-master was sailing with a fair wind, there suddenly appeared above the surface of the water the head and part of the body of a huge marine monster.

Every man on board from Capt. George Brooks to the cook saw the animal, and they are willing to take oath to the fact. They declare that it was no hallucination, and any suggestion that the monster may have been a whale or porpoise is resented. Capt. Brooks declared it was the worst looking "animal" he had ever seen and the other six men bear him out.

Capt. Brooks was averse to telling the story to reporters, fearing ridicule, but finally gave the facts. The skipper has never been a believer in sea serpents and has never before seen anything in his long years at sea that could in any way be mistaken for one. . . .

"At first I thought it was a big gas buoy adrift. It was slanted at a sharp angle and the water appeared to be boiling under it. Then it lifted its great head which resembled more than anything the head of a horse. It gradually rose out of the water until we could plainly see fully 25 feet of its enormous back. The mate sprang for his glass and ran up the rigging to get a better view, while most of the crew followed him.

"I stood on the deck too astonished to move. Suddenly the monster plunged beneath the surface and its entire body disappeared. In an incredibly short time it came up directly ahead of the schooner and closer than before. . . .

"I gave the wheel a twist to swing the schooner away from the monster, and just as we changed course he disappeared, stirring up the water for some distance. If I had a camera I could easily have taken a snap shot of the creature."

Capt. Brooks was so impressed by what he saw that he told the boarding officer about it. He said in his opinion the animal must have been 75 feet long.

Capt. Brooks is about 45 years of age and is a respected citizen of Weymouth, N.S. The crew is composed of seasoned mariners who have long followed the sea.

The next account appears in its entirety, in part because it has not seen print since its original publication in the *Boston Sunday Herald* of July 18, 1915, and in part because of the writer's style. This is a one-of-a-kind account that offers the reader a glimpse of a waterfront world that has all but disappeared, a world where characters such as Jig Field and Cap'n Eddie spun their yarns from a settee at the end of the wharf.

SEA SERPENT APPEARS TO GURNET'S CAPTAIN
Long Black Mane Sticking Out Like Yacht's Pennant, Eyes Rolling and Foam Churning as Leviathan Crossed Steamer's Course at Great Speed, as Skipper Edson Tells It

Whenever there appears the suggestion of a sea serpent in the public print, two sorts of people begin to scoff. These are scientists who insist that there is no such thing, and skeptics who immediately look for the name of a summer hotel in the story, scenting the ubiquitous press agent.

But there is no hotel advertising on this page, and anyone, scientific or otherwise, who insists that the sea serpent is non-existent has only to walk down to Otis wharf and interview Capt. Edward E. Edson of the steamer *Gurnet*. Capt. Edson has seen one, and he knows.

And if he had been a little quicker with a folding pocket camera which was a little slow in the unfolding, being rusted by sea damp, Cap'n Edson could have shown you a picture to prove it. As it is, he will swear on a stock of volumes as high as the custom house tower that he saw this sea monster, and he will be borne out by Quartermaster Roy Litchfield, who first sighted the leviathan. There's no doubt that the *Gurnet's* ship's company had the good fortune, which comes only once in several years, of seeing the sea serpent which now and then chooses Massachusetts bay in which to disport himself.

Not a Stranger

This monster has been seen before. Several independent skippers have come into port and reported him. They can't all be liars. Marine skippers, Kipling, Connolly, Robertson, Jacobs, Marryatt, and Clarke Russell to the contrary, are not all romancers. Most of them are a hard headed lot of floating businessmen who are too busy making both ends meet, especially under the new La Follette shipping act,[5] to indulge in fictitious loggings of their maritime experiences. And the sea serpent is down on the *Gurnet's* log. That settles it.

Cap'n "Jig" Field, the wharfinger of Welch's wharf, at Scituate, where the *Gurnet* docks, who has his finger on the pulse of the water front and knows more about maritime affairs than some people in Scituate, says he knew something was wrong the day the *Gurnet* sighted the sea serpent, because he heard her whistle blowing outside long before she hove in sight from behind Barker's hill.

"I surmised," said Cap'n Jig, "that something was up. Cap'n Eddie don't ever whistle till he gets inside the breakwater and heads up on the dock, but this day he was a-blowing all the way down from Minot's, and I knew something was up."

Something undoubtedly was up, as it appeared to the gaping crowd on the dock as the steamer swung alongside the pier and warped in. Cap'n Eddie Edson never mixes business with pleasure or anything else, and not a word could anyone get out of him until the craft was securely tied to the dock and the passengers ashore, although Cap'n Jig Gardiner [Field] nearly burst with curiosity. Then Cap'n Eddie came ashore and sat down on the settee on the end of the dock.

"Sighted Her, by Crikey!"

"Well, by crikey," said he, "we sighted her."

"Sighted her?" asked Cap'n Shady Barry, who is harbormaster and pilot and is always looking for a piloting job. "Sighted her? Sighted who?"

"Sighted the sea serpent," said Edson. "Run right across her. Pretty near come aboard of us. I could have reached out and tickled her under the chin we were so close. Yes, sir."

"I want to know," said Cap'n Jig Field.

"Yes, sir," said Cap'n Eddie. "We spoke to her all right."

"What did she look like?" asked Cap'n Shady as the crowd pressed closer.

"Yes," chorused the crowd. "Tell us about it."

"Oh well," modestly went on Cap'n Eddie Edson. "It wasn't much of a thing after all. It was this way.

"We was on our way down and somewhere about off to the east'ard of Black Rock when I was below and Roy had the wheel, I heard him let out a yell and I ran on deck."

Could Have Spit on Her

"'For the Lord's sake, what is it?' he was saying, and well he might. About two point off our starboard bow making for the open sea on a course that I saw would just clear us was the darndest looking craft I ever put an eye on. I yelled to Roy and he gave the chief the signal to reverse her—just in time, too. When the *Gurnet* slowed down, that sea serpent ran under her bow so close that I could have spit on top of her head. Yes, sir."

"I want to know," said Cap'n Jig Field.

"Yes, sir. And what's more she was alashing the water in a way to make you sit up. You've seen a big freighter coming in light with her screw about half out and the way she'll throw water. That's the way this sea serpent did and she threw some stream, believe me, some stream!"

"I want to know," said Cap'n Jig Field.

Some Speed

"Yes, sir! And speed! Well I've seen torpedo boats and racing motorboats and these flying boats but I never see[n] anything cut water like that sea serpent. I wouldn't estimate her speed. I wouldn't expect you to believe me. But I tell you this. When that sea serpent saw that we was going to cut her in two if she didn't change her course, she gave herself four balls and a jingle and forced draught and she walked past us and don't you forget it, she flew! The long black mane stuck straight out from the back of her neck like a pennant on a yacht and she rolled her eyes horrible and the drool was running off her cruel mouth like foam. She was wicked. Yes, sir! She was wicked. I picked up a belayin' pin and walked for'ard and brought that belayin' pin down across her stern but there—before it hit her she was nine fathoms away. She was a-sailing!"

"I want to know," said Cap'n Jig Field.

But Capt. Edson sticks to his tale and Roy the quartermaster sticks to his and there it stands.

Cap'n Jig Field says he doesn't believe the story and he'll be durned if he don't ride back and forth on the *Gurnet* until he sees one himself before he'll believe it.

Still anyone who doubts has only to go down to Otis wharf and take the *Gurnet* to Scituate. On the way down make friends with Cap'n Eddie Edson and perhaps he'll show you the log. There it is in black and white. And a ship's log has to be believed.

This journalist, who unfortunately received no byline, has certainly made the most of a slender story. Despite some of the more sensational details of the creature's appearance, whether provided by the witnesses or supplied by the writer, the story is probably essentially true. It will be six years before there is another.

An article in the *Gloucester Daily Times* of November 18, 1919, states that, "A very interesting talk was given before the historical section of the Cape Ann

Scientific and Literary Association at Red Men's Hall last evening, the principal speakers being Nathaniel Babson and George W. Woodbury." The topic was sea serpents, the two men each having a turn at recounting the history of local sightings and pedigrees of the witnesses. Babson spoke first.

> He said in opening that there is no reason for disbelieving in the existence of the sea serpent while there is undisputed authority for its existence in the testimony of respectable witnesses and such magazines as Harper's Magazine and Atlantic Monthly . . . while a book on the subject published in Holland gives a record of 165 different appearances which are vouched for.[6]

Woodbury evidently introduced the sighting made by the late Joseph Proctor (see page 101), then gave "an authentic list of over a score of recorded appearances of the sea serpent in localities ranging from Sable Island to the Gulf of Mexico as well as more distant waters, between 1886 and 1913."

At the conclusion of the talks, Mrs. Fanny F. McLean stated that her two cousins, Albert and Robert Wass, encountered a sea serpent in 1909 about thirty miles below Bar Harbor. Woodbury followed up the lead, the result of which is the original testimony of Albert Wass on pages 147–48. It was not until September 9, 1921, that the *Boston Herald* ran this story of a sighting from the *Calvin Austin*:

SEA SERPENT SHOWS UP OFF SCITUATE
Skipper of *Calvin Austin* Saw It—A Hideous Monster

The annual sea serpent yarn has been spun a little late, but Capt. W. T. Holmes of the steamship *Calvin Austin*, whose veracity in 43 years of seafaring has never been questioned, uncorks a gem about what he saw off Scituate the other morning. He was bound here from New York when through the fog a ship's length ahead he observed a creature with a head as big as a cask and glassy eyes. The barnacled body, that tapered to a tail with a knob, was propelled by two flippers. The body was about 29 feet long and may have weighed a ton. If it's wrinkled warty mass could be appraised in years it may have antedated Methuselah. Capt. Holmes speaks about the creature reluctantly and refers to the pilot, lookout and quartermaster, who were equally amazed that Boston bay should be invaded [by] so repulsive a monster.

The *Boston Transcript* ran a similar story bearing the headline "Sees Strange Fish Off Cape: Captain Holmes of the *Calvin Austin* Reports Remarkable Creature in Cape Cod Bay."

Because this sighting took place late in the season and the creature described was only thirty feet long, it is tempting to ascribe it to some sort of unusual whale, except that one would expect a mariner of forty-three years' standing to be able to recognize a whale even if he did not know the exact species. Furthermore, the knob at the end of the tail, previously mentioned by the captain and crew of the *Gold Hunter* (1826) and the *Warren M. Goodspeed* (1909), where the flukes should be argues against a whale but does nothing to aid in identification.

The details reported in an article in the *Boston Herald* of May 28, 1925, about the creature spotted on May 24 by the crew of the *Foam* aren't all that much better.

SEA SERPENT, HEAVED UP BY QUAKES, CIRCLES ABOUT TRAWLER *FOAM*: FACT

Returning to this port yesterday after a weeks fishing in South Channel, Captain Richard Tobin and the crew of the steam trawler *Foam* told of seeing a 125-foot sea serpent last Sunday afternoon, when the *Foam* was about 85 miles southeast of Boston Light. They insisted it was no "pipe dream" and expressed belief that the sea monster had been forced out of its lair by an upheaval of the bed of the ocean during one of the recent earthquakes in this part of the world.

Capt. James Doyle, acting mate of the trawler, was the first to see the serpent. It came to the surface about 100 yards off the starboard bow of the *Foam,* and at first view he thought it was a naval submarine out hunting rum smuggling craft. But when about 20 feet of the submarine's bow bent upward at a right angle to its body, he gave a shout that brought every man on deck.

They shook like aspen leaves or juniper berries in the November winds, while the monster, propelled by eight fins on each side of his eel-like body, approached near.

As it rapidly swam a circle about the trawler, the men observed that it had an almost perfectly smooth skin, battleship gray, excepting for a stretch of 15 feet at the back of the head and 10 feet of the tip of the tail. On these parts were green scales about the size of tea trays.

The trawler steamed for a while in the wake of the serpent but soon lost sight of it. Capt. Doyle estimated that the serpent was 125 feet long, but Capt. Tobin believes it was nearer 150. It was the first sea serpent to be reported off the New England coast this season.

The story of the 125-foot-long eel-like creature that circled the *Foam* has an overall familiar ring to it; there are, however, two features that match no other description. Did Captains Tobin and Doyle really see eight fins on each side (for a total of sixteen) of a creature most people describe as having none? And how are we to interpret the tea-tray sized (approximately eighteen- by thirty-inch) green scales? The location given for the "scales" along the back of the creature is somewhat consistent with what others described as a frill or a finlike structure; however, because this report gives no information concerning weather conditions, or how close the *Foam* got to the creature, or how long the crew had it in view, and because it is not absolutely clear whether the writer spoke directly to the witnesses or obtained the story secondhand, we should perhaps maintain a healthy skepticism regarding the details. Modern accounts are almost never accompanied by sketches, but this is one instance where an illustration would have proved most helpful.

On August 17, 1929, "The Wit's Weekly" section of *The Saturday Review of Literature* announced its sixty-sixth competition, offering a prize of fifteen dollars for the best lyric called "The Sea Serpent." The results were published in the October 12 edition, where the editor noted that this particular competition had been extremely popular, having brought in nearly two hundred entries, an unusually high proportion of which were up to prize-winning standard. Clinton Scollard won the competition with the following entry:

> She was trig and trimly sparred,
> As fine as a brig might be,
> Yet she was evil-starred,
> For there crossed her bows at night,
> In a spindrift smother of white,

The serpent of the sea.
The lookout saw the thing,
Yet, he knew not what he saw—
Ominous, soul-stirring,
But he gave it a long-drawn hail,
"Ahoy! Is that a sail?"
This with a touch of awe.

A sail, my man? Not so!
Rather a shape of dread:
Eyes that burn and glow,
Twin inhuman fires—
Carnivorous desires—
Set in a scaly head.

And a body long and lithe,
Monstrous, jaws agape,
That seem to oscillate, writhe;
Spewed from the uttermost caves
Of the deep, with its yawning graves,
A murk incredible shape.

Nay she will never come back
To the watchful hearts that yearn,
For a portent has crossed her track;
She will lie erelong, that ship,
Warped to an oozy slip
In the Port of No-Return!

The motif of sea serpent as portent is an unusual one, though not unheard of, particularly among sixteenth- and seventeenth-century Norwegians. Sailors and fishermen tend to be superstitious and once followed all kinds of seemingly peculiar rituals and customs. A silver coin placed under the masthead, for instance, is said to ensure a profitable voyage. Conversely, it is unlucky to set sail on a Friday, to board a vessel left foot first, or to look back once your ship has left port. Porpoises are a good omen, and it is unlucky to kill them. Some seabirds carry the souls of men lost at sea and so must be left unmolested. Count the fish you've caught, and you'll catch no more that day.

An admittedly superficial investigation reveals that apparently the only ship to have met with disaster after an encounter with a sea serpent is the HMS *Hilary*, which was torpedoed within days of having used one innocent victim for target practice during the First World War. The crew of the *Hilary* killed the poor creature, and it could be argued that they got their just desserts.

After the crew members of the *Hilary* were rescued, it transpired that the officer of the watch on duty at the time of the creature's death was the only one who had been prepared for disaster and packed a bag. That officer, who "had been brought up at sea as a youngster by a captain who had an extensive knowledge of, and a firm belief in, many old sea superstitions," had apparently made a strenuous appeal to the navigator, Lieutenant Harris, not to make the entry of the encounter with the sea serpent in the log. When Harris protested that he'd been ordered to do so by the captain, the older officer is said to have replied: "Well, that makes it a certainty anyhow—we shall never reach port again."

Maybe it's the reluctance of some captains to enter their sightings in the log that has saved them from a similar fate.

Chapter 7 Notes

1. Halibut Point is named not for the fish but for the fact that here, at the northernmost point of Cape Ann, it was necessary for sailing vessels to "haul about" to continue their course.

2. On August 22, there was a further sighting at Cape Ann that received scant attention. This time the creature was seen, in a now familiar manner, by several men in a boat. The men thought they saw a spar in the water, but when they approached, it raised its head six feet above the surface, then quickly disappeared.

3. Curiously, Sanderson and Bernard Heuvelmans separately came up with the term *crypto-zoology*, the study of "hidden" animals.

4. In his research for *In the Wake of the Sea-Serpents*, which remains the definitive volume on the subject, Bernard Heuvelmans located only seven authentic reports (that is, not obvious misidentifications) for this period, two of which reported sea serpent fatalities.

5. The La Follette Seaman's Act (not "shipping" act, as in the newspaper clipping), sponsored by liberal reformer Robert Marion La Follette of Wisconsin, is a massive and comprehensive act that provides the merchant marine with a basic charter of employment rights. It passed on March 4, 1915, becoming part of the U.S. Code of Federal Regulations.

6. He refers here, respectively, to the misidentified basking shark from Eastport, Rev. J. G. Wood's article, and Dr. Antoon Oudemans's book.

8

1930 to the Present

That Much Mooted Question

Your modern man would rather disbelieve something than believe it....
His disbelief flatters his vanity, makes him think he is a superior fellow.
Well, it doesn't make him a superior fellow. Any fool can
disbelieve in sea serpents....

—Archie Wills, editor, *Victoria Daily Times*, 1933

In 1930, Rupert T. Gould published *The Case for the Sea-Serpent*, devoting forty-three pages to the "New England Sea Serpent" and concluding that the early–nineteenth-century sightings were generally quite believable.

> A town whose population chiefly consists of fishermen is not usually electrified by the visit of a whale, or shark, or a school of porpoises, or any other common object of their daily life. There can be no doubt at all that the thing seen, whatever its nature, was a most unusual—a unique—sight. If no other evidence had ever come to light elsewhere, I for one should be inclined to hold that that afforded by the appearances off Gloucester and Nahant in 1817 and 1819 would amply warrant the deduction that the existence of a marine animal of unknown species with serpentine head and neck, and about a hundred feet in length, was an established fact.

It was not, unfortunately, an established fact, for most of the twentieth century sea serpent reports from the North Atlantic are scattered and sporadic. It had been five years since the last New England sighting when on

June 7, 1930, a creature was spotted on Georges Bank, as reported in this unsourced clipping from the Woodbury scrapbook.

150-FOOT "SEA EEL" SEEN ON GEORGES

A prolonged hot spell can be depended upon for an old-fashioned sea
serpent tale, and that's just what the schooner *Pollyanna*, Capt. Cecil Moul-
ton of Gloucester, brought in from Georges yesterday. It was the first "sar-
pint" yarn of the 1930 season, a bit early, but bristling with thrills.
Twenty-three men of the *Pollyanna's* crew vouch for a spectacle seen two
weeks ago when a 150-foot something with a head like a horse and poised
above a smooth sea appeared alongside like a huge eel, moving at least 10
knots and never casting an eye on the schooner. It disappeared to the
westward still going strong when last seen. The thing was a greenish-
black with a buff underbody and about the size of a gasoline drum
through its middle. The *Pollyanna's* company undoubtedly breathed easier
when the stranger straddled the horizon, for it might have taken possession of the little vessel and rolled its keel up in a jiffy. Be that as it may,
old-timers at the fish pier wink slyly at mention of sea serpents with a
guess that the *Pollyanna* fell in with a school of porpoises, [which look] for
all the world like a huge snake as they leap, roll, dive and wallow.

One year later the creature was back near Georges, according to this newspaper clipping from the Woodbury scrapbook, source unknown.

REPORT FIRST "SEA SERPENT" OF YEAR

Report of the first "sea serpent" of 1931 was the news of the day at the
Boston Fish Pier—and vouched for by twenty-three fishermen, the captain
and crew of the Gloucester schooner *Catherine Burke*. They all had a look at
the "serpent," or what you will, last Monday, twenty miles east of Boston
Lightship while bound for Georges Bank.

The creature described as forty or fifty feet long, with a head about five
feet long resembling that of a horse, appeared on the surface 100 yards
astern the schooner. It remained in sight several minutes traveling at [an]
estimated speed of seven to eight knots an hour. In this interval, the "serpent" sounded twice, giving the fishermen a view of its "broad black back
and shark-like tail." It was a clear morning and observation was perfect, ac-

cording to Captain Ray Marsden's report of the incident to the secretary of
the Boston Fish Bureau.

It may be that the Great Depression had created a need for an entertaining diversion, or perhaps it was the repeal of Prohibition. Whatever the reason, 1933 was the beginning of a boom in sightings of mysterious aquatic
creatures, especially after reports of a sea serpent in Cadboro Bay, British Columbia, began making headlines.

On October 11, the *Philadelphia Enquirer* ran a short editorial calling for a
scientific investigation. "Now that five Canadians have reported the presence of a sea serpent in Cadboro Bay, Victoria, science should treat this *lusus
naturae* [a monstrosity, or freak of nature] more seriously than it has hitherto
done." Referencing Captain M'Quhae's report of the *Daedalus* creature as
"credible testimony," the writer goes on to state, "Still, skepticism as to the
reality of the sea serpent prevails. Even the researches of the now disbanded
Sea Serpent Club of Marblehead did not dissipate it." [1]

The reports of a sea serpent in the Pacific Northwest continued to filter
in during the fall of that year, prompting the *Boston Herald* and the *Boston
Transcript* to run editorials, which appeared on October 21.

The article in the *Herald* under the title "A Sea Serpent Afar" had something of a chauvinistic tone:

> The Pacific coast has annexed what was once a New England specialty.
> Back in 1818 there was active competition among such towns as Portland,
> Gloucester and Salem for the glory of sighting and describing that elusive
> marine monster. . . . Now with some chagrin it must be recorded that the
> best accounts of these creatures are coming from the Pacific side. Two of-
> ficials of the government of British Columbia are in the press with ac-
> counts of a monster with coils like a snake, its head ten feet out of the
> water, and clearly seen at different times.

The writer goes on to indulge in a little "mine's bigger than yours" competition, stating that, "Anyhow, the New England serpents were bigger than
anything yet recorded from the far coast," and then bemoaning the fact
that "New England has not produced a good sea serpent story for a long
time. The Northwest has had one almost every year since 1926. What about

New England spirit? Rum Row ought to have produced such monsters in abundance. . . ."[2]

The *Transcript* piece, under the title "Sea Snakes and Squids," took up the cause of the sea serpent with a less parochial attitude.

> We must not be swept off our feet by these stories of the Great Western Sea Serpent that are broadcast from Seattle. The first impulse, of course, is to discredit them, to impute them to the jealousy of the West Coast inhabitants wishing to belittle the Great Eastern Sea Serpent whose home is in the primeval ooze of the deeps off Nahant. But that is an ill natured assumption. We are distinctly on the side of the sheep-nosed sea serpent that has been observed in the waters of British Columbia and Washington by eyes that see clear, described by lips that know not the touch of the rum tankard. Nor is it unlikely that the creature has been looked upon by many who doubted the evidence of their own eyes, like the farmer who, seeing his first giraffe, declared vehemently, "They ain't no sich animile!" And there are others, timorous of soul, who have seen it but deny it, lest they be laughed at.
>
> The whole argument against the sea serpent is that a sight of it is so rare. Yet, of the countless millions who people this globe, how many have ever seen a whale? A mere handful. Perhaps one in a hundred million. To all the rest the whale would be fabulous, except that Jonah vouched for it. Fewer still are the children of men who have looked into the awful countenance of the giant squid, that terror of ancient mariners, that monster whose malignant powers are so vividly depicted in Hugo's "Toilers of the Sea." It can be said for the whale that its bones are preserved here and there in museums, but where is there to be found the framework of the giant squid? Apparently there is not a single specimen of it, this creature which the encyclopedias tell us is "the largest invertebrate animal," with its sinister eyes like automobile lamps and its hideous arms more than fifty feet in length.[3] In old books you see pictures of the giant squid grappling with ships and dragging them down to the unfathomable caves of the ocean, where it can feast at leisure upon the bodies of their crews. Is this horrendous creature not as fabulous as the sea serpent? Until we see a giant squid weaving its tentacles in an aquarium or stretched out on the

dissecting table of a zoologist,[4] we shall keep an open mind as to the existence of the sea serpent, at the same time nourishing a hope that some-
day one will be captured and brought ashore to confound the skeptics.

Before long, the "Great Western Sea Serpent" (also known as Caddy) and
its New England relation were to be upstaged.

The first reports of a creature in Loch Ness, Scotland, were published in
August and September 1930 in the *Northern Chronicle*, but it wasn't until May
1933, when the *Inverness Courier* ran the story of a sighting by Mr. and Mrs.
John Mckay of Drumnadrochit, that the public showed interest. Perhaps the
Courier's descriptor—monster—had something to do with it.

By October of that year, *The Scotsman* had a correspondent on the scene.
London newspapers quickly followed. Reports were sometimes quite sensational and included all kinds of misinformation calculated to make the
scenario that much more mysterious. The loch, which "would not give up its
dead," was reputed to be bottomless, its sides honeycombed with under-
ground caverns, the rear tunnels of which led to the sea. Thus Nessie was
a sea serpent that had somehow found its way into the loch and been
trapped.

In reality, the loch is for much of its length seven hundred feet deep (although depths of over nine hundred feet have been recorded in some
places). And as Steuart Campbell points out in his 1991 book, *The Loch Ness
Monster: The Evidence*, because the loch is sixteen meters above sea level,
any tunnel large enough to accommodate Nessie would significantly drain
the loch.

Commander Rupert T. Gould went to investigate the loch and in 1934 published *The Loch Ness Monster*, the first of many books on the subject. (An in-
formal count indicates at least a dozen books devoted solely to Nessie and
more than a dozen others with chapters about the creature.)

Hugh Gray snapped the first photograph of the serpent in November 1933,
but it was the famous "Surgeon's Photo," supposedly taken the following
April by Dr. R. K. Wilson, that put Nessie on the front page above the fold.

For sixty years this was believed by many to be the best proof that a large
unknown marine creature did in fact live in Loch Ness. However, in a

Head and neck, or hoax? For sixty years this photo, supposed to have been taken by Dr. Kenneth Wilson, was presumed to be the real thing. Then in 1993 Christian Spurling claimed he'd made this Loch Ness monster from plastic wood and a toy submarine. (Courtesy of J. Richard Greenwell, International Society of Cryptozoology)

deathbed confession in 1993, ninety-year-old Christian Spurling (stepson of the improbably named Marmaduke Arundel Wetherell) claimed it to have been a hoax planned and perpetrated by Wetherell, then foisted upon the public with the complicity of Dr. Wilson.

Big-game hunter "Duke" Wetherell, Fellow of the Royal Geographical Society and the Royal Zoological Society, had discovered footprints (which turned out to have been created using an ashtray made from a hippopotamus foot) on the shore near the loch while on expedition there in the fall of 1933. Wetherell became a laughingstock, though it is not certain whether he was hoaxer or hoaxed.

According to Spurling, his chagrined stepfather had asked, "Can you make me a monster?" and Spurling complied, producing a one-foot-high model of a serpent head atop a toy submarine.

Why Dr. Wilson, a respected Harley Street gynecologist, went along with the hoax is anyone's guess; he was known to be a bit of a joker, and some suggest that he joined in on the fun not realizing it would get so out of hand. Still, there are some who think that Spurling would have done better to have gone to his grave, as the others did, without revealing the truth. If truth it was—there are several inconsistencies in Spurling's story, which, though widely credited in the press, remains in dispute.

Whatever the photograph depicts, the mysterious creature in Britain's largest freshwater lake remains elusive. Years of intensive study by, among others, Tim Dinsdale, Robert Rines, and Roy P. Mackal, the use of sonar scans and underwater cameras, and thousands of tourists streaming to the two visitor centers have so far failed to produce conclusive evidence to confound the skeptics.

"Harvard Man Battles 'Sea Serpent' Fifty Feet Long in Vineyard Sound," ran the headline on an April 1934 narrative written for the United Press. A lengthy leader summarized the story: "Ratcliffe Bashes Monster With Oar, but Foe Moves Serenely On, Coast guards and fishermen saw Thomas G. Ratcliffe, Harvard junior and member of a prominent St. Louis family, seize an oar and strike at an object in Vineyard Sound yesterday. Ratcliffe thus became the first person ever to engage in actual combat with a sea serpent—if sea serpent it was."

It was not. The clues to the true identity of this unfortunate creature are sprinkled throughout the story, in the headline above, and in the selections that follow.

> I saw an object and thought it was the body of William Hulton, who was drowned a week ago. I said to Eric, "That must be the boy's body." We started for it and then saw that it was a serpent. . . .
>
> When I first saw the thing close to, my first thought was of Lochness, but I said to Eric, "There's no Scotch mist here." Remembering the days when knighthood was in flower, I socked it on the head. The head was not defined from the body but tapered to a snub nose. When we got within ten feet of the monster, we noticed for the first time a tail out of the water about twenty feet away. . . .
>
> After it was struck, it slowly slipped down under the water, apparently arching its body, though it was never completely out of the water. It

slipped alongside the boat for probably 15 seconds and we had ample time to see the monster but I did not strike it again because by that time I had realized what I had done.

As the tail came slowly along, I noticed that it tapered to a point and appeared to carry a fin. The body did not lash or writhe and the beast simply sounded, like a submarine or a whale. . . .

The center of the body was about three feet in diameter. It was quite large and about 30 feet in length.

Clues to the correct identification of the "serpent" include its serenity, the shape of its head, and its length. The following day, the *Boston Transcript* identified the Ratcliffe's sea monster: "Cape Cod Sea Serpent Is *Ceporinus Maximus*" ran the headline. The writer seemed a bit disappointed.

Less than 24 hours after . . . Harvard undergraduates reported seeing a "sea serpent," The Woods Hole Oceanographic Institute announced the monster undoubtedly was a specimen of *Seporinus Maximus* [sic], the basking or bone shark. Sea serpents haven't a chance within miles of the Oceanographic Institute. . . . *Ceporinum Maximus* [sic] attains a length up to 45 feet, but is sluggish, inoffensive and fond of sunning itself at the surface. . . .[5]

These large plankton feeders are related to and resemble their more fearsome shark cousins. They may also account for a small number of sea serpent sightings, as noted in a related article for which the writer consulted with Dr. Charles O. Fish, of the Buffalo Museum of Science, who was visiting in the area when the incident occurred.

There is nothing mythical about the basking shark, and stuffed ones are to be found in various museums of natural history. But it is the basis of most sea-serpent yarns, Dr. Fish said, because its habit of swimming with its friends on the surface, frequently two or three in tandem, with their dorsal fins held high, affords the illusion of fabulously long sinuous monsters to seafarers with active imaginations.

Here again is the slight to seafarers and the assumption of tandem swimming. The basking shark bears no resemblance to the sea serpents reported in the Gulf of Maine. It has no neck and it moves quite slowly. Yet it is not only in life but in death that it seems a monster.

In fact, basking sharks account for most reported sea serpent carcasses.

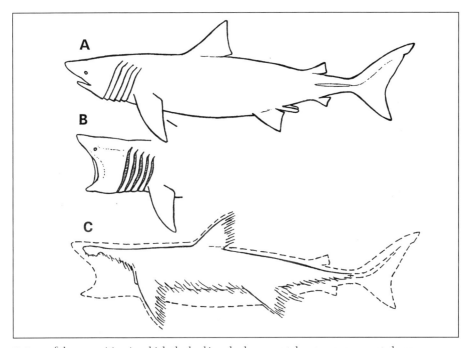

Pattern of decomposition in which the basking shark carcass takes on a sea serpent shape. (Courtesy of Glen J. Kuban)

(Other creatures frequently identified as sea serpents in death are the oarfish and occasionally whales.) A distinct pattern of decomposition in which the gill apparatus, lower jaw, and lower lobe of the caudal fin fall away, leaving only a small skull and what appears to be a long neck, have led to many misidentifications of basking shark carcasses as sea serpents.

On August 21, 1934, the Sandy Bay Historical Society and Museum held its Fifth Annual Meeting and Open House at the Community House on Broadway in Rockport, Massachusetts. Perhaps prompted by increased interest in the sea serpent phenomena generated by the "Surgeon's Photo" and Commander Gould's books, the symposium that followed the meeting was entitled "The Sea-Serpent Comes to Rockport"; it was followed by a social hour and refreshments. George Woodbury was not on the list of speakers, but he was pretty surely in attendance, because there is a copy of the program in his scrapbook.

Naturally, the *Rockport Daily News* covered the event. The first speaker of the evening was Dr. Marshall H. Saville, who provided the introduction and the story of the 1817 sightings mentioned in Commander Gould's recent book. Saville was followed by William E. Eldredge, who reviewed the appearances at Nahant and Swampscott. The testimony of Dr. John E. Sanborn (see pages 137–38) was then read by Frank Tarr, after which Dr. Saville read a letter written by Judge Sumner D. York describing his sighting in the summer of 1886.

My dear Professor Saville—

I understand that the meeting of the Society tomorrow evening is Sea-Serpent Night, and is to be in measure devoted to a discussion of that much mooted question, the existence of the sea-serpent.

Agreeably to my promise, I am pleased to state to you the facts in so far as such an animal has ever come to my notice, as published in the Cape Ann Advertiser July 30th, 1886.

The latter part of July of that year, 1886, Charles A. Russell of Gloucester, Edward C. Battis of Salem, and myself were vacationing near Gully Point, occupying the cottage now known I believe as San Souci Cottage.

On the afternoon of the twenty-fourth day of that month while at dinner, between the hours of six and seven o'clock, Albert W. Tarr . . . excitedly called us out to see some strange sea animal which he pointed out to us closely following the contour of the shore and moving moderately in a westerly direction. . . . Mr. Tarr I think had been watching this object through marine glasses for some while before calling us.

Thereupon we all hurried to the edge of the upland bordering the shore which is considerably elevated above the sea level where it gave us an excellent view with the naked eye as the animal approached us so closely that I endeavored to reach him with a stone, but failed by some distance. After reaching a point nearly opposite from where we were standing, possibly disturbed by the sound of our voices as we were shouting to passersby, or of its own volition, the animal turned and took a northerly course in the direction of Pigeon Cove shore. In line with him and at considerable distance in advance two men were in a dory, either fishing or

Woodbury's X, marking
York's vantage point

Boat +

THE "MARMION WAY" SHORE FROM "OLD GARDEN BEACH" TO "STRAITSMOUTH POINT"
ROCKPORT, MASS.

How Woodbury came by it is unknown, but a signed copy of Judge Yorke's letter found its way into his scrapbook along with this postcard. On the back Woodbury wrote, "This card given me June 2, 1937 by Judge Sumner York shows where he saw the 'Sea Serpent' in 1886. He with others was on land near X and saw serpent move to 'boat' where men were pulling up lobster pots. At about that time the serpent sank & disappeared. People on shore called to attract attention of lobstermen but on account of distance were not heard." (Cape Ann Historical Association)

pulling their traps. We shouted to them, hoping to call their attention to the approach of this animal, but evidently our voices did not reach them, as they kept right on with their work. Before reaching the dory, however, by a considerable distance the animal submerged and passed from our sight.

His head was close to the water. It was, as was so much of the body as we were able to see, of a dark brown color, his movement a vertical one. From the number of ridges in his movement and the distance between them which could be seen at the same time, together with his wake and the trail of his tail, we estimated his length to be from seventy to eighty feet. We did not see enough of his body to form any judgement as to its size. The sky was clear, a little air stirring, and the water smooth; in other words it was dead calm. . . .

My knowledge of sea animals is limited to what I have seen in and about Gloucester and Rockport, and I can say that never before nor since have I seen anything of its kind.

As may be imagined, when the report of the incident became public we were subject to the usual ridicule suffered by others who had been said to have seen the sea-serpent. Personally I was asked what sort of glass I saw the animal through, whether one or more, large or small, and I am almost inclined to think that many friends, solicitous as to our reputation for the truth and veracity, regretted the incident. However, if any of you or your friends wish to preserve your peace of mind, I would suggest that if you ever see anything of an animal of this character, unless you can produce the animal in evidence, never mention the fact.

One of the most fascinating details in Judge York's otherwise fairly straightforward account is that the two fishermen in the dory did not see the seventy- to eighty-foot creature or hear the calls of those on shore. Even at "considerable distance," one would think they would have noticed such an immense creature (and almost certainly would have if it were a whale or a line of dolphins), but perhaps the creature spotted the dory and quietly submerged.

Following Judge York's report, an audience member, Mrs. Arthur W. O'Neill (née Brewer), of Pigeon Cove and Chestnut Hill, recounted how she'd "been brought up on the sea serpent story and [was] greatly pleased at having such an intelligent audience give consideration to it."

Another audience member, Mrs. John M. Wetherell (née Tarr), recalled that she was eleven years old at the time. As the *Rockport Daily News* reported: "Her memory was of the excitement of her elders in rushing her down to the waterfront from the big rock where they had all gathered to view the strange apparition in the water. Mrs. Wetherell said it was most exciting but that no one ever believed it all, when you told them about it."

Indeed one senses a certain underlying bitterness in the judge's words. It is not, after all, pleasant to have one's truthfulness questioned or one's character impugned with suggestions of drunkenness. But Judge York never recanted. In 1947, when York was well over ninety years of age, he was interviewed by Irma Kierman for her booklet *The Sea Serpent of Cape Ann*. He told her, "You know, I've always had the idea in the back of my mind that there was some sort of food along these shores the serpent especially liked. Perhaps it was ripening sea weed . . . or some sort of small fish, like herring."

On September 12 and 13, 1935, the *Boston Transcript* and *Boston Globe* published accounts of the Gloucester schooner *Imperator* having encountered a sea serpent off the fishing grounds south of Nova Scotia.

Boston Fish Pier is agog over the story brought in by Adelbert Langthorne, a fisherman with nearly forty years at sea behind him . . .

Out on Western Bank, to the south of Nova Scotia, where the vessel was jogging while the crew laid trawls for halibut, a fruitful "hole" was found. A marker "planted."

Between the marker and the vessel, some twenty feet away, Langthorne said he sighted a monster rise from the waves. Shouting to fellow members of the deck watch for a harpoon, hoping to bring to port the first genuine sea serpent for scrutiny.

Before a harpoon could be secured, however, Langthorne's objective disappeared, wiggling like a huge eel.

Langthorne spun the yarn today to Frederick F. Dimick, secretary of the Boston Fish Bureau. Captain Albert Williams of the *Imperator* had not seen the monster, but half a dozen of the crew supported Langthorne's narration.

The serpent had a round body about eight inches in diameter, dark brownish-blue in color, large round eyes, and a long snout, Langthorne said. He added that while alongside the vessel, it raised its head and about fifteen feet of its body above the sea, gazed nonchalantly around, apparently ignoring the *Imperator* entirely, then glided away.

The *Imperator* is 106 feet long and the length of the big fish was estimated by the size of the vessel.

Langthorne said it was the first time in his long career at sea that he had seen anything of the sort.

Almost a year later, in August 1936, the *Boston Herald* carried three stories, each successively more bizarre, of sightings from the Canadian Maritimes. The first report, datelined August 11, Liverpool, Nova Scotia (on the Atlantic side, about seventy-five miles south of Halifax), gives no descriptive details but has a familiar feel to it.

BIG SEA SERPENT IS REPORTED OFF
NOVA SCOTIA COAST

A huge elusive sea serpent was described last night by hundreds of bathers who saw it sporting off Summerville Beach near here.

Immediately after the monster was sighted Alben Roy took a party of men out in his 28-foot motor boat and attempted to drive it ashore. But the serpent eluded them for hours before it disappeared, diving under the boat as it approached and appearing hundreds of yards away.

Once it speeded directly across the bow of a large steam yacht owned by Dr. J. L. Brinkley of Del Rio, Texas.

Many of the people who witnessed the threshing of the monster were prominent business men, willing to vouch for their eyesight and veracity.

The next report came from St. John's, Newfoundland, on August 19. This too seems reminiscent of other reports even though the creature's size seems exaggerated.

150-FOOT SEA MONSTER SEEN OFF NEWFOUNDLAND

The Newfoundland natural resources department announced today [that] fishermen on the west coast of Newfoundland had reported a second appearance of what they said was a 150-foot sea monster.

The department said fishermen at Portauport [sic] sent messages to the department last week saying the reported monster has scared boats away from fishing grounds in that vicinity. [Port au Port is near Stephenville on the Gulf of St. Lawrence.]

Another report, dated August 21, is also from St. John's:

SEA MONSTER 200 FEET LONG
Newfoundland Fishermen Say Head Stuck 60 Feet Out of Water

Newfoundland fishermen told vivid—but unconfirmed—tales tonight of a sea monster on the west coast that stuck its head 60 feet out of the water and snorted blue vapor from its nostrils.

Sharp-eyed fishermen produced a collective picture of the monster like this: At least 200 feet long and 18 feet in diameter, eyes as big as an enamel sauce pan and spaced two feet apart; a mane larger than that of any horse.

The fishermen even claimed the monster was so big it set up waves that
rocked fishing boats, and for days no boat dared venture to sea. . . .

One wonders what to make of this account, coming as it does on the
heels of two fairly routine reports. *Vivid* is certainly the right word for the
tale. The great size of the eyes and the snorting of blue vapor would seem to
argue for a giant squid, but the longest known specimen is a scant fifty-five
feet, not two hundred. Perhaps the fishermen had actually seen something,
then—finding an eager audience—decided to have a little fun.

Whatever it was, it was not reported again that year, though the *Boston
Evening Transcript* ran a piece on August 28, asking, "Sea Serpent or Squid?"

Is it not rather late in the summer for the hotelkeepers of Newfoundland
to try to attract visitors to her rocky coasts by sending out stories that the
largest sea-monster of all time is disporting itself in the icy waters of Port
au Port Bay on the west coast of the island? Should we give more credence
to the account because it can serve no ulterior purpose, cannot bring summer folks to the island in shoals to gaze upon the creature? . . .

In northern latitudes sea serpents invariably appear off shore before
mid-July. They come up at dusk to gambol in the moonshine and sink to
the abysmal ooze at dawn. That is why they are rarely and dimly seen. By
the end of August they are well on their way South to more genial waters.

One can't help but speculate that this must be the same writer who, three
years earlier, argued the case for the sea serpent, also in the *Transcript*, and
under an almost identical title, especially because the writer goes on to suggest that the creature

. . . may be a giant squid—one of those enormous octopi which inhabit the
waters off that island. . . . An octopus of that size, swimming on the surface of the sea with its long arms in action, might easily be taken for a sea
serpent if seen at a distance through a Newfoundland fog. . . .

(Squid are not, as the writer suggests, "octopi," although both are cepha-
lopods. These invertebrates share some characteristics, such as intelligence
and long arms, but their habitats and physiognomy are entirely different.[6])

The giant squid *Architeuthis,* with recorded lengths of as much as sixty feet
(with the tentacles), dinner plate-sized eyes, parrotlike beak, and tongue
equipped with teeth, is a true monster of the sea. Still, when giant squid

began turning up on Grand Bank and washing ashore on the Newfoundland and Labrador coasts in the 1870s, the first response of the fishermen was to cut them up as cod bait or feed them to their dogs. If not for the interest and intervention of yet another clergyman, the Reverend Mr. Moses Harvey, it is likely that no parts of the Newfoundland specimens of the giant squid—previously believed to be a myth of ancient mariners—would have been preserved.

A report datelined Nantucket, August 7, 1937, from an unknown source in the Woodbury scrapbook claimed, "The 1937 sea serpent and marine monster season was officially opened to-day. Fisherman Bill Manville came in here Friday night, pop-eyed at what [he said] he had seen a couple of miles sou'east of this island. In Bill's own words it was a 'green sea monster' which reared its briny head several times off his starboard bow before turning seaward."

Two days later, the *Christian Science Monitor* carried the story on page nine of its Atlantic edition.

"SORT OF HORNED HEAD" RAISED
BY NANTUCKET SEA MONSTER

Raising a "sort of horned head"—much larger than the girth of its neck—12 feet above the shimmering waters off Smith's Point as the fog lifted at 9:30 on Sunday morning, a sea monster about 120 feet in length was recognized three quarters of a mile at sea by Gilbert Manter, prominent business man here.

At the time, Mr. Manter said this morning, he was trying to catch his first bluefish of the season, but there was no boat at hand in which he could have gone out to view the monster at closer range—had he been so inclined. Since then he has seen nothing more of the remarkable marine visitor.

He described the apparition as being of a grayish green color and in shape more like a thick serpent than a whale.

On the previous day—also in the morning hours—Charles Manville and his son Charles, both out in a fishing boat, reported catching sight of a sea beast of the same description—but with "blazing eyes" as an additional detail.

Another year passed before the *Portland Press Herald*, datelined Pleasant Point, August 20, 1938, reported another sighting.

INDIAN FISHERMEN ARE ARMED TO TEETH
AS SEA SERPENT APPEARS OFF QUODDY

This quiet Indian village of 400 inhabitants is all agog over the visit of the far famed sea serpent first reported off Grand Manan several months ago.

Eye witnesses to the unusual and fearsome sight were Peter Moore and Joseph Socoby, who, a few minutes previously touched the Pleasant Point shore in their dinghy after a fishing trip on Passamaquoddy Bay.

The serpent was first seen less than a thousand yards off shore as the fishermen cleaned their catch near the waters edge, and Moore admits he shivered and the chills ran through his spine when he thought of being out in the bay with the ugly reptile for company. With eyes fairly protruding, Moore and Socoby stood as if mesmerized, their eyes riveted on the fast moving creature that was, to all appearances, pursuing a school of porpoises. The "humps" of the serpent's body were plainly visible as the snake-like creature drove through the water. Both men declare that in all [their] years of experience on Passamaquoddy and St. Andrews Bays, they have never before witnessed such a spectacular and weird sight as the creature, 40 or 50 feet long, glided through the water, its head protruding at times nearly two feet above the surface.

Although without glasses, it was difficult to make a close estimate of the size of the sea serpent's body, the men thought it larger [even] than a 10-quart water pail. The length of this fearsome inhabitant of the sea was judged by the number of "humps" of its body that were visible, and the distance between them. The animal sort of "slid through the water, and we could see seven or eight humps or curves of its body. It cut the water very fast," said one of the eyewitnesses.

"We don't mind whales," continued the narrator, "for we often see them near our boats, and they will do no harm, but I do not want to be on the water with that creature within a hundred miles."

A few days before the serpent was seen off Pleasant Point, a similar creature said to be sixty feet long was seen off The Wolves. The three Indians
who observed the giant reptile in St. Andrews Bay were John Polis,
Richard Sacobasin, and Sabattus Francis. The serpent, swimming with a
portion of its black back showing above the water, sank beneath the surface of the bay, apparently as the sound of a boat engine came within its
hearing. One who witnessed the last reported appearance of the serpent
off Pleasant Point said, "It may not be for a thousand years that the serpent, or whatever it is, will come this way again, but that will be plenty
soon enough."

Bernard Heuvelmans writes that Charles Ballard, a resident of Sydney,
Nova Scotia, also reported seeing the creature in 1939. In a letter written to
Ivan T. Sanderson in 1947, Ballard described seeing an eighty-foot-long creature that resembled a "gigantic eel" swimming along about three hundred
feet from the shore in the harbor between Sydney and North Sydney.

Folklorist L. D. Geller collected the following story in 1969 from Captain
Albert Franklin Pierce. Pierce had spent most of his ninety-two years as a
fisherman on the Grand Banks and as a lobsterman. He told Geller that
some thirty years earlier he had encountered an unusual creature.

I was hauling lobster pots at High Pine half way up to Brant Rock from the
Gurnet with a fellow named Smith. I saw a serpent with three bends between the waves. It was a light grey in color. He was headed away from
us so we couldn't see his head. He was pretty big. I wanted to get near
enough, but Smith said he was as close as he wanted to be. At Marblehead,
lobster fishermen saw it three days after and reported it all around. . . . I
used to laugh when they talked about sea serpents but when I saw this
one I was convinced. He was at least sixty feet long and he had fins five
to six feet high out of the water. I saw him for about five minutes, while
I was hauling one pot it settled right down. The water was all greasy
where it went down. It was about one and a half miles off shore. . . . No
one has seen it lately, but they are sure to turn up again.

A rare report of a sea serpent in New England during the Second World
War appears in this article that Woodbury clipped from *American Weekly*,
May 18, 1941:

NEW EVIDENCE THAT SEA SERPENTS ARE THE REAL THING?

The hard-headed residents of Grand Manan Island, far out in the Bay of Fundy, are seeing sea serpents again. There's no doubt about it according to the weather-beaten lobstermen and herring seiners who swear it's the real thing.

The creature, described by fishermen who've actually seen it, appears to have a great and ugly head like a dragon. It swims at breakneck speed, throwing its head from side

The Hard-Headed Natives of Grand Manan Island Are Sure That the Thing They Have Seen in the Waters of the Bay of Fundy Is a Monstrosity of Enormous Proportions.

This illustration accompanied the article in *American Weekly*, May 18, 1941.

to side as it gulps down bushels of fish from the great schools of herring that are swarming around the island just now.

The hardy and usually unexcitable fishermen of Grand Manan can't classify the queer critter that has upset their lives, so they just call it a sea serpent.

A few of the islanders believe that the sea beast that has kicked up all the fuss and excitement may be two or three huge basking sharks swimming tandem and in single file. Since these fish are often 50 feet long, they could, together, create the illusion of something approximating the proportions of the so-called sea monster.

But this theory doesn't go down with the men who have seen what some of them call "the thing." They say the head of the monster looks like no sharks ever found in these waters. And they clinch their argument by saying there aren't any sharks in the Bay of Fundy at this time of year.

The article goes on to report that in 1883 "this monstrosity" had appeared in the Bay of Fundy "to terrify fishermen by suddenly rearing its wicked looking head. . . . For more than a month the fishing industry was at a standstill." Then on November 23, Welchpool resident "Barnacle" Mitchell came across the creature stretched out on the beach on Campobello Island, apparently asleep. Having an axe handy, he "crept up on the freak and drove the blade of his axe into its skull. Then he ran for his life."

When Mitchell returned with a neighbor, the creature was dead. Mitchell and his companion measured the scaly carcass, which was described as slim except in the middle (at ninety-two feet) where there was a distinct "paunch." They then chopped the remains (which they claimed contained seven or eight sheep) into twenty-three pieces, which they ferried over to Eastport and sold to a fertilizer plant.

This tale of "Barnacle" Mitchell's sheep-poaching serpent is extremely doubtful, but it may have a kernel of truth at its core. Perhaps there was a sea serpent terrorizing the fishermen that year, and maybe Mitchell killed something, but it is hard to believe that he would have sold a sea serpent for fertilizer when the whole creature would have brought a far greater profit.

On September 3, 1947, during an unusual run of small herring on the north shore of Massachusetts, Medford piano tuner John Ruhl and his daughters saw off Lynn Beach a fifty-foot creature with black coils every six feet. Ruhl swore it was not a whale. "I know nobody will believe me, but I saw the serpent and my daughters saw it, and I'm no fool."

That December, the Grace Line steamer *Santa Clara* logged in red (it is customary to record unusual incidents and accidents in red in the log) a collision with an unknown creature just southeast of Cape Hatteras. Chief Officer William Humphreys, Third Officer John Axelson, and navigating officer John Rigney were about to take noon sightings when Axelson spotted a snakelike head rising out of the water off the starboard bow. Apparently the submerged portion of the smooth-skinned dark brown creature was directly in the path of the steamer, which was unable to effect a course change. According to the message received by the U.S. Hydrographic Department on December 30, the *Santa Clara*

STRUCK MARINE MONSTER EITHER KILLING OR BADLY WOUNDING IT PERIOD ESTIMATED LENGTH 45 FEET WITH EEL LIKE HEAD AND BODY APPROXIMATELY THREE FEET IN DIAMETER PERIOD LAST SEEN THRASHING IN LARGE AREA OF BLOODY WATER AND FOAM

According to the narrative written by the captain, John Fordan, the creature was spotted in calm conditions under a clear sky with light winds. No fins, hair, or protuberances were noticed by any of the witnesses. The collision with the creature sent a shudder through the ship, which brought additional crew and passengers on deck, all of whom witnessed the creature's death throes until it sank in the ship's wake.

A report of the event published in the *New York Times* of December 31 drew the usual skeptical commentary. Dr. Christopher Coates, of the New York Aquarium, suggested, "It's possible what they saw was a large porpoise, but more likely it was an oarfish."

The oarfish, *Regalecus glesne,* also known as "King of the Herring" or the ribbon-fish, is a flattened silvery creature reaching lengths of about twenty feet. It has a coral-red crest along its spine and two long pectoral fins, which widen out at the ends like tiny oars. Nothing that is known of this fish in any way corresponds with what the crew of the *Santa Clara* all agreed they'd seen; it seems even less possible that it was a large porpoise. Nevertheless, the *Santa Clara* incident was regarded by some as a hoax. Others suggested that there had been drinking involved, even though the captain was an avowed teetotaler and would scarcely have tolerated a significant portion of his crew being drunk before noon.

The following summer, on August 26, Harold Robie, his wife, Wava, and their friends Deering and Edna Roberts boarded the Robie's cabin cruiser *Wava E.* on a cruise to Gloucester from York, Maine. At eleven that morning, in a glassy sea, they passed an enormous school of mackerel near the Isles of Shoals, off the New Hampshire coast. Shortly afterward they encountered what they at first thought was a reef, yet there should have been at least a hundred feet of water in that vicinity. They put the boat in neutral and quickly pulled out their charts. The "reef" sank as they watched, then reappeared at the stern with three humps showing, then swam rapidly away. "All four of us saw a sea serpent that August day of 1948," Deering Roberts later told historian Edward Rowe Snow. "It was an awesome spectacle that left us very quiet and thoughtful for some time afterward."

About eight years were to pass before the next report, which tells of an encounter in 1956, from West Point, Prince Edward Island. Raeford MacLean and John Ellis saw a creature they estimated to be forty to sixty feet long from a distance of about two hundred yards. MacLean described the creature as dark in color and generally serpentine in shape but noted that there appeared to be a large hump at some distance behind the head. As it turned out, both men had family members who had seen a similar creature in the past. MacLean's father had seen one in 1938, also in the vicinity of West Point; Ellis's brother and a friend had seen another off the western end of the island.

On Tuesday, September 3, 1957, the crew of the scalloper *Noreen* spotted an unknown creature 120 miles east of Georges Bank near Nantucket. Joseph H. Bourassa, the cook, retired from twenty years of service in the U.S. Navy, gave this account to the *New Bedford Standard Times*.

> At 4:25 PM today a strange object was seen surfacing off the starboard quarter about 100 yards from the ship. He had a peculiar look about him. He had a large body and a small alligator-like head. The neck seemed to be of medium size, matching the size of the head. The body was shaped somewhat like a seal. There was a mane of bristly hair or fur which ran down the middle of his head.
>
> He would surface the upper part of his body and glide out of the water with the lower part of his body remaining submerged. The portion of his body which was visible measured about forty feet in length. We estimated his weight to be between thirty-five and forty tons overall.
>
> At no time did the whole body show. He stayed on the surface no longer than forty seconds at a time. You could hear the heavy weight of his upper body when he dove below, creating a large splash and a subsequent wake. He surfaced four times in twenty minutes, during which we were trying to stay clear of him. The captain changed course to steer away from him and the queer fellow surfaced on our starboard beam.
>
> We changed course again and he then rose off our starboard bow, keeping his same distance from us. The Captain ordered the drags be brought in. Once the drags were on deck, the Captain turned the boat and steamed at full speed to the west, away from the queer fellow. . . .
>
> Another peculiar thing about him was that when he'd surface he would

turn his head looking toward us and it seemed to us he was playful and curious. Another point was that on the upper part of his body there were two flippers, similar to those of a seal. The weather was clear and visibility was good. The sea rough and sloppy. The wind was coming from the west-southwest at about 30 miles an hour.

Twenty years later, cryptozoologist Gary S. Mangiacopra confirmed this report with the *Noreen*'s captain, Robert M. Smith, who stated: "It was a strange looking creature different from the usual shark, or whales, porpoise, swordfish, etc., we often see every trip. It didn't spout like a whale and seemed to stay on the surface of the water most of the time just gliding along with us."

The next account was collected in 1985 by well-known cryptozoologist Loren Coleman.[7] An elderly Dane, Ole Mikkelsen, told Coleman that on June 5, 1958, half an hour after sunrise, he and his partner, Ejnar Haugarrd, saw the creature about five miles off Cape Elizabeth, Maine.

Suddenly, we saw an object coming toward us out of the haze. We took it to be a submarine, but as it came closer we discovered it was some live thing, light brown like a cusk [a large edible fish related to the cod] with a tail like a mackerel's. It looked well over 100 feet long. Its head stuck out of the water and was broader than the neck it was on. I was not sure of its ears or eyes, but it could hear. Every time the foghorn on the lightship *Portland* sounded, she turned her head in that direction. As it came still nearer it dove down and a tail came up out of the water, and slowly it went down again. In about three or four minutes it surfaced again, came near us and dove again. Then it came up once more about 125 feet away from us, stopping as if to look us over.

Both were experienced fishermen, but neither wanted to get any closer. They considered themselves fortunate when the creature disappeared to the southeast in the haze.

On July 7, 1960, the passengers and crew of the charter boat *Julyntha* saw a creature seventy feet long off Cape Ann. One of the passengers, Richard Laupot, of Great Neck, New York, told the *Gloucester Daily Times* that the creature "looked just like a sea serpent . . . slithering along on top of the water. It was grayish with dark rays and black sails on the top of it. It had a head like a gigantic snake. We circled it for about 10 or 15 minutes. Then we came on in."

Mrs. Laupot added, "The minute I saw it I . . . knew exactly what it was . . . a sea serpent. . . . It had these sails on top of it with yellow dots. Its head was like a dinosaur."

The *Julyntha*'s skipper, Captain Ellis Hodgkins, described the creature quite differently: "I have no idea what it was. I have never seen anything like it before in my life. . . . It looked like a camel half out of the water."

Another sighting that summer took place one foggy morning when a Manchester fisherman and his crew were visiting their fish trap in a small boat at about 5 A.M. They came upon what they thought was a partially sub-merged overturned boat in the vicinity of Egg Island, off Gloucester. On closer approach they realized it was an unknown creature thirty to forty feet long with a prominent backbone. It held a horselike head with protruding eyes about six inches above the water, circling the boat and the fish trap for several hours.

All told, it appears that the creature spent about ten days that summer in the vicinity of Cole's Ridge between Twin Lights and Marblehead, having been seen a few days before by other Manchester fishermen and afterward by two fishermen from Marblehead.

On July 25, 1962, United Press International carried an account of the sea serpent, datelined Marshfield (Massachusetts), which reported that fisher-men aboard two boats, the *Vincy* and the *Carol Ann*, had seen a sea monster with a head like that of an alligator, a body shaped like a nail keg, and two large fins protruding from its tail area. One of the fishermen, Archie Lewis, said the creature "was gulping up the fish in the area and did not concern itself with [the] fishermen in any way." Lewis added that he had seen all types of whales "but never one that resembled this creature."

By the mid 1970s, the only sea monster on most New Englanders' minds was *Carcharadon carcharias*, the great white shark. Peter Benchley's book *Jaws* was *the* beach book in the summer of 1974, and the brilliant and terrifying portrayal of a man-eating "rogue" shark in the movie version, directed by Stephen Spielberg, kept many swimmers watching for the dreaded bullet-

shaped head as they warily waded in a few feet of water. Others stayed out
of the ocean altogether. Sportfishing for shark became more popular, with
the great white the ultimate prize.

The ancestors of these formidable predators first roamed the world's
oceans 300 million years ago, evolving into a recognizable form about 200
million years later. Although often portrayed as mindless (even malevolent)
man-eaters, of the more than 350 species of sharks known today, many are
much too small to be a threat to humans, and the two largest are plankton
feeders. Still, it seems that humankind cannot resist the temptation to do
battle with and slaughter any creature whose historic role makes it seem so
worthy an opponent, an attitude with truly terrifying potential for harm to
the marine ecosystem.

In 1976, another shark made headlines when it was caught off Hawaii. It
was a fifteen-footer, and no one had ever seen anything like it. In fact
Megachasma pelagios, the megamouth shark, turned out to be a new species altogether, and the only known member of a new family. Eleven specimens of
this previously unknown filter feeder have since been caught, the most recent of which turned up in the Philippines in February 1998.

On April 25, 1977, the Japanese fishing vessel *Zuiyo-maru* hauled up an
enormous rotting carcass while trawling for mackerel about thirty miles
east of Christchurch, New Zealand. No one on board had any idea what it
was, though some crewmen thought it looked like a giant turtle without its
shell. It stank, and fearing that any effluent might spoil their catch, the crew
agreed that it should be returned to the sea. In the process of maneuvering
the thirty-three-foot, four-thousand-pound carcass overboard, it was acci-
dentally dumped on deck. Michihiko Yano, a thirty-nine-year-old graduate
of the Yamaguchi Oceanological High School, used this opportunity to
quickly measure, photograph, and take samples of the carcass before it was
consigned to the deep.

About three months later, on July 20, 1977, the Taiyo Fish Company Ltd. of
Japan held a press conference to announce its extraordinary find. Professor
Yoshinori Imaizumi, director of animal research at the Tokyo National Science Museum, was one among many who weighed in with a theory. His was
quoted in the *Asahi Shimbun* newspaper: "It's not a fish, whale or any other

A basking shark carcass hauled up by the *Zuiyo-maru* on April 25, 1977, while trawling for mackerel. It displays the characteristic pattern of decomposition that has led many to misidentify such remains as evidence of sea serpents. (Photographed by Michihiko Yano. Courtesy of Glen J. Kuban.)

mammal. . . . It's a reptile, and the sketch looks very like a plesiosaur. This is a precious and important discovery for human beings. It seems to show these animals are not extinct after all."

The story and Yano's photographs were soon making their way around the globe as cryptozoologists and a good many others held their breath. Could it be that this was proof at last of a living dinosaur, confirming once and for all that sea monsters do exist?

Unfortunately, the Taiyo Fish Company had acted a bit hastily. Only a month later, the preliminary report on the analysis of Yano's tissue sample seemed to indicate that it was "similar in nature to the fin rays, a group of living animals." It was in fact a shark—as subsequent research was to show, a basking shark.[8]

North American sea serpent sightings from the 1970s to the present come almost exclusively from the Gulf of Georgia, in the northern Pacific.[9] In 1933,

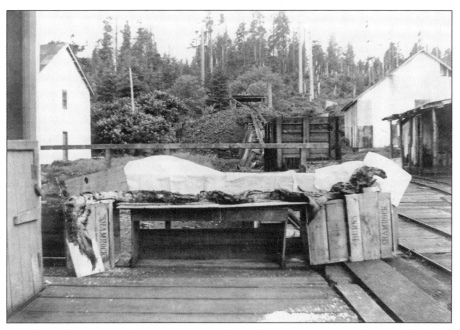

An infant Cadborosaurus? The whale men at the Naden Harbor station, Queen Charlotte Islands, who took this carcass from the belly of a sperm whale in 1937 had never seen anything like it. Regrettably, no part of the specimen was preserved. (G. V. Boorman photo. Used by permission of P. LeBlond.)

the Boston papers called it the "Great Western Sea Serpent," but the creature is familiarly known as Caddy because of numerous sightings in Cadboro Bay, British Columbia. Since 1881, Cadboro Bay has been the source of some of the most consistently curious encounters with an unusual marine creature. (Actually, there is evidence in Native American folklore and craft that the creature was "known" far earlier than the nineteenth century.)

There were some twenty-odd sightings of Caddy in the early twentieth century, but the 1930s were its heyday. In 1933, the creature acquired a champion by the name of Archie H. Wills, managing editor of the *Victoria Daily Times*, who eagerly gave "his sea serpent" plenty of ink. Indeed, Wills is presumed to be the author of this October 7, 1933, editorial:

> There is abundant, unimpeachable evidence that some strange marine
> monster either has its home in the Gulf of Georgia or frequently visits
> those waters. The detailed reports of responsible citizens of what they

have seen of the stranger and its activities transfer it from the world of fiction to that of reality.

If only that were true. Despite more than a hundred years of eyewitness testimony and photographs of what was possibly a juvenile found in a sperm whale's belly, Caddy is as easily dismissed by some as is the New England creature.

Caddy and the New England creature share more than skeptics. Although size varies with the reports (as it does in the Gulf of Maine), Caddy is usually thought to be twenty to forty (though sometimes a hundred) feet in length. Its color is most often brown, but black, green, gray, and even blue are also described. It has a long neck and a head like a horse (or a dog, cow, camel, or giraffe), and there are occasional mentions of stripes or streaks of a lighter color. It has a long, serpentine body and a serrated, or saw-toothed, back sometimes described as a fin. Like the New England creature, Caddy appears to undulate vertically "like a caterpillar," showing between three and five humps separated by five to eight feet. It is fast (some say forty knots), and it can sink down "as if something pulled it under." Though it is not as clearly seasonal as the New England creature, it is frequently associated with similar prey, particularly herring.

Caddy witnesses frequently mention a mane of something that looks like kelp. Horns and ears are often mentioned, as are large eyes, and the creature is occasionally described as furry. It can be noisy and sometimes spouts water or air upon surfacing. Like its North Atlantic counterpart, it does not attack humans or their boats, even when fired upon. It has, however, been seen to feed on ducks and other seabirds.

Unlike its New England counterpart, Caddy is still very much in evidence, having been spotted at least twenty times in the 1990s. Credit for the record of these reports of Caddy, and continuing scientific investigation into the phenomenon, must go to scientists Dr. Paul H. LeBlond and Dr. Edward L. Bousfield, both of whom have pursued their "eccentric" interest in Caddy to the point that they have produced a record of reliable sightings in their book *Cadborosaurus: Survivor from the Deep* and proposed a scientific name for it: *Cadborosaurus willsi*.

Dr. LeBlond, professor emeritus of the University of British Columbia, is also one of the world's best-known authorities on marine cryptozoology. In 1997, he was contacted by his friend Jon Lien, a whale expert and professor at Memorial University in Newfoundland, who recognized the description of an unknown creature in the *St. John's Evening Telegram* on May 6.

The story stated that at about noontime on Sunday, May 4, 1997, two fishermen, Charles Bungay and C. Clarke, were out fishing in Fortune Bay, on the southern coast of Newfoundland, when they saw what appeared to be floating garbage bags. Deciding to haul them aboard, they got within fifty to sixty feet when something reared its head.

"It turned its head and looked right at us," Bungay is quoted as saying. "All we could see was a neck six feet long, a head like a horse, but his dark eyes were on the front of its face . . . like a human. . . . He just looked at us and slid under the water and disappeared."

Dr. LeBlond contacted Bungay, who estimated the creature's length at between thirty and forty feet, adding that it had ears or horns six to eight inches long, and scaly skin.

Have the creatures returned to the Gulf of Maine after an absence of thirty-five years, or was this a misidentification of a known species? There is no way to know. Unless, of course, people begin to see others.

CHAPTER 8 NOTES

1. Information concerning the Sea Serpent Club is scanty. What is known is that it was a group of journalists and officials who held annual "chowder meetings" at Naugus Head presided over by Marblehead's historian, Samuel Roads, Jr.

2. Rum Row was not, as the term might imply, a string of waterfront taverns. Rather it was a floating wholesale liquor enterprise initiated in 1921 by Floridian Bill McCoy. McCoy imported only the best—"the Real McCoy"—which he sold from his ship, the *Henry L. Marshall*, while cruising the coast just outside territorial waters. Swampscott was a favorite landing spot for the rum runners, who were themselves run off by the Coast Guard in 1925 (at least for the time being) when "Silent Cal" spent the first summer of his presidency there at "White Court."

3. There was one, a specimen washed ashore at Trinity Bay, Newfoundland, on September

1877, a cast of which is still on display at the American Museum of Natural History, in New York City.

4. Sixty-five years later, on June 11, 1998, the *New York Times* reported the arrival of a twenty-five-foot-long juvenile giant squid that had been caught in New Zealand and frozen before being shipped to the American Museum of Natural History for examination.

5. The *Transcript*'s multiple mangled spellings aside, the correct name is *Cetorhinus maximus*.

6. Richard Ellis has fascinating chapters on both in his book *Monsters of the Sea* (Alfred A. Knopf, 1994).

7. Coleman's latest books on the subject are *The Cryptozoology Handbook: Loch Monsters, Sasquatch, Chupacabras and Other Authentic Mysteries of Nature* (Fireside/Simon and Schuster, 1999), and *Field Guide to Bigfoots, Yetis and Other Mystery Primates Worldwide* (Avon Books, 1999). His Web site is included in the Web Sites of Interest section of the bibliography (under *The Cryptozoologist*).

8. For a thorough and evenhanded account of the research, see Glen Kuban's *Sea-monster or Shark?*, published in Reports of the National Center for Science Education, May/June 1997, or visit his Web site, listed in the Web Sites of Interest section of the bibliography.

9. There have also been a number of sightings of the sea serpent Altamaha-Ha on the south Georgia coast near Darien. These creatures, like those reported in the North Atlantic, have been seen in fresh- and saltwater and are commonly described as snakelike. Author-artist Ann Davis wrote a book for children about Altamaha-Ha and maintains a Web site, which is listed in the bibliography.

9

Evolution, Extinction, Ecology, and Overfishing in the Gulf of Maine

It would be a sad (but perhaps not altogether surprising) comment on human beings if a creature which had come down unchanged and unharmed from prehistory was to be finally exterminated by modern man.

—Gerald Durrell, Foreword to *The Loch Ness Story*, 1974

Oddly enough, for a creature that many people have never heard of (and far fewer believe ever existed), the New England sea serpent has been given no less than four scientific names.

Technically, not one of them represents a valid species. According to the International Commission on Zoological Nomenclature, founded in 1895, in order for a species to be considered valid it must have a scientific description and a registered holotype—a physical specimen (or at least a confirmed part of a specimen)—available for study at an accredited museum or institution. This commission did not exist, however, in 1817, when the first of these binomials, *Scoliophis atlanticus* (Atlantic humped snake), was offered for the Linnaean Committee's specimen of the supposed offspring of the eighty-foot creature seen in the harbor at Gloucester.

That same year, the French American naturalist Constantin S. Rafinesque-Schmaltz published a description of the Gloucester monster in *American Monthly Magazine* under the title "Dissertation on Water-Snakes, Sea-Snakes and Sea-Serpents." Rafinesque-Schmaltz proposed the name *Megophias* (big snake), basing his description of the creature on sketches and not on a specimen, confirmed or otherwise.

> It is evidently a real Sea Snake, belonging probably to the genus *Pelamis* and
> I propose to call it *Pelamis megophias*, which means great sea snake Pelamis.
> It might however be a peculiar genus, which the long equal scales seem to
> indicate and which a closer examination might have decided: in that case
> the name of *Megophias monstrosus* might have been appropriate to it.

Seventy-five years later, in his book *The Great Sea Serpent*, Dr. A. C. Oudemans modified the name to *Megophias megophias*. Oudemans was persuaded by the evidence he assembled that the sea serpent was not a reptile but a mammal. He based his assessment on, among other things, the fact that some witnesses had described a mane or whiskers on the creatures and that he did not believe a reptile to be capable of sustaining life in cold water. Bound by the rules of scientific priority, which hold that the first published description and name will outlast any future understanding of a creature's nature, the "great snake" proposed by Rafinesque-Schmaltz would now stand for a giant long-necked seal.

In 1965, Bernard Heuvelmans published *In the Wake of the Sea-Serpents*, in which he examined 587 sea serpent sightings worldwide and concluded that no one description would fit them all. He identified nine different types of sea serpent based upon specific determining characteristics. Heuvelmans separated the New England creature from the pack and offered for it the name *Plurigibbosus novae-angliae* ("that with many humps, of New England").

> I think the name *Megophias monstrosus* must be abandoned once and for all.
> It was originally used by Rafinesque to describe the Massachusetts Bay
> sea-serpent, that is, the Many-humped, but without a sufficiently detailed
> description for it to be recognized. And when Oudemans took it over and
> modified it to *Megophias megophias* it was based on descriptions of several
> different animals.

Although he disagreed with the name, Heuvelmans concurred with Oudemans that long-neck sea serpents were actually mammals related to the pinnipeds, though Heuvelmans did not rule out sirenians. For these he proposed the name *Megalotaria longicollis* ("the big sea-lion with a long neck").

When Commander Rupert T. Gould weighed in on the subject with *The Case for the Sea-Serpent* in 1930, he too had a theory. Not being a scientist, he offered no new names or descriptions, but he did conclude that as many as three distinct types of sea serpent were possible. He believed that there could be a giant long-necked seal and perhaps also a gigantic turtlelike creature, but the majority of sightings might, he thought, be explained by a known marine creature that had been presumed extinct for many millions of years. He offered as one explanation "a creature . . . resembling in outline and structure the *Plesiosaurus* of Mesozoic times. I do not suggest that the last named is actually a *Plesiosaurus*, but that it is either one of its descendants or has evolved along similar lines."

Among those who have disputed the notion of a long-necked mammal and favored the plesiosaur proposed by Gould and others is Dr. Karl P. N. Shuker, a zoologist by training and one of the world's leading cryptozoologists. In his *In Search of Prehistoric Survivors* (1995), Shuker wrote, "In my view it is unnecessary to invent an entirely new animal (i.e. one that has no palaeontological predecessors of any kind) to explain long-necked water monsters when there are reasonable explanations for the morphological differences between such creatures and fossil plesiosaurs."

Consider then this portrait of the plesiosaur written in 1824 by the Reverend W. D. Conybeare.

> It may perhaps have lurked in shoal water along the coast, concealed along the sea-weed, and raising its nostrils to a level with the surface from a considerable depth may have found a secure retreat from the assaults of dangerous enemies; while the length and flexibility of its neck may have compensated for want of strength in its jaws and its incapacity for swift motion through the water, by the suddenness and agility of attack which they enabled it to make on every animal fitted for its prey, which came within its extensive sweep.

Indeed, of all the creatures known to have inhabited the earth's oceans, it is the plesiosaurs whose "outline and structure" seem to best correspond with *some* descriptions of the sea serpent. But what was it that made Gould suggest this apparently long-dead species as the likeliest candidate?

The marine reptile theory had been put forth in the past by both scientists and witnesses.[1] As early as 1833, British geologist Robert Bakewell wrote in his *Introduction to Geology:*

> I remember one of the most particular descriptions of the sea serpent was given by an American captain, who saw the animal raise a large portion of its body from the water: he reported it as of great length, and about the bulk of a large water cask; it had paddles somewhat like a turtle, and enormous jaws like a crocodile. This description certainly approaches, or may be said to correspond with, the ichthyosaurus, of which the captain had probably never heard.

Heuvelmans noted that he was unable to discover the report referred to here, but it is possible that the sighting, like so many others, was never written down. He further points out that the *Ichthyosaurus* bears no resemblance to the sea serpent. Ichthyosaurs resembled most closely a sort of fierce, oversized dolphin, but, as Heuvelmans also pointed out, the name means "fish lizard," which has probably been the cause of the confusion.

Professor Benjamin Silliman added this note of polite one-upmanship to the American edition of Bakewell's book:

> Mr. Bakewell's very sensible conjecture that the sea-serpent may be a Saurian agrees still more with the supposition that it is a *Plesiosaurus* than an *Ichthyosaurus*, as the short neck of the latter does not agree with the common appearance of the sea-serpent.

In 1841, German zoologist Heinrich Rathke suggested the reason that the sea serpent remained elusive:

> It is possible and probable that when it stretches out its long neck it usually sticks only the tip of its nose out of the water, and then only for a very short time, keeping the rest of its body under water, which cannot make it easy to see among the movement of the waves.

Eight years later, in the aftermath of the *Daedalus* controversy, Louis Agassiz stated his support of the plesiosaur theory:

> The truth is . . . that if a naturalist had to sketch the outlines of . . . *Plesiosaurus* from the remains we have of them, he would make a drawing very similar to the sea-serpent as it has been described. . . . I still consider it probable that it will be the good fortune of some person on the coast of

Norway or North America to find a living representative of this type of reptile, which is thought to have died out.

But what is the likelihood that the unknown creature inhabiting the Gulf
of Maine was a marine reptile believed to have vanished with the dinosaurs
at the end of the Cretaceous period?

Scientists are divided on what brought about the demise of the dinosaurs. A whole host of factors may have been involved, so there are many
theories.[2] Most scientists, however, agree that the evidence suggests that the
dinosaurs were well on their way to extinction before the volcanic eruptions
of the Deccan Traps in India and/or the meteor hit near Chicxulub on the
Yucatan Peninsula between 65 and 67 million years ago, at what is known as
the K-T boundary (the end of the Cretaceous period and the beginning of the
Tertiary period). Whatever the cause or causes, the reign of the dinosaurs
concluded with cataclysmic changes to the earth and its atmosphere that
wiped out an estimated two-thirds of the species then living.

Some species did cross over into the Tertiary period, and their descendants are alive today. Crocodilians came through, as did sharks, amphibians,
turtles, mammals, and birds. Why these species survived and others died
out is a matter for conjecture. Species survival, whether at the K-T boundary or today, is inextricably tied to the health of the ecosystem and the bal-
anced distribution of predator and prey. A healthy ecosystem ensures that
a sufficient number of any given species are able to attain reproductive maturity and produce enough surviving young to guarantee the continuation
of the species.

When the stability of an ecosystem is threatened by environmental
changes, habitat destruction, or some other factor, species lacking the ability to adapt quickly become endangered. A highly specialized species may
find itself facing the threat of extinction. Modern examples of this can be
found in (among others) orangutans, koalas, and giant pandas, which because of their small populations, specialized diet, and diminished habitat
are dangerously threatened.

In order to come through the changes at the K-T boundary, the species
that persisted must have drawn on all their resources to adjust to a dra-

matically altered environment: a world grown suddenly cold, dark, and hostile, with food in short supply and an atmosphere laden with sulfur dioxide. As did land species, the creatures of the Cretaceous seas suffered mass extinction, although some did come through, including sharks, sea turtles, horseshoe crabs, and at least one ancient fish.

One of the most astounding finds of the twentieth century, the discovery of the coelacanth (hollow spine) in 1938, startled the scientific world. Not only was there no hint until then that this 400-million-year-old fish might still exist, but fossil evidence suggested that it too had perished at the end of the Cretaceous period.

On December 22, 1938, the fishing trawler *Nerine*, working at the mouth of the Chalumna River, on the east coast of South Africa, hauled up an unusual blue fish. Arriving in port, the skipper, Captain Hendrik Goosen, as was his practice, had a clerk at the fishing company contact Marjorie Courtenay-Latimer, the thirty-two-year-old naturalist and assistant curator of the East London Museum, to see if she wanted to examine his catch. Goosen's arrangement with Courtenay-Latimer and with the local aquarium provided both facilities an opportunity to add new and unusual specimens to their exhibits, in her case to the fledgling museum's meager holdings.

Courtenay-Latimer briefly considered not going, but because it was almost Christmas she decided that season's greetings were in order and went down to the dock. Captain Goosen was gone when she got there, but one of the crew pointed out the specimen pile, which at first seemed uninteresting. Then a curious blue fin attracted her attention. It belonged to an unfamiliar fish, five feet long, with heavy scales and large, peculiar fins. Because the specimen was completely unknown to her, Courtenay-Latimer decided to take it back to the museum.

Her library was no help in identifying the fish, nor was the chairman of the board, who dismissed it as a rock cod. Still, as she recalled in a 1989 interview with cryptozoologist J. Richard Greenwell, "It was this idea of mine that it was something very primitive, and I thought to myself, this must be a ganoid fish, with these strange scales. But then a ganoid fish to me was a fossil fish, and how could it be a fossil when this thing was alive? . . . I had to save this thing, whatever happened."

Naturalist Marjorie Courtenay-Latimer with the newly discovered coelacanth in 1939. Ichthyologist J. L. B. Smith described this species and gave it the name *Latimeria chalumnae* in her honor. (East London Museum. Used by permission of J. Richard Greenwell, International Society of Cryptozoology.)

Courtenay-Latimer spent the remainder of the afternoon trying to find someone who would help her preserve the specimen. The hospital morgue turned her down, as did the Cold Storage Commission. At wit's end, she finally decided she had no alternative but to place the specimen in the care of the local taxidermist, Robert Center, with whose help she wrapped the fish in a sheet soaked in what little formalin was available. She then waited through five days of South African heat before regretfully admitting that skinning the fish and saving the skull offered the only hope of its preservation.

In the meantime, she sent a sketch of the strange fish to Rhodes University chemistry professor James L. B. Smith, an amateur ichthyologist with whom she was on friendly terms. From the sketch, Smith, much to his considerable astonishment, identified the fish as a coelacanth. By this time, however, the internal organs of the fish had long since been consigned to the rubbish heap, preventing Smith from a detailed examination.

Professor Smith spent the next fourteen years in search of another specimen. Leaflets offering a reward for the fish were distributed, but the only results were tantalizing reports by fishermen claiming to have seen one at some time or another. The Second World War intervened. Not until 1952 would Smith have his prize.

Ahmed Hussein, fishing from a canoe near the Comoro Islands, in the Indian Ocean, had hooked a large, fierce fish and upon arriving at market the next day was told it looked like the picture in the leaflet. Smith was contacted. After a frantic journey, during which he lived in continual fear that the fish would rot and be discarded before he could get to it, he found himself face-to-face with a descendant of the ancient world.

The coelacanth is not a fossil fish, as has sometimes been reported, but a highly specialized descendant. It has a hollow cartilaginous tube in place of a backbone, and its digestive system resembles that of a shark, yet it has a bony head, teeth, and scales. It gives birth to live young and has a joint that allows it to raise its top jaw while lowering its bottom jaw to increase its gape. Yet with all that is known, still more is literally beyond reach: Its habitat is between 650 and 2,000 feet below the surface of the sea.

More than a hundred of these coelacanths have since been caught and examined by scientists. In December 1997, the *Boston Globe* reported that the single relic population, located off Grand Comoro, was critically endangered and possibly on the verge of extinction.[3] Despite protection offered by the Convention on International Trade in Endangered Species (CITES) and a government ban on catching the fish, the combination of pesticides, overfishing of its prey species, and its unfortunate habit of taking bait meant for other edible fish have reduced the population of coelacanths from between five hundred and six hundred in the late 1980s to an estimated two hundred in 1998.

The coelacanth, dubbed "old four legs" because of its fins, breathed new life into the question of the sea serpent as plesiosaur, as Professor J. Z. Young noted in his book *The Life of Vertebrates* (1962).

> Although it has often been suggested that tales of sea serpents indicate the continued survival of plesiosaurs, since the discovery of the coelacanth fish Latimeria zoologists have become cautious about rejecting such possibilities.

In the September 24, 1998, issue of *Nature*, three scientists—Dr. Mark Erdmann, a postdoctoral fellow from the University of California at Berkeley;
Roy Caldwell, professor and chair of integrative biology at Berkeley; and M.
Kasim Moosa, of the Indonesian Institute of Sciences—announced that a
second population of coelacanths had been discovered off North Sulawesi,
Indonesia. The Indonesian coelacanths, which are brown rather than blue,
had been discovered the year before by Erdmann in a fish market on the Sulawesi mainland while he was on his honeymoon. Nearly a year later, with
the help of funding from the National Geographic Society, Erdmann located
a second specimen caught off Manado Tua, about which he comments:

> The biogeographic importance [of this find] is enormous. Even if the Su-
> lawesi population is the only other area where the coelacanth is found,
> the fact that it could escape detection from the scientific community in
> an area well studied by ichthyologists for over 100 years is wonderful. It is
> a humbling and exciting reminder that humans have by no means con-
> quered the oceans, and provides fodder for our imagination about other,
> as-yet-undiscovered "sea monsters" and oddities from the deep. And it
> underscores the importance of protecting our oceans, lest we lose things
> forever which we have not yet even discovered!

Indeed, the remarkable discovery of a second population of coelacanths
is proof positive that smallish creatures from the late Cretaceous period survived unknown until late into the twentieth century. But what are the
chances for a forty-foot-plus plesiosaur?

In spite of the fact that plesiosaurs inhabited the earth's oceans for nearly
as long as the dinosaurs ruled the land, comparatively little is known about
them. Studies in marine vertebrate paleontology have suffered in contrast
to those of their glamorous land-dwelling counterparts, the monsters of the
prehistoric seas having failed to capture the imagination of the public in the
manner of, say, *Tyrannosaurus rex*. Even the men who discovered the sea-
dwelling monsters get short shrift.

In *The Great Dinosaur Hunters and Their Discoveries,* Edwin Colbert mentions
Rev. William Conybeare only in passing and his associate Henry De La Beche,
with whom Conybeare conducted much of his research on ichthyosaurs

and described the first plesiosaur, not at all.[4] Perhaps Conybeare, a gifted, imaginative, and collegial gentleman geologist who suggested the names for at least four of the first fossil reptiles described, suffers for having discovered a marine saurian instead of a land dweller.

What is known, or thought to be known (we have ample evidence that science is a fluid art and many things are "known" only until they are proved incorrect), is that the plesiosaurs first appeared in the Early Jurassic period, having evolved from the nothosaurs of the Triassic period or the pistosaurs, also Triassic, and continued to evolve throughout the Jurassic, becoming larger and more specialized during the Cretaceous period. One family, a long-necked elasmosaur, reached more than forty feet in length and flourished until the end of the Cretaceous.

That is what the fossil record yields, or seems to yield anyway. This ancestry has been challenged by paleontologist Dr. Robert Bakker, who in 1993 suggested that the long-necked plesiosaurs of the Jurassic died out, whereas the short-necked pliosaurs of the Jurassic independently evolved into the long-necked elasmosaurs of the late Cretaceous.

Whatever their lineage, elasmosaurs were magnificently adapted to their marine environment. Described by the Reverend Mr. Conybeare as "snakes threaded through the bodies of turtles," elasmosaurs reached a known length of forty-six feet, more than half of which (about twenty-six feet) was neck. Their four highly specialized oarlike flippers moved up and down like wing beats, enabling the beasts to "fly" through the water in a manner similar to that of sea turtles and penguins.

Elasmosaurus is thought to have been an ambush predator, using its long neck to swoop up prey before its presence was even sensed. But that long neck is believed to have presented a problem when it came to speed. Theoretically, any movement of the head while swimming could cause a course change; the creature is therefore presumed to have been a comparatively slow swimmer.

Elasmosaurs had slender, pointed, somewhat curved teeth, suggesting that their prey would have had soft flesh and been impaled and swallowed rather than chewed. It has also been suggested that elasmosaurs may have swallowed stones (gastroliths, which have been found in fossilized speci-

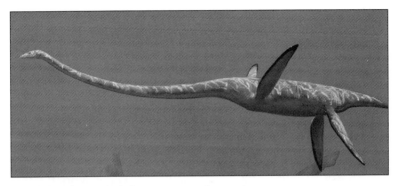

Flight of the long-necked plesiosaur. © Douglas Henderson.

mens) to aid in digestion. Another explanation suggested for the gastroliths is that they may have acted as ballast, as in modern crocodiles.

Unlike the ichthyosaurs, for which there is fossil evidence suggestive of live birth (as in the specimens collected at Holzmaden, in southern Germany), elasmosaurs have traditionally been considered oviparous and were presumed to have laid their eggs on sandy beaches, as sea turtles and crocodiles still do. This viewpoint has been challenged, with good reason. If elasmosaurs did indeed lay eggs, the process was likely clumsy and dangerous. Supporting a twenty-six-foot neck without the water's buoyancy while preparing the sand and depositing eggs would have been a Herculean feat, not to mention placing the animal in an extremely vulnerable situation.

Nothing is known of elasmosaurs' external appearance except what can be theorized from examination of fossil remains. Coloration, skin texture, and the presence or absence of frills or other nonbony appendages are mostly a matter for conjecture. Reconstruction of the head suggests something snakelike, although the creature's nostrils, which are comparatively small, are closer to its eyes than to the front of the face.

One reason for the sketchy knowledge of plesiosaurs is that their fossilized remains are seldom found and even more rarely are they still intact. Fossilization in and of itself is rare and requires a combination of factors wherein an animal dies and is quickly buried by sand or silt under the right conditions to be preserved.

In North America, some of the best examples of fossilized plesiosaurs have been discovered in an area that was once a large inland sea (the Western Interior Sea) stretching from the Arctic to the Gulf of Mexico and en-compassing the now landlocked states of Kansas, Nebraska, Oklahoma, and the Dakotas as well as parts of Montana, Wyoming, Colorado, Minnesota, and Iowa. This inland sea was also populated by squid, sharks, bony fishes, ichthyosaurs, and mosasaurs.

Fortunately for the science of paleontology, it was an elasmosaur from Kansas nicknamed Dr. Turner's Dragon that, according to legend, played an important role in what became known as the Great Bone Wars. The wars began, so the story goes, in 1869 when Othniel Charles Marsh[5] (O.C. to his friends) pointed out that Edward Drinker Cope had made a critical error in his description of a new plesiosaur, *Elasmosaurus platyrus*.

Talented and ambitious young men, Cope and Marsh began their associa-tion as friendly rivals. Each was able to indulge his passion for fossil hunt-ing and scientific research, Cope through the support of his father, a wealthy Philadelphia shipowner, and Marsh through the patronage of his uncle, George Peabody.[6]

Cope's reconstruction of *Elasmosaurus platyrus*, which was published in the *Transactions of the American Philosophical Society*, was indeed extraordinary, but only, according to Marsh, because Cope had put the head on the wrong end of the beast.

To be fair, it should be pointed out that Cope was reconstructing a speci-men that had been excavated and shipped to him piecemeal by a young army doctor, Theophilis Turner, stationed at Fort Wallace in Kansas. Turner had found the fossilized skeleton in a ravine while on a hunting trip and communicated its discovery to Cope at the Academy of Natural Sciences of Philadelphia. Cope had the doctor elected a corresponding member of the academy and nicknamed the specimen "Dr. Turner's Dragon."

To Cope's bitter embarrassment, Marsh was absolutely correct about the misplacement of the head. Cope had a significant ego, and his humiliation was proportionate. He bought up all the copies of the *Transactions*, had a new engraving made, and paid for republication, but Marsh held on to his copy as proof of Cope's ineptitude.[7] The battle was well and truly joined, and for the remainder of their lives the two men pursued each other relentlessly,

Edward Drinker Cope's reconstruction of *Laelaps aquilunguis* confronting *Elasmosaurus platyrus* with its head on the wrong end. From *American Naturalist*, vol. 3 (1869), "The fossil reptiles of New Jersey." (Courtesy of the Linda Hall Library, Kansas City, Missouri)

employing sabotage, subterfuge, and slander, and all the while advancing science.[8]

Almost thirty years later, the plesiosaur theory was still the most popular explanation for sea serpents. In a letter to *The* (London) *Times* in 1893, Thomas H. Huxley wrote, "There is no a priori reason that I know of why snake bodied reptiles, from fifty feet long and upward, should not disport themselves in our seas as they did in those of the Cretaceous epoch, which geologically speaking is a mere yesterday."

A mere yesterday indeed, but how to reconcile the description of the long-necked, broad-bodied elasmosaur with the more snakelike appearance customarily described by witnesses of the New England creatures, particularly those who had the best opportunity to view it for considerable periods of time in Gloucester Harbor in 1817?

The long, slender body with humps or bunches "resembling a row of casks" or the "buoys of a seine" can scarcely be said to resemble the known skeletal remains of elasmosaur, especially because not one of the witnesses, even those who had seen it in shallow water (only partially submerged), ever mentions flippers.

Were the early witnesses, perhaps led by the term *sea serpent*, unwilling to report any features that did not appear to them to be snakelike? Could they possibly have missed significant features such as the broad torso and long paddles? Were the later witnesses who described an appearance resembling an overturned dory responding to the suggestion of a marine saurian, adding adornments to fit a popular theory? Whose testimony do we consider suspect? The only features common to both appear to be a long neck and a snakelike head lifted sometimes many feet above the water.

Did a species of plesiosaur survive the environmental disaster at the K-T boundary and evolve over time into a more elongate, more flexible, more specialized creature, capable of sustaining life in cold water? Is it a reptile at all?

Although some naturalists and cryptozoologists have willingly subscribed to the plesiosaur theory, others then and since have believed the likeliest candidate to be *Basilosaurus cetoides* (also known as *Zeuglodon*), a primitive Eocene whale.

Harvard zoologist Samuel Kneeland was one who subscribed to the theory that the sea serpent was one of these Eocene whales. Another was Rev. J. G. Wood, who, in his article "The Trail of the Sea-Serpent," in the *Atlantic Monthly* (June 1884), concluded that the sea serpent "does not correspond with any contemporary animal at present known to zoologists." He goes on to suggest that it could be "a surviving being belonging to a race verging on extinction . . . but that the survivor (or survivors) belongs not to the saurians, but to a cetacean animal, which if not an actual zeuglodon, has many affinities with that creature."

The long, probably flexible body of *Basilosaurus* fits quite nicely with many descriptions, and Heuvelmans suggested that his *Plurigibbosus novae-angliae* might be a descendant. The one feature it did not have, however, is a long

Believing its bones belonged to an immense marine reptile, Dr. Richard Harlan described the first of these ancient whales in 1843, giving it the name *Basilosaurus* ("King of the Lizards"). Sir Richard Owen later recognized it as a mammal and renamed it *Zeuglodon*. (Courtesy of Florida Geological Survey, Tallahassee, Fla.)

neck. But if elasmosaurs could have spent 60-odd million years becoming more streamlined, then *Basilosaurus* could have spent the last 20 million years extending its neck. However, as Matthew Bille pointed out in an article about the *Valhalla* creature in *Strange Magazine* (1994), "The objection to this is that zeuglodons were in fact evolving in the other direction, resulting in the almost total disappearance of the neck in modern whales." Curiously, Dr. Oudemans once suggested that the sea serpent might be a creature possessing the features of both, a hybrid creature he proposed to call *Zeuglodon plesiosauroides*, though he later recanted.

The arguments for a whale ancestry are compelling. In the marine environment, only mammals—otters, seals, manatees, dolphins, and whales—propel themselves with vertical movements.

Basilosaurus is generally depicted as long and streamlined, with its tail tapering to an unlikely point, and sometimes with smallish crescentic flukes. And as Heuvelmans indicated, "With their relatively small mouths they could not have trawled for their food like the whalebone whales: they must have hunted their prey—fish and squids—at top speed, and therefore have been built for the chase." But to do this they would have needed a stabilizing dorsal fin (for which there is no fossil evidence) to prevent them from yawing from side to side. Heuvelmans addressed this as well. "Of all known cetaceans, they need a big dorsal ridge the most. It could be a single dorsal fin, either tall and narrow or low and long; it could be a combination of the two, a small dorsal fin followed by a row of small humps. This would agree with the arrangement on the Massachusetts Bay sea-serpent."

Another candidate for the ancestor of the New England creatures is the mosasaur, which seems to have made only a brief appearance in the ancient world, filling the niche left by the demise of the ichthyosaurs. The first of the mosasaurs was discovered in 1780 in Maastricht, the Netherlands, where it was put on exhibit until Napoleon's forces carried it back to Paris as a spoil of war. The great French comparative anatomist Baron Georges Cuvier used "la grand animale de Maastricht" to support his then revolutionary theory of extinction, but it was not until 1822 that Rev. William Conybeare gave it the name *Mosasaurus*.

As early as 1869, Edward Drinker Cope suggested that there were similari-

In the Cretaceous sea, the twelve-foot mosasaur *Clidastes* makes a meal of *Calcarichelys*. © Dan Varner.

ties between mosasaurids and snakes. More recent analysis has shown this to be true, although mosasaurs bore a striking resemblance to a giant crocodile. The fact that mosasaurs were marine dwellers might mean that the first snakes were too and that the New England creatures descended from them.

In 1938, Roy Chapman Andrews, a zoologist with the American Museum of Natural History, wrote a short article debunking sea serpents in which he used a mosasaur instead of a plesiosaur to illustrate his point. "Sea Serpents Always Get Away" ran the headline for the article (unsourced in the Woodbury scrapbook).

> For some reason everyone wants to believe that somewhere in the ocean depths there are strange creatures, survivors of the Age of Reptiles, still living. . . . Arguments are of no avail. Therefore I do not hope to convince anyone—especially newspapermen—for serpent yarns make much too good copy.
>
> . . . There is not a shred of scientific evidence to show that any of the great monsters of the Age of Reptiles still exist. No one could ask for a better sea serpent than the thirty-foot mosasaur but unfortunately it has been extinct for about eighty million years. . . . [T]heir fossilized bones are never found above the beds of the upper Cretaceous age. Then sharks[,] whales[,] and seals became the dominant giant marine types and it is these that give rise to most of the sea-serpent stories that are not pure fabrication.

The humorous illustration by G. de Zayas that accompanied Roy Chapman Andrews's article debunking what he called "sea serpent yarns."

Another possibility is that sea serpents are an unknown species of giant eel. In 1955, oceanographer Dr. Anton Bruun, director of the University Zoological Museum of Copenhagen, announced at the International Congress of

Zoology that sea serpents do exist. He offered as proof a six-foot eel larva (*Leptocephalus*) caught in the southern Atlantic in 1930 by the deep-sea expedition ship *Dana*.

Bruun's reasons for suggesting that sea serpents are in fact giant eels were compelling. Knowing that eels in their adult form can be as much as thirty times larger than in the larval stage, Dr. Bruun reasoned that a six-foot larva might grow to be as much as a hundred or more feet in length. Moreover, Dr. Bruun's larva had been caught at latitude 35 42' south, longitude 18 37' east, not far from where Captain M'Quhae and the crew of the *Daedalus* had their famous sighting of the sea serpent.

Naturally, there were objections to Bruun's theory, one being that just because some eel larva metamorphose into much larger adults does not necessarily mean that all do. Nor does the eel theory answer the most perplexing element of the sea serpent identity—the vertical undulations. Despite the fact that some witnesses described the creature as resembling a giant eel, the fact is that eels, fish, and water snakes all move horizontally with a left-to-right flexure. In order for an eel to move like a sea serpent, it would have to be swimming on its side. Curiously, Dr. Maurice Burton and Roy P. Mackal both observed eels doing precisely that at different times in separate locations. Still, an eel swimming on its side on the water's surface produces considerable commotion that does not match the descriptions of the sea serpent gliding along at high speed with its head out of the water.

Another theory is that the sea serpents are misidentified giant squid and that the head and neck are actually a tentacle raised above the water. Although this explanation may account for an occasional sea serpent sighting, using one creature once presumed to be mythical to explain another seems a trifle too convenient. Moreover, the common descriptions of the New England creatures do not fit this explanation.

Ancient whale, marine reptile, enormous eel, or giant squid—whatever the New England creature is or was—why has no one ever captured one on film or found a carcass washed ashore? Both are perfectly reasonable questions, with perfectly reasonable answers that will satisfy no one.

A picture may have once been worth a thousand words, but in this age of

Sandra Mansi took this picture while picnicking on the shore of Lake Champlain near North Hero, Vermont, in 1977. Experts agree that the photograph shows no signs of tampering, but just exactly what it depicts remains a mystery. (Sandra Mansi/Gamma Liaison)

photomanipulation it would be proof of absolutely nothing with regard to the New England creatures. Nor, as has been seen in the case of the Loch Ness monster, would it preclude the accusations of a hoax. The sightings that offered the best opportunity for photographic evidence—those at Gloucester in 1817-18 and Nahant in 1819—took place when photography was in its infancy. Small, portable, affordable cameras, though available in the late 1880s, did not come into widespread use until the early twentieth century. Even with that, few people, unless they were photojournalists or on holiday, walked about with a camera dangling from their neck. Fewer still would have had the presence of mind to quickly capture on film something they were not expecting to see. And most of the twentieth-century sightings were by fishermen, who almost never took cameras along on their voyages.

Although it appears that no one has ever captured ocean-dwelling sea ser-

pents on film, there are numerous still and videotaped images of lake creatures. Perhaps the best of these is the photograph taken of the Lake Champlain creature by Sandra Mansi in the summer of 1977. The case of the Mansi
photo is instructive; it has been analyzed by experts, who concluded that
the photo had not been tampered with and is probably of a living creature,
but just what they cannot say.

The question of a carcass is another matter. Large oceangoing creatures
rarely wash up on beaches where they might be found (and thus examined).
When one does, it is usually because the animal died relatively close to
shore and was carried in on the tide as decomposition began and gases built
up and floated the carcass. As often as not, it is carried out again by the next
high tide. Whales (particularly pilot whales) sometimes strand in considerable numbers, but the reason seems to be related to a breakdown in their
ability to echolocate; their internal sonar system goes haywire and the result is fatal. But these occurrences are relatively rare, and the animals in
question are usually common. The chance that one of a small population of
sea serpents that apparently travels widely in open water would wash
ashore is necessarily small. If the creatures were related to plesiosaurs and
had the added weight of gastroliths, the likelihood is further reduced. So
the absence of a sea serpent carcass is not proof positive that none exists.

In the absence of an actual specimen, all is conjecture. But, if we dismiss
the various "explanations"—seals, seaweed, and any number of large fish or
selachians swimming in a line—offered for the New England sea serpents
and take as a matter of faith that this was not a hoax of two hundred years'
duration or a mass hallucination, we are left with creatures that many individuals with significant collective knowledge of the sea and its inhabitants
have described as unknown to them.

As a basis for discussion, we can state that the New England creatures are
(or were) elongate marine animals (class unknown) reaching an average
length of between sixty and eighty feet. Their coloration, dark above and
lighter below, is consistent with that of many marine mammals and most
large reptiles. Witness testimony concerning skin texture ranges from
smooth and shiny to scales the size of a tea tray, making it impossible to

arrive at any conclusion. A more consistent feature is what may possibly have been a long, low dorsal fin described by early witnesses as bunches or protuberances and later as humps or a fleshy fin. The rare mention of a tall crest or finlike adornment on the back could be explained by sexual dimorphism, meaning that only the males or only the females possessed this feature.

The creatures' behavior has led witnesses to describe them as shy (perhaps cautious would be more accurate), curious, and sensitive to mechanical and human sounds. There appear to be no reliable cases of the New England creature exhibiting any aggression toward humans or boats, even when fired upon. Its defensive response is flight, which is accomplished either by sinking out of sight or swimming away rapidly. Recurrent descriptions of the creatures resting on the surface of the water suggests near neutral buoyancy and could be related to the regulation of body temperature. Observations of this behavior and others where the creatures are seen nearly aground in shallow water may mean that the New England creatures basked on the surface in order to collect and store up the warmth of the sun, especially if they were reptilian, and thus ectothermic.

Ectotherms (cold-blooded creatures) obtain most of their body heat from external sources, whereas warm-blooded animals (endotherms) generate a constant body temperature using their own metabolism. There are, however, a combination of physiological anomalies collectively known as gigantothermy, which allow extremely large ectothermic creatures (more than 2,200 pounds) to maintain a high body temperature at a low metabolic rate.

The creatures appear to have favored the Gulf of Maine for summer feeding and may have retreated to the warmer water of the Gulf of Mexico during the winter months in common with many other large Atlantic species, notably the humpback whale and the bluefin tuna. They may also have migrated to southern waters for breeding.

The largest of the marine mammals reach reproductive maturity at about twelve to fifteen years of age and thereafter give birth once every two to three years; they care for their young for a period of about six months to a year. As large predators the New England creatures can be presumed to have had few natural enemies (until the nineteenth century, when everyone

began taking potshots at them), so it is likely that they too had a comparatively old reproductive maturity and gave birth at similar intervals.

Unlike the whales, the New England creatures do not seem to have been
nurturing parents. If the creatures were gigantothermic, as Dr. Shuker has
posited, the juveniles (like those of the leathery turtle *Dermochelys coriacea*)
might have remained behind in more temperate southern waters until
reaching a size that would permit them to withstand the cold North Atlantic. Another possibility is that they grew at a rate comparable to whales,
which would account for observations of smaller (forty-foot) creatures.

Because they were seldom seen in pairs or groups, we can conclude that
the New England creatures were not especially social with their own
species, although some reports mention seeing them in the company of
pilot whales or dolphins, which could indicate a symbiotic relationship of
some kind.

Sightings were so frequently associated with herring and mackerel that
we can assume that their preferred food source was small and mid-sized
midwater schooling fish. These fish are highly seasonal, and their abundance or absence (which may be influenced by water temperature) is subject to considerable fluctuation from year to year.

The New England creatures appear to have followed the fish to the fish-
ing banks on a seasonal basis, most notably an area known as Stellwagen
Bank. In 1853, Captain Henry S. Stellwagen, a hydrographer with the U.S.
Navy and assistant in the U.S. Coast Survey, was conducting soundings in
Massachusetts Bay when he came upon an underwater plateau, which he
described in a letter to Superintendent Alexander Dallas Bache.

> I consider that I have made an important discovery in the location of a 15
> fathom bank lying in a line between Cape Cod and Cape Ann—with 40 and
> 50 fathoms inside and to the northward of it and 35 fathoms just outside
> of it. . . . We have traced nearly 5 miles in width and over 6 miles in length,
> it no doubt extending much further. . . . We are all very much interested
> in pursuing the discovery still further to determine if it is a continuous
> bank or a detached knoll.

Five days later Stellwagen added, "I find the Bank is known by [the] vague term of Middle Bank but little is ascertained about it except that it is a good fishing ground."

A good fishing ground indeed; the creatures seem to have found it so, for it is within the area of Stellwagen Bank and the adjacent coastal waters of Massachusetts Bay that the majority of the sightings took place. Today, Stellwagen Bank is protected under the National Marine Sanctuaries Reauthorization and Improvement Act of 1992 and provides a haven for endangered and nonendangered aquatic life and seabirds. But the legislation that protects its intricate ecosystem, championed by Senator John Kerry and Congressman Gerry E. Studds of Massachusetts, may have come thirty years too late for the sea serpent.

As Glen Kuban has suggested, if one or more types of sea serpent did roam the oceans until recently (which he considers plausible but not certain), their demise might be likened to the proverbial canary in the coal mine, their disappearance having been an early warning of the dangers represented to marine life by a lack of responsible stewardship of ocean resources.

Intense pressure from increasingly efficient fishing methods; the use of nonselective fishing gear; the heedless disposal of human and industrial waste, pesticides, and dredge spoils; fertilizer runoff; and accidental spills of chemicals and petroleum are only the most obvious factors that may have contributed to the disappearance of the New England creatures. The biological reality is that habitat destruction and overfishing can in a disturbingly short space of time reduce a species from viability to extinction. Even species that were once plentiful in the North Atlantic have been depleted to a point that would have been unimaginable to the early explorers.

It is said that John Cabot, upon his return to England in 1497, reported that, "The Sea there is swarming with fish which can be taken not only with the net but in baskets let down with a stone." In 1602, Bartholemew Gosnold renamed Cape Cod (which Verrazano had called Pallavisino) for the fish that "pestered" his ship there. Twelve years later, John Smith, though noted for overstatement, does not seem to have been exaggerating when he wrote that there was hardly "any Baye, shallow shore, or Cove of sand, where you may not take many Clampes, or Lobsters, or both at your pleasure; and in many places lode your boate if you please. . . . And in the harbors we frequented, a little boy might take of Cunners and Pinnacks and such delicate fish, at the ship's sterne, more than six or tenne can eate in a daie; but with casting a net, [a] thousand when wee pleased."

Dozens of once abundant species—among them the Atlantic cod, halibut, swordfish, Atlantic salmon, bluefin tuna, haddock, pollock, sea scallops, three kinds of flounder, half a dozen kinds of shark, and that most ancient creature of the seashore, the horseshoe crab—have been dangerously depleted and are in urgent need of a chance to rebuild their population levels. Sadly, the almost total absence of recent sightings of sea serpents in New England waters may mean that they are gone, or nearly gone, for good.

Once, though, not so very long ago, these creatures commanded the attention of the finest scientific minds, enticed the curious, and confounded the doubters, eluding both capture and classification. Perhaps their story is best summed up by Granville Putnam, writing some 112 years ago:

It has been my belief for some years that there is some fitful, gigantic wanderer inhabiting the ocean; . . . I shall not attempt to classify it. Whether it belongs to the mammalia, reptilia or pisces, whether it be ophidian, cetacean or saurian, I must leave it to the naturalist to determine. I am no stranger to the sea. A love for its beauty and grandeur, in calm and storm, as well as a fondness for the study of its teeming life, both animal and vegetable, minute as well as gigantic, has led me to spend eighteen years upon its very verge. This experience makes me sure that no one who saw what I did would ever entertain the suggestion that it was a school of porpoises, a grampus, or a horse-mackerel. Because some have been deceived by these, or a floating spar or a mass of seaweed, it does not follow that others have not seen a genuine monster. . . .

I stoutly claim that when one has thrown aside as worthless all the yarns of sailors and the stories of landsman upon which rest the taint of suspicion, there still remains a residuum of evidence which cannot justly be ignored. My own firm belief is based both upon what my eyes have seen and upon the unimpeachable testimony of many men, whose word upon any other subject would be taken without a question.

Chapter 9 Notes

1. Among the eyewitnesses, Rev. Arthur Lawrence, Nathan Chase, and Second Officer Batchelor of the *Corinthian* all suggested a marine saurian as the best explanation for what they'd seen.

2. For a thumbnail survey of recent opinions, see Louis Psihoyos's witty and wonderful *Hunting Dinosaurs* (Random House, 1994).

3. Three marine biologists who have undertaken an intensive study of the creatures (Mike Bruton, of the Two Oceans Aquarium, and Hans Fricke and Karen Hissman, of the Max Planck Institute) warn that if something is not done, and soon, the fish discovered only sixty years ago will soon be lost forever.

4. Technically, plesiosaurs and the other marine reptiles of the ancient ocean are not dinosaurs.

5. While conducting research at Yale University in 1972, Gary S. Mangiacopra discovered a copy of Oudemans's *The Great Sea Serpent* inscribed with the name O. C. Marsh. Tucked inside the book was a yellowing newspaper account of a sea serpent sighting in Long Island Sound.

6. Marsh persuaded Uncle George to endow a new museum at Yale University, with a provision that Marsh be named professor of paleontology.

7. It's not as if old Othniel was above the occasional error of his own. In his rush to describe the immense amount of fossil material being shipped to him by his workers in Como Bluff, Wyoming, he occasionally gave different names to separate specimens of the same creature. (Actually, Cope and Marsh both did this, once giving twenty-two names to the same species.) Marsh also put the wrong head on one skeleton; thus, the Brontosaurus beloved of schoolchildren must by scientific priority become *Apatosaurus*.

8. Despite their bitter antagonism, Marsh and Cope are forever united by their enormous contribution to the study of vertebrate paleontology. Between them, they found and described 130 new species in a period of only twenty years.

THE SEA SERPENT

The sea-serpent, in languor curved
About a rock, the world observed,
How all the beasts and birds
And fishes too, from near and far
Were pigeon-holed by genera
And tagged with Latin words.

"They lose thereby, each one," said he,
"His individuality
And influence to boot
The others mark his spot or stripe,
Ignore the beast but not the type
And pitch their praise to suit."

So sailormen he shunned, save such
As a double grog had drunk too much
And had a mighty bun on.
"For these," said he, "will ne'er agree"
Some give me one head, some say three,
And some that I have none on.

"They credit one with variation,
A virtue in intoxication
As excellent, as rare."
And then he swore, while life was his,
To be just sui generis,
A fearful oath to swear.

For still the world in anger raves
Not half so hard at cheats and knaves,
Its anger all is turned
On harmless chaps whose end and glory
Is not to fit a category:
This truth our hero learned.

In boat and plane and submarine
Bewhiskered pundits, students keen
Pursued him day and night,
Inventing terms of barb'rous Latin
That Julius Caesar could not chat in
Or Cicero recite.

At last, of food and sleep bereft—
No leisure more or refuge left—
Of long pursuit he tired,
And softly murm'ring e'er he died,
"Thank God, I die unclassified!"
Resignedly expired.

—Claudius Jones, "The Wits' Weekly" contest entry
Saturday Review of Literature, October 12, 1929

APPPENDIX A: SIGHTINGS TABLE

YEAR	DATE	LOCATION	VIEWED FROM	WITNESSES	PAGE
~1638		Cape Ann, MA	Boat	4 +	36
~1641		Lynn, MA	Shore		36, 75
~1746		New England coast			47
~1751	May	Muscongus Island, Broad Bay, ME	*Intrepid*	J. Kent	25
~1773		Boothbay, ME		Capt. Reed	23
~1776-81		Muscongus Bay, ME			23
~1776-81		Meduncook (now Friendship), ME			23
~1777-78		North Haven/Vinalhaven Is., Pen. Bay, ME			25
~1779		Penobscot Bay, ME	Shore	Capt. Crabtree + S. Tuckey	25
1779	Summer	Penobscot Bay, ME	*Protector*	Cmdr. Williams, Preble, & crew	26
1780	May	Round Pond, Broad Bay, ME	Cutter	Capt. G. Little	24
~1784		Ash Point, Penobscot Bay, ME		Crocket	23
1787		Gut of Canso, Cape Breton, NS	Schooner	W. Lee	27
1793	June 20	Mt. Desert Island, ME	Sea	Capt. Crabtree	28
1793	August 3	Kettle Island, Gloucester/Manchester, MA			29
~1794		North Haven/Vinalhaven Is., Pen. Bay, ME	Shore	Inhabitants	23
~1799		North Haven/Vinalhaven Is., Pen. Bay, ME	Shore	2 young men	23
1802	July	Islesboro/Cape Rosier, Pen. Bay, ME	Boat	Cummings + 3	21
1809		New England coast		Capt. Lillis	29
1809		Penobscot Bay, ME		Miller	29
1811	End of July	Faeroe-Iceland Ridge, North Atlantic		Capt. Brown +	30
1815	June 20-21	Warren's Cove, Plymouth, MA		Capt. Finney +	31
1817	July	Penobscot Bay, ME	Shore	Inhabitants of Mt. Desert Island	
1817	August 6	Gloucester Harbor, MA	Shore	2 women, coaster	37
1817	August 10	Ten Pound Island, Gloucester Harbor, MA	Shore	Wonson, Story, Stover	38
1817	August 12	Ten Pound Island, Gloucester Harbor, MA	Shore	S. Allen III	39
1817	August 13	Gloucester Harbor, MA	Shore	S. Allen III	39
1817	August 14	Gloucester Harbor, MA	Boat, shore	Gaffney, Ellery, Nash + 30	39, 47
1817	August 15	Kettle Island, Gloucester/Manchester, MA	*Hazard*, shore	Lee, Mansfield	41, 44
1817	August 17	Gloucester Harbor, MA	Shore, sea	Foster, Saville, Johnston	41, 44
1817	August 18	Off Webber's Cove, Gloucester, MA	Sailboat	Pearson, Collins	42
1817	August 18	Gloucester Harbor, MA	Shore	Perkins, Lee, etc.	42

YEAR	DATE	LOCATION	VIEWED FROM	WITNESSES	PAGE
1817	August 22	Gloucester, MA	Shore	Mr. & Mrs. Mansfield	49
1817	August 23	Gloucester Harbor, MA	Shore	A. Story	49
1817	August 25	Kettle Cove, Gloucester/Manchester, MA	Sea		50
1817	August 28	Eastern Point, Gloucester, MA	*Laura*	Bragg, Somerby, Toppan	51
1817	August 28	Kettle Cove, Gloucester/Manchester, MA			50
1817	September 10	Half Way Rocks, Marblehead, MA	Sea	Fishermen	53
1817	October 3	Scotch Caps, Mamaroneck Harbor, NY	Shore	J. Guion	54
1817	October 5	Rye Neck, Long Island Sound, NY	Shore	T. Herttell	53
1818	June 19	Sag Harbor, Long Island, NY			57
1818	June 21	Cape Ann, MA	*Delta (Delta)*	Shubael West	56
1818	June 27	Casco Bay, Portland, ME		Fishermen	57
1818	July 1	Salem, MA	Several boats		57
1818	July 2	Portland, ME		Hamilton, Webber	57
1818	July 11	Portland Harbor, ME			57
1818	July	Gloucester, MA	Shore	L. Wonson	57
1818	July	Muscle Point, Gloucester, MA	Shore	J. Moores	57
1818	July 25	Gloucester, MA		W. Sargent	57
1818	July 26	Gloucester, MA			
1818	July 29	Gloucester, MA	Boat	Fishermen	57
1818	July 30	Gloucester, MA	Whaleboat	Capt. Webber, etc.	57
1818	August 12	Between Newburyport and Gloucester, MA	Boat	T. Hodgkins +	59
1818	August 16	Annisquam Lighthouse, Ipswich Bay, MA		Many people	59
1818	August 19-20	Squam Bar, Ipswich Bay, MA		Capt. Richard Rich	59, 63
1819	June 6	Off Cape Ann, MA	*Concord*	Bennett, Wheeler	68
1819	June 11-12	Cohasset, MA			69
1819	June 30	Scituate, MA			69
1819	Mid July	Massachusetts Bay, MA			
1819	August 14	Long Beach, Nahant, MA	Shore	Cabot, Prince +	70, 72
1819	August	Long Beach, Nahant, MA	Shore	N. Chase +	75
1819	August 26	Gloucester Harbor, MA	Schooner's boat	Rev. Felch +	77
1819	August	Ft. Independence, Boston, MA	Shore	Soldiers	69
1820	Summer	Nahant, MA	Shore	Perkins +	80
1820	August 5	Little's Point, Swampscott, MA	Shore/boat	Reynolds +	80
1821	May	Cape Ann	*Minerva*	Capt. Crows	

YEAR	DATE	LOCATION	VIEWED FROM	WITNESSES	PAGE
1821	Summer	Nahant, MA		Francis Joy	82
1821	Summer	Nantucket, MA	Whaleboat	Duncan +	82
1821	August 2	Portsmouth, NH	Cash	Capt. Beal +	82
1821	August 12	The Graves, Massachusetts Bay, MA	Shore	Perkins +	82
1822	Summer	Nahant, MA		Weston	83
1823	July	Plymouth Bay, MA	Boat	F. Johnson, Jr.	83
1823	July 12	Lynn/Nahant, MA			83
1823	August 6	Squam Bar, Cape Ann, MA	Shore	50 +	83
1823	August 7	Sandy Bay Harbor, Rockport, MA	Shore	Ruggles family	83
1824	August 11	Plum Island Beach, Newburyport, MA			84
1825	July 15	Little Boar's Head, Cape Cod Bay, MA	Shore, boat	Goreham +, Barry +	84
1826	June 17	Halifax Harbor, NS	*Silas Richards*	Holdredge, Wharburton +	87
1826	June 19	41'30 N, 67'32'W (vicinity of Georges Bank)	*Iris*	Capt. Goodspeed + 7	89
1826	June 19	S. of Cape Cod, MA	Boat	Capt. Dagget +	89
1826	Summer	S. of Cape Cod Light, MA			89
1826	December 25	Nahant, MA	*Gold Hunter*	Capt. Knowles +	90
1827	July 29	40'30 N, 63'W	*Levant*	Capt. Coleman +	90
1830	June	Off Gay Head, Vineyard Sound, MA			91
1830	July	Boothbay Harbor, ME			90
1830	July 21	New England coast			91
1831	June	Kennebunk R., Kennebunk, ME	Boat	Gooch +	91
1831	June	Boothbay Harbor, ME	Shore	Smith + 14	91
1831	Summer	Boothbay Harbor, ME	Shore	Chandler	92
1832	July 27	SE. of Nahant, Massachusetts Bay, MA	*Detector*	Capt. Walden +	92
1832	August 2 or 9	Nahant, MA	Boat	W. Johnson + 3	92
1833	May 15	Mahone Bay, Halifax, NS		150	93
1833	May 18	20 miles from Cape Cod Light, MA	Boat	Ince + 5	94
1833	July 5	NE. of Nahant, Massachusetts Bay, MA	*Mechanic*	T. Bridges +	95
1833	July 5	E. of Nahant, Massachusetts Bay, MA	*Connecticut*	Capt. Porter +	96
1833	July 5	Lynn/Nahant, MA	*Charles of Provincetown*	Cook, Needham	
1834	Early August	Nahant, Massachusetts Bay, MA		40-50 people	96
1834		Castine, Penobscot Bay, ME	Packet	Capt. Goodrich + 30	96
1834		Gloucester, MA	Schooner		96

YEAR	DATE	LOCATION	VIEWED FROM	WITNESSES	PAGE
1835	Spring	Off Race Point Light, Cape Cod Bay, MA	Mangehan	Capt. Shibbles +	96
1835	June 17	Off Chatham Light, Nantucket Sound, MA	Mary Hart	Nichols +	96
1835	October	Great Point, Nantucket Sound, MA			96
1835	November 17	Half Way Rocks, Marblehead, MA	Dove	Capt. Peabody	96
1836	August	Mt. Desert Rock, ME	Fox	Capt. Black + 2	97
1839	July 10	Between Cape Ann and Boston, MA	Hamilton	Capt. Sturgis	97
1839	July 22	Wells Bay, ME	Boats	Fishermen	97
1839	Early August	Portsmouth, NH	Schooner	4 fishermen	97
1839	August 19	Between Kittery and York, ME	Shore	Chapman	97
1839	August	Kennebunk Harbor, ME	Boat	Fishermen	97
1839	August 13	Cape Neddick, ME	Boats		97
1839	August 15	Whale's Back Light, Piscataqua River, NH	Boat	G. Bell	98
1839	August 23	Deer Island, Boston Harbor, MA	Boat	Lt. Bubier +	98
1839	August	Nahant, MA	Shore	T. Colley Grattan +	99
1839	September 3	Southern Maine coast	Columbia	Patten	100
1839	September 7	Off Seguin Island Light, ME	Planet	Capt. Smith +	100
1839	November 2	Boon Island, Newburyport, MA	Alfred	Capt. Sawyer	100
1840	March	Massachusetts Bay, MA	Phoenix	Capt. Fears	101
1840	July	Cohasset, MA	Shore	5 +	101
1843	May 12	Off Cape Ann, MA	Brilliant	Fishermen, Capt. Cotton	101
1844	August	Manchester-by-the-Sea, MA	Boat	Proctor, Fears, Gaffney	101
1844	Summer	Boothbay, ME			101
1844	October	Arisaig, NS	Shore	Barry	102
1845	August	Merigomish, NS	Shore	2 observers	102
1845	(prior to)	Gulf of St. Lawrence, PEI		Fishermen	102
1846	Summer	Faeroe-Iceland Ridge, North Atlantic	Ship	Capt. Christmas	104
1846	Summer	Western shore of St. Margaret's Bay, NS	Schooner	Wilson, Boehner	103
1846	Summer	Hackett's Cove, St. Margaret's Bay, NS		G. Dauphiney	104
1846	July	Nantucket, MA	Whaleboat		
1846	August	Cape Cod, MA		B. H. Revoil	
1848	August 6	24 44' S, 9 22' E	HMS Daedalus	M'Quhae, Drummond, Sartoris +	107
1849	Summer	South West Island, St. Margaret's Bay, NS	Shore	Holland, Kedy + fishermen	118
1849	August 3	Swampscott, MA		J. Marston	119
1852	June	Off Race Point, Newfoundland	Fishing vessels		

YEAR	DATE	LOCATION	VIEWED FROM	WITNESSES	PAGE
1852	(prior to)	Manomet, Cape Cod Bay, MA	Boat	D. Webster	120
1852	August	Rockport Light, Rockport, MA			119
1852	August	Hull, MA			119
1856	March 30	29 11'N, 34 26'W (Mid-Atlantic)	*Imogen*	Capt. Guy + 3	119
1869	November	38 16'N, 74 09'W (off Delaware Bay), MD	*Scottish Bride*	Capt. + crew	125
1870	May 6	Grant's Island, Hudson River, NY			125
1875	July 17	Plymouth, Cape Cod Bay, MA	*Norman, Roman*	Capt. Garton +	126
1875	July 30	Swampscott/Egg Rock, Nahant Bay, MA	*Princess*	Rev. Lawrence + 6, Kelsoe, Thomas	127, 128
1875	Early August	Gloucester, MA			128
1875	August 22	Off Matinicus Island, ME	*Emily Holden*	Capt. Fredrick York	129
1875	August 30	Salisbury Beach, MA	Shore	Hervey, Butler, Tepney +	129
1875	August 30	Isles of Shoals, NH	*Everett*	Capt. Coffin	129
1875	August	Mt. Desert Rock, ME	Boat	Capt. & crew	129
1875	September	Race Point, MA			129
1875	September 15	Portland Harbor, ME			129
1877	July 15	Gloucester, MA	*Gulnare*	G. Wasson, B. L. Fernald	130
1877	July 15	Nantasket, MA	Shore	J. T. Gardham	131
1877	Summer	Long Island Sound			131
-1878		Plum Island, Newburyport, MA	Shore	G. Whipple	132
1878	August 29	Off Race Point, Cape Cod Bay, MA	*Drift*	R. Platt	133
1878	September 2	Long Island Sound, NY		Kelly	132
1878	September 3	Black Rock Light, Bridgeport, CT		Murphy, Spielman	132
1879	January 2	Captain's Island, off Greenwich Point, CT	*Jane Eliza*	Capt. Dalton + 2	134
1879	June 20	Cape Ann Light, MA	*Aeronaut*	Capt. Wells	134
1879	July 29	Pictou Is., Gulf of St. Lawrence, NS	*Louisa Montgomery*	Capt. Samson	134
1880	June	Minot's Light, Massachusetts Bay	Shore	H. Goodwin +	134
1880	August	Merigomish, NS	Boat	Fishermen	134
1883	Autumn	Bay of Fundy, NS		Fishermen	199
1884	February 18	Cape Henry, NC	*Edward Waite*	Officers & crew	134
1884	Summer	Gulf of St. Lawrence	*Silkworth*		135
1886	July 24	Gully Point, Rockport, MA	Shore	Tarr, York + 9	137, 190
1886	August 12	Pigeon Cove, Rockport, MA	Shore	Brewer, Henderson, Putnam, Pool	139
1886	August 19	Pigeon Cove, Rockport, MA	Shore	Putnam, Brewer	141
1886	August 22	Rockport, MA	Boat	Brown, McCormack, Scott, Worth	179

YEAR	DATE	LOCATION	VIEWED FROM	WITNESSES	PAGE
1886	August 29	Kingston Point, Hudson River, NY	*Mary Ann*	Addison, Brush +	143
1886	August 31	Hudson River, NY	*John H. Cordts*	Capt. Conkling	143
1886	September 2	Bearden Island, Hudson River, NY	*Lotta*	Capt. Hitchcock	143
1886	September 8	Long Island Sound, near Cromwell, CT		Col. Stockwell, Sage, Capt. Phelps + Reed	143
1886	September	Herring Cove, Cape Cod Bay, MA		Young women	143
1886	October 13	Between Norwalk and Westport, CT			143
1886	October 17	Between Southport and Westport, CT	Sailboat	Sanford, Stroud, Keys	143
1886	November 5	Flushing Bay, NY	Shore	Thompson, Vaugh	143
1886	December 10	Off Nantucket, MA	*Thingvalla*	Capt Laub, Hanman +	143
1887	February 7	Middle Ledge, near Fisher's Is. Sound, CT	Boat	Capt. Paine	143
1887	July 22	Ft. Popham, ME	Shore	Neilson, Ziegler	143
1887	July	Eaton's Neck, Long Island Sound, NY	Schooner	Capt. Smith	143
1887	July 29	Nahant Bay, MA	Sea, shore		143
~1888		St. Croix River, Passamaquoddy Bay, NB			154
1888	March 23	Connecticut River, CT	*Coral*	Capt. Stanson	144
1888	June 3	Jones Beach, Long Island, NY	Boat	Capt. Sherman	144
1888	June 18	Nags Head, NC		Russel, Smithson	144
1888	June 20	N. of Georges Shoal	*Alice Hodges*	Thomas	144
1888	July 30	Watch Hill, Block Island Sound, RI	*Venetian*	Muir	144
1888	August 4	Point Judith, Block Island Sound, RI	*Sanford*	Howard, Nalty, Walsh	144
1889	May 4	44 N., 42 40 W (Mid-Atlantic)	*Mary Lane*	Capt. Delory & crew	144
1889	May 28	Hudson River, near Newburgh, NY	*British Princess*	Capt. Smith	144
1890	September	Brant Rock, Marshfield, MA	Shore	Nathaniel Lyons	144
1891	August 9	ESE. of Cape Ann	Boat	Edson, Whidden	144
1891	Summer	Vineyard Sound, MA	*Gold Hunter*	Opt. Jacobsen & crew	145
1893	August	Long Island Sound, Barlett's Reef Light, CT	Boat	Borden	145
1893	December 2	SW. of Grand Bank 43 55'N~56W, NF	*American*	Logan, Waldorf	145
1895	July	Long Island Sound, CT	*Connecticut, City of Lowell, New Hampshire*	Peters	145
1895	July 23	Hempstead Harbor, near Sea Cliff, NY	Boat, shore	Burrows, Stokes, Lewis, Speed	
1896	February 4	Long Is. Sound, near Port Washington, NY	Shore	Forrest, Terry	
1896	June	St. Andrews Bay, NB	*Terrapin*	Capt. Brooks	145
1896	June 17	St. Andrews Bay, NB			145
1896	July	Centerville, Bay of Fundy, NS	Boat	Lewis	145

YEAR	DATE	LOCATION	VIEWED FROM	WITNESSES	PAGE
1896	July 19	Lighthouse Pt., New Haven Harbor, CT	Shore, boats	200 +	146
1896	August 10	Egg Rock/Swampscott, Nahant Bay, MA	Yacht	Mohr & son	147
1897	July 10	Half Way Rocks, Marblehead, MA	Boat	J. Kirk	147
1897	August 7	Long Island Sound, CT	Yacht, shore		147
1898		SW. of Schoodic Pt., Frenchman Bay, ME	*Nancy Hanks*	Wass brothers	147
1899	July 25	45°37′N, 58°09′W, off Newfoundland	*New England*	Passengers & crew	149
1901		Long Island Sound			151
1901		Hudson River			151
1902	Early July	Mark Island, ME	*Kitty Lawry*	Chapman, Drinkwater	151
1902	July 9	Islesboro, Penobscot Bay, ME		Sherman	151
1902	July 10	Sydney Harbor, NS		J. J. Hill +	151
1902	July 11	Nahant Bay, MA	*Waccouta*	L. Wagniere	152
1902	July 14	Nahant Bay, MA	Shore	E. Brann	152
1902	August 10	City Island, Long Island Sound, NY	Yacht	Capt. Banta	153
1903	July	Cape Hatteras	Boat	J. Ostens Grey	153
1903	August 5	St. Croix River, Passamaquoddy Bay, NB	*Tresco*	Greenlaw	154
1903	August 18	Louisburg, Cape Breton, NS		Schooner	153
1903	Summer	Wood Island, ME		3 women	154
1904	December 1	Off Sable Island, Gulf of Maine	*Columbian*	Dawes +	155
1905	July 10	Simons Farm Beach, Hull, MA	Boat	H. E. Hatch & wife	157
1905	July 12	Cohasset, MA	Boat	G. Cole	158
1905	August 5	Wood Island Light, ME	Boat	Merriam	158
1905	December	off Parahiba, Brazil	*Valhalla*	Nicoll, Meade-Waldo	160
1907	September 1	Passamaquoddy Bay, ME	Boat	Carver, Gillespie +	162
1909		Casco Bay, ME	*Bonita*		164
1909	October	Highland Light, Massachusetts Bay	*Warren M. Goodspeed*	Perry +	163
1910	August 20	Brown Cow, Casco Bay, ME	*Bonita*	Capt. & crew	164
1911	July	Nantasket, MA			164
˜1912		Portland, ME	Steamer	Mrs. F. W. Saunderson	164
1912	August 18	Off Cape Porpoise, ME	*Philomena*	McKinnon +	165
1913	August 30	Grand Bank	*Corinthian*	Ayers, Batchelor	168
1914	June 9	Thatcher Island, Cape Ann, MA	*Flora M.*	Brooks +	170
1915	July	Black Rock, Cohasset, MA	*Gurnet*	Litchfield, Edson +	171
1921	September 8	Scituate, Cape Cod Bay, MA	*Calvin Austin*	Capt. Holmes +	175

YEAR	DATE	LOCATION	VIEWED FROM	WITNESSES	PAGE
1929		Montauk Point, NY	*Foam*	U. S. Coast Guard	176
1925	May 24	South Channel, Massachusetts Bay	*Pollyanna*	Capt. Tobin +	182
1930	Late May	Georges Bank	*Catherine Burke*	Capt. Moulton + 23	182
1931	May 18	E. of Boston Lightship, Mass. Bay	*Imperator*	Capt. Marsden + 22	193
1935	Early September	Western Bank	Sea, shore	Langthorne + 22	194
1936	August 10	Summerville Beach, Liverpool, NS	Sea	100 +	194
1936	August 19	Port au Port, Gulf of St. Lawrence, NF	Sea	Fishermen	194
1936	August 21	Newfoundland coast	Shore, fishing boat	Fishermen	196
1937	August 6-7	Off Smith's Point, Nantucket, MA		G. Manter, C. Manville & son	197
1938	June	Grand Manan, Bay of Fundy, NB		Fishermen	197
1938	Early August	The Wolves, Passamaquoddy Bay, ME	Sea	Polis, Sacobasin, Francis	197
1938	August 18	Pleasant Point, Passamaquoddy Bay, ME	Shore	Moore, Socoby	202
1938		West Point, PEI		MacLean	198
1939		Sydney Harbor, NS	Shore	C. Ballard	198
~1939		High Pine, Cape Cod Bay, MA	Fishing boat	Capt. Pierce	198
~1939		Marblehead, MA		Lobstermen	198
1941	Early May	Grand Manan, Bay of Fundy, NB		Fishermen	198
1947	September 3	Lynn Beach, MA	Shore	John Ruhl +	200
1947	December 30	188 miles E. of Cape Lookout, NC	*Santa Clara*	Axelson, Fordam, Humphreys	200
1948	August 26	Isles of Shoals, NH	*Wava E.*	Robie, Roberts	201
1956		West Point, Egmont Bay, PEI	Shore	McLean, Ellis	201
1957	September 3	Off Nantucket, MA	*Noreen*	Bourassa, Smith + 2	202
1958	June 5	Off Cape Elizabeth, ME	Fishing boat	Mikkelsen, Haugarrd	203
1960	Summer	Egg Island, Manchester, MA	Fishing boat	5	204
1960	Summer	Cole's Ridge, Marblehead, MA	Fishing boats	Fishermen	204
1960	July 7	Gloucester, MA	*Julyntha*	Hodgkins, Laupot +	203
1962	July 25	Marshfield, MA	*Carol Ann, Vincy*	Fishermen	204
1997	May 4	Fortune Bay, Newfoundland	Fishing boat	Bungay, Clarke	209

The Linnaean Committee's Questions

1. When did you first see the animal?
2. How often and how long a time?
3. At what times of the day?
4. At what distance?
5. How near the shore?
6. What was its general appearance?
7. Was it in motion or at rest?
8. How fast did it move, and in what direction?
9. What parts of it were above the water and how high?
10. Did it appear jointed or only serpentine?
11. If serpentine, were its sinuosities vertical or horizontal?
12. How many distinct portions were out of the water at one time?
13. What were its colour, length and thickness?
14. Did it appear smooth or rough?
15. What were the size and shape of its head, and had the head ears, horns or other appendages?
16. Describe its eyes and mouth.
17. Had it gills or breathing holes, and where?
18. Had it fins or legs, and where?
19. Had it a mane or hairs, and where?
20. How did its tail terminate?
21. Did it utter any sound?
22. Did it appear to pursue, avoid or notice any thing?
23. Did you see more than one?
24. How many persons saw it?
25. State any other remarkable fact.

ACKNOWLEDGMENTS

First and foremost, my immense gratitude to my husband, William F. O'Neill, whose indefatigable faith, support, and good counsel have been crucial to this project and whose love and friendship are so essential to my happiness. And to Maeve, the best assistant anyone ever had.

I am profoundly indebted to my mother, June Elizabeth Pusbach, who, in the short time we had together, stretched her slender resources to foster and promote a love of books, science, music, and history and my fascination with the Loch Ness enigma. The influence of her guiding spirit, intellect, and lifelong love of learning is everywhere expressed in this book.

My enormous gratitude to cryptozoologist Gary S. Mangiacopra, who generously shared years of painstaking research along with his encouragement, insights, and goodwill. And to those without whose publications mine would not have been possible: Dr. Antoon Oudemans, Commander Rupert T. Gould, Bernard Heuvelmans, and George W. Woodbury, whose scrapbook filled out the record.

Thanks to my families—the Hogans, O'Neills, and Palumbos—and to my friends Beth Ader, Pamela Sheehan Carden, Glen Gillen, Sudi Jacobs, Nancy Jones, Danna Lopez, Anna Palumbo, Ray Perkins, and Maria Porco, who, each in his or her way, contributed more than they know. Thanks particularly to Bill Bandon, Tricia McKeogh, and Susan Golden, who read and commented on early chapters.

My deepest thanks to my most faithful and patient cybercorrespondents—Mike Everhart and Glen Kuban—for reading the manuscript and contributing their expertise and advice. Many thanks to Dan Varner and Douglas Henderson for bringing the Cretaceous seas to life and for generously allowing me to include their work.

To the many people who have kindly shared their research and material: Wayne Wilcox; Swampscott historian Louis Gallo; Ellen R. Nelson, librarian and archivist of the Cape Ann Historical Association; Calantha Sears, of the

Nahant Historical Society; Paul V. Heinrich; Nathan R. Lipfert, library director of the Maine Maritime Museum; Karen MacInnes, of the Marblehead Historical Society; Muriel Sanford, of the Fogler Library; Matthew Bille; Janet Bord, of the Fortean Picture Library; Bruce Bradley, of the Linda Hall Library; and cryptozoologists Loren Coleman, J. Richard Greenwell, John Kirk, and Paul LeBlond.

Also Roslyn Strong and Peter Waksman, of the New England Antiquities Research Association. And Romantha Burrow, of the Waponahki Museum and Research Center, for putting me on the trail of the "dragon" at Embden.

To my mentors Virginia Van Brunt Fossel, W. Clapham Murray, Dr. and Mrs. Montford H. R. Sayce, and especially Mom-Pat Brown.

To the staff of the Katonah Village Library and the members of the Katonah Rotary Club.

Thanks also to my road crew—Auntie B., Maeve, and Tucker—for the treasured memories, especially that sparkling morning we spent amid the tide pools and the heart-stopping afternoon at Pemaquid Point.

Betty says not to thank her and Francis for looking after Maeve, but without them this book would never have been finished, so thank you both for being such wonderful grandparents to the daughter I love so dearly.

Abundant thanks to my excellent editor, Barbara Feller-Roth, for all her "picky little queries."

And finally to Karin Womer of Down East Books for taking a chance and setting me off on this adventure in the first place.

Bibliography and Web Sites of Interest

AUTHOR'S NOTE: *Books containing significant factual errors have not been included in this bibliography.*

Almy, Kenneth J. "Thof's Dragon and the Letters of Capt. Theophilus Turner, M.D., U.S. Army." *Kansas History Magazine*, Vol. 10 (1987): 170-200.

American Council of Learned Societies. *Dictionary of American Biography.* New York, N.Y.: Schribner's Sons, 1932.

Babson, John J. *History of the Town of Gloucester, Cape Ann.* 350th Anniversary Edition. Gloucester, Mass.: Peter Smith Publishing, 1972.

Bakker, R. T. "Plesiosaur Extinction Cycles: Events That Mark the Beginning, Middle and End of the Cretaceous," in *Evolution of the Western Interior Basin.* W. G. E. Caldwell and E. G. Kaufman, eds. Geological Association of Canada. Special Paper 39 (1993): 641-64.

Bigelow, Jacob. "Documents and Remarks Respecting the Sea Serpent." *American Journal of Science and Arts*, Vol. 2, No. 1 (1820): 147-64.

Bille, Matthew A. *Rumors of Existence: Newly Discovered, Supposedly Extinct, and Unconfirmed Inhabitants of the Animal Kingdom.* Blaine, Washington: Hancock House, 1995.

———. "The Definitive Sea Serpent." *Strange Magazine* (July 1994).

Bright, Charles. *Sea Serpents.* Bowling Green, Ohio: Bowling Green State University Popular Press, 1991.

Brown, Chandos Michael. "A Natural History of the Gloucester Sea Serpent: Knowledge, Power, and the Culture of Science in Antebellum America." *American Quarterly*, Vol. 42, No.3 (1990): 402-36.

Callaway, Jack M., and Elizabeth L. Nicholls. *Ancient Marine Reptiles.* San Diego, Calif.: Academic Press, 1997.

Citro, Joseph A. *Passing Strange.* Shelburne, Vt.: Chapters Publishing Ltd., 1996.

Colbert, Edwin H. *The Great Dinosaur Hunters and Their Discoveries.* New York, N.Y.: Dover Publications, 1984.

Coleman, Loren. *Mysterious America.* New York, N.Y.: Faber and Faber, 1983.

Colonna, B. A. "The Sea Serpent." *Science*, Vol. 8, No. 189 (1886): 258.

Cooper, James Fenimore. *Lives of Distinguished American Naval Officers.* 1846.

Cronon, William. *Changes in the Land: Indians, Colonists, and the Ecology of New England.* New York, N.Y.: Hill & Wang, 1983.

Devens, R. M. *Our First Century.* Volume II. Springfield, Mass.: C. A. Nichols & Co., 1876, pp. 575-82.

Dexter, Ralph W. "Cape Ann Visits of the Great Sea Serpent 1639-1886." *American Neptune* 46 (1986): 213-20.

Dingus, Lowell, and Timothy Rowe. *The Mistaken Extinction: Dinosaur Evolution and the Origin of Birds.* New York, N.Y.: W. H. Freeman and Co., 1998.

Ellis, Richard. *Monsters of the Sea.* New York, N.Y.: Alfred A. Knopf, Inc., 1994.

Erickson, Evarts. "When New England Saw the Serpent." *American Heritage,* Vol. 7, No. 5 (April 1956): 26-27.

Farlow, James O., and M. K. Brett-Surman, ed. *The Complete Dinosaur.* Bloomington and Indianapolis, Ind.: Indiana University Press, 1997.

Fish, John Perry. *Unfinished Voyages: A Chronology of Shipwrecks.* Orleans, Mass.: Lower Cape Publishing, 1989.

Garland, Joseph E. *Down to the Sea: The Fishing Schooners of Gloucester.* Boston, Mass.: David R. Godine, 1983.

———. *The North Shore.* Beverly, Mass.: Commonwealth Editions, 1998.

Geller, L. D. *Sea Serpents of Coastal New England.* Plymouth, Mass.: Cape Cod Publications 15, 1979.

Gordon, John Shand. *Sea Serpent: A collection of scientific articles and newspaper reports.* 1926.

Gould, Rupert T. *The Case for the Sea-Serpent.* London: Philip Allan, 1930.

———. *The Loch Ness Monster.* London: Geoffrey Bles, 1934.

Greenwell, J. Richard. "The Coelacanth: 50 Years Later." *The International Society of Cryptozoology Newsletter,* Vol. 8, No.1 (1989).

Hawke, David Freeman. *Everyday Life in Early America.* New York, N.Y.: Harper & Row, 1988.

Hay, John, and Peter Farb. *The Atlantic Shore.* New York, N.Y.: Harper & Row, 1966.

Heuvelmans, Bernard. *In the Wake of the Sea-Serpents.* New York, N.Y.: Hill & Wang, 1965.

History of the Town of Rockport. Rockport, Mass.: Rockport Review Office, 1888.

Hobbs, Clarence. *Lynn and Surroundings.* c. 1886.

Holder, J. B. "The Great Unknown." *Century Magazine* (June 1892).

Hotchner, A. E. "Are There Sea Serpents, Really?" *This Week Magazine* (Aug. 14, 1955).

Jenks, Rev. William. *Letter to Linnaean Society* (September 17, 1817).

Kenny, Herbert A. *Cape Ann: Cape America*. Philadelphia and New York: J. B. Lippincott Co., 1971.

Kierman, Irma C. *The Sea Serpent of Cape Ann*. Self-published, 1950.

Kipling, Rudyard. *Captains Courageous*. New York, N.Y.: Doubleday & Co., 1896.

Kuban, Glen J. "Sea-monster or Shark? An Analysis of a Supposed Plesiosaur Carcass Netted in 1977." *Reports of the National Center for Science Education*, Vol. 17, No. 3 (1997): 16-28.

Kurlansky, Mark. *Cod: a biography of the fish that changed the world*. New York, N.Y.: Walker and Co., 1997.

LeBlond, Dr. Paul H. *British Columbia Scientific Cryptozoology Club Newsletter*, No. 29 (July 1997).

LeBlond, Dr. Paul H., and Dr. Edward L. Bousefield. *Cadborosaurus Survivor from the Deep*. Victoria, B.C., Canada: Horsdal & Schubart Publishers Ltd., 1995.

Mackal, Roy P. *The Monsters of Loch Ness*. Chicago: The Swallow Press Inc., 1976.

Mangiacopra, Gary S. "The Great Unknowns of the 19th Century: Sightings of Sea Serpents Along the Northeast Coast of North America. Part I: 1869-1879." *Of Sea and Shore* (Winter 1976-77): 201-5,228.

——. "The Great Unknowns of the 19th Century. Part II: 1880-1888." *Of Sea and Shore* (Spring 1977): 17-24.

——. "The Great Unknowns of the 19th Century. Part III: 1892-1899." *Of Sea and Shore* (Summer 1977): 95-104.

——. "The Great Unknowns of the 19th Century. Part IV: Comments and Conclusions." *Of Sea and Shore* (Fall 1977): 175-78.

——. "The Great Unknowns into the 20th Century: Observations of Large Unknown Animals Along the Northeast Coast of the North American Continent. Part I: 1900-1913." *Of Sea and Shore* (Spring 1980): 13-20.

——. "The Great Unknowns into the 20th Century. Part II: 1919-1939." *Of Sea and Shore* (Summer 1980): 123-27.

——. "The Great Unknowns into the 20th Century. Part III: 1947-1980." *Of Sea and Shore* (Fall 1980): 193-96.

———. "The Great Unknowns into the 20th Century. Part III Continued: 1947-1980." *Of Sea and Shore* (Winter 1980-81): 259-61.

McGowan, Christopher. *Dinosaurs, Spitfires, and Sea Dragons.* Cambridge, Mass.: Harvard University Press, 1992.

Moore, Gary. "The Gloucester Monster: The Sea Serpent That Attacked New England." *Boston Herald American* (January 9, 1977).

Morison, Samuel Eliot. *The Oxford History of the American People.* Oxford University Press, 1965.

Nagel, Paul C. *John Quincy Adams: A Public Life, A Private Life.* New York, N.Y.: Alfred A. Knopf, 1997.

Nicolar, Joseph. *The Life and Traditions of the Red Man.* Fredericton, New Brunswick: Saint Annes Point Press, 1979.

Ocko, Stephanie. "The Gloucester Sea Serpent." *American History,* Vol. 17, No. 2 (1982): 36-41.

A Particular Account of a Monstrous Sea-Serpent, The Largest Ever Seen in America. Brattleboro, Vt.: The Brattleboro Bookstore, 1817.

Psihoyos, Louie, with John Knoebber. *Hunting Dinosaurs.* New York, N.Y.: Random House, 1994.

Remich, Daniel. *History of Kennebunk from Its Earliest Settlement to 1890.* N.p., n.d.

Report of a Committee of the Linnaean Society of New England Relative to a Large Marine Animal Supposed to be a Serpent Seen Near Cape Ann, Massachusetts in August 1817. Boston, Mass.: Cummings and Hilliard, 1817.

Rich, Louise Dickinson. *The Coast of Maine.* New York, New York: Thomas Y. Crowell Co., 1956.

Roesch, Ben S. "A Review of Alleged Sea Serpent Carcasses Worldwide." *The Cryptozoology Review,* Vol. 2, Nos. 2 and 3, and Vol. 3, No. 1 (1998).

Safina, Carl. *Song for the Blue Ocean: Encounters Along the World's Coasts and Beneath the Seas.* New York, N.Y.: Henry Holt, 1997.

Sargent, C. L. *The Sea Serpent, Evidence About It.* Unpublished manuscript, Cape Ann Historical Association Archives, Gloucester, Mass., 1818.

Shuker, Karl P. N. *In Search of Prehistoric Survivors.* London: Blandford, 1995.

Snow, Edward Rowe. *Legends of the New England Coast.* New York, N.Y.: Dodd, Mead & Co., 1957.

——. *Supernatural Mysteries and Other Tales*. New York, N.Y.: Dodd, Mead & Co., 1974.

——. *True Tales and Curious Legends: Dramatic Stories from the Yankee Past*. New York, N.Y.: Dodd, Mead & Co., 1969.

Thompson, Waldo. *Swampscott: Historical Sketches of the Town*. Lynn, Mass.: Thomas Nicols Press, 1885.

Thoreau, Henry David. *Cape Cod*. Introduction by Henry Beston. New York, N.Y.: W. W. Norton, 1951.

Thorne-Miller, Boyce L., and John G. Catena. *The Living Ocean: Understanding and Protecting Marine Biodiversity*. Washington, D.C.: Island Press, 1991.

Ward, Nathalie, ed. *Stellwagen Bank: A Guide to the Whales, Sea Birds, and Marine Life of the Stellwagen Bank National Marine Sanctuary*. Camden, Maine: Down East Books, 1995.

Wilcox, Wayne H. M. "The True Story of the 'Sea Monster' Killed in Eastport." *Quoddy Tides* (April 23, 1996).

Wilson, Fred A. *Some Annals of Nahant*, 1928.

Witchell, Nicholas. *The Loch Ness Story*. Baltimore: Penguin, 1975.

Wood, John George. "The Trail of the Sea-Serpent." *Atlantic Monthly* (June 1884):799-814.

Woodbury, George W. *Scrapbook #15*. Gloucester, Mass.: Cape Ann Historical Association, 1933.

Zimmer, Carl. *At the Water's Edge: Macroevolution and the Transformation of Life*. New York, N.Y.: The Free Press, 1998.

Publications & Web Sites of Interest

Michael J. Everhart
Oceans of Kansas, marine reptiles
http://www.oceansofkansas.com

Paul V. Heinrich
Primitive Eocene whales
http//intersurf.com/~heinrich/basilosaurus/.html

Glen J. Kuban
Sea monster or shark? Analysis of a supposed Plesiosaur carcass netted in 1977
and links to many, many paleontology sites
http://members.aol.com/gkuban/glenk.htm

National Audubon Society Living Oceans Program
550 South Bay Avenue
Islip, NY 11751
http://audubon.org/campaign/lo/

New England Antiquities Research Association (NEARA)
www.neara.org
Roslyn Strong's analysis of the Embden petroglyph
http://www.neara.org/ROS/dragon.htm

Cryptozoology

Altamaha-Ha
http://www.gate.net/~anndavis/sightings.htm

The Anomalist
P.O. Box 577
Jefferson Valley, NY 10535
http://www.anomalist.com

CRYPTONEWS
British Columbia Scientific Cryptozoology Club
John Kirk, Editor
6141 Willingdon Avenue, Suite 89
Burnaby, BC, Canada V5H 2T9
http://www.ultranet.ca/bcscc/
e-mail: bccryptoclub@yahoo.com

The Cryptozoologist
Loren Coleman
http://www.agate.net/~cryptozoo/cryptohome.html

The Cryptozoology Review
Ben S. Roesch, Editor
166 Pinewood Avenue
Toronto, ON, Canada M6C 2V5

Ben S. Roesch On-Line Cryptozoology Archive
http://www.ncf.carleton.ca/~bz050/HomePage.cryptoz.html

Exotic Zoology
Matt Bille, Editor
3405 Windjammer Drive
Colorado Springs, CO 80920

FATE Magazine
P.O. Box 64383
St. Paul, MN 55164-0383
http://www.llewellyn.com/fate/main.htm

Fortean Times
Subscriptions:
3330 Pacific Avenue, Suite 404
Virginia Beach, VA 23451-2983
888-428-6676

ISC Newsletter
International Society of Cryptozoology
J. Richard Greenwell, Editor
P.O. Box 43070
Tucson, AZ 85733
http://www.izoo.org/isc/

The Shadowlands
http://www.theshadowlands.net

Dr. Karl P. N. Shuker
http://members.aol.com/karlshuker

Virtual Institute of Cryptozoology
http://perso.wanadoo.fr/cryptozoo/welcome.htm